KIRENAI FATED MATES

KIRENAI FATED MATES BOOKS 1-3

(INTERGALACTIC DATING AGENCY)

TAMSIN LEY

Twin Leaf Press

Cover by The Book Brander

Paperback version
ISBN-13: 978-1-950027-49-1
Copyright © 2021 Twin Leaf Press
All Rights Reserved.

Twin Leaf Press
PO Box 672255
Chugiak, AK 99567

Kirenai are an all-male species of shapeshifters with a natural form (resting state) like an amoeba who usually assume a bipedal shape to interact with other species. Until the discovery of humans, Kirenai required a permanent pair-bond with a female of another species to produce offspring. All Kirenai traits are dominant and located on the Y chromosome; male offspring are fully Kirenai, while female offspring are fully of the mother's species.

Birth rates have been historically low, and over the ages, the population has been dwindling. Human females proved to be exceptionally receptive to impregnation, and do not require formation of a pair-bond to conceive. This has made Earth a target for black market slave traders who deal in "breeders." The Emperor has been making attempts to protect the population.

Regardless of the shape a Kirenai is in, he will be recognized as Kirenai by his skin and hair color. The most common hue is blue, although colors can be anywhere from mint green to lavender. Rare individuals called *burendo* can effect coloration outside this range. Kirenai blood is clear or slightly milky unless infected, when it grows murky to almost solid white.

All Kirenai have empathic abilities called Iki'i which make them capable of reading emotion and desire, as well as identifying individuals within their own species regardless of shape. This is the only Kirenai trait sometimes passed on to female progeny. The ability also makes the species as a whole consummate lovers because they can take actions and form attributes their partner finds most appealing. Bonded mates assume a permanent form pleasing to their mates; rarely can they force themselves into an alternate shape after bonding.

The average Kirenai life-span is approximately eight hundred human years. When a pair-bond is formed, a Kirenai passes a small genetic marker to his mate that mitigates the aging process, giving the mate a lifespan to match his own.

GLOSSARY

Ahen - an opiate-like drug.

Amai wood - a rich golden brown wood sought after for its buttery texture and sweet scent. The resin is used as an aphrodisiac on the planet Hy.

Ayabe - slightly astringent fermented leaves humans might think resembles cole slaw.

Bacca - a game that resembles frisbee golf.

Burendo - a Kirenai who excels at shapeshifting and is able to not only assume the form of other species, but coloration as well.

Fogarian - aliens with red hair and sideburns who live on a rocky, mountainous planet.

G'nax - a species that uses light to communicate attraction and arousal. They also have a symbiotic relationship with an eight-legged insectoid.

Hage - bald, wide-eyed alien that looks much like the iconic alien humans have circulated.

Happa trees - blue fronds resembling palms.

Hypawa - species with magma-colored eyes.

Ijin'en - four-legged herd animal raised for meat and well known for its stupidity.

Iki'i - empathic power.

Irn - a unit of measure. One planetary rotation around the Kirenai's sun.

Itoshi - beloved. Term of endearment.

Jiro - a unit of measurement equivalent to approximately two Earth hours.

K'ogai - the town near the palace on Kirenai Prime.

Kazhitu - nuts that look like sticky buns when baked. High in sugar, and tastes buttery and fruity.

Khargal - gray, horned aliens with stone-like skin and wings from the planet Duras ;)

Khensei - a toxin that causes Kirenai to denature into their resting state.

Kikajiru - my distracting one - a term of endearment.

Kirenai Prime - the Kirenai home planet. Purple and blue with swirling white clouds.

Klen - aliens who communicate via scent.

Kuro - a type of bitter, very black tea.

Kuzara - shit, damn, fuck.

Kryillian death swarm - tiny insectoid creatures that can kill a man within seconds by sucking his blood.

Matrix/cellular matrix - the term for a Kirenai's cellular mass.

Nezumi - a small downy animal with a stumpy tail and floppy ears found on most space stations.

Nilgawood - a tree used to make resin.

Oritsu - An expression of awe.

Popotan - the plant used to line ship interiors that provides oxygen, recycles water, is highly resistant to radiation, and can regenerate itself if damaged.

Qalqan - a species known for their healers. Good bedside manners due to their resistance to emotional fluctuation.

Resting state - a Kirenai's amorphous shape, like nakedness to humans, it is shown only to family or trusted friends.

Senburu - a galactic conglomeration of merchants who oppose the emperor's rule. Individual members are called *Senbur*.

Sireta Prime - a popular party planet.

Supo cloth - smart fabric for clothing that doesn't need buttons or zippers.

Teozhisa - a cart to carry people.

Tolonovone - a device that creates lighted markings on the skin. Used by G'naxians as part of their mating rituals.

Ukimi ice - beloved dessert with cool, spicy flavor like sweet mint.

Vatosangans - species with alabaster skin and blue or green hair who tend to be stocky or rounded. Planet is called Vatosang.

Zhinku weed - common in the popotan fields.

ARAZHI

An alien prince needs to sire an heir, and human females are rumored to be good breeders, so he heads to Earth and buys a date at a charity auction. Now he thinks he owns her...

CHAPTER ONE

Georgie flinched as the black lab on her grooming table shook water from his fur. The big oaf was one of the lucky ones headed to the feed store for adoption day, and she'd volunteered to help groom and transport them from the shelter. She wiped her glasses off on her sleeve and finished rinsing the pup, who thanked her with one of his signature slobbery kisses. If she wasn't living in a tiny one-bedroom apartment with her dad at the moment, she would've considered adopting him herself, but there was barely room for the two of them as it was.

In the nearby kennels, a dog started barking, which soon escalated into a chorus. The Jack Russell Terrier Lora was grooming on the next table over started crying, writhing against the leash. The poor baby had anxiety issues, and Lora tried to distract it with a squeaky toy.

"I think you're stressing her even more, Lora," said Georgie, making a face at the added noise.

At the third dog washing station, Maise had already finished with an older German Shepherd who now lay placidly at her feet. She owned Yappy Hour, the pet boarding and grooming business they were using to clean up the dogs, and was a pro with the wash station. She leaned against the table, long dark ringlets obscuring her face as she looked at her phone. "What about this one, Georgie? Intergalactic Dating Agency seeks capable human to coordinate first ever alien matchmaking event. All applications considered."

"You've got to be kidding," said Lora, ceasing her squeaky toy distraction and looking at Georgie. "Aliens?"

Extraterrestrials hadn't been seen on Earth since a singular appearance over forty years ago—if that was even to be believed. The ships had landed at Beijing Daxing International Airport in China, spoken to government officials there, and departed again before the other nations could even respond. Despite photographs and eyewitness accounts, many people believed the visit had been a hoax—a myth created by governments to justify spending on defense and outlandish space research.

Yet in the years since, people still claimed to have been abducted, including Georgie's mom. Her mom had died several years ago from a head injury after falling from a ladder, but Georgie'd always wanted to believe her mother's story.

"Maybe they're checking in on us," Georgie said.

"To ask for dates to the movies? How desperate can they be?" Lora snorted. "Keep scrolling, Maise."

"No, wait. I want to know more," said Georgie, wiping her hands off on a towel.

If this was an actual, paying gig, she couldn't dismiss it

without at least reading the fine print. She'd been trying to get her event planning business off the ground for months now, but every time she thought she had a lead, someone snagged the contract out from under her. The only people who said yes couldn't pay her, and one guy who wanted a bar mitzvah for his son had even had the balls to say she should be grateful for the "exposure" planning his son's event would get her. Asshole.

Problem was, she was desperate enough to consider it. Since her divorce, she'd been living with her dad to save money, sinking all her savings into getting her business off the ground while working part time as a cashier at the grocery store. She had to do something soon, or she was going to go crazy.

"Maybe it's just a cosplay party or something. Let me see your phone." She held out her hand.

Maise handed over her cell, and Georgie looked over the advertisement. An alien matchmaking event did sound hokey, but it wouldn't hurt to ask for more information and submit a proposal. Heck, an alien-themed party could be really fun. She typed in her email address and handed the phone back.

"How cool would it be to plan the first ever party with actual aliens?" asked Maise, pocketing the phone and grabbing a towel to help Georgie with the lab.

"I just want to know how much they'll pay." Georgie fixed a collar around the dog's neck and led him to the floor.

"You couldn't pay me enough to go on a date with an alien." Lora scooped the shivering terrier into her arms.

As they headed to the shelter's van to load the dogs for transport, the breeze coming off the pulp factory made Georgette want to gag. It was particularly bad today. She'd just closed the lab into a kennel and shut the door when her phone pinged with an incoming email. She glanced at it.

"It's them," she said, surprised to have a response so quickly, then read the email out loud. "Thank you for your interest in the Intergalactic Dating Agency. Please send proposed Earth time frame, location and cultural requirements."

Lora readjusted her sagging auburn ponytail. "Earth time frame? Really? They're certainly playing up the alien angle, aren't they?"

"Just staying in character, I guess." Georgie chuckled. A plan was already forming in her head. "At least I know they want me to keep things weird."

"What the heck are cultural requirements?" asked Maise.

"I don't know, but it sounds fun." Georgie squinted at the fine print at the bottom of the email. It was hard to read, so she expanded the text.

Her jaw dropped. "Holy crap, listen to this! Upon acceptance, the coordinator will be paid ten thousand Earth credits in the monetary unit of their choosing plus expenses upon receipt."

"Earth credits?" asked Maise as she climbed into the van's front seat. "What are those?"

"I think they mean I can choose dollars or yen or whatever currency I want." Georgie bit her lip. "And look, the return email is from a dot gov site." She let out a slow breath. "I think this really is a solicitation from aliens."

Lora scrunched one eye doubtfully and moved to the driver's side. "Highly questionable."

Questionable or not, Georgie needed the money. "I have an

idea. Let's host a charity auction where aliens—or alien wannabes or whatever—bid on dates, and the proceeds benefit the shelter. The client foots the bill for the party, with food, dancing, and booze. The aliens meet women, and the shelter earns some money. Win-win!"

"But who are you going to auction?" asked Maise, scooting across the bench and buckling into the middle seat.

Georgie gave her a devious smile and climbed in behind her. "People who support the animal shelter, of course."

Lora shook her head and started the engine. "Count me out. I'm not into green slime."

"They're not slimy," insisted Georgie. "They look sort of human. See?" She did a quick search and found one of the old images that had been all over the news. A slim alien with bluish skin looked into the camera with big eyes.

"They're sort of cute," said Maise.

Lora glanced at the image, then put the van into drive. "He looks like my grandpa."

Georgie released a heavy sigh. "I'm not asking you to marry one, Lora. Just go out to dinner. Or coffee. Look at it as an opportunity to make new friends."

"I usually do more than make friends on my dates." Lora gave her a sardonic look.

"Slut." Maise elbowed her in the ribs with a smile.

Lora laughed. "Whatever."

"Please?" begged Georgie. "I really need this contract."

"I'll run security for you. You might need someone to fend off death rays or something." Lora was a police officer and always assumed there'd be trouble.

"I can hire security," Georgie said. "I need women for the auction."

Lora raised an eyebrow. "Who says they want women?"

"Oh." Georgie opened up her email. "You're right. I'd better ask."

"What about you?" asked Maise. "Are you entering?"

"I have to run things." Georgie was already researching possible venues, caterers, permits...

Lora snorted and turned onto the highway. "Right. The perfect excuse."

Georgie looked up. "Fine. If I enter the auction, will you agree to do it, too?"

"Can I bring my dogs?" asked Maise. "If it's a pet event, we should include pets."

"Great idea," Georgie said. "We can hold it at Covey Park."

"Aliens, come run with our animals at the dog park!" Lora called toward the ceiling.

"So you'll help?" asked Georgie, batting her eyes beseechingly at her friend.

"I guess," said Lora. "But at the first sign of slime, I'm out."

Georgie finished drafting her proposal while they drove. Normally, she would take this home to think about it. But she'd had opportunity snatched out from under her too often.

This time, she was going to be first.

She hit send and set her phone on her lap. Once she had a contract, she'd worry about getting more volunteers for the auction.

To her surprise, her phone buzzed before they'd even reached the feed store. She swallowed, hardly able to believe the response. *Your terms are acceptable. Women matches only. Please find your fee in your monetary storage account. Additional funds available upon receipt. Send updates to this address.*

Wondering how they'd accessed her bank account, she logged on to find she was now ten thousand dollars richer. "Holy shit," she breathed. "I just got the contract."

"You did?" Maise asked.

Georgie showed her the bank balance.

"Wow! That was fast!" Maise grinned and raised her hand for a high five.

Georgie gleefully smacked her palm as reality settled in.

She had an event to plan.

CHAPTER TWO

Prince Arazhi descended the ramp from his private ship onto the dark stone tiles of the landing pad outside the palace. As he walked, his limbs shifted, becoming heavily muscled to match his mother's species, while his blue-skinned features coalesced into the bored-but-responsible look he tended to wear for his family. He'd received an urgent request to attend his father, Emperor Ozhin, and he wasn't happy he'd been dragged away from his latest dalliance with a Hypawa female with eyes like liquid magma and a mouth just as hot.

Like most of his liaisons, she'd hoped to secure a prince as a mate. And like all of his liaisons, he'd enjoyed the game, teaching her how to entice a partner without allowing himself to be enticed. An all-male species, Kirenai were well known across the galaxy as being able to bring great pleasure to their partners, using their empathic Iki'i senses to know exactly what a female desired. But Arazhi had no intention of attaching himself to a jealous, power-hungry female.

Guards stood posted outside the palace courtyard, their various bipedal shapes encased in full body armor, despite the heat. They greeted him with nods as he passed. He strode through the gate into the courtyard where towering blue happa fronds shaded the mossy path to the palace's main door.

A bondservant met him at the threshold. "Welcome home, my prince. Would you like me to prepare your room?"

"I won't be staying, but thank you." He intended to go straight back to the Hypawa's waiting arms once this meeting was over.

Arazhi strode down the arched stone hallway toward the throne room. Even when there was no court in session, his father preferred to conduct life from the vantage of his throne, and Arazhi was surprised to find the emperor's dais vacant.

A teal-skinned guard in traditional happa bark body armor stood at the base of the platform. He pointed toward the back to the royal chambers.

Unshielded anxiety pulsed from that direction, nudging his Iki'i senses, and Arazhi moved toward the door, concern building in his chest; most of the time he had to be nearby to sense someone's emotions.

The royal sitting room was vacant, and the doors to the bedroom stood open. The fruity scent of regeneration fluid filled the air. Concern transformed to worry, and he hurried forward.

"...can't be certain," someone in the bedchamber was saying, followed by a murmur he didn't catch.

Inside the chamber, Arazhi found Elthos, the royal healer and the emperor's most trusted advisor, standing near a regeneration pod that must've been brought in from the clinic, pink-scaled features as unreadable as ever. Arazhi's dam sat next to it, one alabaster hand resting on the lip of the gray, trough-like container that brimmed with green regeneration fluid.

Arazhi's heart constricted. Kirenai required periods of rest when they allowed their bodies to relax into their natural, amorphous state, but regen fluid was reserved for the seriously ill or injured who couldn't maintain a humanoid form to consume sustenance.

He hurried forward. "What's going on, Damma? Is Father hurt?"

His damma rose, a tight smile on her pale white face. She was a Vatosangan, small and slight, with deep blue hair and rounded features. "My child, we're so glad you're here."

The regen fluid in the pod roiled as his father's pale blue face appeared just above the surface. "Hello, my son." The emperor's usually melodious voice had a gravelly quality. "It's good you've come."

"Tell me what happened." Arazhi leaned over to look into the pod. The blue, amoeba-like form floating inside showed no outward signs of illness or damage.

Damma shrugged, blue lashes damp with unshed tears. "He cannot keep to his upright form. The healers say he's been poisoned."

"Poisoned?" Arazhi sucked in a breath. That explained the

regen fluid. He looked to the nearby healer. "When? By who? Is there an antidote?"

"We are working on one," Elthos said with a bow. As a Qalqan, he possessed a machine-like calm that was immune to a Kirenai's Iki'i, but a Qalqan's objectivity also made them the best healers in the galaxy. "The palace guards are investigating suspects."

Damma nodded to the healer. "Thank you, Elthos. Please keep me updated on what you find."

"Of course, empress. I'll get back to work." Elthos bowed again and turned to leave.

Arazhi watched his father's face dip below the surface and back up again. Normally, his father was excellent at shielding his Iki'i, but pain now leaked from him in undulating waves.

Damma rose from her cushion and looped her arm through his, drawing his attention. "You must produce an heir immediately."

Arazhi bit his lip. This was not the discussion he'd prepared for, especially now that he knew his father was ill. "I don't want to talk about that now, Damma. I'm still young, and I've met no one who makes my shape want to settle, let alone solidify." That was only partly true—there had been a female on Sireta Prime who'd kept him enthralled for almost two irns when he was younger. But she'd continually compared him to other men, no matter how he adjusted his form, and eventually left to marry a G'nax nobleman. He'd avoided that sector of space ever since.

Emperor Ozhin sighed. "The Senburu are on the verge of a coup. They want to nominate a new successor to the throne."

The Senburu were powerful merchants who dominated the galactic consortium of planets and disagreed with the emperor's trade policies. They'd been trying to relegate his father's position to nothing but a figurehead since before Arazhi was born. "They can't do that. The planetary governors support our dynasty."

Damma took his hand. "Kirenai are bonding less frequently, and even bonded pairs produce fewer and fewer offspring. Everyone wants to be sure the royal line is secure. The consortium won't allow you to ascend the throne without an heir."

"That's ludicrous." He pulled his hand free. "I have plenty of time to produce an heir."

Most Kirenai waited until late in their long life to settle, enjoying their capacity to assume different forms as long as possible. Once a Kirenai bonded, his form would permanently assume the most pleasing shape for his mate.

Voice strained, his father said, "The consortium has already put forth Senbur Aguno as a candidate."

Arazhi stiffened. Aguno was his father's second cousin and only known blood relative. "He would turn on you like that?"

"He's found a mate," Damma said softly. "And it's rumored she's already with child."

Arazhi frowned. He'd seen Aguno at a recent ball, and there'd been no mention of a mate, let alone a child. "How is that possible?"

"His mate's from a planet called Earth, where the females are said to be like ijin'en, going into estrus and out again as easily as breathing," said his father.

Ijin'en were herd animals that symbolized stupidity. "What

sort of heir can such a union produce?" Arazhi scoffed. "The Senburu can't possibly consider such a species worthy of the throne."

"Earth's inhabitants are primitive, but not unintelligent," his father said.

Damma added, "Their planet was supposed to be closed to trade, protected until the species was more technologically developed. But since it's now public knowledge that Aguno has successfully bred with one, your father was forced to authorize limited social access."

Arazhi scowled. "If the planet was supposed to be closed, how did Aguno end up with a mate? We should arrest him for breaking the trade edict and be done with it."

"It's not that easy." Damma's voice held a note of disgust. "Aguno rescued her from black market slave traders. Apparently, they've been abducting Earth females and forcing them into servitude without contracts."

Arazhi's throat tightened. Slavery was legal in this part of the galaxy, but only if a person enslaved themselves—and they always had the right to buy back their own contracts. Most of the palace bondservants entered contracts merely to enjoy the prestige of working for the emperor, and would be retired with a stipend when they were no longer able to work.

"What's important now is how this affects our dynasty," his father grated out, voice becoming more gravelly every time he spoke. "Humans are capable of producing children without a permanent bond."

Arazhi shook his head. His father must be delusional.

Kirenai could only reproduce after forming a permanent bond. "Didn't you say Aguno was mated?"

Damma answered, "He is, but other rescued females had already been impregnated without being mated to their captors."

"Are you certain the progeny are Kirenai?" Arazhi asked.

Kirenai could breed with a female of any species, producing male children that were always purely Kirenai, with empathic and shapeshifting abilities. The female progeny were of their mother's species, although a few did also inherit Kirenai Iki'i power.

"The healers assure us none of the women have the genetic signatures of a mate bond, and the male offspring are Kirenai."

A sense of unease filled Arazhi's stomach. "So what do you want me to do?"

"Go to Earth, find a willing female, and produce an heir. Quickly."

Arazhi took a step back. He'd pleasured his share of women, but never imagined doing so with the intent to produce a child. And he knew nothing about these humans. What if they really were as stupid as ijin'en? "How am I supposed to do that? Seduce my way across the planet until one of them gets pregnant?"

"Humans have agreed to hold an auction of willing females. Select one and do your duty. Now go. I must rest." His father's face disappeared beneath the surface, leaving behind only a ripple of green waves.

Arazhi turned to his damma. "He can't possibly be serious."

"He is." She once more took his hand, a worried smile on her pale face. "I've met a few of the captured human women, and they appear to make good mothers. Many insisted on remaining here on Kirenai Prime with their offspring. I've established a foundation to house them and help raise the children. My hope is that you find a female worthy of bonding while you are on Earth. Please say you'll at least try?"

"I shouldn't have to try." He scowled, thinking of those two years on Sireta Prime. "When I meet the right person, I'll just know."

"Shed your anger, Arazhi. Your heart has been closed for a long time. All I suggest is you open it again, or true happiness will never find you."

He swallowed and glanced at his father's pod. How was he supposed to pleasure a woman while his father might be dying? He rubbed his chin. "You think it was the Senburu who poisoned him?"

"That would make sense. They put forth a replacement, though his condition has not been made public."

"I'm going to track down who did this and punish them." He clenched his fists.

"We will. And the healers are doing their best to find an antidote for your father in the meantime. But right now, your job is to ensure our enemies can't seize power before we can finish the investigation, and the only way to do that is to produce an heir."

He sighed. He knew his duty. If humans were as willing to produce offspring as his father suggested, perhaps he wouldn't be gone long. Then he would see to the investigation himself and find revenge. "All right," he said. "I'll go to Earth and meet these humans."

CHAPTER THREE

Arazhi's ship orbited the blue-green planet called Earth, waiting for his security officer, Zhiruto, to report back. The Intergalactic Dating Agency that had coordinated the auction charged exorbitant amounts to attend their events, which meant any other attendees would be either royalty or diplomats, like him, but after the attempt on the emperor's life, Zhiruto had insisted on checking the venue out first.

While he waited, Arazhi read over the list of cultural requirements the IDA had provided in their Earth orientation packet.

- Leashes required.
- Must be licensed and vaccinated.
- Feces must be cleaned up by owner.
- Control excessive barking.
- Fill in any holes created in lawn.

- No swimming in fountain.
- Do not interfere with wildlife.

Arazhi had been to many diverse planets and attended many interspecies functions, but leashes? Barking? Feces? What sort of race were these humans? No wonder his father had tried to keep the planet closed until the natives matured. Although Arazhi also couldn't deny that there was a certain appeal to the shape of the species' females now that he'd seen the images.

He practiced assuming the form of a human male once more, looking at himself via one of the camera feeds in his intergalactic vessel's living quarters. Human men seemed to prefer wearing long coverings for their legs and torsos, leaving only their hands and heads bare. Even their feet were covered, and he hadn't acquired any local clothing. Adjusting both color and shape wasn't easy, but he thought he'd done fairly well emulating long dark blue slacks and a blue collared shirt that matched his skin.

His communicator beeped, and Zhiruto's face took over the image on screen. "I've secured the area. All guests are accounted for. The universal translators are still updating hundreds of local languages, but it's safe for you to transport down, Prince Arazhi."

"All right, thank you." Arazhi didn't care for the transporter, preferring to land in the comfort and dignity of his ship, but non-essential technology was prohibited on newly introduced planets in order to keep it from ending up in the hands of natives who might not be ready for it.

He moved to the transport room and engaged the system.

The computerized voice said, "Please prepare for deposition in aqueous habitat."

He hesitated. Humans were supposed to be land-based, but they hadn't yet formed a single language to share, so perhaps they hadn't yet settled on being land-based, either. And these were the same coordinates Zhiruto had used. He'd never learned to swim as a biped, and hated water-based landings in that form.

Releasing a breath, Arazhi relaxed into his amorphous resting state.

The familiar cold tingle of dematerialization swept through him, and his view of the transport bay blinked out. An instant later, he was surrounded by fresh, flowing water. Bright lights flickered from blue to red to purple below the surface, and below him, a tiled floor had been littered with metallic disks. No other beings appeared to be in the water.

He pulled himself into his human form, water running off his shoulders and down his sides. Once he'd fully coalesced into his upright shape, he looked around. The pool only reached his knees, and a jet of water spouted into the night air. A pounding beat of Earth music came from somewhere nearby, and several humans gaped at him from beneath strings of lights draped along a nearby concrete path. One pulled out a small device and began flashing a light at him. Was she signaling for him to approach?

He stepped over the edge of the pool toward them.

The humans were all female, wearing various colored gowns that showed a lot of brown or pink legs. They all held leads connecting them to small, furry quadrupeds. One quadruped was making a sharp, repetitive sound, its body jerking with each burst of noise. *Ah,* he thought. This explained the cultural requirement about leashes. The people on G'nax had a symbiotic relationship with an eight-legged insectoid. Did humans have quadruped symbiotes?

Before he could get close enough to ask, the females hurried away.

He didn't mind. It gave him a moment to smell the moist night air and watch a tiny insect with pale wings flutter against one of the lights. The path he stood on was edged with green vegetation, and he bent to touch the curiously even blades.

"My prince." A tall blue figure approached along the path from the direction of the music.

Although the form was unfamiliar, Arazhi recognized Zhiruto's Iki'i. His security officer had assumed the shape of a broadly muscled and bare-chested human, with thick blue hair falling in waves down his back. He carried a delicate flute of golden liquid in one hand.

"I was growing worried." Zhiruto said as he came to a halt. "Why didn't you use the updated coordinates I sent you?"

"I didn't receive them." Arazhi stood.

Zhiruto grimaced. "Sorry. The security systems have been getting some feedback and interfering with comm signals. I'll get that fixed right away."

Eyeing Zhiruto's half-clothed figure, Arazhi asked, "Do all males in this region dress like this?"

"No, but you know how I am with emulating clothing." Zhiruto winked. Clothing was the most difficult aspect Kirenai integrated into their shapeshifting. "And the females seem to like my current figure. Come, we don't want to miss the first bondservants up for auction."

They left the trail, cutting across the shorn blades toward a brightly lit dais where a band played. As they moved, Arazhi shifted again, emulating Zhiruto's easier-to-maintain form.

The band's melody was interesting, upbeat, reminding him of the balls he'd been to on Sireta Prime. At the base of the dais, several round tables hosted a smattering of Kirenai in human form, a pair of horned Khargals, and a single red-haired Fogarian with massive sideburns. Humans in black-and-white clothing moved between the tables carrying trays.

One of the female servers with brown hair pulled into a bun approached, carrying a tray filled with flutes of golden liquid. Her smile was nervous, but genuine. "Kan eek helf een?"

Arazhi frowned. "Excuse me?"

Zhiruto gestured toward the tray in the woman's hands. "She's offering you a drink."

He removed one of the flutes from her tray and nodded, taking note of her interest in Zhiruto's large muscles. He didn't even need to use his Iki'i to sense her attraction. She kept glancing over her shoulder toward them as she departed.

"You've garnered some attention, I see." Arazhi readjusted his musculature to more strongly resemble his security officer's.

"She's not one of the ones for sale," replied Zhiruto, pulling out a chair at a table in front of the stage. He was usually more interested in the females they met, but tonight he was all business. "The females we're after will be displayed for us there."

Arazhi looked toward the stage where several humans stood

at the side, clustered around a female in a dark blue dress. His breath caught in his throat. The female's pale blonde hair was pulled up on top of her head, but tiny wisps had come loose along the sides, framing smooth rosy cheeks and glossed lips below a pair of glass lenses that accentuated her striking blue eyes. The neckline of her dress draped modestly over her collarbone, but left her shoulders and arms bare and did nothing to disguise her ample breasts and well-rounded hips.

She was stunning. But even more captivating was the way she directed the people around her.

He sighed and looked away. She was totally his type, but she wouldn't be one of the females for sale, not with a bearing like that. She was undoubtedly a princess or dignitary. If he was going to buy a slave, he'd do best to select the meekest one. A female who would have no designs on becoming queen once she bore his child and earned her freedom.

He sampled the carbonated liquid in his flute, recognized it as alcohol, and downed it in one swallow. At least these humans had good taste in beverages. As he was looking around for the woman with the tray, the lights went out, and a voice came over the speaker. The words were garbled in his translator, but he caught enough to know the auction was about to begin.

On stage, a single spotlight popped to life, and the woman in the blue dress stepped into it. Once more, his breath caught in his throat.

She held a mic to her mouth. "Dang fur kom, ederon."

Her voice was like a song, and a shiver ran through him, as if a lover had just stroked his pleasure line. *Oritsu*, she was amazing. He stopped trying to decipher her words and simply allowed the cadence to float over him. Why couldn't she be for sale?

She handed the mic to a human male with a double chin and a patch of fur over his mouth who moved to a podium at the front of the stage. Lights popped on behind her, illuminating a cadre of females all dressed in gowns of sparkles and silk. Quite a few held animals in their arms or led them by leashes.

He leaned over to Zhiruto. "Are these creatures they carry symbiotic?"

"Not that I'm aware of." Zhiruto shrugged. "I believe they are for sale, too."

The quadrupeds were definitely gaining some interest from the Khargals, but not the kind he thought humans would appreciate. He nudged Zhiruto. "I get the sense these animals are precious to humans, not food. Go tell the Khargals before they try to eat one."

Zhiruto grumbled, but rose to speak with the gray-skinned aliens.

Arazhi settled back against his seat and watched the females parade across the stage in some sort of synchronized march, quadrupeds in tow. The music ended, and the women filed off stage. A tall woman with a sharp chin remained, and the man at the podium began chanting in a singsong voice.

The Fogarian at the next table raised a hand. "Eight thousand."

The double-chinned man pointed at him, and the woman nodded in his direction.

The auction has begun, Arazhi realized. He considered raising his hand, buying the woman, and getting this whole ordeal over with. Except he couldn't seem to take his eyes off the woman in blue standing at the edge of the stage. One after another, women appeared, were bought, and descended to meet their new owners. One after another, Arazhi couldn't bring himself to bid.

"Do none of these females entice you at all?" asked Zhiruto, who'd won a bid for a tall woman in a black dress.

Arazhi sighed and raised his hand to bid on the current offering, only to be outbid by the Fogarian.

Then the woman in the blue dress stepped forward once more, giving the audience a wide smile, one hand on her hip. His stomach sank. The auction was over, and he'd missed his chance. He glanced at the next table where a woman held a small quadruped on her lap and smiled nervously as the Kirenai reached out to stroke its fur.

At the podium, the auctioneer once more began his chant, and Arazhi's attention snapped back to the stage in disbelief.

The woman in the blue dress was for sale.

A Khargal raised his hand. "Nine thousand."

The woman smiled at him and made a small curtsey.

Arazhi was determined to have that smile all to himself. He raised his hand. "Ten."

The Khargal raised his hand again. "Fifteen."

This auction was pointless. Arazhi knew what he wanted, and money was no object, not when the fate of his dynasty was on the line. Plus, the mother of his child deserved recognition of her worth.

He rose from his seat. "Five hundred thousand."

The woman's eyes went round behind her lenses. She

glanced at the auctioneer, who seemed just as stunned as she was.

The Khargal growled but crossed his arms and slumped back against his chair, shaking his head. "She's all yours, Kirenai."

For a moment, the entire world seemed to hold its breath.

Then the auctioneer banged his gavel. "Sold!"

And every human in the area burst into thunderous applause.

CHAPTER FOUR

Georgie carefully made her way down the stage stairs, trying not to trip in the Louboutin stilettos she'd bought to go with her dress. She'd never owned shoes this expensive, not even for her wedding, but the Intergalactic Dating Agency had not only paid her up front for planning the event, it had reimbursed her for every receipt she submitted, including her formal wear. They seemed made of money, and she'd even secured stipends for her volunteers to buy gowns, which had made recruiting so easy, she'd eventually had to turn women away.

Every one of the aliens seemed to be rich, their bids escalating with every date auctioned. She almost wished she'd gone ahead and accepted every woman who'd volunteered. But that would be greedy. As it was, the shelter wouldn't need to worry about funding for the rest of its existence, especially with that final bid. *Five hundred thousand dollars!* And it had been for her.

Blinded by stage lights, she hadn't been able to see her bidder, but her date could have fins and fangs for all she cared. Heck, with the money they'd brought in, even Lora better not complain about this event, slime or no slime. Not that that was a worry. The aliens she'd glimpsed while coordinating the auction weren't bad to look at. A couple had horns, and she'd spotted one terrifying guy who reminded her of Arnold Schwartzenegger with fangs and a wild mop of crimson hair. But the rest just looked like humans with blue skin. Not scary at all.

Picking up a nearby bottle of champagne and an empty flute, she minced across the lawn toward his table, trying not to let her heels sink into the grass. Women sat with aliens at every table, some looking uncomfortable, others laughing or showing off pets. With the auction complete, it was time for the guests to get to know each other.

The alien who'd bid on Georgie was unmistakable as she wove between the tables toward him. His gaze remained fixed on her. She moved slowly, taking time to look him over. He was shirtless, and except for his blue skin and strangely dark eyes, he looked human. *Gorgeously human.* She gulped and forced a smile, wondering why he was shirtless. His broad shoulders and god-like chest and arms made it difficult for her to raise her attention to his face.

When she did, she was equally stunned. His square jaw was the epitome of handsome. Midnight blue eyes with no white seemed to bore directly through her. And a sensuous mouth smiled at her without actually turning upward, as if he knew a great secret only they shared.

She paused at the chair next to him and stuttered, "Thank you for your generosity. You've helped a lot of homeless pets." She lifted the bottle. "Shall we celebrate?"

He nodded and extended his empty champagne flute.

She filled it then her own before sitting down next to him.

He downed his in a single gulp, then resumed silently staring at her as the band began playing a popular Country Western song.

Her stomach fluttered. She downed her champagne, too, hoping it would calm her erratic nerves. She'd never expected an alien to be so handsome, much less seem to be interested in her.

The moment she set her glass down, he refilled it.

Strong silent types were definitely her thing, and everything about him had her mind going to naughty places. She hadn't been on a date since her divorce, so perhaps it was just easy for a man to turn her head, but to be fair, the guy had just dropped half a million dollars for a date with her and also looked yummier than any Chippendales model she'd ever seen.

Except this wasn't just any date, and he wasn't just any guy.

He was an alien. He might look human, but that didn't mean they were remotely compatible. Her gaze fluttered down toward his lap, suddenly wondering what alien peen might look like. Did he even have one?

She felt his smile on her, and heat crept up her cheeks again. Dragging her gaze back to his, she thrust out a hand. *At least learn his name first, girl.* "My name's Georgette, but everyone calls me Georgie." She had to half shout to be heard over the band. "What's yours?"

"Name," he said, as if feeling the word on his tongue. His voice was deep and smooth—another of her weaknesses. "Arazhi," he rumbled.

She gulped. "Good to meet you, Arazhi."

He looked like he wanted to lick her all over as he reached out and took her offered hand. The contact sent a jolt of awareness through her, and she immediately recalled Lora's quip about doing more than making friends on a first date. Georgie tended to be more reserved, but for this guy...

Gripping her hand gently, he lifted it toward his mouth as if to kiss it. But instead of a kiss, his tongue flicked out along the slit between her index and middle finger, dipping in at the apex in a way that totally had her thinking of other slits. Was this how aliens greeted each other? Her panties felt suddenly wet.

"Oh, my," she whispered, voice drowned out by the roll of the auctioneer. She clenched her thighs together and glanced around, worried someone might somehow notice how turned on she was, but everyone's attention was elsewhere.

All attention except Arazhi's. His thumb traced the trail his tongue had left, sending another shiver straight to her core.

She laughed uncomfortably and pulled her hand away, picking up her champagne. She really shouldn't drink more, not when she hadn't eaten all day. The alcohol was going to her head. That had to be why her body was responding this way. Her heart raced and her skin felt flushed.

There were supposed to be hors d'oeuvres at the event, but she hadn't noticed any pass their way. Where the hell were the servers? She glanced around for one, but there were none in sight.

She set the glass on the table and stood. "I need to go check on something."

Arazhi stood with her, putting a hand on her elbow. "Hungry."

She wasn't sure if he was saying he was hungry, or somehow sensing she was, but all the guests were likely feeling peckish by now. Hangry aliens were the last thing she needed. "I'll be right back with food."

But her alien apparently didn't understand he didn't need to tag along and trailed her between the tables toward the caterer's tent. She found a harried looking woman in a white caterer's jacket opening more champagne. "Why isn't there any food out there?" Georgie demanded.

The woman wrinkled her nose. "We served the early arrivals, but those aliens with horns ate everything we had ten minutes after they'd arrived."

Crap. Georgie glanced through the darkness toward the table in question. A horned, gray-skinned alien had apparently won the bid for Maise, who now sat between him and another like him, clutching her dog against her chest as if worried they thought it was the main course.

"Why didn't anyone tell me?" Georgie glowered at the caterer. This was exactly why her being in the auction had been a bad idea. She needed to be available to make sure everything ran smoothly. "Send one of your people out to pick up cheese and vegetable trays or something. Put it on my account. I have a feeling these aliens aren't picky."

"Yes, miss. Right away." The caterer rushed off to do as instructed.

Georgie turned to find Arazhi grinning at her, once more looking like he knew a secret. He had a dimple on one cheek. God, she was a sucker for dimples. Was it possible for him to get any sexier? She swallowed and smiled back.

"Come," he said, and once more took her elbow, guiding her away from the auction toward the park.

"I really shouldn't leave." She looked over her shoulder toward the stage where another auctioned woman in gold sequins was holding up her cat like Rafiki in *The Lion King*.

Arazhi's hand remained firmly on her elbow, propelling her toward the fountain. "Please, keep talking."

What a strange request. "About what?"

He tapped a finger to his ear. "Translator is learning."

"Oh." She hadn't even given a second thought to whether or not aliens spoke English. *Shit, what if he didn't know how much he'd actually bid?* Wouldn't it be just her luck to learn the aliens were spending their version of Monopoly money? "Have you understood what's going on tonight?"

He stopped and turned her to face him, his dimple once more in place. "Money is good."

She was relieved to hear it. Still, she pretended to wave away her concern. "Oh, I wasn't worried about that. I just want to make sure you're having a good time."

He stepped closer, forcing her to look up.

She inhaled a nervous breath. He smelled amazing, slightly sweet and a bit like good tobacco.

With one hand, he brushed a tendril of hair from her face,

looking down into her eyes with a fierce possessiveness that made her legs feel like jelly. His baritone voice repeated, "Good time."

Is he going to kiss me?

Even as she thought it, one powerful arm circled her waist, pulling her against him.

Her nipples tightened, and the place between her thighs pulsed with need. He was warm, hard muscles to her soft curves. She let her head fall back, closing her eyes.

The explosion of sensation when his lips met hers left her dizzy. It was as if unadulterated desire poured into her bloodstream. His kiss was soft yet firm, his tongue sliding hotly between her lips like ambrosia filling her mouth. He plundered her for what felt like an eternity, yet ended too soon. His big hand splayed at the small of her back, keeping her pressed against what was very obviously a throbbing erection.

At the edge of her awareness, sounds penetrated her fog of desire. A dog was yipping. Something crashed. Screams filled the air.

Jolted from the dream-like kiss, she pushed off Arazhi's chest. Something was wrong.

Several party guests ran past her toward the parking lot.

She grabbed the arm of one woman who ran past. "What's happening?"

"The aliens are shooting death rays or something! A bunch of them dissolved into goo!" The woman jerked away and kept running.

"Oh, God!" This was not a contingency she'd planned for.

What should I do? She hiked up her dress and kicked off her shoes, preparing to go back and stop the chaos.

The blue alien who'd been sitting next to Arazhi ran toward them, shouting something.

Behind her, Arazhi said, "Danger."

Before she took another step, he jerked her back against his chest.

"Put me down!" She struggled. "I have to stop this!"

But his grip was like an iron band. Then, it was as if she was suddenly encased in shrink wrap. Everything went blurry. She couldn't move, couldn't breathe. The ground seemed to wobble and shift.

And she was no longer standing in the park.

CHAPTER FIVE

Arazhi's security officer wasn't one to exaggerate danger, so when Zhiruto shouted for the prince to transport off the planet, Arazhi'd quickly encased Georgie within his matrix and signaled his ship for pickup. Not the most elegant way to get her on board his vessel, but his transporter didn't yet have her genetic signature, and he wasn't about to leave her behind.

They rematerialized on the bridge, and Georgie stumbled forward, gasping. His Iki'i picked up on her shock, which was understandable; she came from a primitive species after all. She likely had no idea where they were or how they'd arrived.

While she stood with her back to him, gaping at the view screen displaying a portion of Earth's blue-green horizon, he reassembled his matrix into the human form she preferred. He'd been making slight adjustments to his features all night and believed he'd achieved her standard of attractive. The next step would be assessing her likes and dislikes when it came to the more personal aspects of his anatomy.

He moved to the communication console. He needed to find out what had happened on Earth. Where was Zhiruto? His security officer should've arrived on deck right behind him.

"Zhiruto, are you still planet-side?"

A familiar blue face appeared on screen. "Yes. I've ordered all transporters blocked to prevent suspects from escaping."

"Do you think someone was trying to assassinate me?"

"We must assume so." A dog was barking, and the image canted sideways as Zhiruto glanced over his shoulder toward a woman in a crimson gown restraining a gangly, russet-furred quadruped.

Georgie pushed up beside Arazhi, placing her fingers against the screen. "Lora! Aryou kay?"

The universal translator seemed to be catching up, but still wasn't perfect. The woman in the uniform turned to face the camera, looking over Zhiruto's shoulder. "Georgie? Where are you?"

The screen resumed its focus on Zhiruto. "My prince, you must leave orbit immediately. I don't know how many assassins there are or if any escaped back to their ships before the shutdown. You could still be in danger."

"I'm not leaving without you." Leaving his security officer behind was a huge breach of protocol, not to mention Zhiruto was his friend.

"I'm going to keep searching here. I'll be fine, but you cannot be compromised. Now go!"

Arazhi hesitated, then hit the button that would execute the pre-programmed escape route. He hated leaving Zhiruto behind, but he trusted his security officer knew what he was doing.

A small shudder preceded the change of trajectory, then the view screen went black as they entered FTL.

Georgie grabbed his arm. "Call them back. I need to know if my friends are okay."

Putting a hand gently on her shoulder, he transmitted calm. "Communication is impossible while the Faster Than Light drive is active, but my security officer has everything in hand. Don't worry. We'll find out more after we reach Kirenai Prime."

"K-kirenai Prime? What's that?"

"My home planet."

"The hell?" She shrugged off his grasp. "I'm not going to another planet. I need to get back to Earth! Turn us around right now."

He sensed that she was focusing on her responsibilities in order to keep her mounting panic at bay. Staying in control made her feel secure. *She is going to be an impressive mother to our children*, he thought. He smiled and radiated pleasure, anticipation, and an innuendo of desire. He couldn't help the last part. Something about her made him want—need—to make her happy. Though she'd sold herself as a bondservant, he planned to treat her like a princess. "We can't stop until we reach our destination. Come. We will eat now."

She took a step back. "I don't want to eat. I want off this ship. Take me back to Earth this instant."

Now her stubbornness was becoming a nuisance. It was her job to make him happy, not the other way around. He set his jaw and wrapped one hand around her elbow to guide her from the bridge. "Your responsibility is only to me from now on."

"What are you talking about?"

He frowned. Why did she continue to radiate confusion? She'd come to his table after he'd purchased her contract. "I purchased your contract. You belong to me now."

She gasped and stumbled, even though she no longer wore those ridiculous pointy shoes. "You thought you were buying a slave?"

He blinked. "Of course."

Her mouth dropped open. "It was a charity auction, for God's sake! A benefit for our animal shelter. You bought a *date* with me, not a lifetime of servitude."

He narrowed his eyes. He'd spent an exorbitant amount on her, and while money wasn't the issue, he wasn't about to let things go. She was perfect, and he wanted her more than he'd ever desired a female before. "Earth was only allowed to join the consortium because they offered us willing females. Did you not accept my bid?"

"Well, yes, but—"

"Then, as a royal bondservant, you'll be treated well. I'll even grant you freedom after we successfully breed."

A spike of arousal wafted from her, at odds with the sharp tone of her voice. "Breed? As in make babies?"

"Yes. I require a male child."

She laughed harshly. "Well, joke's on you, buddy. You won't be getting a kid out of me, male or otherwise."

He tilted his head. Georgie's emotions were a whirlwind of contradictions through his Iki'i. She wanted to be with him and seemed to desire a child. But she also resisted her desires. "I'm offering you great pleasure."

Her lips parted a moment, and she exhaled slowly before saying, "If you truly want to please me, take me home."

Perhaps he was being too soft with her. Little was known about human mating habits, but many species required an interested male to press his advance until the female relented. Taking her shoulders, he backed her toward the lavender wall. "You'll enjoy our breeding, I promise."

Sexual energy flowed like a current between them. She did enjoy his forcefulness. Yet still she protested. "You don't understand. This factory's out of order. Condemned."

He didn't understand her idiom. *The universal translator must still be updating*, he thought. But language didn't always require words.

Running his hands down her arms, he inserted his thumbs between her fingers the way she'd liked at the party. Her blue eyes had darkened, and her cheeks were flushed as pink as the sun on Hynodae. Dipping his head, he brushed her soft lips with his.

She sucked in a startled breath, body perfectly still.

Hovering a breath away, he opened his Iki'i, searching for her true desire. Bondservant or no, he wouldn't breed with an unwilling female. There was something in her emotions he didn't understand, a fear of something other than him. But even stronger was the sense that she enjoyed his mouth on hers.

He lifted one hand to her throat, tilting her face toward him. He slid his tongue along her parted lips, gently exploring the contours. She put her palms against his chest, as if intending to push him away. But she didn't try to move him. Instead, her fingers slid across his pecs, exploring the muscles he'd created.

A brief flicker of gratitude that he'd followed Zhiruto's lead in choosing a form ran through him, then his tongue was pressing inside her mouth. Her lips softened and opened further, accepting his slow, questioning strokes. He delved deeper, his Iki'i thrilling with her rising desire.

She tasted like morning dew on happa fronds, slightly sweet with a hint of musk. No wonder the black market was abducting human females. Were they all this intoxicating? He didn't think so. He hadn't felt remotely attracted to the other women he'd seen at the auction.

The only one he wanted was Georgie.

He palmed her waist, loving the curve while at the same time imagining his child swelling within her. Never in all his experience had a woman made him think like this. Made him feel so right inside his skin. Georgie was special. He'd been right about his first assessment of her—she wasn't meant to be a bondservant, and he wouldn't enforce her contract.

But he was going to convince her to be his lover.

CHAPTER SIX

Making a baby had been a fantasy of Georgie's for as long as she'd known about sex—a fantasy that had been ground to dust by years of fertility treatments, with the remaining particles blown away by her divorce. There would never be a baby for her. Yet Arazhi's talk about breeding swept through her like a drug.

He prodded his tongue between her teeth, muscular chest pressing her against the curved alien wall behind her. A tingle of desire raced from her nipples to her center. She wasn't small or dainty, but the way his body covered hers, the way his big hand cradled her head as he kissed her, made her feel more feminine than she'd ever felt before. Like she was made for kissing.

His kissing.

She raised her chin to meet him, sliding her hands up his bare chest to explore his muscles. He was ripped, without an ounce of fat on his body, and the fact that he wanted her was mind-boggling. He obviously didn't understand that she couldn't bear him a child, but she'd been honest, so for now, she was going to enjoy the pleasure he'd promised. It wasn't as if she could do anything to help her friends from here, anyway.

His palm slid up her waist until his thumb stopped at the crease below one of her breasts.

Nipples aching for his touch, she arched her back.

He cupped her breast, thrusting his tongue into her mouth with quick, sure strokes.

She couldn't remember the last time she'd been so thoroughly kissed. It was making her dizzy. Her hands slid around the solid muscles along his ribs as if he was the only thing holding her upright.

His thumb stroked over the fabric covering her nipple, making it harden in response. She could only imagine how much better it would feel on her bare skin.

As if of the same thought, he slid the spaghetti strap of her gown off her shoulder and down her arm, exposing the top of her strapless bra.

She tilted her head, letting his questing tongue lave her skin. Shudders of delight coursed through her at his touch. She hadn't been with a man since Josh had left her, and her hormones were on fire.

Arazhi tugged the strap, breaking it in half, and she snapped back to reality. This gown had cost a fortune. She grabbed his hand. "What are you doing? Don't rip my dress."

Arazhi stepped back so quickly she nearly collapsed. His

eyes were wide as he looked at the broken shoulder strap. "Have I harmed you?"

She held the severed edge of the strap, trying to determine if it could be repaired. "You could've used the zipper."

"What is a zipper?"

She let out a slow breath and bit her bottom lip. He didn't know what a zipper was. *He's an alien, what did you expect?* She shouldn't be making out with him, anyway. She had to focus on getting home. Swallowing, she smoothed one hand up the front of the gown to cover her exposed bra. "How long until we reach your planet?"

"Approximately sixteen jiros."

She really hoped jiros translated to minutes. "Uh, can you give me that in Earth time?"

"I believe it is almost two of your Earth days."

Her stomach cramped. *Two days?* Double that if she counted the return trip. And she still had no idea if her friends were okay. "Can we go any faster?"

"Not appreciably, no." He tilted his head, as if listening to something. "You are hungry. Come, I will show you the galley." Without waiting for her to agree, he turned and exited the room.

She was hungry, and if she was about to face multiple days of space travel, she should probably eat. As she followed Arazhi, she glanced at the strange pastel walls around her, nervous about what aliens might consider food. She'd seen several episodes of Star Trek where aliens ate live worms or other gross items.

Reality suddenly hit her—she was on an alien spaceship. And everything was completely different from anything she'd ever imagined. The walls weren't metal, but ribbed like giant leaves and glowing with pale lavender light, like something out of a fairy story. The air smelled sweet and slightly like wintergreen, with a warm current of fresh air flowing from the curved hall Arazhi had entered.

She ran her fingertips along a thick support rib running the length of the hall. The surface felt warm and leathery, almost alive. "What is this wall made of?"

"The interior walls are grown from a variant of popotan." He looked over his shoulder at her, his dimple flirting with the edge of his almost smile. "I look forward to showing you the farms where we grow it on Kirenai Prime. The rolling hills there are lovely."

She dropped her hand from the wall and glared at him. "We will not be going on a field trip to some farm. The moment we reach your planet, we're going to contact the IDA and straighten this out."

"Of course." He returned his attention to the hallway ahead. "I'm simply saying you would find the farms enjoyable. I used to play there as a child."

Her footsteps slowed. She was trying to be angry with him, to resist the lure of a dream that could never come true. But what if his species had technology that would allow her to bear a child? *A tiny Arazhi would be so cute*, she thought, picturing a chubby blue toddler playing among rows of purple leaves. *And making that baby with Arazhi...* Her insides tingled with the memory of his hand on her breast.

She let her gaze follow the muscular curve of his blue shoulder to the planes of his back. Alien or not, he pushed all the right buttons for her. Tall, deep-voiced, muscular, and that dimple when he smiled—she was continually on the verge of forgetting everything and letting him pleasure her like he promised.

She shook her head, refusing to follow her thoughts. Arazhi wasn't asking to marry her and have a family. He wanted to *breed* her as if she was livestock. He'd even said he'd grant her freedom afterward, which could only mean he intended to take the child from her. No way was she going to have a baby only to give it up. But leaving Earth to live on an alien planet? No way. She had parents, friends, and a life—such as it was.

Arazhi entered a door to the left, and she paused at the threshold. Storage shelves were inset between the ribs in the walls here, and a brushed gold table rested in the center, surrounded by plush violet captain's chairs. A heavenly scent reached her, reminding her of roast pork with apples as Arazhi set an oval platter on the table.

Her stomach growled, and she looked at the orange glistening lumps sitting on top of something that might pass for rice. Despite her growing hunger, her concern about eating alien food returned. "Are you sure humans can eat your food?"

He smiled, his dimple once more making her insides flutter. "I verified that everything here is compatible with human physiology." He set a basket of round red fruits that looked like plums with pointed ends next to the platter. "Let me show you how we eat this dish."

Transferring a fruit to a shallow bowl, he deftly squished it into a paste with a utensil that looked like a small spatula. He turned the spatula around and poked the pointed end of the handle into one of the orange lumps, dipped it into the paste, then returned the paste-covered morsel to the platter where he rolled it around to pick up the pale brown grain.

Holding it toward her mouth, he said, "Try it."

Jaw tight, she shook her head. "You first."

He laughed and ate it, then repeated the process, offering the next bite to her. "You may spit it out if you find it distasteful."

The food smelled edible, and he seemed to enjoy it. And she would have to eat something before they got back to Earth. Might as well do it now. She opened her mouth and let him place the food on her tongue.

An explosion of flavor filled her senses—sweet and rich with a hint of spice. It was crunchy on the outside and soft and juicy on the inside, somewhat like fried chicken. The delicious flavor flowed down her throat before she could even think to stop it. "What is this? It's amazing."

"A dish called akeno. It's a root with a glaze of urebi, one of my favorites."

"I can see why." She reached for the other spatula utensil, but he already had another bite up to her mouth.

This time she took the utensil from him to feed herself, relishing the flood of flavor. As she finished chewing, he slid a cup in her direction. "This pairs well. Try it."

She sniffed the bubbly liquid. It smelled like alcoholic Sweet Tarts. She took a tiny sip. The hint of sour was a perfect complement to the akeno, and she took a bigger drink. "This is refreshing. Thank you."

"We make it from zhupakuri fruit. It's native to Kirenai Prime."

Relaxing into her chair, she let him feed her another bite. She hated to admit it, but she could get used to treatment like this. "What do your species call themselves? Kirenai?"

He beamed at her. "Correct."

Damn. Why did she like his smile so much? She took another sip to hide her distraction. "Why did you leave your friend behind?" She hadn't understood their language, but she'd sensed the tension between them during the call earlier. "The people that ran past us near the fountain said something about aliens turning into puddles of goo."

Arazhi's eyes flashed, and he sat up straighter. "You mean they destabilized?" Before she could answer, he rose, his face a grimace of anger. "*Kuzara*, the food."

Georgie put a hand over her mouth as she remembered how quickly the hors d'oeuvres had been eaten. "Oh, God, I never imagined our food might be harmful to aliens."

"Human food is not harmful to us. The IDA verified compatibility before the party."

She let out a shaky breath. "Then what do you mean?"

He paced to the other side of the room and back. "It was an assassination attempt. Someone poisoned the emperor the same way. Now they're after me."

"You? Why?"

He paused his pacing. "I'm his sole heir."

She gulped as the implication sank in. If Arazhi was the son of an emperor, that could mean only one thing.

She'd been purchased by a prince.

Arazhi stood still, watching Georgie's expression shift as her roving emotions teased his Iki'i. Women always fell all over him the moment they learned who he was, and he expected no different from this gorgeous Earth woman.

But when she met his eyes she asked, "Is your father all right?"

Her sincere compassion sliced straight to his heart. He was used to doling out empathy, not receiving it. All the anxiety he'd bottled up since learning of his father's condition threatened to break loose. "I don't know," he said, keeping his voice even. "Our healers were still looking for an antidote when I left."

"I'm sorry." Georgie knitted her brows. "Are you two not close?"

"Why would you ask that?" He frowned, affronted by her question. Family meant everything to Kirenai; from the moment they bonded, they lived and died for mate and children. Kirenai children honored and cherished their parents. "Of course we're close. He's my father."

She shrank back in her seat, embarrassment wafting toward him. "It's just that you're here, not with him. If it was my father, I'd want to be with him every moment to make sure he was all right."

He grimaced, suddenly realizing his hands were balled into fists. He didn't want to frighten her. Relaxing his posture, he returned to his seat in the chair next to her. Perhaps if she understood the true reason he needed her, she would stop resisting. "We are close. But if I don't produce an heir before he dies, my family will lose the throne."

"Oh." Her brow furrowed. "Why come all the way to Earth? Don't you have any women on your planet?"

This conversation was taking an unexpected turn, and he didn't feel like getting into a biology lesson about shapeshifting and pair bonding right now, so he kept things simple. "Kirenai require a female of a different species to reproduce. Humans are reported to be the most prolific, and I need a female who can conceive and bear a child quickly."

Her body tensed, and she shook her head. "I don't know any women who'd be willing to have a baby and just hand it over like that, especially to someone who lives on another planet. Visitation rights would be a nightmare."

"I wouldn't dream of separating a mother from her child. Part of the reason I came to Earth was that I was told humans make excellent mothers."

"Oh." She looked away. Regret floated like a sour miasma around her. "In that case, I'm sure you can find a woman willing to have your baby as soon as we get back to Earth. There were quite a few volunteers for the auction who I had to turn away."

He frowned. He thought he'd been paying her a compliment, assuring her he trusted her to become a mother to his child. Why did she continue to deny her own desire? Was this trait unique to Georgie, or were all human females this difficult? He placed a gentle hand on her arm. "But I don't want another female. I want you."

She shoved away from the table and stood, regret now consumed by searing hurt and anger. "You aren't listening to me. Unless you have a way to fix broken hardware, you need to find someone else to make alien babies with, okay?"

Again with the undecipherable idioms. "I don't understand."

Her eyes glistened as she pointed to her stomach. "I'm barren. Infertile. Broken. Defective." Her voice cracked. "Unable to have children. Understand?"

He didn't need to use his Iki'i to feel her pain. He could see it in her eyes. "Ah." He shifted his gaze to her middle. "Is it physical or genetic?"

"I don't know!" She turned away. "The doctors ran every test they could and couldn't fix me. Just take me back to Earth and swap me out. I'm sure an alien prince as hot as you are won't have any trouble finding someone else."

Pain and angst welled over him in waves, filling the room like the bitter scent of nilgawood resin. All he wanted was to soothe her. "Human physiology is new to the galactic consortium, but there are healers among the Qalqan who—"

She sliced a hand through the air. "I tried to have a baby for eight years, and I'm done with heartbreak. I can't handle another failure. Besides, you don't have time for tests and treatments. You need someone to pop out a kid quick."

Then he understood—she wasn't resisting him so much as she wanted to do the right thing. She was being honest. But her sincerity only made him want her more. "You let me worry about that."

Hope flared against his Iki'i, but died almost as quick. "Worry all you want, but leave me out of it. I've moved on."

He could tell she hadn't moved on; she still yearned for exactly what he was offering, regardless of her refusal to see a healer. And he wanted her regardless of her capacity to bear children, even if only for a single interlude of passion. "Then let's not talk about it anymore. I'd still like to give you pleasure if you're willing. We won't reach Earth again for several of your days, and I can think of no better way to spend that time."

She squeezed her eyes closed, wiping angrily at a tear that escaped one corner.

It wasn't a yes, but it wasn't a no, either, and he could sense she was tempted. He stood to face her and gently tucked a strand of hair behind her ear, letting his fingertips trail lightly down the side of her neck to her shoulder. Her indecision felt like a sheet of brittle ice melting in the sun. He leaned closer, letting his breath heat the skin where his fingers had touched. "What do you have to lose?"

Biting her bottom lip, she shrugged. "I guess I've got nothing better to do." She lifted red-rimmed eyes to meet his. "As long as you understand there'll be no babies."

He smiled and pulled her into his arms. "Think only of pleasure."

He was going to make her forget all about pain and regret.

CHAPTER EIGHT

Toward the end of Georgie's marriage, sex had become so focused on getting her pregnant, it had felt like a chore. Arazhi was offering her a chance to enjoy her own body again. And it had been so long since she'd felt desirable.

She relaxed into his arms, still worried she was making a mistake. She could enjoy being with him now, before he moved on and found a suitable woman. One who could give him everything she couldn't. She'd been relieved to learn he didn't intend to take his child from its mother, but it was a bittersweet relief. *Why can't it be me?*

Arazhi kissed her softly, as if sensing her need for tenderness, stroking her hair, feathering butterfly kisses over her cheeks and eyelids. Then he pressed his forehead to hers, just holding her and letting his presence wash over her.

After a few calm moments, he said, "Come."

Taking her hand, he led her down the purple-veined

hallway to another curved room. A circular bed made up with sheets that looked like iridescent mirror glaze sat in the center. Shelves lined the walls, filled with an assortment of odd items. Her gaze snagged on a flickering cube with the image of a blue man with his arm around an alabaster-skinned woman. Arazhi's parents? But before she could ask, she was pushed back onto the bed.

The shimmering covers felt buttery soft against her bare arms and shoulders. All thoughts of his family photos left her as she looked up at the perfectly cut muscles of Arazhi's torso and abs. His midnight dark eyes were sexy as hell, and the way he was looking at her made her breath catch in her throat.

He placed his hands on her thighs and slowly slid up her gown, letting the air caress her legs. By the time the hem reached the top of her thighs, her entire body trembled with anticipation. He let his thumbs slide between her legs, stroking softly upward in exactly the way she'd imagined when he'd licked between her fingers.

She let out a shaky breath and relaxed her legs, letting them part beneath his touch as he worked his way up. His fingertip bumped against her panties, and she flexed toward him involuntarily.

Chuckling, he ran his thumbs over the lace covering her hips, sending shivers of delight straight to her core.

"I want to see you naked," he said. "Show me how to remove your gown."

Although she felt ready to rip her panties off and let him take her, she complied and rolled over onto her stomach. "Pull down on the metal tab."

His knees sank into the mattress on either side of her as he straddled her hips, then the warmth of his hands met her back. He lowered the zipper until it stopped at the base of her spine. "Intriguing closure."

She chuckled. "I thought you were an advanced species. How can you be unfamiliar with a zipper?"

"We use *supo* cloth. No need for zippers." His hands slid along her back beneath the bodice and over the strap of her bra, easily discovering how to release the constricting elastic. With a deft pull, he detangled her from the gown and flipped her onto her back once more, leaving her in nothing but her panties.

He licked his lips, hungry gaze roaming her body.

She breathed shallowly, letting her own attention run down his gorgeous body. Her eyes widened at the sight of his bulging crotch. She swore she could see the actual outline of his dick beneath his pants. Heat flooded her panties. What did he look like?

She sat up and reached for his waistband. "I want to see you, too."

He took her hands in his, stopping her. "Do not be alarmed."

His words made her gulp, eyes locked on his bulge. "I wasn't until you said something."

Whatever was under his clothes was pulsing—actually pulsing. She was about to see an alien cock. What if he was too big for her? Or shaped strange? She didn't mind a little kink, but just how kinky was this about to get? Were they even compatible?

Then, right before her eyes, his pants seemed to melt away,

and she was looking at a thick blue shaft between heavily muscled legs. It looked like her favorite vibrator, a pronounced head with ridges along the top of the shaft and a clit tickler at the base—except this piece of masculinity was very much alive. A small bead of pre-cum glistened at the tip.

She gasped and raised her eyes to his. "Your pants were an illusion?"

He laughed. "I guess you might say that."

She ran one finger along the top of his curved length. His skin was hot, and he grunted softly at her touch, thrusting his hips forward. She leaned in, inhaling his clean masculinity. She'd never wanted to taste a man like she wanted to taste him. Circling her tongue over the turgid head, she wrapped one hand around the base of his shaft. His taste was rich with a hint of spice that was potently male.

He remained perfectly still as she explored. Mouth opening wide, she took him in deeper. As her fingers circled his dick, she felt another protrusion below his shaft, between his ball sack and dick. Her pussy clenched, imagining what that might be for.

Flattening her tongue against the sensitive underside, she sucked in her cheeks and drew back.

He groaned, a low, deep sound that sent heat straight to her pussy and spread up her abdomen to her nipples.

She took him in again until his cock bumped the back of her throat. He was the perfect length, thick and solid.

His fingers released her hair from its messy bun, threading through the strands as she worked his shaft, losing herself in his flavor and heat.

Suddenly, he pulled away, urging her backward onto the

soft iridescent sheets. He slid a knee between her legs, spreading them under his hungry touch.

Her nipples were rock hard, and wetness soaked her panties. His breath fanned over her inner thighs as he pulled her panties from her, then kissed his way up the inside of her legs to her center. He pushed a finger inside her, his tongue circling her clit as he drew out, then thrust back in. Out. In. Long thick finger driving in until his knuckles met her outer lips, hot tongue flicking over her clit. Her juices coated her thighs.

An orgasm rose inside her, hot and tight, and she bucked her hips in time to his plunging finger. She couldn't remember ever needing to come this fast. As she strained to reach the crest, he pushed in hard, and she felt a firm probing at her back hole. Before she could clench, he'd entered her there.

She screamed as the wave broke, pleasure shuddering through her as he continued plunging in and out with both fingers.

When she came down enough to regain her senses, he crawled up her body, sucking in one nipple, then the other. "Are you ready for me, Georgie?"

"Yes," she gasped. She needed more of him. Needed to be filled completely.

He settled between her legs, thick cock pressing her entrance. It stretched her opening almost to the point of pain. But he didn't hurt her. Pushing in shallowly, he locked eyes with her, rocking in and out, sinking deeper. Deeper. She could feel every ridge along his shaft as he entered.

When his hips met hers, he let out a long sigh. "So hot."

She panted against his shoulder, hands clawing his back. That part of him she'd thought was a clit tickler did exactly that, cupping and kneading her swollen bud and making her squirm with pleasure. The smaller protrusion below his main shaft prodded her ass without entering, which was good. His cock alone was huge, and she wasn't sure she could take more of him inside her.

He eased back, tilting his hips in such a way that kept his tickler on just the right spot, then thrust in again. She gasped, bucking in time to his increasing rhythm. As her muscles spasmed, she tossed her head against the covers. Her hands clutched his shoulders. All she could do was hang on as ecstasy flooded her.

He drove forward, hips slamming into hers. Heat exploded against her inner walls, and he grunted.

Riding out her own wave, she managed to crack her eyes open and watch his abs flex as he continued to pulse inside her. He was staring at her, his intensity sexy enough to make her orgasm flutter once more.

When she could breathe again, he lowered himself on top of her and murmured into her neck. "Next time will be even better. I promise."

She couldn't imagine better. Her body felt like a giant marshmallow floating in a sea of hot chocolate. But hell if she was going to say no to a next time.

CHAPTER NINE

They made love several more times before Georgie could no longer stay awake. She'd never lost herself so deeply to any experience. Her brain was in a heavy fog as she lay on her side with Arazhi's body curled around hers. She was surprised by how safe she felt as she drifted to sleep.

She didn't know how much time had passed when she opened her eyes and stretched to find herself alone. Her heart constricted. She'd hoped to find Arazhi next to her, smiling with that sweet dimple. To spend a few lazy hours in his bed, talking and getting to know him. But that wasn't what he'd promised. He'd offered her a mere few hours of pleasure, nothing more. Now she'd return to Earth, and he'd find a woman who could provide what he wanted—a baby.

Get over it, Georgie, she told herself. She wasn't meant to be a mother, and she barely knew Arazhi, anyway. When she got home, she'd see what she could salvage of her wrecked event planning business, get out of her parents' apartment, maybe adopt a dog, and get on with her life—assuming the chaos with the poisoned aliens hadn't caused the end of the world.

Thinking about Earth again got her blood flowing, and she once more worried about her friends. No longer wanting sleep, she reached for the floor near the bed, searching for her glasses. She didn't remember taking them off, and hoped they hadn't gotten crushed. Thankfully, they were fine, folded neatly and waiting for her by the bed on a low table she hadn't noticed earlier. She settled them on her nose and spotted her dress hanging against the opposite wall. She would've liked to wear something more comfortable, but none of the shelves held clothing, only the curios and image cubes she'd noted earlier.

Rising, she went over and pulled down the garment. The strap had been repaired as if by magic, with no sign of damage. Arazhi's ship must have some sort of fabric repair technology she wasn't aware of. That had been nice of him, at least. A parting gift before he sent her on her way. Her bra and panties lay folded on the shelf nearby.

She stepped into her dress while examining a nearby cube with flickering images. In one photo, a blue-skinned man stood between two aliens with green and yellow scales. He bore a slight resemblance to Arazhi, but she couldn't be sure if it was him or a close relative. The next image was a different blue-skinned man with his arm around a short woman with alabaster skin and dark blue hair. The woman wore a crown that looked like it was made of interwoven diamonds and gazed at the man with obvious adoration. *Arazhi's parents?*

The image shifted to a short video of the same woman, only

without a crown this time, bouncing a small blue toddler while the blue man watched with obvious love in his gaze. Double moons hovered over rolling purple hills in the background. *That must be a young Arazhi and his parents visiting the fields he mentioned.* Georgie's chest tightened at the thought of Arazhi taking his new family on a trip, his dark eyes filled with love as he watched over the mother of his child.

Enough torturing myself. Turning away, she went to the lavatory and cleaned herself up. At least a lavatory was a lavatory, even on an alien ship. When she returned, soft music was playing, and a small table and two chairs had appeared in the room. A rich, buttery smell with hints of fruit wafted from a covered plate on the table.

Arazhi entered carrying two glasses. He set them on the table. "I was hungry and thought you might be, as well. Please, sit."

A wave of giddiness passed through her. *He didn't just use and abandon me.* Or even leave a servant to see to her. He'd come back to take care of her himself. Suddenly ravenous, she gladly took the seat beside him, wondering what alien delicacy he had for her today.

He lifted the lid, exposing what looked like sticky buns. "Baked *kazhitu*. A type of nut that grows on my mother's planet." He picked one up with his fingers and put it on a small plate in front of her. "I believe you will like it."

There were no utensils in sight, so Georgie picked up a bun with her fingers. She took a small nibble, surprised by how soft it was as it all but melted on her tongue. The sticky glaze tasted like apple pie filling. "Oh, wow."

Arazhi smiled and took one himself, devouring half in a single bite. He poured them each a large glass of what looked like orange juice and took a deep gulp.

Cautious about chasing the sticky bun sweetness with sour juice, Georgie took a cautious sip. A flavor like sweet cream, only cleaner and more refreshing, hit her tongue. She took a bigger drink, realizing how parched she was. Not surprising, considering how active she'd been for the last few hours. Heat crept into her cheeks at the memory.

A warm hand covered her thigh, sending a jolt of awareness straight to her tired pussy. She looked up, startled. Arazhi's midnight eyes made her want to fall into them and never come out.

"You're very sexy when you enjoy your food, *kikajiru*," he murmured.

The heat in her cheeks intensified. "Uh, thanks." Why was he still trying to charm her? She'd been very clear about their situation. She was tempted to set him straight again, but another part of her just wanted to enjoy being pampered. "What does *kikajiru* mean?"

"Distracting one."

Unsure if that was a compliment or not, she changed the subject, pointing toward the picture cube she'd looked at earlier. "Is that your family?"

He raised his eyebrows. "Yes. But I'm surprised you recognized them."

She shrugged. "I was just going off the fact that the man and baby were blue. What species is your mom?"

"She's a Vatosangan, from a planet two solar systems away from Kirenai Prime."

"Do Kirenai always buy their females? Like you tried to buy me?"

He laughed. "No, my parents met at a game of *bacca*. She accidentally hit him with a disk. He, of course, fell immediately in love."

Georgie took another drink. So aliens could fall in love. *Just not with me.* She pointed to an ornately carved pink box on another shelf. "What are all those other things?"

Arazhi rose and picked up the box. "Things I've collected during my travels. This is a *G'naxian tolonovone*. An antique."

He traced a raised curve on the lid and the box seemed to open like the petals of a rose. Pulling one petal free, he ran the slightly pointed tip down the outside of her arm, leaving a trail of golden light on her skin.

Shock rippled through her. She ran her fingers over the light, expecting it to wipe away, but it seemed to be embedded beneath her skin like a tattoo. She had a black tattoo of rosebuds in a wreath of leaves around her ankle that was supposed to be in color, but the needle had hurt too much, and she'd never gone back to finish it. "That's amazing. How long does it last?"

Arazhi selected a second petal and tapped it alongside the line, creating glowing pink dots this time. "With this device, the patterns only last a day or so. New technology can make them more or less permanent, though you must be careful with your patterns."

"Why?"

A dimple appeared on Arazhi's cheek as he removed a third

petal and made small orange swishes around each of the pink dots. "G'naxians use light to communicate attraction and arousal."

She found it suddenly hard to breathe. The way his fingers held the petal, dancing it across her skin, was mesmerizing. She wanted him to paint her whole body. "What is the pattern you're painting now?"

"I'm not familiar with their traditional patterns." He traced one finger over the swirling lines. "I simply enjoy making my own." His midnight eyes rose to meet hers. "Will you allow me to use more of you as a canvas?"

She nodded mutely, accepting his hand to help her stand. He moved behind her and slid her zipper down, loosening the straps of her dress, letting the fabric slide down her body to the floor. He unfastened her bra and dropped it, too, then rolled her panties down her hips.

Breathless, she stepped out of them, feeling his gaze assess her naked body before he began painting, dappling her shoulders, outlining her buttocks, painting her toes. He smoothed wide swathes of gold light up the sides of her belly, circled her navel, and tipped her nipples in pink. The only touch he made to her face was her lips, a brief flutter of sensation, and she didn't even know what color they might be.

He stepped back and smiled, closing the petals back into a box. "You look like a G'naxian goddess."

Georgie looked down her front, taking in the vibrant display of color. "Do you have a mirror?"

"Of course." Arazhi moved to the wall and touched it. The spaces between the ribs in the walls, floor, and ceiling suddenly changed from lavender to reflective, like hundreds of mirrors.

"Whoa." She took a step back, slightly dizzy as she was faced with a thousand versions of her glowing self. "This feels like a funhouse."

"What's a funhouse? The word implies enjoyment, but you do not sound pleased."

"It's okay, I was just startled." She stepped closer, focusing on one image of herself. It was hard to get a true picture when there were reflections upon reflections of multi-colored glowing lines. "A funhouse is something they have at carnivals. Kind of hard to explain, but the gist is to disorient people. A lot of them have a mirror room, but they also have obstacle courses, moving stairs or halls, and the spooky ones have creatures that jump out and try to frighten you."

"That does not sound fun at all." The mirrors disappeared.

"Humans enjoy a bit of adrenaline now and then. A funhouse is pretty benign compared to other things thrill seekers do." She smiled. "Can you put a mirror on just one wall?"

"Here. I'll show you how." He took her hand, pulling her to where he'd been standing, and placed her palm on the wall. "Do you feel this?"

All she could pay attention to was his warm skin against hers, but she tried to feel what he was talking about. "I'm not sure."

He guided her fingers over raised bumps of differing sizes and shapes. The sensation reminded her of braille on an elevator button. "You can see the texture difference, as well."

She circled one bump with her fingertip, and the lighting in the room brightened. "How do you tell which ones do what?"

"By size and shape, of course."

Of course, she thought wryly. She squinted at the bumps and ran her finger across an elongated oval. A slight breeze wafted through the room, smelling of wintergreen.

"That's ventilation. This is the mirror control." He pointed to a cluster of three small bumps. "To get a single mirror, touch one raised spot twice."

She did as instructed, and one wall became a mirror. Smiling, she turned and looked at herself once more. The glowing lines over her skin weren't as garish as she'd first imagined, but the outlines along her hips and breasts definitely accentuated her curves. "Do you have any photos of G'naxians? I'd like to know who I'm ruling over if I'm going to be a goddess."

He laughed. "I believe so." He went to one of his shelves. "Let me see..."

As he was looking, a voice seemed to come out of nowhere, uttering syllables she didn't understand. Then the floor shuddered as if they were having an earthquake.

"What just happened?" Georgie clutched her arms over her naked breasts, moving toward her discarded clothing.

Arazhi turned to her with a smile. "We have arrived."

CHAPTER TEN

Arazhi let Georgie dress and then led her to the bridge where the view screen showed the curved blue and purple horizon of Kirenai Prime. *Home.* He was anxious to find out if his father was all right, but torn because his time with Georgie felt far too short. Now it would be back to duty for him, searching for a woman to bear his child. And as the first human arriving on Kirenai Prime through official channels, Georgie would be sought after as a rare bed partner.

Jealousy rose in him as he thought about her in another Kirenai's bed.

Georgie moved close enough to brush shoulders with him and looked at the view screen. She let out an appreciative sigh. "Is that your planet?"

He loved having her at his side. Loved feeling her awe. He would like nothing more than to show her the universe, if only to experience it again through her eyes. "Yes. Welcome to Kirenai Prime."

"It's beautiful." She traced a swirl of white clouds obscuring the surface of the planet with one fingertip. "I wish I could stay and see it, but I really want to check on my friends. How soon can we turn around?"

Arazhi's heart fell. He'd hoped their time together might've made her want more. *Just put her on a ship and send her home.* But he balked at the idea of her spending the return trip with another Kirenai. If he had to go back to Earth for another female, he might as well be the one who took her. "Would you mind if I visited my father first?"

A dark wave of guilt flooded his Iki'i. "Of course," she blurted.

Her compassion moved him. She hardly knew him, and yet she cared. He wanted to ease her guilt. "The communication system can sync now. Let me see if I can contact my security officer. He's still on your planet and should be able to provide an update."

The connection took a few moments before Zhiruto's image appeared on the screen. He was still bare-chested, but his features had shifted, so he now had a slightly crooked nose and what looked like a scar above one eyebrow. "My prince. You're safe at home?"

"We've reached Kirenai Prime, yes. What's happening on Earth?"

Zhiruto scratched his head. "The transporters are still locked down, and all but one of the IDA guests are accounted for—thirteen Kirenai are dead."

Arazhi closed his eyes a moment. "That's terrible. Any survivors?"

"The Khargals and the Fogarian are fine. Three Kirenai are alive but in critical condition. A human doctor has been consulting with one of our healers in orbit and administering treatment. No prognosis yet. Any word on your father?"

"We're still in orbit. I'll contact you again after I see him."

Zhiruto nodded. "Arazhi, I believe our suspect may be a *burendo*. It's the only explanation for how he's evading detection."

Arazhi frowned. Although Kirenai could assume different forms, altering one's coloration outside of various hues of blue was a rare skill. *Burendo* could change color as well as shape, allowing them to blend in with local populations with extreme success. They were often hired as spies or assassins. "I thought the IDA had screened the guests. How did a *burendo* get an invitation?"

"I don't know yet." Zhiruto pulled back to show a woman sitting on a sofa next to a large, furry reddish quadruped with floppy ears and a long muzzle. The creature had its head in her lap, and she was rubbing its ears. "This human is a member of local law enforcement. She has a plan to get us back onto the site to look for leads."

Georgie shouldered in closer to see the screen. "Lora?"

The woman's eyes widened, and she shot to her feet, moving next to Zhiruto. "Georgie? Where are you? What's going on with your skin?"

"Oh." Georgie looked at her glowing forearms. "It's painted

on, don't worry. I'm fine. What's happening there? Is everyone okay?"

"Depends on your definition of okay. No humans are dead, but the aliens are understandably upset. It doesn't help that the NSA quarantined everyone for nearly two days. The aliens who are still alive are locked down." She shot a wary glance at Zhiruto. "Except this one. He managed to escape and asked for my help finding the murderer." She frowned, scanning the background through the camera. "Where are you, anyway?"

"I'm currently orbiting an alien planet, believe it or not." Georgie laughed, sending a shiver of discomfort across Arazhi's Iki'i. "I'm heading back to Earth now. I should arrive in a few days."

"Girl, don't." Lora held up a palm. "The NSA's been looking for you. They consider you a person of interest, and they're assholes. You do not want to end up in their hands. Plus, if more aliens show up, they'll tighten security again and mess up my plan to get back inside the park."

Arazhi allowed himself a smile. As much as he wanted to grant Georgie's wish to be reunited with her friends, he wouldn't be upset if this woman convinced her to stay with him longer.

Georgie looked at him. For a moment, he worried she knew what he was thinking. Then she turned back to the screen. "I guess I can stay here a while. But I'll be in touch. Take care of yourself, okay?"

"You, too." Lora blew her a kiss.

Zhiruto's face took over the screen again. "Glad to see you got your human off planet."

Arazhi nodded. Though he'd mistakenly assumed Georgie was to be his bondservant, he was glad he'd spirited her away from the trouble back on Earth. With an assassin on the loose, who knew what might've happened to anyone connected to the prince? Now he just needed Zhiruto to return safely, as well. "Stay safe, my friend, and keep me informed."

"I will."

The screen went dark.

There was nothing more he could do, so Arazhi turned to Georgie with a smile. "Sounds like you're going to stay a while. Perhaps I can interest you in a tour of the popotan fields after all?"

CHAPTER ELEVEN

Georgie stood inside the ship's airlock, staring down the landing ramp at the alien landscape. The sun outside seemed brighter, more white than yellow, and the plants she could see tended toward blue and purple rather than green. Her chest felt tight, and she realized she was holding her breath, even though Arazhi had already opened the door and taken a few steps down the ramp.

He'd reassured her she'd be safe, but she was about to set foot on an alien planet. What if she couldn't breathe? What if gravity made it hard to walk? At least astronauts had space suits —she had nothing but a ball gown and bare feet, since she'd kicked off her shoes back on Earth.

Arazhi held out a hand and encouraged her to follow him with a small gesture.

Nerves tingling, she thought, *here goes nothing*, and took a small sip of air. When she didn't keel over, she exhaled and took a larger breath. The humid air smelled earthy and slightly metallic. Placing one foot firmly on the ramp, she stepped out under the alien sun.

Rolling hills covered in blue foliage spread as far as she could see. Mishmashed structures poked above the tree line, everything from clusters of thatched domes to sparkling glass high rises. Directly across the stone platform where the ship had touched down, a massive building set with fantastically curved spires looked as if it was being overrun by vines. It reminded her of pictures she'd seen in National Geographic of ruins in Thailand or South America, except the plants were the wrong colors. At the bottom of the landing ramp, a double column of guards formed a pathway toward the building.

"Is that the palace?" she asked.

"Yes. Welcome to my home." He wiggled his fingers. "Now come, *kikajiru*. The sun is hot. I want to get you inside."

Gulping, she took one step, then another, and grabbed his hand to let him lead her down the ramp. The ground was hot against her bare soles, but not unbearably, and she glanced over her shoulder at the ship she'd just left, getting a good look at it for the first time. It resembled a pale purple rosebud, the outside made of the same veined leaves as the inner walls.

Arazhi paused near the first guard to say something she didn't understand. The guard answered in the same language. He was blue like Arazhi, but his face looked more like the snout of a dog than a man, and fine blue hair covered what she could see of his skin. In fact, all the guards were as varied in shape and size as the nearby city. One had what looked like antennae sprouting from his forehead, and another had huge bird claws for hands.

Every one of them was staring at her.

She edged closer to Arazhi. "What kind of aliens are these?"

He flicked a glance at the nearest one, then back to her. "They are Kirenai."

He'd said it as if it explained everything. She looked at the one with bird claws. "I don't understand."

"We're shapeshifters, remember? These are their chosen forms."

Her stomach dropped, making her stumble. "Shapeshifters?"

Arazhi caught her by the elbow. "Did the IDA not tell you?"

She tried to recall any mention of shapeshifting in the numerous pages of the contract she'd signed. "I don't remember reading anything about shapeshifters..." Her attention slid involuntarily down his chest as the implications sank in. *Arazhi is a shapeshifter.* What did he really look like? "So... this isn't your real body?"

Eyes glittering, he laughed and put an arm around her, pulling her along with him toward the palace. "It's entirely my own body. One I hope pleases you."

Well, that certainly explained why he looked so hot. If she could choose what to look like, she'd want a supermodel body, too. "What do you look like for real?"

"We don't show our resting state to strangers." He kept walking without glancing at her.

A wash of disappointment filled her as she recalled the

intimate ways he'd touched her, not once, but many times. He'd even painted her in tattoos that still glowed upon her skin. "Oh. I thought we were more than strangers."

He sighed and leaned closer, his arm still around her. "I prefer not to talk in front of the guards."

His words eased her concern enough to keep her moving.

He dropped his arm from her shoulders, nodding at the guards as they passed. Entering a large gate in the stone wall, they moved through a courtyard shaded by a thick canopy of blue leaves. A tiny brook trickled between scaled gray tree trunks, and clusters of white and yellow flowers grew here and there. The path they were on looked like white pea gravel with a pearly sheen, and she bent to pick one up. She could swear to God it was an actual pearl. "Is this real?"

Arazhi had continued on without her, apparently anxious to check on his father. "Is what real?"

"Never mind." She clasped the pearl in her fist and hurried after him. She would ask him about it later.

He pushed open a door that looked similar to the same leaf-like material of the ship. A diminutive person of indistinct gender met them, bowing low and jabbering something.

Arazhi nodded and nudged Georgie forward. "Deshel will show you to my room. I'll be along soon."

Then he strode away without a backward glance.

Georgie gaped after him. She'd thought she'd be meeting his father. Instead, she felt like she'd been kicked to the curb. *Of course he doesn't want me with him.* His father was dying, not in a state to receive guests, let alone meet a stranger. Plus, the emperor of the galaxy probably didn't agree to see just anyone.

Even so, she felt a little salty that Arazhi would ask her to have his baby, yet disregard inviting her to meet his parents.

A gentle hand on her elbow drew her attention down to the little alien called Deshel. The being reminded her of a house-elf without ears. Waving a slender blue hand, Deshel gestured for Georgie to follow, a string of nonsense streaming from its tiny mouth.

Georgie took one last glance at Arazhi's retreating form, then followed the alien down a stone hallway. It wasn't as if she had anywhere else to be at the moment.

Deshel blabbered the entire time they walked, leading Georgie to a large room with floor to ceiling windows and strange items scattered in clusters like furniture. There were chairs and tables, but other items were baffling. There was a plush, banana-shaped structure the size of a compact car, and three chair-sized metal buckets perched on six delicate feet.

As she took it in, she realized Deshel had gone silent. She turned to find the alien's large eyes looking at her as if waiting for something.

Does he want a tip? Georgie shook her head. "I don't understand. I'm sorry."

Deshel let out a small sigh and spoke a string of obviously frustrated words before tapping his-or-her forehead with one finger.

Is this alien saying I'm stupid? Georgie narrowed her eyes and crossed her arms. "I just got here and don't speak alien, all right?"

Shrinking back, Deshel bobbed as if in apology, then once more gestured for Georgie to follow.

They passed through a bedroom into a third room that looked like it was tiled in the same pearl stone that made up the path in the garden. Light filtered between the blue fronds shading the windows, and beyond them she could see more of the rolling hills and strange buildings in the distance. In the center of the room rested a round, sunken basin brimming with water.

Still speaking a never-ending stream of syllables, Deshel made a flourish with one hand, making it very clear she was to bathe.

Georgie glanced longingly at the huge tub. The lavatory on the ship had been adequate, but a nice hot soak sounded divine. She nodded and stepped toward the basin. The tub looked like it was fed by a natural hot spring, the surface rippling slightly where the water entered and exited on opposite sides. But unlike any hot spring Georgie had ever visited, there was no lingering scent of sulfur. In fact, the smell here reminded her of gardenias and vanilla.

She turned to thank Deshel and discovered the small alien had already gone. *Well, all right, then.* At least he'd given her privacy.

Glancing around one last time to be certain she was truly alone, she stripped out of her dress and underthings, then stepped into the tub. The water engulfed her in warmth, scented steam curling around her face like a caress. As she relaxed, she couldn't help but wonder if she was trapped in a dream. Everything she liked seemed to come her way the moment she wanted or needed it. Even Arazhi's lovemaking had been the epitome of perfect.

She bit her lip, remembering Arazhi's revelation about being a shapeshifter. How had she missed that in the IDA paperwork? And why hadn't Arazhi mentioned it? It seemed like it should've come up in conversation at some point. Was he hideous behind that gorgeous façade?

She shook her head. It didn't matter. She wasn't some princess destined to kiss a frog and turn him into a prince to get her happily-ever-after. Arazhi was already a prince, and he hadn't offered to marry her, even if she could somehow offer him a baby.

The thought made her throat tighten, and she ducked beneath the water, wetting her hair. She could find no shampoo or soap, but the water smelled great on its own, so she rose, looking for a towel to dry herself. Dripping water, she moved to one wall, thinking perhaps there were buttons on it like on the ship—a compartment where they kept towels or something. As she moved over a spot on the floor, a strong breeze hit her, seeming to come from all directions at once.

She stopped and laughed, turning in a slow circle to let the air dry her off. "Like a car wash for people," she said aloud, finger-combing her hair and enjoying the subtle flowery scent surrounding her.

Though she wasn't thrilled to put her dress back on, it was all she had, so she returned to the edge of the tub where she'd dropped it. The floor was bare, her dress nowhere in sight. Had it blown away? She searched the corners of the room but found neither dress nor undergarments. Had that little alien come back and stolen her things?

Frustrated, she peeked around the corner into the bedroom.

Something that might be clothing lay neatly on the foot of the bed. "Oh, thank God."

As she stepped into the room, a scaled pink man with large slitted eyes rose from a chair tucked in one corner. His chest was bare, and he wore black straps that resembled suspenders holding up a black ankle-length skirt.

Georgie let out a squeak and stumbled back, arms crisscrossed over her front to hide her private parts. "Who the hell are you and what are you doing here?"

He held up two long-fingered hands. "Don't be afraid." His voice was raspy. "My name's Qantina. I've been instructed to provide you with a universal translator."

Georgie looked from the alien to the clothing on the bed. "Do you mind turning around so I can get dressed first?"

Qantina tilted his head, large eyes blinking, then spun to face the other direction. A line of bony ridges ran down his spine, and a stubby scaled tail protruded from his backside through a hole in the skirt.

Georgie edged toward the bed and snatched up the cloth. It was a sheet of soft, thin fabric, the same shade of blue as her dress. Not clothes, but it would do. She wrapped it around herself like a towel. It was a little short on the lower end, but it covered all the important parts. "All right."

The pink alien turned around, no expression on his lipless mouth. "Excellent. I'm not yet familiar with your species. If you would allow me, I would like to perform a scan so I may ascertain where the translator should be installed."

"How come I can understand you, but not that other alien who escorted me here?"

"The device works with the recipient's speech centers to facilitate both speaking and understanding, utilizing thousands of language databases. Once one is installed, it will not matter if those around you have an implant. Deshel is new here, however, and bondservants do not always have the latest technology when they arrive. I will see to it at once."

Bondservants. Wasn't that what Arazhi had called her when he thought he'd purchased her? "I'm not a bondservant," she said. "Arazhi is taking me back to Earth as soon as he's visited his father."

"Yes, he told Deshel this."

That was reassuring. "Okay."

Picking up a device that looked a bit like a TSA wand, Qantina stepped forward. "Remain still, please."

Starting at the top of her head, he pressed the wand against her and began making widening circles around her skull. After a few moments, he pulled out something that looked like a gun and pressed it behind her ear. A stinging sensation made her flinch. "There. All finished."

"That's it?" She touched the spot behind her ear gingerly. "I'll be able to understand everyone now?"

"Once the program has uploaded, yes."

If aliens could give her the ability to understand any language, was it possible they could restore her fertility as Arazhi had said? Swallowing her fear, she asked, "Are you a healer? A—" she stumbled over remembering the word Arazhi had used. "A Qalqan?"

"That is correct." Qantina placed the device back in his bag.

"What sorts of things can you heal?"

"We are skilled at determining the causes of many ailments. Why do you ask?"

Georgie smoothed the silky fabric over her hips. So Arazhi hadn't told the Qalqan of her problem conceiving. Part of her was grateful he'd respected her wish not to be disappointed again. Another part regretted being so insistent. These were aliens, after all, with superior technology. What if they really could fix her?

I could bear Arazhi's child. But it wouldn't be hers. He'd said he didn't intend to separate mother from child, but he'd made it very clear the child would be his. Which meant that if she had his baby, she'd basically be agreeing to become his bondservant.

She forced herself to smile and shook her head. "Never mind. Thank you for the translator."

CHAPTER TWELVE

Arazhi hurried through the palace corridors to the throne room. The guard he'd spoken to on the tarmac hadn't had any news of his father; obviously the royal council was keeping his condition secret. *It could be good news as easily as bad,* thought Arazhi as he burst into the royal living quarters. He wouldn't put it past his father to hide a miraculous recovery just to keep their rivals off balance.

The royal sleeping chamber was empty when he arrived, but the air still smelled of regeneration fluid. His gaze settled on his father's resting pod; the green liquid was calm as glass.

Arazhi's heart plummeted. He hurried to the edge of the pod, looking down at the indistinct blue form beneath the surface. "Father?"

Small ripples disturbed the surface as the blue shape at the bottom moved, but his father didn't rise to greet him.

Looking around the empty room, Arazhi called out, "Hello? Where is everyone?"

His mother entered from the balcony doorway. "Arazhi? No one told me you'd returned." She rushed forward to wrap her arms around his waist, then pulled back to look up at him. "You're so much taller than usual."

He kissed the top of her head, realizing he was still in his human form. Altering it now would be pointless, so he simply said, "This is the form my human prefers."

Her eyes lit up. "You found one, then?"

"We can talk about that in a moment." He wasn't ready to reveal that the female he'd selected didn't suit his parents' purpose. "How's father? Have the healers made any progress on an antidote?"

She nodded, but worry railed against his Iki'i. "Yes. They've halted the poison and Elthos says he will live."

He narrowed his eyes. "That's good news, right?"

"Indeed." She placed a finger to her lips. "He needs his rest. Come to the balcony so we can talk."

He followed her trail of fear outside to the far end of the stone balcony. A small table beneath the shade of the happa fronds still held a half-eaten meal, and potted yellow *kanzo* blossoms drooped in the heat nearby.

She took both his hands. "Tell me about your female. Is she carrying your child yet?"

"Why does it matter? If father will recover, there should be no rush for me to produce an heir." He bent his head so he could look directly into her eyes. "I sense a lie here."

Her brows knit, and she shook her head. "I'm not lying.

Your father will live. But..." She swallowed and tears brimmed in her eyes. "Elthos says he may never again be able to shift out of his current form."

Arazhi's stomach squeezed, and the brief moment of relief he'd felt about his father's escape from death felt like ash at the back of his throat. In their resting form, Kirenai couldn't easily communicate with other species. Which meant that his damma faced a future bonded to a mate she couldn't speak with. She'd have to rely on intermediaries. "Oh, Damma."

She swiped at the tears streaming down her cheeks. "He doesn't know yet, and I fear he may give up the will to live when he finds out. But he was clear about one thing the last time we spoke—he's counting on you to produce an heir and carry on our dynasty."

Arazhi looked away, staring at an insect with its face buried in the *kanzo* blooms. "The human I selected believes she is infertile."

Damma remained silent for a heartbeat, then sighed. "You were supposed to find a mother for your child, not another bedmate."

"By the time I found out, we were already on our way here." Not that he'd been interested in any of the other humans he'd seen while on Earth. "You're the one who told me to keep my heart open."

Damma's eyebrows shot up. "So she's your mate?"

Her direct question put him on edge. He didn't want to admit it, but the deepest part of him knew. *I'm meant to be with Georgie.* "All I know is that there's something between us. I want to make her happy."

Sighing, Damma looked him over, as if assessing his current form for flaws. "Well, I suppose that explains why you showed up in human form." She tapped her chin thoughtfully. "Earth's technology is primitive. Just because she believes she's infertile doesn't mean the problem can't be corrected. Did you take her to the royal healers?"

"Not yet," Arazhi said, remembering Georgie's conflicting emotions. "She said she tried to have a child for a long time and is afraid of being disappointed again. I need time to convince her."

"Arazhi, you know what's at stake. You're not bonded yet, so if she's not viable, you must leave her. Return to Earth and find another who is willing to produce your child."

The thought of taking another human to his bed stuck in his throat, no matter the stakes. At least he had a valid excuse for delaying. "I can't go back to Earth. Someone tried to kill me at the party."

"What?" Damma's alarm sliced through his Iki'i like a blade.

Arazhi described what had happened and how he'd been forced to leave his security officer behind. He glanced toward the door to the royal chambers. "Whoever poisoned the food is probably the same person who tried to kill father. Zhiruto has the transport web locked down until he finds the traitor."

"That's horrible." Damma sat heavily in her chair, her grief weighing against his Iki'i. Then a thoughtful look settled over her features. "You know, Earth isn't the only place to meet human females. Some women we rescued from the slave ship are still with us. It's how we know about their frequent estrus cycles—"

"Mother!" His shock at her pending suggestion overwhelmed anything his Iki'i might be receiving from her. "You can't be serious?"

"I'm not saying we should force anyone. But you are a prince and quite charming. I'll bet you could convince one to become the mother of the future emperor of the galaxy."

"No." He rose abruptly from his seat. "They've been through enough. I won't treat them like breeding stock."

She looked up, her voice rough. "I don't suggest it lightly. But these are desperate times. If Aguno takes the throne, the Senburu will control the galaxy, and if that happens, rest assured that more than a handful of primitive Earth women will be forced into slavery—including this woman you're so intent on having as your mate." The intensity of her emotions was like a gale force wind. "You have no time to waste on an infertile female. Keep her as a concubine if you wish, but you must take another who can bear a child. You have more to consider than yourself, Arazhi. Your duty must come first. The fate of the galaxy is in your hands."

Arazhi's teeth ached from grinding them. He knew his duty. But he also understood Georgie well enough to know she'd refuse to become a mere concubine. With her, it was all or nothing. He felt the same way. "Georgie would never accept that role."

Yet a sickening feeling was growing inside him, one he knew he couldn't fight. His mother spoke the truth. He mustn't allow his heart to cause the downfall of the galaxy. But he was unable to picture a future without Georgie. "Give me a few days. I'll try to convince her to see a healer. And if I can't, I'll consider a surrogate."

Damma pursed her lips. "I suppose we can keep your father's condition a secret a while longer. But you must hurry. As soon as word gets out about your father's prognosis, the Senburu will make their move."

Lowering his head in acknowledgement, Arazhi turned and strode from the royal chambers, heading to his quarters where Georgie waited. He'd spent a lot of time with women and knew how to please them. Yet he'd never had to worry about how they actually felt about him. Never had he felt as nervous as he did right now. Was he being a fool, like he had all those years ago on Sireta Prime? The disappointment of that youthful encounter still twisted in his chest.

You don't even know if she's the one. But there was a way to be certain.

Taking a detour to the courtyard, he strayed from the path to a jutting rock garden. The sun still glanced off the top of the highest rocks, and he stepped onto the first sharp ledge, letting his feet sense the hardness of the stone. He'd often played here as a boy, pretending to be a Fogarian explorer, and now he relaxed his matrix, imagining the sharp noses and facial hair common to the species. Looking at his hands, he tried to form a Fogarian's short claws and broad palms.

Although his human features had softened, he couldn't seem to grasp the shape he was seeking. Thinking he might need to start from scratch, he looked around to verify no one was watching, then let himself sink into his resting form before once more pulling himself upright as a Fogarian.

But when he looked at his hands, they had the blunt nails of a human. He touched his cheeks, finding smooth skin. And his nose was the same aquiline shape he'd worn for the past few days. Human.

Which could only mean one thing.

Georgie was his mate.

CHAPTER THIRTEEN

Georgie stood on the veranda outside the suite and gazed into the vivid alien forest beyond. Towering blue trees grew right up to the palace walls, while farther out between the tree trunks, ground-hugging underbrush ranged from mahogany to midnight blue. Through a small clearing in the trees, she could see a road snaking through the forest, alive with oddly organic-looking vehicles, and more traffic moved overhead in the azure sky. Yet despite the activity, there was no roar of jets or rumble of wheels. The air was impossibly quiet; the only sound was the occasional whirr, hum, or rustle of local wildlife.

She edged farther along the short railing, keeping to the shade as the sun sank toward the trees. The few minutes she'd been exposed to the blazing white orb's rays had made her fair skin prickle, and she'd quickly recognized how easily she'd burn under this alien star. At least a gentle breeze from the forest tempered the heat.

Inhaling the slightly metallic smelling air, she reminisced about how only a few weeks ago she'd been arguing with Maise and Lora about whether or not aliens were real. Now, here she was—in an alien palace, no less—waiting for her alien lover to return. She glanced down at the paint still glowing faintly on her arms, recalling how he'd created the patterns with almost reverent attention to every inch of her body. She wasn't the kind of girl who swooned, but damn if that hadn't made her come close.

"Georgie," Arazhi's deep voice drew her attention.

She looked up to find him standing stiffly in the doorway, features slack as if in shock. Concerned that he'd received bad news, she hurried over. "How's your dad?"

He put both arms around her and pulled her close, bending to inhale deeply at the top of her head. "Not well."

She wrapped her arms around his waist and squeezed. "I'm so sorry."

He held her like that for a long moment, then sighed and kissed her forehead before pulling away. "You're a great comfort to me."

She smiled up at him. "I'm glad I'm here for you, then."

"So am I." He sighed heavily. "But I need to talk with you."

Her stomach lurched. His tone reminded her of when Josh had given her the news he was leaving her. "Of course."

He led her inside to the large bed and sat on the edge, pulling her to sit next to him. "You know that in order to become emperor, I must produce an heir."

Yep. Pretty much the same conversation I had with Josh.

Why couldn't she be worth more to Arazhi than her ability to breed? "Of course. I understand."

His fingers tilted her chin toward him. "Will you please reconsider seeing our healers? Time is of the essence, and with the situation on Earth, I'm uncertain when I can return you."

To exchange for a new female, she finished the sentence in her mind. Jealousy jabbed her heart like a white-hot poker, and she had to remind herself to focus on the good things she had on Earth. Parents who loved her, friends, a business... well, she hoped she still had a business after the debacle at the auction.

But what if his healers can actually fix me? Arazhi was gorgeous, wealthy, artistic. He even knew how to be forceful without being an ass—something most human men never learned. And the way he tended her every need told her he'd make a wonderful father.

Looking into his eyes, she saw hope there that mirrored her own. She bit her lip, resisting the urge to say yes and chance another heartbreak. Yet she also couldn't seem to say no. The silence stretched. *Yes. Say yes.* But the word remained a lump in her throat.

As if sensing her teetering, he released her chin and made a sweeping gesture toward the palace. "I promise that as the mother of the future emperor, you'll live right here in the palace and be lavished with the finest things the galaxy can offer."

It was as if a guillotine dropped, severing any urge to agree. This wasn't a romantic offer or even an offer of partnership as a co-parent. He was offering to pay her to produce his child. She yanked her hand from his and stood, looking down on the muscled blue alien. "I have no desire to become a brood mare, well-kept or not. I want a husband."

He rose slowly, eyes becoming slits. "I should've known."

Alarmed at the sight of this new side to Arazhi, she asked, "Known what?"

"You're no different than the others." His lips curled into a sneer. "Only better at distracting me from your lies with your emotions. Are you truly even barren? Or is that just a ploy?"

She frowned and shook her head. "A ploy? For what?"

He stepped forward until he loomed over her, looking down into her upturned face. "To become queen."

"To..." She gaped at him. "You think I orchestrated all of this to become a queen?" Planting her hands against his chest, she shoved. He remained solidly in place. She glared, refusing to back down. "You're the one who abducted me, remember?"

His fathomless dark eyes bored straight into her soul. "You were in charge of the auction."

"So? I didn't force you to bid on me." Her breath heaved. How dare he put her through all this, then accuse her of being deceitful? "I didn't even know you were a prince until we were already on route to your planet."

His nostrils flared, as if trying to sniff out the truth. Then his brows drew together, and he took a step back. "Do you truly have no desire for the throne?"

"I couldn't care less about some throne in a galaxy far, far away." She waved a hand at the darkening sky out the windows, noting the fading swirls of light Arazhi'd tattooed on her skin. She'd been a fool to imagine he wanted more than her body and its ability to bear children. *Inability*, she reminded herself, covering her mouth with one hand and fighting a blur of tears. Her heart felt like it was about to break into pieces. "I want a husband who loves me—regardless of whether I can bear him a child or not."

Arazhi's features softened, and he stared at her as if awestruck. "I've misjudged you."

She dropped her hand from her mouth, balling it into a fist and trying to summon more indignation. But her words only emerged as a whisper, "Damn right you've misjudged me."

Slowly sinking to one knee in front of her, he took her clenched hand. "Can you forgive me?"

She jerked her fist away, wishing she was ballsy enough to punch him in the face. "Why should I?"

"Because I love you."

Time stopped for a moment. She blinked. Mere seconds ago, he'd accused her of deceit. Then there was the fact they'd only just met. How could he love her? "You're only saying that so I'll go see the healers. The moment they confirm I'm barren, you'll kick my ass to the curb."

He tilted his head. "I don't know what this curb is you refer to, but rest assured I would never, ever kick you."

His sincere confusion almost made her smile. Almost. "It means you'll throw me away like trash. Discard and abandon."

"Never." He shook his head, his midnight eyes full of integrity. "I wish to give you everything your heart desires. I was wrong to doubt your intentions. You are my mate."

Taking her hand again, he pressed his forehead to her knuckles, then once more met her gaze. "I, Prince Arazhi, first in line of the Yazhu dynasty, offer myself for your pleasure for the rest of your days. Georgie, in the manner of the Kirenai mate-bond, will you become my queen?"

Her breath caught. Was he serious? "Are you... are you asking me to marry you?"

He nodded. "More than marry. Mate. Kirenai pair for life, *kikajiru*. What I'm asking is not trivial."

"But you need an heir. What if the healers can't fix me?"

There was a hint of worry in his tone as he said, "We have other options. We could use a surrogate to bear my child, though that's not something I want to think about now. All I know is that I can't live without you. Please say yes."

Her heart urged her to agree, but her brain cautioned her with common sense. This was happening too fast. Maybe it was normal among aliens to fall in love so quickly, but she was human, and she'd never believed in love at first sight. "Can I have time to think about it?"

He frowned and tilted his head down. "If that's what you need."

She swallowed, guilt creeping in that she couldn't freely return his feelings. "For humans, love takes more time." Before she could stop herself, she added, "Let me see the healers first. If they can't help me, you'll have a chance to change your mind."

His gaze connected to hers like a bolt of lightning. "Nothing they say will change my desire for you."

Her skin flushed with warmth and her knees grew weak. God, she wanted him to touch her right now, to stand and pull her close. It was as if every one of her nerve endings caught on fire. But it wouldn't be right to give in to him, not until they had an answer. If he still wanted her when they confirmed her infertility, then she'd say yes. She lifted her chin in defiance. "It might not change your mind, but it could change mine."

That same almost-smile he'd worn at the auction softened his features, as if he'd just glimpsed her deepest secret. "Then we shall see the healers. But no matter what, you'll be my bride."

She nodded slowly, still unsure.

He let his attention drift slowly down her body, and she became hyperconscious of the fact she wore no underthings below the thin fabric wrapped around her like a towel. He ran a finger along the seam of cloth falling down her front, taking the bottom edge and rubbing it between his fingers so it gaped open by her thigh. "You're beautiful in this."

A draft teased her nether regions, and she gulped air that suddenly felt thick with desire. "Thank you. But I'd like some real clothes before we go anywhere. I'm worried this might fall off at an inopportune moment."

With a quick tug, he pulled the wrap free. "I see what you mean."

She scrambled to grab it before it fell to the floor. "Arazhi!"

Both his hands engulfed hers, freezing her in place so she remained completely naked before him. He looked down at her breasts. "Many species wear no clothing at all, you know."

Her skin felt electrified, and her pulse raced. His mouth was close enough to kiss. *Do it*, her heart urged. Or was that her pussy? He had her hormones in an uproar. And he obviously wanted her again, even if she couldn't get pregnant. "But you're the one wearing clothes."

"Am I?" His deep voice made her want to melt.

She glanced down between them and sucked in a breath—his pants were gone, and his dick was thick and ready. Her insides fluttered. "Oh."

His fingers still around hers, he pulled them to his heated cock. Guiding her touch, he pushed down until the head of his shaft nudged between her thighs.

Unable to resist, she tilted her hips and let him slide between her legs. Her juices were already flowing, and she shuddered at the sensation of his ridges bumping along her clit. An unintelligible moan escaped her lips.

Tugging her hands free of his, she grabbed his ass, pulling him forward until their hips met, his shaft clamped between her legs.

His length throbbed against her lower lips.

She let her head fall back. "How are you so freaking hot?"

Lightning quick, he flung her onto the bed and thrust one knee between her thighs as he climbed up her body, forcing her legs apart as he moved. Reaching her mouth, he dipped down and claimed a kiss, his tongue demanding and urgent.

She let herself sink into the pleasure of the moment as his muscular thigh ground against her heated center. One of his hands moved to her breast, massaging and tweaking the nipple to aching awareness. His tongue plundered her mouth, filling her again and again while she writhed against the pressure of his thigh.

He brought his other leg up, spreading her wide until the head of his cock probed her slit. Teasing her opening, he spread her slickness with his length, circling, throbbing, pulsing. Then, with a single, sharp thrust, he drove his long hot shaft inside her.

The motion brought her to the edge of an orgasm almost immediately. She cried out, clawing her fingernails against his ass.

With small thrusts, he continued kissing her until the aftershocks ended. Then he drew back and filled her again, beginning a pounding rhythm. Each time he pistoned forward, she gasped, the pleasure surging in growing waves as a second climax built inside her.

His hands cupped her face, and he kissed her until she was helpless under the onslaught. When her orgasm broke, it came like a storm, a flash of lightning and a roll of thunder that made every muscle in her body convulse.

She'd barely come down when Arazhi's release triggered her third climax. His hot seed spilling between her thighs was pleasure itself as he ground his hips, ejaculating deeply inside her. He shuddered and slumped on top of her, breathing hard.

They remained locked together, his weight a comforting pressure, his fingers tangled in her hair as he supported himself on his elbows. When their breaths had slowed, he nuzzled her ear and feathered kisses down her throat, keeping his arms around her like a protective cage. "I am never going to let you go."

CHAPTER FOURTEEN

The next morning, they sat on the veranda again, enjoying a small breakfast together before the sun crept over the horizon. The soft sounds of animals and insects among the trees created a song Arazhi realized he'd missed during his time away. Being here with Georgie felt more right than he could've imagined. He'd made love to her all night, struggling against his need to take the final step in their bond. She didn't yet grasp what his commitment meant, and though he was under pressure to sire an heir, he intended to give her all the time she needed to recognize him as her mate.

He placed another *kazhitu* bun on her plate. "How do humans bond with a mate?"

Georgie shrugged. "A couple usually holds a wedding and invites all their friends and family to hear their vows of eternal love." A wave of bitterness flooded his Iki'i. "But most humans don't actually bond for life."

He nodded slowly, getting the sense he was broaching a sore subject. "There are many species like that. But for a Kirenai and his mate, there is no breaking the bond once it is set."

She made a non-committal sound and took a bite of her bun, looking out at the forest.

Reaching out, he took her hand, drawing her attention back to his face. "I sense you doubt me. But we exchange more than vows when we select a mate. To form a pair bond, a Kirenai passes along a small genetic marker that grants a mate an extended life—usually enough to match his own."

Georgie's brows drew together. "Extended life? Do Kirenai live a long time?"

He leaned back in his chair. "It's not uncommon for us to live eight hundred to a thousand of your Earth years."

The bun she was holding dropped back to her plate with a soft thud. "How old are you?"

"I'm still young, not yet two hundred. We'll have a long and wonderful life together."

Incredulity rendered her silent, and he gave her a few moments to mull everything over. Few species lived as long as Kirenai, and he understood the time span could be daunting.

Finally she whispered, "I definitely need to see the healers before we do anything you'll regret."

She still worries I'll reject her. His heart ached. He'd hurt her by doubting her motives. And although he, too, worried about how he was going to produce an heir, he wasn't willing to give up the woman who'd claimed his heart. "That has no bearing on our bond. We have plenty of time to see the healers."

"Earlier, you said time was of the essence to produce an

heir. I think it's only fair you know what your options are going to be." She pressed her fingers against some crumbs on the table and deposited them back on her plate. "Let's tear off the bandage and get it over with."

The universal translator still had trouble with her idioms, but he thought he understood her. "You need to put that worry behind us."

She nodded.

"If that's what you need, then we'll see the healers immediately."

She pushed away her plate. "I'm ready whenever you are."

He rose. "Afterward, I want to take you to the popotan fields for a picnic. I think you'll enjoy them."

He led her through the palace to the clinic and let Georgie explain what the doctors on Earth had told her. "Spare no effort," he instructed Elthos, his father's personal healer. "And do it quickly. You understand what's at stake."

"Of course, Prince Arazhi." The pink-scaled Qalqan nodded and asked Georgie to accompany him to the scanning chamber.

While Georgie was being scanned, Arazhi made arrangements to visit the popotan fields, hoping to give her something else to focus on while they waited for the results. Normally, he'd take his private transport, but he wanted Georgie to experience the raw charm of the rural district in the same way he had as a child. He arranged for an airlift to drop the public viewing area, and selected a handful of palace guards to go with them; normally, Arazhi travelled with only Zhiruto, but recent events had made him more cautious, and he wanted to enjoy the day with his mate without distraction. From the palace kitchens, he coordinated a picnic lunch that would be suitable for a human for when they arrived. He wanted everything to be perfect, yet still have enough spontaneity to allow Georgie to make her own choices.

By the time Georgie emerged from the healing wing looking flushed, he was satisfied their day would be perfect.

"They said they need a few days to analyze the data and come up with a treatment," she said. He'd given her a selection of clothing, and she now wore a flowing white tunic and breezy, loose-legged pants that still managed to show off her delectable curves as she walked.

"There's nothing you can do now, so let's enjoy our day together." Leading her to the airlift, he handed her a wide-brimmed hat to keep her cool under the fierce Kirenai sun. "Here, you'll want this when we're not in the shade."

They climbed on board the small airlift, and two security guards slid discretely into jump seats behind the pilot. Four more followed in another airlift behind them.

He settled into the plush seat next to her, pointing out the window as the craft lifted into the air. "Keep an eye out for places you'd like to hold a wedding."

"I haven't said yes yet, Arazhi." She frowned at him, yet warm affection bathed his Iki'i. Turning to look out the window, she added, "But planning an alien wedding could be fun."

Thinking perhaps she was homesick, he said, "We can hold our wedding on Earth, if you like. Or if you prefer, I'll have our fleet bring your friends and family here."

"They can come here?" She gave him a doubtful look. "All

of them? Because my Aunt Billie has at least a dozen cousins and their families she'll want to invite."

"Invite as many as you like, *kikajiru*. You can plan the entire event."

The short flight to the mountainous region where the popotan grew was smooth, and he pointed out a few key landmarks poking up from the thick vegetation covering the planet.

They landed near the public tourist clearing with a grand view of the mountainside, and he escorted her toward a shaded area where people gathered to eat and enjoy the vista. The cool, spicy scent of *ukimi* ice drifted toward them from a nearby food cart.

She kept close to his side, clearly self-conscious under the open stares of the other visitors. "Are we going to eat here?"

"Not here. I'm going to take you to where we used to picnic when I was a child. But I wanted to give you the full experience." Family picnics were one of his fondest memories of childhood, and he hoped Georgie would be willing to continue the tradition once they had a child of their own.

He pointed toward the rows of massive, lavender leaves lining the contours of the mountain like spiny dorsal fins. "The popotan plants always face the sun. I got lost among the rows once as a child because they'd rotated. I thought it was a great game, but my parents were terrified. They sent out half the palace guard to find me."

Georgie smiled. "Sounds like me and my mom when she'd take me clothes shopping at K-Mart. I loved hiding among the clothes racks, and she'd get so mad."

Taking her elbow, he led her toward the path that zig-zagged up the mountain to the fields. Along the trail, the clear domes of *teozhisa*—traditional bubble-shaped hover carts—trundled between the foliage. Normally, he'd take a private craft to the picnic, but he wanted Georgie to have the full experience. "Would you like to walk? Or we can take a *teozhisa*." He gestured to a waiting cart, its driver nearly hidden in the small compartment below the passenger cab. The bubble-shaped cab itself allowed passengers a full view of their surroundings.

Arazhi planned to stop at an overlook off the beaten path. There was a lovely waterfall nearby, and the popotan were exceptionally vibrant in the area. Two guards had taken the airlift to get there ahead of them and set up a picnic lunch.

"I'd prefer to ride. I'm still not used to this heat." Her pink cheeks glowed with perspiration, reminding him of how she looked after intense lovemaking. His human anatomy stiffened, and he had to reign in his desire. Time enough for that once they'd reached his private picnic area.

"Of course." He signaled one of his guards to make arrangements.

Two of his men boarded the first *teozhisa*, starting out ahead. The guard bowed toward Arazhi and stepped away from the next driver, signifying the fare had been paid, and moved to the next driver in line to arrange transportation for himself and his partner.

One hand against the small of Georgie's back, Arazhi guided her forward and opened the door, revealing a padded bench seat inside.

The slim Kirenai driver peeked up from his compartment,

obviously nervous about driving his prince but hiding his emotions well.

Arazhi acknowledged him with a nod, then squeezed in next to Georgie, placing his arm around her shoulders as the *teozhisa* started forward with a small lurch. The forest to either side was verdant with deep violet vines and mahogany flowers with yellow throats, and they passed quickly by several groups hiking up on foot as they followed switchback after switchback.

The passenger compartment tilted precariously each time, and Georgie clutched his arm. "Does he have to go so fast?"

"He's probably nervous about transporting royalty." Arazhi spoke into the intercom, asking the driver to slow down.

Either the intercom was broken, or the driver was too nervous to comply. They broke from the forest into the lower edge of the fields, rounding another corner onto a rocky ledge. The view down the mountainside opened up, showing an ocean of blue forest with the occasional spire or cluster of rounded huts.

"It's amazing that you can build spaceships out of these plants," Georgie said.

"It has something to do with their sensitivity to light. I can arrange for you to speak with a scientist if you're interested."

She laughed. "I probably wouldn't understand most of what he said."

The *teozhisa* rocked again, and Arazhi scowled. It had been a long time since he'd been here, but he was fairly certain they'd taken a wrong turn. The guards must not have been clear in their directions.

I miss Zhiruto. He pounded harder against the floorboard. "Where are you taking us? We don't need to leave the trail."

The driver didn't stop. In fact, he seemed to speed up.

"What's happening? Where are we going?" Georgie clung to his arm. Her fear stabbed into his Iki'i and made his already racing heart pound faster.

He opened the door a crack and leaned down to look into the driver's compartment. The compartment was empty, and the rocky ground was flying by at breakneck speed.

"*Kuzara,*" he swore, pulling himself back into the cab. "Something happened to the driver. I need to engage the brakes."

But it was too late. The ground suddenly dropped out from beneath them, and they were no longer hovering—they were falling. The *teozhisa* tilted, flinging them both forward against the windshield. Below, jagged rocks loomed like teeth.

There was no time to think. He had to protect his mate. Relaxing into his resting state, he engulfed her.

He could only hope his own body was enough to save her.

CHAPTER FIFTEEN

Georgie opened her eyes to find a scaled pink muzzle filling her view. She gasped, and the Qalqan drew back, forcing her to squint against the bright lights overhead. Last she remembered, they'd been hurtling over a cliff, then she'd felt like she'd been encased in shrink wrap, the same sensation she'd had when Arazhi'd transported her to his ship. Now she was in the palace clinic, reclining on the same small bed she'd been on earlier for her scans.

The healer who'd woken her held a strange, multi-pronged device, and in a raspy voice like nails on a chalkboard said, "She's conscious."

A second Qalqan moved into view, his black skirt and suspenders the same as the first one wore. Were these the same healers who'd done her scans earlier? She wished they wore nametags or something. She was embarrassed to admit she couldn't tell them apart.

"What happened?" Her eyes felt watery, and every muscle in her body was on fire.

"You were in an accident," the first healer said. "You've been unconscious for two days."

The other healer rasped, "I'll let the security team know you're awake. They want to speak with you."

"Two days?" The last thing she remembered was the ground rising toward them at breakneck speed. It was a miracle she was alive. *Those bubble carts must have some seriously high-tech safety measures.*

She wiggled her fingers and toes, lifting both hands to see if anything was broken. Although she ached, she appeared to be intact. Grimacing, she sat up. Two blue-skinned guards stood near the exit, and another pair stood at the opposite doorway. The rest of the room was empty.

"Where's Arazhi?" she asked.

"He's in a regen pod right now. He took an extraordinary amount of damage and will require time to recover."

The pit of her stomach churned. How was he hurt so badly if she was fine? She pushed off the bed, pain lancing her knees as her feet took her weight. "Can I see him?"

The nearest healer nodded. "Of course. This way."

She gritted her teeth and hobbled past a pair of guards to the next room where what looked like four concrete bathtubs full of green liquid lined a wall. The air smelled like strawberries, and a slight humming sound came from wall panels scrolling with unrecognizable text.

The healer pulled something that looked like a hovering surfboard over next to one of the tubs. "Here, sit. He's sedated and may be slow to respond, but he can hear you. I'll send the security team in here when they arrive."

She moved closer to the tub and peered into the glossy green liquid. It reminded her of Jello before it had set, only instead of fruit and marshmallows floating in it, a blue sludge covered the bottom. She frowned. Where was Arazhi?

"I think this is the wrong one." She glanced over her shoulder, but the healer had already gone.

Legs trembling, she leaned on the floating stool and limped to the next tub, peering into it. The green fluid in this one was completely clear. She moved to the next one. It appeared to be empty, too.

She turned to move back down the row to the tub at the other end when a short woman with alabaster skin and dark blue hair entered the room and hurried to the first tub Georgie'd been sitting by.

The woman gripped the edge and stared down into the green fluid. "Arazhi, you need to wake up."

Georgie's brows drew together. Had her eyes been playing tricks on her? Maybe she had a concussion. Or perhaps Arazhi was somehow concealed in the blue layer at the bottom. "Is Arazhi in that one?"

The woman's head jerked up, her gaze instantly shrewd. "You must be Georgie."

"Yes." The woman's posture and tone made Georgie want to take a step back. Who was this person, and why did she seem so hostile? A vague memory of the photos Arazhi'd had on his ship popped to mind—a blue-haired woman wearing a crown of interwoven diamonds. "Are you his mother?"

Gaze flicking over Georgie's body as if judging and finding her lacking, the woman said, "I am Empress Vella."

Realizing she was standing face-to-face with the empress of the entire frickin' galaxy, Georgie attempted an awkward curtsy. Then she felt silly. Did aliens even curtsy to royalty? "A pleasure to meet you, your highness. Is that the correct title?"

"I have no time for titles." Empress Vella turned back to the tub. "Leave us."

Indignation prickled along Georgie's spine. She understood a mother's concern, but Arazhi was important to her. "I was in the accident with him. I need to know he's all right, then I'll go."

Still facing away, Empress Vella's shoulders remained rigid. "He'll be fine. But he almost died because of you."

"Me?" Georgie put a hand against her chest. Where was this woman's anger coming from? "I didn't cause that crash."

"Not directly, but it was aimed at you." With a glance over her shoulder, the empress all but threw daggers from her eyes.

Georgie sucked in a breath. "Why would anyone want to kill me?"

"Because they think you're going to bear Arazhi's heir." Empress Vella turned to face her. "It would be one thing if you were, but you can't. He could've died protecting you, and you can't even give him the one thing he needs."

Nausea rolled up Georgie's throat. "We don't know that yet. He says the healers can probably fix me."

The woman's indigo lips pursed. "I just spoke to the healers. They say they can't."

The room seemed to tilt, and Georgie caught herself with

one hand against the stool. *Guess there's no such thing as HIPAA when it comes to alien doctors.* "Did they say why?"

Empress Vella crossed her arms. "Only that you aren't compatible or you'd be pregnant already."

Hating the hope Arazhi had created inside her, she said, "That's not fair. Arazhi and I have only known each other a few days."

The woman crossed her arms. "Do you know where we got most of our data about humans? From females who were abducted by black market traders to become breeders. We rescued them from slavery, but all the humans on board that ship who'd been pleasured by Kirenai had already conceived. It seems that humans are uniquely receptive to Kirenai insemination." Arazhi's mother stepped closer. "Or they're not."

The woman's words snapped Georgie's tenuous hope, sending pain crashing into her like a ten-thousand-pound steel beam. She couldn't breathe. This was exactly what she'd feared when Arazhi'd suggested they try to let the healers fix her.

Ripples shuddered across the surface of the green fluid behind the empress. The surface parted, and Arazhi's face appeared. His eyes remained closed, but his lips moved. "Damma, stop."

Empress Vella didn't even look in his direction. "You can't protect her, Arazhi. She deserves to know what will happen." She moved forward again until she stood an arm's length away from Georgie. "You have more than your own future to consider. Remember the slaves I mentioned? If my son fails to produce an heir, our enemies will seize control of the galaxy, and the first thing they'll do is force every fertile female on your planet to become a breeder. A slave."

Cold shock crashed into Georgie. Then she remembered the auction, and her shock turned to anger. "Isn't that what your son already tried to do at my auction?"

This time Arazhi spoke, his face still the only part of him showing. "That was a misunderstanding. A bondservant willingly enters a contract, and I relinquished my claim to you when you clarified our terms."

"Our enemies make no such contracts," Empress Vella added. "They take what they want by force. That's why an heir is so critical. You have to let my son choose another and fulfill his destiny."

Georgie realized she was shaking her head in denial and stopped. Over the past few days, her feelings had grown for Arazhi. Grown into something she wasn't sure she was ready to admit. And his insistence that he wanted her regardless of whether or not she could bear children had almost broken down her resistance. She wanted to be his wife. To learn to love him and spend the rest of her life at his side. But if Earth's future was really at stake, it changed everything. How had she suddenly become responsible for the fate of the galaxy?

Arazhi said softly, "Damma, she is my destiny. My form has settled."

The empress's alabaster skin flushed pink, and she spun to look into the tub. "You already bonded with her?"

"All but the final step."

What was he talking about? What final step? And why could she only see his face? Although he'd told Georgie that his people were shapeshifters, she'd never had a chance to ask what his real form looked like. Now he was claiming to have settled. Did that mean she'd never get to see his true shape? She stepped closer to the tub to peer into the green liquid. But although the face at the surface was Arazhi's, the body connected to it didn't look like a body at all. It looked like a lump of blue modeling clay.

Georgie took a step back, uncertainty roiling in her gut. "What happened to your body? Did the accident cause this?"

His eyes opened for the first time, seeking her out. "This wasn't how I wanted to introduce you to my resting state."

"Resting state? You mean this is your Kirenai form?" She took another backward step. "Are you going to look like this from now on?"

"No. Once I'm recovered, I'll be as you saw me before. As you prefer." The surface of the liquid sloshed against the sides as if he was moving beneath it.

The anxiety that had been crawling up her throat subsided, but only a fraction. Seeing him as a disembodied head was disturbing. She took another step backward until she could no longer see anything but his face.

Empress Vella spoke in a low voice, less angry and more desperate. "I understand you must bond with her. But before you do, you must sire a child with another. There are other females in the palace who'd be willing surrogates."

"I'll find no pleasure in another," Arazhi growled, the liquid sloshing more violently. "Georgie, please don't go."

"You're not doing it for your pleasure," the empress insisted. "You're doing it for the fate of the galaxy."

"Empress Vella." The familiar, raspy voice made Georgie jump. At the doorway stood one of the healers, small pink tail twitching rapidly back and forth. "The emperor has urgent need of you."

The empress's eyes widened. "I'm coming." She cast a final glance at Arazhi. "You know what you must do."

Then she stormed out without another glance at Georgie.

Georgie stood frozen for several heartbeats, uncertain. Half of her wanted to flee, to leave Arazhi to make his own decisions. The other half wanted to rush to the tub to be near the man—alien—who claimed to love her.

"Will you please come closer, *kikajiru?*" Arazhi asked. "I want to see you. I worried I wouldn't be able to protect you from the fall. Are you all right?"

Slowly, she approached, the final moments of that fall now making sense. Arazhi's arms around her. The sudden sensation of being encased in something. He'd literally enveloped her with his own body, taking all of the impact to protect her. "Thank you for saving me."

"You're my mate." The blue figure under the liquid now had a semblance of arms and legs, although it certainly wasn't the body she remembered. "I need a little more time in the regen fluid, but I'll soon look the way you want me to. I promise."

She smiled, surprised she wasn't more put off by his current appearance. "Hey, I'm no princess first thing in the morning either."

"I like how you look in the morning." He grinned.

Her smile slipped. "Why didn't you tell me about the human slaves?"

"I meant to. It just hadn't come up yet. I'll take you to see them as soon as I can get out of this pod."

"Wait. They're still here? On Kirenai Prime?" She frowned. "I thought your mother said they'd been freed."

"They are free, but we set up a community here on Kirenai Prime where they can raise their children. Kirenai don't do well raised without their own kind to teach them."

She gulped and looked at his body once more. "Are the babies shapeshifters from birth?"

"They're born looking like their mother's species, but the males will fall in and out of a resting state soon after birth. It takes them time to develop the ability to shift to other forms."

She'd be terrified if her baby suddenly melted to blue slime in her arms. "That must've been quite a shock to those women."

"Yes. But humans appear to be wonderfully resilient." He grew more somber. "I'm sorry the healers didn't have the answer we wanted."

She nodded and looked at the floor, trying to sort through her emotions. "Me too. But at least we can use a surrogate."

"*Kikajiru*, are you certain you're okay with that?" His voice had taken on a rough edge.

She shrugged, still not looking at him. She didn't want him to see her disappointment. "It's not like you're going to sleep with her or anything. I can love your baby as my own."

He remained silent.

She dragged her gaze back to his face. His pained

expression made her sink backward onto the stool. "What are you not telling me?"

His eyes squeezed closed. "Artificial insemination isn't possible for Kirenai. The woman who bears my child will have a bond with me, though not as strong as a mate bond."

She looked at the wall of scrolling text, numbness creeping through her. The woman who carried his child wouldn't be a mere surrogate. It sounded like she'd be a second mate. But how else was he going to have an heir? He had to protect Earth and who knew how many other planets across the galaxy from being enslaved. *I don't want to share him.* She deserved better. And to be fair, the mother of his child deserved better, too.

Standing, Georgie took one last look into the tub. Even though Arazhi's body wasn't currently human, he was still the perfect man. Committed. Understanding. Supportive. He was going to make a wonderful husband and father. For someone else.

Tears filmed her eyes. God, she wanted to kiss him one last time. To feel his arms around her, sense his heartbeat next to hers. But the only way he'd do what had to be done was if she was gone. "I can't stand the thought of sharing you," she blurted.

"Georgie, I—"

"You have to mate with another and become emperor." She took a step back, each word feeling like it was choking her. "Give the mother of your child your heart if you can... It's the right thing to do. I'm leaving, for everyone's sake. Goodbye, Arazhi."

Before he could say anything else, she turned and rushed from the room.

CHAPTER SIXTEEN

Arazhi tried desperately to pull himself into his human form, to get out of the pod and follow Georgie. But the connective tissues in his matrix had been damaged in the fall, and holding a specific shape was nearly impossible. Even the small task of maintaining his facial features while speaking had been excruciating. The sedatives infusing his regen fluid were threatening to force him into sleep once more.

Curse Damma for interfering. Georgie's pain lingered in the room, infusing his Iki'i as strongly as the sedatives flowing through the regen fluid. But he also felt the unyielding titanium of her resolve. She was going to do as his damma had insisted.

Reject him.

"Healer!" he called, hoping his voice was strong enough to carry to the next room. He needed to catch up to Georgie and make her stay, but he couldn't even configure limbs while affected by sedatives. He could endure the pain without them if that's what he had to do.

He dipped beneath the surface, green liquid blurring his vision. He couldn't remember ever feeling this weak or frustrated. Kirenai were strong—nearly indestructible. Damma was right in assuming the accident hadn't been intended to harm him—it had been aimed at Georgie. But that meant the Senburu had spies in the palace. How else would they have known she was here and what she meant to him?

Kuzara, what if they tried again? And here he was trapped in a regen pod. He had to find the strength to get out. Struggling to pull himself together, he surfaced once more.

A pink-scaled Qalqan stood looking down at him. "Go back to sleep, my prince."

Arazhi was having difficulty keeping his eyes open, let alone his face above the surface, but he recognized the healer as Elthos, his father's personal healer. "Turn off the sedation. I need to get out."

"No." Elthos's flat denial was jarring, but his lipless mouth and slitted eyes remained as unreadable as ever.

Arazhi fought to put authority into his voice but ended up slurring, "As your prince, I command you." The healer had to obey a direct order. "I need to reach my mate immediately."

"I fear I cannot allow that to happen." The scaly pink muzzle lowered to within inches of Arazhi's face. "I always rather liked you, so I'll try to make your passing painless. But the galaxy must come first."

Adrenaline shot through Arazhi. The healer's words made no sense. *Elthos wants me dead?* Not possible. He must've misunderstood. The Qalqan was part of the emperor's inner circle. *He probably just means he can't let me bond with Georgie.* It would make sense for the healer to be aligned with his parents in that regard.

Using every bit of energy he had, Arazhi pulled his form together, trying to ignore the stabbing pain in his matrix. "Elthos, stop. Listen to me."

Elthos reached a pink-scaled hand into the regen fluid and pushed Arazhi under.

A wave of something fungal and bitter flooded Arazhi's cellular matrix. He could feel himself reacting, denaturing. *Poison?* Just like his father. It was all beginning to make sense.

He struggled under Elthos's hand, tried to reform his face at the other end of the tank so he could cry out, but the sedatives had been increased. He was helpless. Dying.

Elthos really intended to kill him. The royal healer had been with the Senburu this entire time.

As Arazhi's respiration slowed and his mind faded, the last thing he thought before blackness took him was that at least when he was dead, Georgie would no longer be a target.

CHAPTER SEVENTEEN

Georgie hurried from the clinic, grateful the hallway was empty as tears blurred her eyes. She'd finally found a man willing to love her no matter what—even if it cost him a throne—and she was being forced to reject him. Leaving him made her feel worse than she'd ever felt before. Her legs felt like they'd been strapped with twenty-pound weights, and she wasn't sure how much of that was because of the accident and how much of it was grief.

Pull it together, Georgie. She stepped into an alcove along the hallway and sank onto a stone bench. Tall windows looked out on a dark, empty courtyard. Stars glittered between the trees, and her breath hitched again. Soon, she'd be headed back into space, back to Earth, where she belonged.

Then she remembered that Arazhi's security officer had said Earth was closed to interstellar travel during the investigation. Even Lora wanted her to stay away. How long would Georgie be stuck here? And where would she live while she waited? Perhaps in the human community Arazhi'd mentioned. *The community he'll probably visit to find a new mate.*

She scrubbed angrily at the tears on her cheeks. So much for not believing in love at first sight. How had her heart become so entangled with his? And why did he have to be the freakin' prince of the universe? She'd never be able to escape his face; an alien prince looking for love would definitely make the tabloids on every magazine rack now that the world knew aliens truly existed.

"Come, human," a deep voice behind her made her flinch.

Turning, she saw one of the palace guards standing at the entrance to the alcove. His gray armor encased what appeared to be a Qalqan body, only with blue scales instead of pink. She'd seen a lot of Kirenai in the shapes of other species, but this was the first she'd seen as a Qalqan. Then she remembered one of the healers had mentioned the security team wanted to talk to her. "Are you here about the accident?"

"Yes." Although his placid, reptilian features showed no malice, this dude was giving her a suspicious vibe.

She shook it off. He was looking for clues about who'd caused the accident, so of course he was suspicious, even of her. Standing, she attempted to calm her topsy-turvy emotions. At least when she'd finished answering their questions, they could take her to the empress so she could ask to be sent home.

She stepped forward to join him, glancing up and down the empty hall. Where was the guard's partner? Didn't they usually travel in pairs?

He wrapped his long, clawed fingers around her arm and pulled her out of the alcove.

A shot of adrenaline spiked through her. No one except Arazhi had touched her since her arrival here—even the healers' scanners had been touch-free. The empress's words came back to her: *The accident was aimed at you.*

The hair on the back of her neck rose. What if this guard was actually an assassin?

She dug in her heels, trying to pull from his grip. "I need to see the empress."

"Not now." His grip tightened, forcing her to keep walking.

She gulped, looking around the empty hall, no longer grateful for the privacy. "Where are you taking me?"

"To the harem, where you belong."

Harem? No one had mentioned a harem. Dread ran cold along her spine. Maybe he wasn't an assassin. Maybe this was something else. How far would the empress go to keep Georgie away from her son?

Georgie trotted along beside the guard, trying to catch his eye as he stared straight ahead. "You don't need to do that. I told Arazhi I won't be his mate."

The lipless reptilian face beside her seemed to smile, then right before her eyes, it pulled into a real smile as the guard's features rearranged themselves. The eyes drew closer together, the muzzle formed into a nose and chin, and two ears and hair sprouted from the guard's head. It was the first time she'd seen a Kirenai shift forms, and it felt oddly personal. *Why is he changing?*

Never breaking his stride, he turned to look at her, a human face on a Qalqan body. "Perhaps you'd prefer me to fill that belly of yours."

Disgust rolled through her at the same moment as realization—the empress hadn't sent him. And he wasn't here to kill her. This was one of the slavers the empress had warned her about. The ones who wanted to make humans into breeders. *They've infiltrated the palace.* She had to get away. To warn Arazhi. "Guess you haven't heard," she said, trying to be flippant. "But I'm infertile. Incompatible, the healers say."

The guard leaned closer, his smile reminding her of a chimpanzee's. "I've heard quite the contrary. I'm told you're special."

She didn't know what that meant, and she had no desire to find out. Glad Lora'd forced her and Maise to take those self-defense courses, she spun toward him and thrust her free palm upward into his nose.

His head snapped back. The grip on her bicep loosened.

Twisting free, she spun again, aiming a kick at his crotch.

He crumpled forward with a choked curse, apparently not accustomed to his new human anatomy.

"Help!" she screamed as she pelted back toward the clinic. Her voice echoed through the empty hallway.

The doors to either side were made of lavender popotan leaves, but not a single one opened. She didn't stop to try them. The rooms behind them might be empty, and she couldn't afford to slow down.

She kept running, terror driving her body past the lingering ache from the accident. Gasping for air, she reached the clinic's double doors and burst through.

Two healers stared at her with unreadable expressions as she stumbled and fell, crashing to her knees on the stone floor.

All four guards pulled weapons from their belts.

She pointed to the open door behind her, barely able to pant out the words. "There's a slaver after me."

The two guards nearest the exit stepped into the hall, while the two standing at the door to Arazhi's room widened their stance, weapons ready.

She couldn't seem to catch her breath. Her skin prickled and burned. And everything in the room felt too loud and bright.

A healer emerged from Arazhi's chamber—Elthos, she thought his name was. She recognized him by the tiny dark spot he had under one eye, and she remembered one of the others saying she ought to be important if the emperor's personal healer was seeing her. He'd made her feel uncomfortable during her scans, but she'd shrugged it off—she was being examined by aliens, after all. Now every hair on her body stood on end.

Something wasn't right.

She scrambled to her feet, filled with foreboding. "Is Arazhi all right?"

Elthos glanced at the guards. "Why is she still here?"

One guard waved his weapon toward the exit. "She said there's someone chasing her."

"Then shouldn't you go look?" Elthos folded his hands, as if waiting expectantly.

The guards glanced at each other, then back to Elthos. "We can't leave our post for any reason. The other two are looking now."

The suffocating feeling was making Georgie see stars now, and it somehow seemed to be coming from Arazhi's chamber. She couldn't take her eyes off the royal healer. He'd just been in there. "You didn't answer my question about Arazhi."

"That isn't your place, human," Elthos said. "You already set his recovery back once. I was forced to increase his sedatives to counteract all the excitement you caused."

If there was one thing being an event coordinator had taught her, it was to always double check the details. She pointed at the other healers. "As his mate, I want a second opinion. Go check him."

"I assure you he's fine." Elthos remained planted in the middle of the doorway.

"Forgive me, royal healer, but perhaps you missed something?" one of the guards said. "I did sense distress from the prince a few moments ago. I must insist that you allow your assistants to double check."

Elthos lifted his chin and stared down his muzzle at the guards. "The emperor will be hearing about this, and I assure you he will not be pleased."

He strode toward the exit as the other healers headed into the room, snatching up a strange medical instrument from a table along the way. He passed Georgie without a second glance.

She wanted to tell the guards to stop him, but had no basis for the request, plus it was taking everything she had to remain standing.

A crash from Arazhi's chamber made Georgie spin, and she rushed forward to find the healers scrambling with loose tubes and wires. They both knelt on floating stools, hovering above the green fluid puddling on the floor. The sickening smell of rotten strawberries permeated the air.

One shouted, "Charge now."

What sounded like a bug zapper filled the room, and light surged from Arazhi's tub.

Georgie gasped. "What's going on?"

"The recirculation unit came loose. He's destabilizing," one said without turning around.

Gripping the doorframe, she watched helplessly while they worked. Her feelings had been right—Arazhi was in danger. He was dying.

The healers argued over the next course of action, speaking too fast for Georgie to understand. All she knew was she needed to see Arazhi. To connect with him, even if only visually.

The green fluid was receding into a drain in the floor, so she stepped inside the room, careful to stay out of the healers' way. "Arazhi, I'm here," she called, hoping he could hear her. "It's me, Georgie. Please, wake up."

Like a man in a coffin, Arazhi lay with his eyes closed and his arms at his sides. He was completely naked, but fully formed, a blue human. He wouldn't look human if he was dead, would he?

"We must try the antitoxin, quickly," one of the healers said.

The second healer picked up what looked like a needle the size of a drinking straw. With barely a pause, he slammed the point straight into Arazhi's chest.

Georgie gasped, her own heart seizing as if she'd just been stabbed.

Arazhi's body arched. His chest heaved. Green foam erupted from his mouth.

"Arazhi!" she called out, panic seizing her. *Don't die.*

The healers blocked most of her view, but between their shoulders, Georgie thought she saw Arazhi's eyelids flutter. His hands rose and gripped the sides of the tub. "Stop him," he groaned.

Shit. She'd forgotten entirely about Elthos. Georgie called to the guards, "Arrest the royal healer. By order of the prince."

She didn't wait to find out if they complied. Arazhi was alive. The healers had stepped back, so she hurried forward to take his hand. "Are you okay?"

"I'll live." He smiled, although she could see how much it pained him. "But promise you won't leave me again."

Her legs felt weak with relief. "I'm right here."

But even as she said it, her heart ached. This didn't change what she had to do. It only altered her timeline. She couldn't be his mate, but she could at least stay by his side until he was well.

CHAPTER EIGHTEEN

Arazhi insisted on transferring back to his own rooms, refusing to relax into his resting state while the healers saw to his recovery. He didn't want to take his eyes off Georgie again, especially after she told him about the slaver in the hallway. His days of being shadowed by a single guard were a thing of the past—not to mention his most trusted security officer, Zhiruto, was still back on Earth.

Almost a week had passed since the accident, and Elthos had so far managed to elude capture. Arazhi had been overseeing the palace investigation, trying to determine how deep the Senburu's infiltration ran. He'd picked a few key personnel who were not only investigating each other, but also every palace guard, healer, bondservant, and dignitary who'd had access to the palace.

"Leave no stone unturned," were Georgie's words, and for once, her idiom made perfect sense.

He gazed at her now from where he sat propped in his bed. She was swinging back and forth in the hanging chair she favored for reading, her bare feet tucked up beside her, pale hair catching rays from the afternoon sun streaming through the window. He wanted to kneel in front of her and kiss every one of her adorable pink toes. But she'd been keeping him at a distance, hovering nearby like a satellite that never landed.

Although his matrix was growing stronger every day, taking less effort to maintain his human shape, he hadn't admitted that to anyone. He knew Georgie intended to leave as soon as he was well. He felt the clock ticking and knew the truth would have to come out soon.

Suddenly, Georgie gasped and looked up from the data pad with bright eyes. She'd been scrolling through the morning updates from his new security team. "They say your father was able to speak to them this morning."

As suspected, Elthos had also been behind his father's illness, or at least his continued decline. Under the guise of keeping the emperor's condition from going public, he'd insisted on being the only healer to treat him. All the while, he'd been continuing to administer the poison.

Arazhi patted the mattress beside him. "Come sit by me so I can read, too."

She raised an eyebrow. "It didn't work yesterday and it won't work today, Sneaky Pete. I'm not getting in your bed."

Leaning forward, he smiled, making sure his dimple showed and enjoying the surge of her attraction flooding his Iki'i. "Don't you humans have an idiom about sexual healing or something?"

She laughed. "That's not an idiom. It's an old song from the eighties."

"Whatever. I'm going to die if I don't get to touch you. Don't make me get up and come over there." Though she'd remained in his rooms, she'd been sleeping on a sofa. She refused to let him touch her, let alone come to his bed. He understood her reluctance to share him with a surrogate—he found the idea equally distasteful. All he could do at the moment was hope for a miracle that would allow them to be together.

Standing, she moved to the chair next to his bed. His momentary elation to have her near faded as she pushed it back just out of his reach before she sat. "Arazhi, I'm here until you're well, but I can't touch you. You need to sire an heir." Her voice grew thick. "And since that has to be with someone else, I prefer to make a clean break sooner rather than later."

"But now that my father's well, my parents could have another child." That was unlikely, but he was willing to hope for anything. "I don't have to be the only one in line to become emperor."

She shook her head, a sad smile ghosting her lips. "You said children are rare among Kirenai, that most couples are lucky to have just one. What's the chance of them having another?"

A raspy voice from the doorway behind Georgie answered before he could, "Possible, but not likely."

Qantina, the new head of the clinic, stood there with a scanner in one hand and a vial in the other. Deshel stood next to him, bowing deeply as apology flowed toward Arazhi's Iki'i. "Pardon us, Prince Arazhi," Deshel said. "I didn't realize you and your mate were busy. I can tell the healers to come back—"

"No, it's all right." Arazhi frowned. "Is it time for my therapy already?"

"We've been concerned about your slow recovery and have a new treatment that should help fortify your matrix more quickly." Qantina stepped forward. "But first, I couldn't help overhear that you and your mate have not yet bonded. This is relieving news."

Georgie aimed a tight smile toward Arazhi and stood. "See?"

Qantina tilted his head at her. "I believe you've been misinformed about your compatibility."

Arazhi sat up straighter. "What do you mean?"

"Our scans revealed Kirenai markers in Georgie's DNA."

Georgie's face paled. "Markers in my DNA? What does that mean?"

Arazhi didn't like where this was going; Kirenai left a marker in a female when they pair-bonded with one. "Impossible. Surely I'd have felt if she was already mated."

"She isn't bonded." The healer set the vials down on the bedside table. "Her father is Kirenai."

Shocked silence filled the room.

Then Georgie took a step back, shaking her head. "What? No! My dad is... Dad. He's as human as I am."

Qantina bowed slightly. "With all respect, the DNA doesn't lie."

Georgie's face went ghostly pale, and he didn't even need his Iki'i to sense her dismay. "You mean it's true? This whole time..."

Concerned she might faint, Arazhi threw back the covers and shot to her side. "What's true?"

She grabbed his arm, seemingly glad for the support. "Mom said she was abducted by aliens right after Dad was deployed the first time. Everyone thought it was just her throwing a fit so he'd come home." She met his gaze. "It happened about nine months before I was born."

Earth was supposed to have been closed, so Arazhi'd never considered that she might have Kirenai bloodlines. *Slavers must've impregnated her mother and then returned her to Earth once they realized she was carrying a girl.* The knowledge made him twitch with anger. But it also finished the puzzle about why Georgie had trouble conceiving; she needed to pair-bond first— with a Kirenai male.

Shock made the air feel fuzzy as Georgie collapsed into a chair. Her voice shook as she asked, "But if I'm half Kirenai, why am I not blue?"

Qantina answered, "Kirenai traits are almost entirely contained on what you humans call the Y-chromosome. Only the Kirenai empathic power is sometimes present in female progeny."

Arazhi nodded. His persistent sensation that Georgie had understood his emotions made sense if she had a trace of the Iki'i. "This is good news, *kikajiru*." He knelt to take her hand. "It not only means we can have children, but that we're more compatible than either of us ever imagined."

Georgie's eyes widened. "How?"

"Kirenai females need a pair-bond to conceive, but if they find a suitable mate, they often have more than one child."

His Iki'i felt a moment of vertigo, then she turned her attention toward Qantina. "So, let me get this clear. I've been unable to have a baby because my Kirenai DNA requires me to be bonded to a Kirenai mate first?"

"Correct," Qantina said.

"If Arazhi and I bond, I'll be able to get pregnant?"

"Considering the human half of your DNA, I theorize you will conceive almost immediately."

Georgie sucked in a breath and gripped Arazhi's hand.

Qantina added, "Once the prince has adequately recovered, of course."

Arazhi could swear he felt mischievous amusement coming from the Qalqan, as if the healer had suspected his improvement all along. Standing, he pointed toward the door. "Thank you for your visit. Now please leave us."

The healers bowed as they departed.

Georgie frowned, looking up at him from her seat. "You shouldn't be out of bed."

Pulling her to her feet, he guided her backward to the mattress. "Neither should you, *kikajiru*."

She sat on the bed and yielded to his hand pressing her back onto the pillows. "You've been faking illness to keep me here, haven't you?"

Her words held only mild reprimand; most of his Iki'i was saturated with the euphoria of love. "I was debilitated by lovesickness." Lying down beside her, he stroked her cheek, looking deeply into her eyes. "Only you can cure me."

She smiled and leaned in to kiss him, the softness of her lips quickly igniting his passion. He slid his fingers into her hair, reveling in the heat of her body against the length of his.

When he finally paused for breath, she asked, "Are you well enough for this?"

"I don't want to wait another moment to make you mine. But there is one problem."

Concern flickered through her. "What?"

"You have not yet agreed to marry me."

She laughed, pure joy rolling from her like sunbeams after a long winter. "Of course I will, Arazhi. I want us to be together forever."

He smiled back. "Then let's make it so."

Inhaling her sweet musk, he kissed her again, moving along her jaw and down her throat as he parted the front of her tunic.

Her hands clawed at the nightshirt he wore—he'd discovered wearing human clothing was far easier than simulating it—and pulled it up over his head. Within moments, they were both naked. His cock throbbed with the need to fill her, but he didn't want to rush this moment. He wanted their bonding to be a memory they treasured. He pushed back onto his knees to look down at her naked body. "You are so luscious."

She spread her knees and beckoned him toward her with both hands. "I want you."

"In due time, *kikajiru*." He bent and sucked in a nipple.

Her back arched to meet him, the bud hardening under his tongue. He loved how responsive she was, the little mewling noises of pleasure that escaped her throat. Her arousal was like a drug threading through his Iki'i, making his heart race and his blood grow hot.

She dug her fingers into his hair, gasping as he sucked hard before moving to her other breast. She wrapped both legs around his backside, trying to draw his hips toward hers.

He resisted, moving lower, scraping his stubble lightly down her ribs, kissing along her belly. Her skin was so smooth and soft, he wanted to taste every inch of her.

When he dipped down to the apex of her thighs, she jerked lightly against his hair. "You don't need to—"

He slid his tongue between her lower lips.

"Oh!" she gasped, hips flexing.

Her sweet musky flavor filled him, like morning dew on happa fronds, and he pulsed his tongue in and out, responding to her desire. He toyed with the small bundle of nerves at the top of her slit as she trembled, then opened like a flower to his caress, thighs spreading wide beneath the gentle pressure of his palms.

Slicking through her wetness again and again, he lapped up her juices until her hips began to buck and her thighs trembled. She was close to her climax, and he slid a finger inside, pumping in and out, his tongue never ceasing its rhythm against her clit. Her inner walls clamped around his finger, pulsing as she cried out her release. He continued driving forward and stroking her with his tongue as she rode out her orgasm. At last, her hips sagged back onto the mattress.

As she lay gulping for breath, he climbed up to cover her with his body. He nuzzled the crook of her neck, his rock-hard cock throbbing against her opening.

She wrapped her arms around him, stroking up and down his back. "I want you. All of you."

He needed no further encouragement. His cock drove inside her with one solid stroke. Her wet heat was exquisite, threatening to tip him over the edge. He pulled back, then ground against her again, the feelers just above his shaft cupping her clit as he filled her.

She moaned, and her pussy pulsed with another orgasm, squeezing him to the brink of ecstasy. He kissed her again, savoring her lips, stroking her breasts, thrusting into her until her juices coated their hips.

"I want to claim you now, *kikajiru.* Are you ready?"

Breathing hard, she opened her eyes. "The bond?"

"Yes."

She nodded, excitement filling her eyes. "Make me yours."

He'd never heard words more sweet. Primary cock buried deep in her heat, he hardened his mating shaft and prodded her back opening.

She gasped, fingers clawing into his back as he eased inside her tightness. He'd never used his mating shaft before, never felt the need with anyone except Georgie. This was the way he'd transfer the marker that would make her his forever. He paused his thrusting, trying to maintain control as the new stimulation scaled his arousal to new heights.

"Don't stop," Georgie choked out, tilting her hips up against him.

He had to grit his teeth to keep himself from coming right then and there, but he drove forward, burying both shafts inside her.

Then he began pumping, moving in and out, fucking her ass at the same time as her pussy. He gripped her wrists and pinned them above her head, looking down into her lust-filled eyes. He'd never felt so connected to another being as he did in this moment.

Georgie's eyes squeezed shut as she made a gargling sound that slowly rose to a scream. Her back arched, and the wave of her pleasure hit his Iki'i like a tsunami.

Unable to stop himself, he sank both shafts as deep as they would go. His mating shaft ejaculated along with his primary shaft, overwhelming him in bliss he'd never imagined possible. The room seemed to spin, and he balanced himself on his elbows above her, breathing hard until his heart resumed a normal pace.

Georgie's eyes fluttered open, cheeks flushed and a small sheen of perspiration glistening along her hairline. "That was... that was amazing."

He brushed a strand of hair away from her eyes, his heart full to overflowing as he grinned. "It was, my mate. I'm now yours forever."

She cupped his cheek, trailing a finger over his dimple. "Good. Because I love you, Arazhi."

He laughed. "So—ready to plan a royal wedding?"

Her responding joy was broad enough to light up the entire room. "Yes!"

EPILOGUE

Georgie had never imagined planning an alien wedding before, let alone her own royal, alien wedding. The event was exactly the opposite of the intimacy of her and Arazhi's pair-bonding, and the amphitheater she'd selected for the event was packed; at least fifty-thousand guests sat beneath an enormous dome of interwoven vines that provided partial shade from the harsh Kirenai sun. Flowers dangled from garlands overhead, catching the dappled sunlight and filling the air with a gentle, sweet fragrance. More flowers lined every aisle.

She stared nervously toward the end of the tunnel into the amphitheater where her father stood, waiting to signal the musicians to begin the processional. He looked dignified in his silk tuxedo, graying hair clipped to a tidy fringe around his balding head. She hadn't told him the truth about her DNA, since it didn't really matter. Dad was the only father she knew, and some asshole slaver who'd abducted her mother didn't deserve to connect himself to the royal family in any way. Qantina had looked into who might've sired her, but it seemed that Elthos had tampered with the Kirenai genetic database before he left, probably to hide any Senburu advocates.

Next to her in the hallway, Lora stood holding Georgie's bridal bouquet, a stunning flow of violet and magenta flowers interspersed with pearls. Lora's bridesmaid dress was a matching shade of magenta, and her auburn hair was pulled away from her face and decorated with the same flowers. "Having second thoughts?"

"Not at all. Just self-conscious about how many people are watching." Georgie smoothed a hand over the front of her gown. The healers had confirmed her pregnancy almost a month ago, but she wasn't yet showing, thankfully. She was delighted to be pregnant, but Kirenai Prime was hot even without direct sunlight, and waddling down the aisle would've been uncomfortable at best. The gown she now wore was gossamer thin, soft and nearly transparent as it molded to her torso and floated in waves down her hips and thighs. Millions of pearls had been affixed to the surface using some sort of alien technology to keep them from weighing the fabric down. She felt like a real interstellar princess.

Arazhi had been confused when she'd picked it out. "You want a dress rolled in pebbles?"

She'd almost reconsidered—the palace courtyards were literally paved in pearls—but the dress was so gorgeous... "Pearls are traditional decorations for wedding dresses on Earth."

He'd shrugged. "Whatever your heart desires. You're exquisite in whatever you choose to wear."

Now she smiled at her friend. "I'm ready."

Lora looked into her eyes as if to verify, then proceeded down the hall, past Georgie's dad, and into the amphitheater. A loud murmur rose in the crowd as she appeared, then died down when they realized it wasn't their new princess.

Georgie was still unable to wrap her head around her new title. How did a supermarket checkout girl trying to build her own business handle becoming not only a princess, but also the galactic representative for the entire human race?

Moving forward, Georgie stopped next to her dad.

He held out his elbow, ready to escort her down the aisle. "You sure about this, Bug?"

His pet name for her made her smile, the sting of tears filling her eyes. "More than anything." She took a deep breath, wishing her mom could be her to see her as the music transitioned to the wedding march. "Let's go."

Together, they stepped out under the dome, her curtain of pearls flowing around her in a cascade that caught the dappled rays of the sun. A collective sigh from the audience drowned out the music for a moment, but Georgie focused on the path ahead. Violet carpet covered the amphitheater floor toward the squat dais where Arazhi waited, wearing the traditional garb of Vatosang, Empress Vella's home world. Georgie'd been trying to build a rapport with his mother, despite how awful the empress had been; spending the next few centuries with a mother-in-law who hated her would not be pleasant.

Arazhi looked strange, but very handsome in the calf-length, burnished gold duster vest with a raised epaulet on his left shoulder. The vest flowed longer at the back than the front, revealing form-fitting black pants with gold piping down the front crease, and was cinched to his waist by a black sash with gold chevron designs. On his head sat a small crown of interwoven diamonds that sparkled when he moved, matched by bands around his wrists and a sprinkle of diamonds along his epaulet.

Next to him stood his Best Man, Zhiruto, wearing a tuxedo from Earth, his long blue hair pulled into a man-bun on top of his head. It was the first time she'd seen Arazhi's security officer fully clothed since he'd arrived on Kirenai Prime. She glanced at Lora, who also waited on the dais. As she'd suspected, Lora wasn't even looking in her direction—she was focused on Zhiruto. Georgie'd been getting a strange vibe from them whenever they were together. Most of the time, they acted as if they hated each other, but then Lora would catch her friend sneaking longing glances.

"Did he do something wrong?" Georgie had asked soon after her friend arrived. She knew Lora and Zhiruto had worked together trying to track down the assassin on Earth.

Lora had looked away, but not before Georgie caught the flash of pain in her friend's eyes. "I can't talk about it yet."

Georgie hated to think Arazhi's best friend might've done something terrible. Even more, she hated seeing her friend like this. "I can ask Arazhi to dismiss him."

"No!" Lora had shaken her head emphatically and grasped

Georgie's hand. "Please, don't say anything to the prince. This is entirely on me."

"What did you do?"

"It's complicated." Lora's lips pressed tightly together, and Georgie could tell she wanted to say more, but something was holding her back. "I promise I'll tell you someday, okay?"

All Georgie could do was nod and continue coordinating her wedding plans.

Now she stepped onto the dais as Arazhi bowed low to her father and took her hand. He met her eyes with a dimpled smile that made her heart flutter no matter how many times she saw it and murmured, "You look magnificent, *kikajiru*."

Still in awe that he loved her, she let her own adoration flow toward him like a beam of light. "I'm so happy."

The minister cleared his throat and rattled quickly through his opening speech. The entire ceremony went by in a blur, and the next thing Georgie knew, Arazhi's lips were claiming hers as the ground shook beneath them with the force of the crowd's roar.

A shower of thousands of lightly glowing balloons drifted down around them like snowflakes, and Arazhi escorted her toward the exit where a convoy of carriages waited. They settled on the carriage's plush seat while Zhiruto and Lora climbed in behind them, taking the facing seat; Arazhi never went anywhere without his security officer anymore, and Lora seemed to have assumed the role of Georgie's bodyguard.

"I can't wait to be alone." Arazhi put his arm around Georgie's shoulders and pulled her close, nuzzling her temple and lightly kissing her ear. "The things I plan to do to you..."

She smiled, her heart full to bursting, and leaned into him, one hand on his muscular thigh as she glanced self-consciously toward their companions. Except Zhiruto and Lora weren't paying attention to their charges in the slightest.

Zhiruto and Lora were kissing.

ZHIRUTO

An assassin is loose on Earth, and Zhiruto must stop him from killing again. Except when the captivating, outspoken police officer assigned to help him turns out to be his one true mate, the murderer decides she's next on the hit list...

CHAPTER ONE

Lora poured two glasses of champagne and offered one to the blue-skinned man sitting across from her at the table. Stars glittered overhead, and a few couples were dancing in front of the stage where a live band played. She had to give Georgie credit—the alien charity auction had so far been a success, raising more money for the animal shelter than all the previous fundraisers combined. She also had to admit that her worry about being set up on a date with a big-eyed, six-tentacled alien from Area 51 had been unfounded.

Every alien at the auction was positively scrumptious—if they even were aliens. She still had her doubts, though their blue skin looked amazingly realistic.

Extraterrestrials had supposedly landed in Beijing several decades ago. They'd showed off for the cameras, talked to a few dignitaries, then disappeared without a trace. Most people believed the visit had been a hoax, but Lora's friend Georgie insisted this Intergalactic Dating Agency thing was legit. Then again, Georgie's mom used to tell stories about being abducted. *Whatever.* Lora was willing to go along with the cosplay to make money for the shelter.

Her date wore a navy blue suit and looked like a broad-shouldered member of the Blue Man Group, bald head and all. However, his stoic silence was giving her a bit of a creepy vibe.

"So, have you been to Earth before?" she asked, trying to initiate alien small talk. She pushed one of the champagne flutes toward him, wrapping Pepper's leash tighter around her free hand. She regretted bringing the gangly Redbone Coonhound along—the guy couldn't seem to take his attention off the dog.

Her date turned his gaze to her, his eyes a solid black that was hard to get used to. "No."

A piercing scream erupted at a table behind her.

At almost the same moment, her date's body seemed to quiver. Not like someone with a chill or even a person with palsy—he actually *quivered*, like his body was made of Jell-o. Then he collapsed inward, reduced to a glob of glistening blue slime in the seat of his chair.

Lora gaped, then stood to pull the hem of her crimson ball gown out of the way of the gelatinous sludge rolling off the seat toward her. *Oh, hell no.* Georgie had promised there would be no slime.

Her date—or what was left of him—landed on the grass with a plop.

More screams were coming from other tables, and she glanced around, heart pounding fast and hard. Everywhere she turned, blue-skinned aliens were dissolving. A white poodle darted past, dragging its leash. A woman ran after it shouting, "They must have death rays!"

Most of the alien guests had looked like blue humans, but the two gray aliens with horns and wings now perched on the stage several yards away. Now one of them flew upward—actually flew!—and batted something from the sky.

Lora gaped, all doubt about these being real aliens dispelled.

A drone smashed to the ground several yards away. A small red light blinked from its underside and letters on one of the rotor arms spelled Mini2. *That's not a death ray.* Just some amateur trying to get footage of the soirée. And definitely not the cause of disintegrations. So who was attacking them and from where?

She turned a full circle, looking for a shooter as she dug out the cell phone she'd stashed in the bodice of her gown. She knew she shouldn't have listened to Georgie's insistence that a police uniform didn't fit the theme for participants in the dating auction. Trying to keep her curious dog from burying her nose in alien goo, she called dispatch.

An automated voice said, "All circuits are busy. Please try your call again later."

"Fuck." She shoved the phone back into her bodice and watched as women in ball gowns tripped over toppled chairs, loose pets, and each other in their need to flee.

Towering well above the crowd, a singular set of broad blue shoulders and flowing navy colored hair was moving toward the park's fountain. He appeared to be the only surviving blue alien at the party. Was he responsible for the attack—or trying to escape it?

Cursing silently at her four-inch heels, she followed him, threading between the abandoned tables. Pepper wanted to stop and sniff every toppled chair and discarded napkin, and she was forced to yank on the lead to make her obey. "Pepper, heel, or so help me—"

Overhead, a pair of helicopters came into view, spotlights panning the tables as they descended to the lawn behind the stage. Someone must've gotten the word to the authorities. But her intuition was tingling about the blue alien she'd seen fleeing.

She hurried along the path toward the fountain, following the string of lights hung between poles to make the evening more romantic. Poor Georgie must be beside herself over what was happening to her premier event.

Pepper spotted a loose dog and veered off the path, trying to drag Lora with her. Lora'd enrolled her in obedience school and had been training her to track scents, but the dog was willful beyond belief. "Damnit, not now." Lora gritted her teeth, keeping firm hold of the leash.

She looked back up to find the blue alien striding toward her. He was tall, towering over her despite the added height of her pumps. Suddenly realizing she had no weapon, no cuffs, not even a radio to call for help, she held up one palm. "Springfield Police Department. Freeze."

He stopped a few steps away. His well-muscled chest was bare, narrow hips clothed in blue jeans, and the light stubble of a beard dusted his jaw.

Her mouth went dry. She couldn't tell where his solid black eyes were focused, but despite the chaos around them, it felt like he was undressing her with his gaze. Unbidden curiosity about how that stubble might feel against the tender flesh of her thighs filled her. *Wrong moment, wrong guy, Lora.* But damn if he wasn't the sexiest man—alien or otherwise—she'd ever laid eyes on.

Curious as always, Pepper surged forward to greet the stranger.

The sudden change in trajectory made Lora stumble, ankle twisting in her heels. The leash was yanked from her grip and she tumbled forward, hands out to catch herself.

The alien somehow averted the dog and managed to catch Lora before she crashed to her knees. His big hands were warm on her bare arms, his naked blue chest right at eye level. *Damn.* He was ripped. He even smelled sexy, like warm spices with a hint of leather. Her knees suddenly felt weak from more than just the tumble she'd almost taken.

She lifted her gaze to meet his glittering dark eyes and swallowed. *Stand up, you idiot.* But her legs felt too wobbly to hold her weight.

"You are injured," he said. His voice had a smoky depth that shot straight to her core.

What was wrong with her? This guy was turning her into a slobbering idiot. At least he didn't seem to intend her any harm.

"I'll be fine. I just need to take these shoes off." Still leaning on his arm, she slid her injured foot out of the pump. But when she tried to put weight on it to remove her other shoe, pain rocketed through her ankle. She fell to one knee on the grass.

Pepper took that as in invitation to play and barreled into her, knocking her flat onto the ground. "Pepper, no! Stop."

God, could this be more embarrassing? She wrapped one

arm around Pepper's neck to keep her under control and managed to push herself up to her knees, trying not to think about the grass stains she was probably getting on her expensive dress.

The alien suddenly stiffened, and she thought she was about to see another guy turn into goo. Instead, he lifted his arm, and a semi-transparent screen appeared above his wrist, just like in a sci-fi movie. Another alien's blue face floated in the air, speaking a language Lora didn't understand.

Then she heard a familiar voice. "Lora! Are you okay?"

"Georgie?" Lora let go of Pepper and grabbed the alien's outstretched arm, dragging herself upright onto her good foot. "Where are you?"

The big blue man frowned and pulled his arm from her grasp so the screen once more faced him. After a few more words with the other alien, the screen disappeared.

Lora reached for his arm again. "That was my friend! What have you done with her? What's going on?"

The alien tilted his head, as if taking a moment to understand. This close, she saw his eyes weren't completely black, but deep blue with no whites. His nose was slightly crooked, as if it had been broken at some point. "Your friend is safe. She's with Prince Arazhi."

"Prince?" Lora gaped. "What prince? What's going on?" She took a hobbling step forward and gritted her teeth against the pain lancing through her ankle.

Without warning, the alien swept her into his arms and strode toward the stage where the helicopters could be heard winding down. "Someone tried to assassinate the crown prince. I must find out who."

Lora clung to his neck. She wasn't exactly a small woman, but he carried her as if she weighed nothing. Before she could ask more questions, a man's voice called out, "Hey! You! Come with us."

Twisting her neck, she spotted a pair of men in black suits approaching along the path ahead. *Probably Feds.* And here she was being carried like a damsel in distress. The guys at the precinct were going to have a heyday when they heard about it.

She patted the alien's shoulder. "Put me down, please."

He hesitated, gaze concentrated on the men, then gently set her on her feet.

Keeping her weight on her good ankle, she reached into her bodice to retrieve her badge. "Springfield P—"

"Gun!" The shorter man shouted, drawing his pistol.

CHAPTER TWO

Zhiruto lunged past the human female and grabbed the man's weapon, forcing him to the ground. The only thing on his mind was protecting the female. *My female.*

The moment he'd touched her, he'd sensed she would be his perfect mate. The feeling had been so distracting, he'd missed his teleportation window off the planet. Now he was stuck here, protecting a female he neither knew nor owned, yet who'd captured his attention in the most primal way possible.

My mate.

The human male he now held pinned was leaking aggression like a Kryillian death swarm. The taller human with him was more nervous than hostile as he pulled his own weapon, so Zhiruto ignored him; if the man fired the primitive projectile, it would now be at Zhiruto, not the female, and a Kirenai's shapeshifting matrix could absorb the impact—he was certain the female's physiology could not.

"Stop!" the female shouted. "Don't hurt him!"

The universal translator was still updating, and Zhiruto wasn't sure if she was talking to him or the other men, but he kept his focus on the grappled man and spoke carefully, "I do not intend harm."

The taller human male spoke in a shaky voice, "Let him go. Now."

Zhiruto's Iki'i—his Kirenai empathic sense—itched with the emotions swirling around the humans. The female had said she was with the police, a human term he recognized as one of authority. He looked at her. "Shall I release him?"

She was clinging to a gold charm shaped like a primitive shield that hung around her neck. "Not yet." She turned her attention toward the taller male. "I don't know what sort of operation you're running, but I was trying to identify myself." She raised the charm. "Lora Griffin, Springfield P.D. Now who the fuck are you?"

A surge of jealousy rose in Zhiruto—she hadn't even bothered to ask his name when they'd met. He needed to remedy that immediately.

The man slowly lowered his weapon and pulled a black wallet from his jacket. "Agent Richfield. National Security."

Loragriffin took a limping step to look closer, making Zhiruto's possessiveness nearly consume him. He needed to get himself under control before his urges made him do something rash.

She examined the wallet, then nodded before looking once more at Zhiruto. "They're NSA. You can let him go."

Reluctantly, Zhiruto relaxed his grip and stepped back. The

human he'd been holding scrambled to his feet and smoothed his hands over the lapels of his jacket. "The alien needs to come with us."

Zhiruto stiffened. He wasn't about to let this NSA—whatever that was—make him look like a nobody in front of Loragriffin. "I am Zhiruto Miru, head of security for Crown Prince Arazhi Yazhu. Take me to your leader immediately."

The shorter human let out a barking laugh. "Seriously?" He turned to the other man. "He just said take me to your leader."

"What's he supposed to say?" Loragriffin stepped in, as confident as a queen issuing a royal edict. "Just take us to whoever's in charge."

Zhiruto couldn't help but smile. She was magnificent.

The shorter man looked her up and down with unconcealed disdain, then glanced at Zhiruto before nodding. "This way."

Zhiruto yearned to put the man in his place, but Loragriffin called for something called "pepper" and emitted a whistle his translator couldn't interpret. *Is that how humans signal they're in pain?* Or perhaps pepper was an analgesic. He didn't have any painkillers on him, but he offered to carry her again.

She refused, continuing to call out as she limped after the man.

Appreciation of her strength rose up inside him. He'd noticed it earlier when she'd been on stage, and would've bid on her if he hadn't already purchased a female—not that he wanted to own a bondservant for himself. Empress Vella had given him orders to purchase a back-up female in case the reluctant prince failed to win one. He'd lost sight of his new bondservant during the chaos, but that no longer mattered.

Now that he knew the prince had secured one of his own, Zhiruto would let her go.

He'd rather spend his time on Earth with Loragriffin.

The NSA men led them past the tables where fallen Kirenai lay puddled on the grass, dull blue and lifeless. None of the formless shapes near the tables appeared to be moving or attempting to reform, and Zhiruto's stomach churned with dismay. As shapeshifters, his people could assume the appearance of any species in the galaxy, but their natural state was an unformed cellular matrix which humans might associate with an amoeba. A Kirenai never used that form in public, but there were some toxins that could force them into it, most notably the poison which had recently weakened the emperor. Could this have been caused by the same poison? And why didn't the IDA have its healers out seeing to the fallen?

Well away from the tables, a cluster of humans and their accompanying quadrupeds stood near the stage surrounded by armed men in camouflage clothing. Several of the quadrupeds barked. Two females sobbed, while another spoke to the guards, demanding something she called a "cell phone." His universal translator was sending him conflicting interpretations of what the word "cell" meant, and he tapped the implant in his wrist, frustrated that humans had so many languages and idioms the translation database had yet to parse.

Loragriffin's quadruped appeared within the crowd, held in check by a female with obsidian hair and a burgundy gown. Relief wafted from Loragriffin. "Can you watch Pepper for a bit, Maise? I'm on duty."

The female called Maise replied, "Sure!"

Pepper is the name of her quadruped, Zhiruto realized.

When he'd first arrived on the planet, he'd assumed the furry mammals were in charge of the females, given the way the humans seemed to defer to them. But after he'd attempted to speak with one he'd realized the creatures were of lesser intelligence. Since human females had strong maternal instincts, he'd concluded that they must need the animals as surrogate children until they could be impregnated. Just the thought of impregnating Loragriffin made his human anatomy swell uncomfortably.

They continued on toward the pale yellow tent that had been used for food preparation. Now, two men in matching black suits blocked the entrance.

Loragriffin lifted her charm in front of their faces. "Springfield Police—"

"We'll take it from here," the shorter of their escorts interrupted. "You can join the others." He pointed back toward the humans near the stage.

"Now hold on..." She protested as a man in a camouflage uniform took her arm.

Zhiruto couldn't read thoughts, only sense emotion, and all he could read on the men at the moment was walled resolution. But Loragriffin didn't trust them, and that made Zhiruto suspicious, as well. He took her other arm. "The female comes with me."

"We've been instructed to segregate the aliens."

"This female has the authority of your police," Zhiruto insisted. "I require her aid."

Loragriffin shot him a surprised glance, and gratitude

warmed his Iki'i. Zhiruto found he liked the sensation. *Don't let yourself be distracted*, he reminded himself, forcing his focus back to the guards. He had to get the situation under control and begin his hunt for the assassin—his prince's safety depended on it.

A man inside the tent said, "It's fine. Let them in."

Zhiruto pulled her inside. Glaring artificial lights cut across the tent from each corner, and the clunky food heating appliances were now shoved to one end. A group of humans stood around a table looking at folding data pads. Beyond them, a paltry pair of human-shaped Kirenai stood submissively under guard along with a pink-scaled Qalqan, the two Khargal guests, and the single Fogarian he recalled from the guest list.

A small measure of relief shuddered through him as he realized he wasn't the only Kirenai left standing.

The human who'd tried to shoot Loragriffin nudged him in the back, speaking toward a man with dark skin and close-cropped silver hair. "This one was wandering around the park."

Zhiruto focused on the dark-skinned man who was obviously in charge. "I am Zhiruto Miru, head of security for—"

The man held up a hand. "We're still coordinating a grounds sweep. Go wait over there with your friends and I'll get to you in a minute."

Zhiruto scowled. This human obviously didn't have a clue about what was happening. "Our healer needs to look for survivors."

"I said, over there. I have my people on it now."

Loragriffin pulled her arm from Zhiruto's grip and stepped up to the man, waving her charm. "Is this how the NSA trains its people to interact with foreign dignitaries? Not to mention he's talking about saving survivors, asshole—"

"I let you in here as a courtesy," the man growled. "If you can't keep a civil tongue, I'll have my men show you out."

The female continued arguing, but Zhiruto didn't have time to wait for the outcome. Loragriffin could obviously handle herself with these men, and he'd already allowed himself to be distracted by her when he should have been escorting his prince back to Kirenai Prime. Now his only task must be tracking down the assassin.

He turned toward the surviving guests at the back of the tent. The Qalqan healer was the head of first aid for the IDA. The Khargals and Fogarian were guests he recognized from the party. And both Kirenai wore IDA badges on white shirts they'd obviously acquired to appear more human; his own clothing was a mere mimicry of human garb.

"Have we checked for survivors?" he asked the healer.

The pink-scaled Qalqan shook his head. "I haven't been allowed a full triage, but the few I was able to scan were deceased." He gestured toward a dull blue matrix lying flat against the grass in the opposite corner of the tent. "That was the IDA's planetary manager. So far, it appears only Kirenai were affected."

Zhiruto's gut clenched. There had been almost twenty Kirenai guests on the list, plus another handful on the IDA staff.

He gestured to the remaining Kirenai. "So why are we still okay?"

"I believe the food was poisoned," said the healer. "Did you eat anything?"

Zhiruto shook his head, glad he hadn't sampled any of the human delicacies during his initial tour of the tent. Had his prince? Dread filled Zhiruto. He couldn't warn Prince Arazhi while the ship's FTL drive was engaged. By the time the ship reached Kirenai Prime, it might be too late.

The taller Khargal fluttered his wings, as if wishing to take to the air. "I sampled the paltry meal and feel perfectly well. Why are we being held prisoner? I demand to be allowed to collect my female and depart this wretched planet immediately."

Zhiruto's Iki'i was swept by unease from the survivors. He gave the Khargal a hard stare. "Nobody's leaving until I have answers."

"You're Prince Arazhi's man, aren't you?" asked the other Khargal, wings furled tightly against his back. "Was the prince harmed?"

Zhiruto narrowed his eyes. As shapeshifters, his species could move among other species without revealing their true identities; only other Kirenai could discern one from another by using their Iki'i. Prince Arazhi had not used his public form— the one the rest of the galaxy would instantly recognize—during his visit to Earth. "How did you know the prince was here?"

"You introduced yourself to the 'humons' as Zhiruto Miru, and everyone knows you never leave Prince Arazhi's side," said the Khargal. "I met you with the prince at a ball on Vatosang."

He didn't recognize the Khargal; but then, he met a lot of people in his travels with the prince. Before answering, he opened his Iki'i for reactions, and he watched the Qalqan for shifts in body language as the species was immune to Iki'i sense.

They were seldom involved in aggression, but Zhiruto wasn't willing to rule anyone out, not when there was a high probability the culprit was standing before him now.

He said, "The prince escaped the planet without injury."

Only relief touched his senses throughout the group, and even the Qalqan nodded in obvious relief. *The suspect isn't one of those here at the moment.* Which meant the culprit had either transported before the window closed or was loose on the planet somewhere. *Could the assassin be human?* That thought sent a chill into his gut.

The Fogarian said, "I'm glad to assist with the investigation."

"Thank you."

The dark-skinned NSA man strode over, a data pad in one hand. "Thank you for your cooperation. My name's Agent Randall. I've been in contact with your IDA representatives, and we're working on getting a shuttle in to pick you up."

Loragriffin stood among the other humans, arms crossed over her chest, a smug smile on her face. She thought she'd helped gain them freedom, but little did she know she may have also given the assassin a way to escape.

"You must not allow orbital traffic until I've finished my investigation," Zhiruto said. "This was an assassination attempt, and the culprit is most likely still among us."

The belligerent Khargal groaned.

The Qalqan made a hissing sound. "Excuse me, but if there are any survivors among the fallen, they will need to be taken to the ship's medical bay right away."

Zhiruto ground his teeth. Finding the assassin was

important, but so was saving lives. There was also a possibility one of the victims had seen something.

"Our medics confirmed all the, uh, remains we've found are dead," Agent Randall said.

"Your healers aren't equipped to deal with our medical requirements," Zhiruto replied. "Please allow us to see to the victims immediately."

Agent Randall's nose wrinkled, but then he nodded. "All right, go ahead. My men are available to help if you need them."

The Qalqan gathered his scanner and scurried from the tent, followed closely by three of the other agents.

Zhiruto slid his gaze to Loragriffin. He needed to speak with the humans who may have seen something, and to do that, he'd need help. "I would like your assistance speaking with the human guests."

Agent Randall started to protest. "She doesn't have clearance—"

"She's the only one I trust."

The man's jaw worked like he wanted to spit, then he shifted his eyes toward her. "I suppose she can be your liaison. Be sure to file a report with us as well as your precinct, Officer Griffin. Understand?"

Wide-eyed, she nodded. "Yes, sir."

Zhiruto hadn't known his request for her help would please her so much, but he felt himself swell with satisfaction. "Come, then." He gestured for her to precede him out of the tent.

CHAPTER THREE

Lora understood Agent Randall's not so subtle hint that she was now working for the NSA, and she wasn't sure how to feel about that. On one hand, it could lead to a promotion or even a new job with the Feds if she performed well. On the other, they were treating the aliens as if they were terrorists instead of the victims of the attack. It was a massive load of bullshit, and if she could help Zhiruto get to the bottom of these deaths, she would.

Trying to hide her limp, she exited the tent ahead of the tall blue alien. As she passed the small agent who'd pulled the gun on her, he muttered, "You've got no business being here."

Zhiruto halted midstep and turned a baleful glare at the man, sending him scurrying back inside.

Lora was really beginning to like Zhiruto, but she couldn't allow him to keep stepping in on her behalf. She put a hand on his arm, surprised by how human his blue skin felt under her palm. "Thanks, but I can fight my own battles."

He gave her a startled look. "You're going to battle?"

She grinned, picturing herself knocking the agent on his ass in kickboxing. She was pretty good in the ring, but she was certain the guy probably had some sort of special ops training a regular cop like her didn't have. Plus, her ankle was currently on fire. "It's just a figure of speech."

"I see." He turned toward the people gathered under the lights near the stage. "This is why I need your help communicating with the humans, Loragriffin."

"Just Lora. Please." It was nice to be appreciated, but his continued use of her name smashed together like that was beginning to feel awkward.

"Lora." He smiled. "A good name for you. It means 'persuasive' in Kirenai."

She had to smile, too. Persuasive sounded a lot more complimentary than the names she was usually called.

As they moved along the line of police tape cordoning off the tables, she watched the pink alien bend over a dark spot on the grass. He was waving what looked like a baton. "What's he doing?"

"Scanning for life signs."

She raised her eyebrows. The jelly-like splotches looked beyond help. Then again, she'd heard rumors the aliens had teleported down to Earth instead of landing in a ship, so maybe they had technology to perform reconstruction. "Can you resuscitate someone who's been disintegrated like that?"

He stopped walking and turned to her. "They were not disintegrated. They were denatured."

"What's the difference?"

He rubbed his chin, the stubble making scratchy noise under his fingers. Was it possible he'd gotten more handsome, or was she just desperate to get laid? It'd been quite a while since she'd been on a date, let alone taken a guy home. She usually preferred her vibrator over the entanglements of bringing a man into her life.

Zhiruto gestured toward a bench on the nearby trail. "If you are going to help me speak to these women, then I must first brief you on the situation."

She sank gratefully onto the bench and he settled down beside her. They were close but not touching, and every inch of her skin seemed hyper aware of his presence. It didn't help that he was still shirtless, his smooth bare chest and abs cut with muscles that flexed with his every move. She worked out at a gym every day with bodybuilders, and not a single one of them could compete with this guy.

Realizing she'd been staring at his perfect little nipples—a darker blue than the rest of his skin—she looked up to find him smiling like a Cheshire cat. *Shit, way to make a fool of yourself.* She planted one hand on the bench and nonchalantly leaned away from him. "So, what about denaturing or whatever?"

He imitated her posture, leaning the other way, which only made his torso seem that much more ripped. "First let me tell you about the emperor's son, Prince Arazhi."

She nodded, trying hard to keep her attention on his face. "The person you work for?"

"Yes. He's the heir to the Yazhu dynasty. His father is ill, and Prince Arazhi will soon take the throne."

"Let me guess. Somebody out there doesn't want that to happen." Overhead, a helicopter circled the night sky, while in the distance a babbling rumble told her a crowd had likely gathered at the park barricades. How much more chaotic would it get once people found out royalty was involved?

"Correct. There is a strong consortium of merchants within the Senburu—our confederation of planets—who oppose the emperor's long-standing trade edicts. They've put forth their own candidate for the throne, and if Prince Arazhi can't produce an heir in the near future, it's likely they will enact a coup and seize power. That's why he came to Earth, to purchase a female to impregnate."

Lora sat up, horror chilling down her spine. Georgie was currently flying to God knew where on a spaceship with an alien who wanted to impregnate her. "Back up. Purchase? Are you saying he thinks Georgie is his slave?"

He tilted his head, as if trying to understand. "He purchased her contract. Did you not sell yourself as a bondservant, as well?"

"Definitely not." She stood, heart thundering against her ribs as she looked down at him. "The auction was for charity. You were bidding on a date, not a woman."

"Yes, a date. This means the delivery of viable bondservants."

She gulped. "There's been a mistake. That's not what dating means on Earth. It means spending time getting to know someone."

"I see." He rose. "This is an unfortunate misunderstanding. I'll see that our universal translator is updated."

"You need to call the prince back and clear this up right now."

"Agreed. However, they are out of communication range while they are traveling to Kirenai Prime. Please rest assured, Prince Arazhi won't harm your friend or force himself on her once he learns of the mistake. But he is short on time to sire an heir. I must ensure he has an alternative." He took a half-step backward, staring at her as if torn. "Would you be willing to have his child?"

She gaped at him. "What the hell? I've never even met him."

"So that is a no?"

"An emphatic no."

He nodded, and she thought he almost looked relieved. Turning toward the cluster of guarded women, he said, "Then let's go talk to the other females."

Thank God he gave up on the baby-making suggestion quickly. He most likely didn't see her as the motherly type. She was simply the first woman presented, and he'd be asking every woman the same question. She shoved aside the odd sense of disappointment threading through her chest. "I'm here to help you find a killer, not find the prince a date."

"Of course." Reaching out, he took her hand and put it on his arm. "Let's proceed with our questioning so everyone can go home."

She didn't want to look like she was being escorted to prom, but she was really feeling the swelling in her ankle, so she gave in and leaned on him to limp toward the group. The NSA guard handed Zhiruto a tablet. "This is a list of human guests. We're still tracking down a few."

"Thank you." Zhiruto passed her the device.

Lora accepted it, and the guard stepped aside to let them pass, body rigid and eyes following their progress like he was watching a snake slither past.

The women, however, were far less suspicious. They surged forward, questions flying from all directions. "What happened? Can we go home now? Are we under attack?"

Maise pushed to the front, multiple leashes clutched in her fists. As usual, she'd assumed responsibility for every stray dog she could find. She now held not only Pepper and her own dog, Bixby, but an enormous Great Dane with striking blue eyes and a caramel-colored labradoodle.

Seeing Pepper again soothed Lora's frazzled nerves, and she rubbed the dog's ears. "Thanks for watching her. Think you can keep an eye on her a bit longer?"

"Sure. Any idea who these belong to?" Maise gestured toward the other dogs in her care. The hem of her burgundy skirt was torn, and her raven curls had come loose from the messy bun she'd worn for the event.

"Sorry, no." The last thing on Lora's mind was tracking down missing dog owners. She turned to the crowd, most of whom she recognized from the pre-auction briefing. "Thank you for your patience, everyone."

She glanced at Zhiruto to find a brunette in a sequined black dress rubbing herself all over him. Well, all right, maybe not rubbing herself, but definitely clinging as if she knew him. Wanted him.

The woman said, "I'm so glad you're all right."

A flare of jealousy made Lora press her lips tightly together. *This must be the woman he thought he was buying at the auction.*

Zhiruto extracted his arm from the woman's grip. "I'm glad you're also unharmed. But in light of recent events, I must nullify our contract. Please step back with the others now."

A hurt look flitted across the woman's face, and she dropped her hands.

Lora's jealousy turned to pity as the woman slunk back to the others. Apparently the guy didn't know how to let someone down easy. But at least he was keeping to business, and she had to approve of that.

He looked at her and said, "Please proceed."

Lora nodded, considering how much to tell the women. She didn't want to fall into the weeds about the whole slavery issue; it wasn't like the aliens in question were in any state to claim ownership, anyway. The important thing right now was finding the killer.

She met the eyes of a woman holding a corgi, then shifted her attention among the women as she spoke. "I know tonight was traumatic, and we appreciate all of you remaining calm. I've been informed that this was an assassination attempt on an alien prince."

Collectively, all eyes turned toward Zhiruto, and the brunette edged a step forward. "You're a prince?"

This time, Lora's jealousy rose burning hot. "No. He's the prince's bodyguard."

Lascivious murmurs about sexy bodyguards forced her to speak louder so she'd be heard. "Ladies, please. Have some respect. Aliens have died and we need your help. Did anyone see anything unusual tonight?"

"More unusual than my date dissolving into a puddle right before my eyes?" asked the woman with the corgi.

Lora put on a stoic face. Even she had to admit she'd been pretty focused on her date when everything went down. "We'd like to speak to everyone individually about the events this evening."

"After that, can we go home?" asked an older woman in a puffy pink gown that looked like it had been a bridesmaid's dress in the eighties.

A scratchy shout came from the area of the tables, making everyone turn.

The pink alien was waving a wand in the air, and the three NSA medics were struggling to push a round cart with a portable MRI scanner across the grass.

"What's going on?" asked Lora.

Zhiruto was already stepping over the police tape. "They've found a survivor."

Lora's stomach flip-flopped, then she limped quickly after him, hoping she wasn't about to see a zombie arm sticking out of one of the blue globs.

CHAPTER FOUR

Zhiruto strode over to the healer, heartened by news of a survivor. The healer was using an anti-gravity field generator to lift the Kirenai's cellular matrix from where it had collapsed on top of a chair. The two IDA representatives were trying to get a hovering transportation creche past the NSA men and their wheeled cart, and a handful of NSA humans crowded around the healer, more curious than helpful as they asked questions. Not only were they in the way, but a Kirenai's resting state was private. This victim deserved dignity.

Holding out his arms as if to block their view, Zhiruto said, "I must ask you to back away so our healer can work."

Agent Randall scowled. "I'm tired of you aliens always treating us as servants. This is an investigation on human soil. We need to be sure there's no threat to our own population."

Zhiruto moved in front of the man, arms crossed. "Is it common practice for your ancillary personnel to gawk at naked human victims? Because right now, this Kirenai is basically naked."

The man had the grace to emit remorse, though his scowl remained. "At least allow us to perform an MRI."

"We have no need of your scanner," said the healer. "Please move your people out of the way." He pointed toward the incoming transportation creche; the organic polymer box was of Qalqan design and would adjust its size to fit the occupant. It would also induce stasis until the appropriate medical facilities could be reached.

Agent Randall glanced at the creche then at Lora, who now stood a polite distance away before telling his men, "Everyone, back to your duties."

To their credit, the men didn't so much as grumble as they stepped away, but Zhiruto could still feel their curious eyes on the scene as they pretended to perform other duties nearby.

Agent Randall took several generous steps backward and continued watching, obviously not considering himself ancillary. There was a sense of avarice coming from him that Zhiruto didn't like, but it was one he'd encountered before—less advanced species often hoped to acquire new technology when they saw it. At least the agent was no longer in the healer's way.

Lora was obviously curious about the fallen Kirenai as well but stayed back.

He signaled her to join him.

She edged closer until she stood beside him, her bare shoulder brushing his arm, and watched the healer transfer the other Kirenai into a transportation creche. Amazement and pity brushed his Iki'i, mimicking his own emotions. That this Kirenai had survived where so many others had not was a miracle. It might also be a curse if the poison couldn't be purged; to be forever relegated to one's resting state would be a terrible fate.

Zhiruto searched for the survivor's Iki'i signature while the healer floated the unformed matrix upward and into the creche. He could sense the victim was alive, but this individual wasn't familiar to him. As the poisoned Kirenai settled inside the creche, the matrix shuddered, convulsed, and pulled into a human-looking face, only to subside once more into a gelatinous resting state.

Lora stumbled backward, wide eyes on the fallen Kirenai. "Holy shit, it *is* alive."

Although Lora's incredulity was strong, the victim's indignation was stronger, almost blinding in its intensity. Zhiruto pulled her aside and leaned close to her ear. "First of all, we say 'he' not 'it'. Second, he can hear you."

Eyebrows drawing together in horror, she nodded. "Oh, God. Sorry. He."

He smiled gently. "It wasn't a reprimand, only a correction. Humans are new to the galactic consortium. We have a lot to learn about each other."

"Is he in pain?"

Now that she mentioned it, Zhiruto was struck by the lack of pain he was sensing. Perhaps the poison also had a numbing effect. "No. He's just unable to rise from his resting state."

"Resting state? What's that?"

Although few had seen it, nearly everyone in the galaxy knew about the Kirenai resting state. "Did the IDA not brief you about the guests? Kirenai are shapeshifters, but we must occasionally allow our cellular matrix to relax."

She gaped, and her attention slid over his body. "You mean this isn't what you normally look like?"

"I can assume the shape of many species, although I'm always this color. I've simply assumed a shape pleasing to... humans." He didn't want to admit that much of what he looked like now—from his crooked nose to the stubble on his chin—was made for her pleasure.

"You're definitely going to need to give me more details on that later." She shook her head, gaze still roaming his chest. "After you finish here."

He nodded, pleased by how quickly she'd overcome her shock and focused back on the job. "I'll be more than happy to tell you more later." Returning his attention to the healer, he asked, "Do you have an ID for the victim?"

The Kirenai kept a genetic database to help track its population, since a Kirenai resumed his resting state upon death and would be unidentifiable any other way. The healer didn't look away from his task. "I will need to get him back to the ship to run a check."

Zhiruto moved forward, extending a hand toward the Kirenai's matrix; his species could share information through their Iki'i when they touched, even in their resting state. He'd simply ask the victim himself.

The healer placed a clawed hand on Zhiruto's arm to stop him. "Don't touch him until I determine if the cause of the condition is transmissible."

That brought Zhiruto up short. "I thought you said it was poison?"

"The poison could transfer between you if you attempt to interface with him."

Zhiruto let out a heavy sigh and dropped his hand. "All right. Just give me a few minutes before you put him into stasis."

Bowing slightly, the healer stepped back to wait. "Please proceed, but keep in mind that the longer he remains unstable, the more difficult it will be to recover."

Moving as close to the creche as possible without touching it, Zhiruto said, "My name's Zhiruto and I serve Prince Arazhi. I'm looking for the person who did this to you. Do you have any information about what happened?"

Anger shot against him like sharp needles along with a sense of affirmation.

Zhiruto's pulse picked up. *He does know something.* The urge to reach into the creche and get the information was difficult to resist. Without touching, he had to rely on yes or no questions. "Was it one of the Khargals?"

Negativity flowed to him.

"The Fogarian?"

Again, negativity.

He had difficulty believing a Kirenai could commit such an atrocity to their own kind, so he asked, "A human?"

A human-looking face formed once more in the matrix, and a single word escaped the Kirenai's lips. "*Burendo.*"

Zhiruto stiffened as the Kirenai relaxed into his resting state once more. All Kirenai could change shape, but *burendo* could change color, as well, and could blend into local populations almost as well as the natives. It meant the culprit was not only Kirenai, but had likely escaped into hiding among the billions of humans here on the planet. And if the *burendo* was a trained assassin, he'd know how to shield himself from another's Iki'i as well. *How am I going to track him down now?*

"What did he say?" whispered Lora, touching his arm.

He gestured for the healer to proceed with sealing the creche—there was nothing more he needed from the victim. Then he turned to Lora. "*Burendo*. It's a Kirenai who can change color and shape. They're extremely rare."

"So the murderer is one of these *burendo*?" Her gaze slid toward a nearby NSA guard. "He or she could look exactly like a human?"

Zhiruto hadn't even had time to consider the assassin could be mimicking not only a human, but a female. Kirenai were an all-male species, but were still capable of assuming a female form if they so desired.

His job had grown exponentially more impossible.

He looked at the gathered humans pressing against the boundary set by the NSA guards. "Do you know these humans personally?"

"A lot of them, yes. Are you suggesting one of them may be a—a doppelgänger?"

His translator took a moment to interpret the word. When it did, he shook his head. "A *burendo* can't assume the look of a specific individual very well, and wouldn't know how to imitate that person without extensive study. Normally, I could detect another Kirenai's Iki'i, but an assassin is likely shielding himself while I'm around. However, if you know these women, I believe it should be easy to confirm each is who she says she is."

She nodded. "All right." Her gaze flicked toward Agent Randall hovering nearby. "But don't tell Randall about the *burendo* or he'll freak out and these women will never make it home. The last thing you want is the NSA to take over. We'd be buried in all sorts of testing and red tape."

Zhiruto didn't know what red tape meant, but he trusted Lora's judgment. "Let's not mention it to anyone. If the assassin finds out we know what he is, he'll be more cautious."

"Good point," Lora said. "Let's make this *burendo* feel comfortable, and perhaps they'll slip up."

He liked that their minds followed the same path. Smiling, he nodded at his partner. "Let's go speak to your friends."

CHAPTER FIVE

Lora was to return to the gathered women and begin questioning them while Zhiruto went to check on the status of the incoming shuttle. She stopped by the restroom on her way over, thinking about everything she'd learned. Zhiruto was not only an alien, he was a shapeshifter. But the hard-muscled blue man she'd been drooling over was nothing like a werewolf in the books she enjoyed. He was actually more like a creature from *The Blob*. *He looks and feels so real.* Hell, he even smelled real, like the best masculine cologne she could imagine. When she thought about it, a shapeshifting blob wasn't really that much more fantastical than a werewolf. Just a bit less cuddly. The thought made her laugh.

She stepped out of the restroom and limped toward the stage. The sky had begun lightening toward the east, and the women all looked haggard and exhausted in their rumpled evening gowns. Even the dogs looked ready to go home, no longer playing or barking, just lying around sleeping or watching their owners with sad eyes.

The women perked up when Lora passed between the guards. Several rushed over and began babbling questions as she approached. "Is one still alive? Are we suspects? Why are they keeping us here?"

She had to use her hard-ass police voice to get them to calm down. "Sit down and be quiet or none of us will be getting out of here anytime soon. To answer your questions, yes, one of the aliens is still alive. He's being taken to their medical facility." She decided to refrain from going into the whole "resting state" thing; it would only cause more questions. "Now if you'll please cooperate, I'm going to try to clear you all to go home."

That got a collective sigh of relief and the ladies trudged back to their seats.

Maise remained standing, three dogs on leashes standing around her like sentinels plus Pepper, who was now whining at the sight of Lora.

"Thanks for hanging onto her. I can take her back now." Lora took the leash, bending down to let Pepper nuzzle her ear. It felt good to have her dog back. She glanced up at Maise, taking in her bleary eyes and drooping bun of black hair. "Why don't I talk to you first?"

Several women grumbled about playing favorites, but Lora ignored them and led the way to one end of the stage where two chairs sat on the grass next to a table that had once held champagne.

Glad to take the weight off her ankle, she sat, tying Pepper to the back of her chair while Maise looped the leashes of the other three dogs on a railing at the edge of the stage. Grabbing two bottled waters from a nearby table, Maise joined her, handing one over. "I haven't seen Georgie since this all happened. Do you know where she is?"

Lora rubbed the back of her neck. "She's, ah, with the prince, I guess."

"Get outta town." Maise's eyes widened. "Where are they? When do I get to meet him?"

"They're on a spaceship, I think. I saw her briefly when Zhiruto Facetimed them or whatever aliens call it."

"A spaceship?" Maise gasped. "Is she okay?"

"Yeah, I think so. At least, Zhiruto says she's not in danger."

Maise gave Lora a scrutinizing look. "I thought you were on official police duty, but you keep mentioning Zhiruto. Is that your alien bodyguard?"

Suddenly reminded of the feel of Zhiruto's muscles and his warm masculine scent when he'd carried her, Lora flushed. "He's not my bodyguard. He's the prince's. And I'm working for the NSA as a liaison."

"A liaison, huh?" Maise smirked. "Leading an investigation with a hot shirtless guy is probably like a dream date for you."

Lora crossed her arms. "Zhiruto isn't my date, and I'm not leading the investigation. Plus, there are more than a dozen dead aliens only footsteps away. Definitely not a dream date or the time to be thinking of hot guys."

"You're right." Maise stopped smirking and dropped her gaze. "This entire thing is awful."

Lora nodded, feeling like a hypocrite—she'd been thinking

about how hot Zhiruto was all evening. "Let's get on with a few questions so I can let you go home, okay?"

Maise nodded.

"Does everyone here seem normal to you?" Keeping the *burendo* a secret was going to make asking questions more difficult. At least she was already certain Maise was really who she claimed to be. "I'm looking for anyone who seemed less shocked than they should be. Or more shocked. Anything strange at all."

Maise thought a second. "I think people are acting pretty normal. Heather's been crying non-stop. Meg's her usual bossy self. I suppose Tammy's been a little quieter than usual, but I think she's in shock. Someone said she and her date were kissing when it happened. She got blue goo all over her when he dissolved, and the NSA confiscated her dress."

Lora shuddered and glanced toward where Tammy sat with her knees drawn up to her chest, wearing nothing but a thin slip with a gray wool blanket draped over her shoulders. "Damn."

"You should probably talk to her next so she can get out of here. I think a bunch of us will need counseling after tonight."

"Thanks, Maise. I'll let the guards know you're clear to leave."

Maise rose and gathered the dogs. "I'm going to take these two to the shelter. Let me know if you talk to anyone missing their dogs."

"You bet."

Lora had just finished questioning Tammy when Zhiruto returned. The poor woman had stuttered her way through the questions, but she was also very clearly the same woman Lora'd met a few times while volunteering at the shelter. She instructed one of the guards to call Tammy a cab as Zhiruto held out a paper cup.

"The humans in the tent are all drinking this," he said. "I thought you might like some." The dark, rich scent of hot coffee wafted from its open top.

"God, yes, thank you." she said, taking a grateful sip. He'd even managed to douse it with the right amount of cream and sugar. She was used to pulling late shifts as a cop, but not without coffee. She closed her eyes with pleasure as the caffeine burned down her throat.

Zhiruto made a small noise that sounded almost like a growl, and her eyes popped back open to find him staring at her with a hungry expression.

Her throat tightened. "Do you, uh, want a taste?"

"More than you know."

She instantly knew he wasn't talking about the coffee, and desire flushed through her, centering deep in her core. She almost couldn't breathe with its intensity.

Focus on the job, you dingbat, she told herself. She had guys come onto her all the time, and brushing them off was second nature. But then, very few of them were built like Zhiruto. Swallowing, she set the coffee aside and turned her eyes to the list of attendees on the iPad the NSA had given her. "Let's stick to business. We have a lot more people to process, so we'd better keep moving."

Zhiruto pulled a chair over from a nearby table and sat. "Please continue. I appreciate your help."

Pepper put her head on Zhiruto's lap and he patted the top of her skull uncertainly. Pepper whined louder.

"Pepper, stop bothering him and go lay down."

"The quadruped isn't bothering me, Loragriffin. She will lie down in a moment."

More tingly feelings raced through Lora as she watched his big hand smooth over Pepper's sleek red fur. Damn, she was a sucker for a guy with a dog. Shaking it off, she called the next person over, trying hard to focus on her questions instead of the towering masculinity next to her.

The rest of the interviews went quickly as the sky above the trees to the east went from pale violet to the gold of sunrise, and the faint whine of morning traffic joined the chorus of birds in the trees. She had little trouble determining that the people she spoke with were who they said they were, mostly by using questions about the animal shelter. A freckled young man with bloodshot eyes who'd been one of the servers gave her a moment of panic when he stuttered out a nonsensical answer about how he'd landed the job, but then she realized it was because he'd lied about being twenty-one.

"I d-didn't touch the champagne. Not even to serve it. I swear."

She handed him back his driver's license. "I'm letting you go this time because we have bigger things to track down. But if we catch you again, you're in trouble. Now go home."

"Yes, officer." The young man stumbled off.

She turned to Zhiruto. "That's everyone on my list except Georgie and someone named Malorie Schmidt."

"We're handling the missing women." Agent Randall's

voice behind her chair made her startle. He stepped into view with three guards behind him. "I've sent agents to their homes and work. From here on out, this is a classified operation. Time for you to go, officer."

Zhiruto rose. "Her assistance is still required. I must find the assassin."

"She's been helpful clearing the civilians, but this is non-negotiable. The order comes from the President himself." Randall speared her with bloodshot eyes. "My men will escort you to your vehicle."

Lora knew better than to argue. She'd only end up in jail, and she'd be zero help in there. "It's okay, Zhiruto. I'll check in on Malorie." She pulled out her cell phone and removed a business card from the slot on the back, handing it to Zhiruto. "Here's my contact information if you need to reach me."

He stared at her with an unfathomable expression that somehow made her chest ache, and she realized this could be the last time she ever saw him. As strange as it was, she wished they were alone so she could kiss him goodbye. *This wasn't a date, Lora,* she told herself. Hell, he probably didn't even find her attractive—after all, he'd bid on another woman.

She held out her hand. "It was an honor working with you, Zhiruto. Sorry your first visit to our planet was a disaster."

"I will contact you, Loragriffin. Thank you for your help."

The way he said he'd contact her made her stomach flutter. She nodded and turned to leave, recalling how Maise had teased her that this had been Lora's dream date. *I really hope he calls me,* she thought. But then again, she wasn't even sure he had a cell phone.

CHAPTER SIX

Zhiruto didn't like the way Agent Randall's men escorted Loragriffin away as if she were nothing more than a stray *ijin'en*, but Agent Randall was clearly finished accommodating Zhiruto's investigation. The man pointed toward the tent. "Your healer says he's completed his scans and there are no more survivors. You need to wait with your compatriots until the ship arrives."

"The assassin may have escaped your park." Zhiruto shot back, his gaze flicking distastefully to the NSA personnel pushing a cart carrying their rudimentary scanning equipment toward another victim. No wonder the emperor had wanted to give Earth more time to mature before opening its borders—the people in charge had no respect for other cultures. "I must be allowed to find him."

"We're handling it. We've got the city on lockdown and we're searching all outbound traffic." Agent Randall glanced over Zhiruto's body. "He can't hide long looking like one of you."

Zhiruto opened his mouth to explain that the assassin could just as easily look human, then recalled Loragriffin's warning not to tell Randall about the *burendo*. He'd gotten to know not only Loragriffin better during the interviews, but her friends, as well. The women had gone safely home, and he didn't want to say something that would cause them pointless trouble. Yet he also couldn't allow the NSA to end his investigation.

He looked at the card Loragriffin had given him. He didn't need it to locate her—he could tap into Earth's interweb database for that—but it was the only thing he had of her if he never saw her again. And he really wanted to see her again. *I could use her help for the investigation,* he thought as Agent Randall nudged him toward the tent.

The smell of death permeated the air inside, and the remaining off-planet guests stood or sat stiffly in one corner, as far from the flattened blue remains of the IDA's planetary manager as possible. The transportation creche holding the survivor hovered at the opposite side next to the healer, its clear rounded walls revealing the murky blue matrix of the Kirenai inside. Multicolored lights winked from the interface on top.

"There's been a small delay getting your ship cleared to land, but we'll get you out of here soon," Agent Randall said in a falsely friendly tone. "Everyone hang tight."

Hang tight sounded like a threat to Zhiruto, but the agent returned to his group of humans without further remark. Zhiruto sighed and went to stand next to the healer. Speaking in Qalqan, he asked, "How is the surviving victim?"

"Stable. I'll have a more reliable prognosis once we get him back to the IDA medical bay."

Zhiruto nodded. "Everyone else feeling all right?"

The taller Khargal stepped forward, furled wings jutting sharply above his shoulders. "I want my female. The humans have overridden my bondservant contract and freed her."

Khargals could get aggressive when it came to females; it would be best to clear up the misconception before things escalated. "I lost my bondservant, as well," Zhiruto commiserated, though he was glad that tie was severed. He'd much rather spend his time on Earth with Loragriffin. "There seems to have been a cultural misunderstanding about the auction. The females were selling something they call a 'date'— an evening of their company—not a bondservant contract."

"What?" the Khargal roared, spinning to glare at the nearest IDA representative. "My introductory documents clearly stated this was a bondservant auction."

The smaller Kirenai tapped his wrist to bring up an interface, reciting a rote response. "Here is the clause at the end of the contract that excuses the IDA from any unforeseen cultural misunderstandings."

The Khargal brought his rock-like fists up, looking ready to pummel the IDA employee into the ground.

The last thing they needed was a fight. The humans would probably try to separate them at the first sign of violence, and Zhiruto needed everyone's help to get him out of here. "We can take that up with the IDA after we get off the planet. Right now, I need to get away from these humans so I can continue my investigation."

"Whatever I can do," the offending IDA representative said, and everyone but the enraged Khargal nodded.

Zhiruto stepped closer to the Khargal. "Once this is over, I will see that the prince recognizes each of you for your help."

The Khargal snarled, but grumbled something Zhiruto's Iki'i understood as agreement.

Running a pink claw over the length of his portable scanner, the healer said, "The humans do not seem capable of detecting life in a Kirenai matrix. Perhaps you could enact your death by entering your resting state. Then the agents would no longer be concerned with your whereabouts."

Zhiruto recalled the way the agents outside were poking and prodding the Kirenai remains. "They're examining the dead fairly closely. I think they'd notice if I dropped dead then went missing."

The Fogarian cleared his throat, running a hand down one bushy red sideburn. "Forgive me, but all dead Kirenai look alike." He looked toward the dead Kirenai in the corner. "If you were to enter your resting state over the top of one, the humans might not notice when you broke away."

Revulsion filled Zhiruto's throat at the thought of mingling with the matrix of a fellow Kirenai, but the plan had merit. He turned to the healer. "Have you determined if the poison is transmissible?"

"Not yet." The healer shook his head. "However, I could place a temporary static barrier over the remains that should keep your matrices separate. Give me a few moments."

Zhiruto followed the healer toward the remains. The sour odor of the dead Kirenai wafted toward him as the healer circled his wand over its gelatinous surface. Leaving the park on his own might not be the best idea, but he also couldn't afford to be locked away with the others.

"The field is in place now," said the healer.

"Thank you." Zhiruto reached out and touched the matrix. The faint, cold sensation of the static field met his fingertips. Even so, he hoped he didn't have to remain in contact long.

He glanced toward the humans at the front of the tent. One of the guards watched him without expression, but Zhiruto could feel twinges of curiosity coming from him. The discussion about the plan had been in Qalqan, so he wasn't worried about the humans catching on, but he did want more eyes on him so the humans would have no doubt about what happened. Roaring as if in pain, he let his cellular matrix come undone and collapsed forward onto the remains, drawing himself into a flat denseness to minimize his size.

The guard shouted for assistance, and Agent Randall along with several more humans rushed over.

A Kirenai's hearing and vision were less refined while in a resting state, but Zhiruto could see the blurry form of the healer blocking the humans. "I warned him the poison might be transferable if he touched the remains." The healer waved his scanner. "But he insisted."

Agent Randall shoved his hands on his hips, the toes of his boots nearly touching Zhiruto's flattened matrix. He was uttering a string of human curse words related to excrement and procreation. "Get our fucking MRI machine in here now! I want every scrap of data we can gather."

Zhiruto remained unmoving, though every fiber of his being

wanted to squirm away. The healer made a few useless attempts to stop the humans from using their machines.

Agent Randall had him escorted back to the other side of the tent. "Stay out of our way. If whatever's causing this is transmissible, I need to make sure it can't spread to humans."

"I assure you, it cannot—" the healer tried to protest.

But Agent Randall called several more guards into the tent, cordoning the healer and the others off from where Zhiruto now lay.

Remaining still, Zhiruto endured many needles piercing his matrix as well as extended magnetic scans, despite the healer's attempts to stop them. Growing increasingly impatient, he waited as the sun passed its zenith. Darkness was approaching by the time the humans admitted that they could find no life signs.

Agent Randall rounded on the remaining group. "No one goes anywhere or touches anything else until you're back on your ship and out of here. I don't need any more mishaps on human soil."

He strode from the tent. The other humans returned to their data pads, and the guards once more assumed watch over the IDA guests.

Slowly, Zhiruto eased his cellular matrix beneath the nearby table and toward the wall of the tent, slipping beneath the edge into the grass outside. The breeze had picked up, and the yellow fabric puffed and billowed like a great beast trying to swallow him. The humans had glaring lights set up across the park, and the short blades of foliage provided little cover. Stretching himself long and thin, he flowed along the tent's perimeter toward the far corner where the shadows were deepest, keeping his Iki'i alert for anyone nearby.

He flowed as quickly as he could toward the trees, continuing through the underbrush until he reached a woven wire fence. On the other side, the land was divided by more fences separating what appeared to be a line of human domiciles. Though it was dark, many of the humans were not only awake, but outside, sitting on chairs in the grass or strolling on the street which ran alongside the buildings.

Zhiruto needed to resume his human form so he could call Loragriffin, but the one thing Agent Randall had right was that blending into the human population would be impossible for normal Kirenai. He eased along the fence, skirting a barking quadruped that radiated deep aggression. When he reached a quiet domicile, he entered along a wooden fence and pulled himself into his human form.

A wall of fluttering cloth stretched between two posts near the building, and it took Zhiruto a moment to realize it was clothing. He had no idea why someone would string clothing like that, and he hoped he wasn't defiling a sacred ritual as he yanked a gray short-sleeved shirt free. Though it hadn't been raining, the fabric was wet and had a pleasant scent.

He pulled the shirt over his head and looked down his front, comparing his emulated blue slacks to a pair of gray ones hanging from the line. *Might as well use everything available.* He jerked the pants from the line, reforming his legs to slide the uncomfortably wet fabric up around his hips.

Most of him looked human now, but not well enough to walk in free view of the humans. A square of yellow fabric printed with pink, long-eared creatures hung with the clothing, and he used it to cover his head and shoulders. He hadn't seen any humans cover their heads like this, but then he also hadn't seen any with blue hair. At least this fabric was human.

Tapping the microchip embedded in his arm, he brought up his comm interface and contacted Loragriffin.

CHAPTER SEVEN

Lora was dreaming of big blue hands running over her skin when her cell phone rang. Groaning, she opened her eyes and groped for the phone. The incoming number was blocked.

"Fuckin' A," she swore, dropping the phone and rolling over. She'd spent the morning at the precinct filling out reports, then went to check on Malorie—who'd already been picked up by the NSA—before being called in to help with a domestic altercation at one of the many alien welcome parties going on around town. By the time she got home, she'd barely managed to take a shower before dropping into bed like a log.

A muffled voice drifted toward her from the sheets where she'd dropped the phone. "Loragriffin, are you there?"

She sat bolt upright. "Zhiruto?"

At the foot of the bed, Pepper groaned and stretched.

Lora located the phone and turned it over. Zhiruto's face

looked back at her from the screen—she must've accidentally accepted the video call when she'd dropped the phone. A thrill raced through her. *He actually called!* God, she hoped she didn't look like a scarecrow. She raked her fingers through her hair, glad she'd put on a nightshirt before dropping into bed, and tried to sound unconcerned. "Hey, what's up?"

"I need you to retrieve me."

"Agent Randall let you go?" She'd been certain the NSA agent would keep the aliens locked down until Judgment Day.

Zhiruto shook his head. "I'll explain everything once you arrive."

She narrowed her eyes. This sounded like trouble, and the last thing she needed was the NSA breathing down her neck for aiding and abetting an alien fugitive. "Where are you?"

"I have transmitted my coordinates to your vehicle. Please hurry."

He hacked into my police cruiser? She shouldn't be surprised. His alien tech could probably access anything. She supposed it wouldn't hurt to hear him out. He was a fellow law enforcement officer, after all, even if he was from another planet. "All right. I'll be there as soon as I can."

She hung up and swung her legs off the mattress, glancing around her disaster of a bedroom. Her gown lay in a heap on the floor near the bathroom, and several days' worth of dirty laundry overflowed her hamper. A matching basket of unfolded clean clothes rested at the foot of her bed. Although she figured the last place he'd be seeing was her bedroom, she quickly shoved everything into her closet and tidied the top of her dresser before pulling on a fresh set of jeans and a black v-neck tank top.

Pepper followed her into the bathroom, watching with hopeful eyes as Lora applied a coat of mascara to her lashes and blush to her cheeks. "You're staying here, girl." She scratched the coonhound's bony skull. "I'll be back soon."

Huffing in resignation, Pepper lay in the hallway with her chin on her paws.

Lora raced downstairs two steps at a time, passing through the outdated kitchen with its dark pressboard cupboards and mustard-yellow refrigerator that refused to die. The house was tiny and needed major renovations, but she'd gotten it for a song, and it was in a decent neighborhood.

Her police cruiser waited in the driveway outside the back door. The sounds of music and voices echoed from neighboring yards where people had gathered in hope of catching a glimpse of the aliens or their ships. She turned on the car's onboard navigation system, and a map appeared with a pinned location near the dog park only minutes away. She started the engine and backed out of the driveway, pulling into traffic.

Small groups of people dressed like aliens peppered the sidewalks. Bobbing plastic antennae, green makeup, and flashy silver clothing seemed to be the favored style, even though they looked nothing like the aliens at the party, let alone the aliens from the old Beijing photographs. The assassin would have no trouble blending into a crowd like this.

Her phone rang, and she glanced at the dash to see Maise calling. Rather late for her friend to call, but she probably wanted the scoop on Zhiruto. With this latest development,

Lora wasn't ready to talk. She declined the call and made the turn onto Maple Street. Every parking space and driveway was crammed with cars, and some lawns had hand-scrawled signs posted with fees to park on the grass. People sat on lawn chairs and picnic tables holding beer bottles and gazing toward the sky.

This is going to get interesting, she thought as she approached Zhiruto's location. She stopped next to a white Toyota Corolla parked at the curb and scanned the nearby houses for a tall blue alien. Porches were full of people, and two houses down there were teenagers playing glow-in-the-dark badminton on the front lawn, but there was no sign of Zhiruto.

Behind her, a green Suburban pulled to a stop. *Great.* Now she was blocking traffic. She didn't want to turn on her lights and draw extra attention, so she rolled down her window and waved for the vehicle to pass. As the SUV pulled slowly by, three kids in the back seat gawked at her.

Just then, the approach of helicopter rotors swelled to a deafening roar. She leaned forward to look through the windshield as a fleet of six military transport choppers passed overhead, heading for the park. *Damn, Agent Randall called in the cavalry.* Were they looking for Zhiruto?

Someone tapped against her passenger side window, and she jerked her head around. Zhiruto's face peered at her through the glass, half-shrouded by a yellow baby blanket covered with pink bunnies. She hit the door lock and he slid into the front seat with graceful ease.

"I suggest we leave the vicinity immediately, Loragriffin."

She shifted the car into drive and pulled onto the street,

thinking he looked comically adorable in the blanket. "What's going on? Are those helicopters looking for you?"

"No one will look for me. Agent Randall believes I'm dead."

She glanced at him in surprise. "How'd you pull that off?"

"I merely entered my resting state and he assumed I was dead."

Thinking of the survivor, she conceded that was entirely plausible. She turned the corner toward her house. "Crafty deception."

Within minutes, she pulled into her driveway. She cut the engine and turned to him, wanting to ask more questions, but he was already getting out of the car.

She scrambled after him as he strode up the two steps to her back door. Much as she didn't like taking a strange alien into her home, she liked standing on an open, exposed porch with him even less, so she shoved her key in the lock and opened the door.

Pepper sat waiting in the darkness, tail thumping against the floor like a club. She was making the throaty, excited whine of greeting she used when her favorite people came to visit.

Zhiruto put a hand on the dog's head, which made Pepper wiggle even harder. The fact that Pepper liked him helped ease Lora's wariness about allowing a stranger into her house.

Stepping past Pepper, Zhiruto glanced around the galley-style kitchen. "Is this your domicile?"

She discreetly nudged an empty pizza box on the counter into the trash before turning on a light. Luckily the rest of the kitchen was clean. "Yes, this is my house. Now please tell me what you want from me. I could get in big trouble for sheltering you."

He let the baby blanket slip down around his shoulders, revealing his long mane of navy blue hair, and moved to peer through the archway into the living room. Somehow, he'd acquired a tee shirt, and it hugged his shoulders and arms in a most flattering fashion. Her gaze slid down his backside to admire the rest of him.

He turned back around and she took a heartbeat too long to return her gaze to his, flushing when she realized she'd been caught staring. She crossed her arms to hide her embarrassment. "There's no one else here, so speak freely."

He crossed his arms, as well. "As you suggested, I didn't tell the NSA about the *burendo*. Agent Randall has men searching outside the park, but they believe they're searching for someone who doesn't look human. The assassin will easily escape their notice. I need your assistance finding him."

She thought about the people gathering outside. "Is he a threat to other people?"

"He has no reason to harm the natives unless he's cornered." The *chop-chop-chop* of helicopters flying low overhead rattled the house, and Zhiruto glanced toward the ceiling. "Your NSA doesn't seem capable of being discreet. It's good Agent Randall doesn't know the truth, or the *burendo* would redouble his efforts to fit in."

She laughed out loud. "The NSA prides itself on operating under the radar." Then she recalled the fleet of choppers and another thought occurred to her. "Unless the government's just covering something bigger."

"What do you mean?"

She pictured secret underground test labs with aliens

floating in tanks. Not wanting to alarm him about the other aliens still in the park, she said, "Just that it might be good you got away when you did."

Zhiruto moved to examine the photos on her fridge. He pointed to the gap-toothed school photo of her niece. "Do you have children?"

"No. Those are my brother's kids." She set her keys and phone on the counter near the door.

He twisted his head to look at her. "Do human siblings care for one another's progeny?"

"If by care for you mean have affection, then yes. But I'm not a caregiver. They live in Houston, so I only get to see them a couple of times a year."

"Why do you not have children of your own?" His gaze was so intense, she wanted to take a step backward. *Or forward.* She couldn't decide.

She settled on a frown. "Not every woman wants kids, you know."

He smiled slowly, his attention sliding down over her breasts and hips. "You would make beautiful children."

Never in her life had she been turned on by baby-making references, but everything about Zhiruto put her hormones into overdrive. *Maybe I should just fuck him and get it out of my system.* Except Zhiruto was an alien. She had no idea if his species even had sex—they were technically amorphous blobs, after all. Yet his present form was so gorgeous, she couldn't help imagining what he might look like naked.

She forced herself to return her focus to his request for help. "Let's go to the living room and discuss your plan."

Moving past him through the archway, she went straight to the curtains facing the street and yanked them closed. The last thing she needed was a nosy neighbor spotting a hunky blue alien sitting on her sofa.

"Please forgive the dog hair," she said as she clicked on a lamp. She turned to find Zhiruto already sitting on the couch with Pepper next to him, the dog's head planted on his lap. An unbidden smile twisted Lora's lips. "And forgive the pesky dog. Pepper, get down."

He smiled back. "Pepper is quite affectionate. I can see why humans are attracted to these quadrupeds."

She nudged Pepper to the floor, then sat at the opposite end from Zhiruto. The coonhound shoved her head into Lora's lap, tail wagging leisurely. "I'm glad you like her."

Zhiruto adjusted his seating, bringing himself closer to her, and reached over to scratch behind Pepper's ears. "I like both of you."

Good Lord, could he be any cheesier? Yet at the same time, Lora was compelled to like him. He was genuine in a way few human men could manage.

"Thanks. We like you, too." She cleared her throat. "So, about this assassin. Do you have a plan to find him or her?"

"I don't believe the assassin will have ventured far from the park. He will take time to learn your customs before trying to blend in."

"You keep saying he. Are you sure it's a man?"

"The assassin is male. All Kirenai are male."

"All male?" She tried to wrap her head around that thought. "How does that work?"

Pepper pulled away and grabbed her chew toy, laying down nearby. Zhiruto dropped his hand to the cushions between their thighs, just touching the edge of Lora's leg. "As shapeshifters, we're able to breed with females of many species."

Alien breeding should be the last thing on her mind. Yet at that moment, with his hand against her thigh, it was all she could think of. Before she knew it, she was leaning toward him.

CHAPTER EIGHT

Desire radiated off Loragriffin, filling Zhiruto like a drug. He knew he needed to focus on finding the assassin, but when she tilted her chin, he was unable to resist. He leaned forward, capturing her lips.

That first moment of contact felt like an explosion that rocked him to his core. This was the sensation every Kirenai dreamed of. The instant a perfect match was made. He no longer cared if he impregnated her and lost his job guarding the prince. This was all that mattered. He opened his mouth and pressed his tongue between her lips, needing to taste her as if she was life itself.

She responded with matching passion, opening beneath his questing tongue in a way that made his human heartbeat quicken. She was the most amazing female he'd ever encountered, and he knew once he had her, there'd be no turning back. His Iki'i was drunk with desire. She was intoxicating. Irresistible. Before he even realized what he was doing, his hand was cupping her breast.

She moaned into his mouth with an abandon that made his cock swell and strain against the human clothing he wore.

He leaned closer, devouring her with his kiss, fingers pinching the taut bud of her nipple through her clothing.

She reached for his waistband, unfastening the button. His cock sprang free with a life of its own, surging toward her groping hand with a need that made him dizzy.

A small noise of surprise escaped her, and she broke the kiss, her gaze going to his crotch. "Good Lord, you're huge."

Her trepidation brought him back to his senses. He couldn't take her like he wanted to. Couldn't risk impregnating her. Kirenai fathers had to focus everything on their children, and his duty to the prince had to come first. He attempted to close his fly, but the swollen shaft was in the way. "We must stop."

She put one hand over his, her desire still pounding his Iki'i. "I didn't mean I don't want you."

"I won't risk impregnating you." His attention dropped to her middle. The thought of putting a child in there made his cock grow harder.

A soft laugh brought his attention back to her face. "You won't impregnate me. That's what birth control's for, and I'm a firm believer in doubling up. I'm pretty sure we can get a condom over you."

His universal translator flooded with information about 'birth control' and 'condoms.' Most species in the consortium struggled to keep birth rates up, but humans were so prolific, it made sense they had developed some form of control over impregnation. He relaxed his grip on the closure of his pants. "You will not get pregnant?"

She pushed his hand away and wrapped her fingers around his shaft. "Don't they have contraceptives on your planet?"

He shuddered in pleasure, barely able to think as she stroked upward over his sensitive crown. "We have no need. Children are rare blessings."

"Wait right here." She pushed off the couch and hurried up a set of stairs behind a huge telemonitor mounted on the wall. Within a few moments, she was back with a shiny square gripped in one hand. She tossed it onto the small table beside where they sat.

"This is the condom you spoke of?"

"Yeah, but we don't have to put it on just yet." She straddled him, the heat between her legs teasing his exposed cock through her pants.

Leaning forward, she set her lips once more to his, fingers threading into the back of his hair.

Now that he didn't need to concern himself with children, his desire returned full force. He placed his hands on her hips and let her have her way.

She kissed him deeply, rocking her hips in a slow rhythm against his erection until he was so hard he thought he might break. She made small moans of pleasure, but he could feel her yearning for something more. He moved his hand to the button at her waist, glad he'd experienced the use of human clothing on his own body.

He deftly flicked it open and slid his fingers inside and over the silken hair of her mons. She gasped, back arching and legs widening as she hovered over his lap. He delved deeper, entering the slit between her legs. Her hot wet nub pulsed beneath his fingers. His Iki'i thrumming with her pleasure, he rubbed his middle finger slowly over the swelling bundle of nerves, loving the way her hips flexed to meet the rhythm.

This was the most primal experience he'd ever had, an instinct he'd never known. He followed the slit deeper, finding a well of moisture. Desire to fill that space—to plunge deeply into her—consumed him.

As he thought it, she broke away, standing to wriggle the fabric of her pants down, exposing herself to his gaze.

His cock pulsed from the gap in his pants, the thick shaft seeming to have a desire all its own as it throbbed in response to her naked bottom half.

She dropped to her knees, and her mouth found the tip of his shaft. The sudden hot, wet heat engulfed him with nearly overwhelming pleasure. Her tongue swirled over the head, making him buck upward, seeking more. Her mouth took in half of his length while her other hand circled his base, pumping up and down.

His eyes rolled back in his head. He'd never had a lover so intent on pleasing him.

Her other hand slid inside his pants beneath his cock, and he knew she was looking for his balls. He had to concentrate on making his secondary shaft subside; the mating shaft was for when the time came to bond with a mate and gift her the genetic markers that would brand her as his forever. *This time is for pleasure alone*, he reminded himself.

She found his balls, and he was once again surprised by the

level of sensation he felt as she fondled them while she sucked. Her groping was awkward, hindered by the pants he still wore. He wanted to feel more, to have her cup them and roll them, to feel them slap against her ass as he penetrated her over and over.

Done with this nonsensical human clothing, he pushed her gently back and stood, peeling the thick fabric off his legs.

Releasing an appreciative breath, she reached for the condom, tearing the small square open with her teeth. She extracted a thin disk. "Here."

Settling the disk over his crown, she rolled the edges down over his shaft. The material encircled him tightly, but it wasn't the pressure he was craving.

He pulled her to her feet then gripped her hips and lifted her until the heat of her center poised over his shaft. "I wish to penetrate you."

Her eyes were round, the black of her pupils nearly consuming the chocolate brown irises. She drew her legs up around his waist and wrapped her arms around his neck, leaning in to kiss him. Her heels dug into his backside, driving him into her slickness as she angled her hips to accept him.

He eased her over his shaft, adjusting his size to meet her pleasure until their hips made contact. *Kuzara*, she was perfect, her desire matching his own. The condom dulled his sensation slightly, but that might be a good thing, considering her effect on him.

She tilted her hips toward him, grinding and squirming delightfully as her walls stretched to accommodate his girth.

"Oh, God, fuck me," she murmured against his lips before once more plunging her tongue into his mouth.

He thrust forward, pulling her against him, then lifted and plunged again. The building friction was like an approaching storm, tumultuous and wild. His rhythm grew more furious until Loragriffin was moaning in time to his thrusts.

Then her channel pulsed and she shouted, "Yes!"

An orgasm rippled through her, but he kept driving, knowing he could take her higher. He was reveling in both her pleasure and his own, focusing the head of his cock against the spot that sent her into ecstasy. He could feel the tension inside her, the need to come building once more. Over and over a small voice in his mind repeated, *My mate. Mine.*

He backed her against the stairway wall, hands cupping her ass cheeks, and thrust deeply, driving into her again and again until she screamed his name. Her slickness coated the fronts of his thighs, and their ragged breathing mingled as if there wasn't enough air in the room. But he continued pumping forward, filling her with the long thickness of his primary cock.

His mating shaft pressed against her ass, slick with her juices. His Iki'i sensed she liked the added pressure, but he forced the shaft into submission. Claiming her wasn't an option. He'd take his pleasure—give her pleasure—and that was all.

Suddenly, her channel clamped down around him with fierce strength. She threw back her head and screamed, "Zhiruto!"

Her juices ran down his legs, and her heels dug into his ass, pressing his hips to hers. His mating shaft jutted forward. Covered in her slickness, it probed her ass. Entered. She moaned again, entire body trembling as her climax rocked her. Buried in her heat, breathing her delicious scent, he shuddered, helpless under the force of his double ejaculation. The sensation was exquisite, beyond anything he'd ever imagined possible.

He held her pressed against the wall for long moments, letting his heartbeat slow. Her breath tickled his ear, and he softly kissed her shoulder before easing his hips back so she could stand.

Then he realized what he'd done.

The condom had done its job, blocking the life force that might create a child.

But there had been no barrier to the shaft that really mattered. The one that set a bond he could never deny.

Loragriffin was now his mate.

CHAPTER NINE

Lora gasped for breath, stars swimming across her vision. She'd had great sex before, but never an orgasm like that. What must've been Zhiruto's finger in her ass had intensified her climax beyond anything she'd imagined possible.

When she finally regained enough focus to look at him once more, the startled look on his face made her sober. "What is it?" She pushed him away, glad the wall was still at her back when her rubber band legs almost refused to hold her. "Did the condom break?"

He looked down to where his cock still stretched the thin sheath to its maximum capacity, the reservoir at the tip now filled with milky blue fluid. "No."

Shit, then what was the matter? Getting pregnant wasn't her worry; her IUD was her primary birth control, and the condom was just assurance against sexually transmitted disease. *Maybe it was terrible sex for him.*

Blanching at the idea, she snatched up her discarded jeans and hurried to the stairs. "I'm going to clean up." She pointed to another door near the kitchen. "There's a bathroom through there if you need it."

She raced up the stairs, thighs slippery and muscles tired. Before she'd reached the upstairs bathroom, she'd stripped out of her shirt and bra. After a quick rinse in the shower, she pulled on a yellow tee shirt and a fresh pair of jeans. She still wasn't ready to face Zhiruto's disappointment. He'd seemed to be enjoying himself, yet there was no denying that horrified expression on his face at the end. *For all I know, he's married.* The idea made her squeamish.

Looking in the mirror, she wiped the residual smudges of mascara from beneath her eyes that the shower hadn't rinsed away. Her cheeks were flushed, her eyes dilated. Usually, that rumpled, satisfied look was a good thing, but right now it made her self-conscious. How could she face him again when he had obvious regrets?

Then another thought occurred to her—what if he'd slipped away already? Only one other time had an evening been so awful that a guy had left without saying goodbye. He'd been an ass to both her and Pepper, and frankly she'd been relieved when he left. Now, all she could think about was making Zhiruto stay.

The toilet flushed downstairs, and she let out a relieved breath. He was still here. *Maybe I can make things better.*

She winced and turned away from the mirror. That inner voice sounded too much like her mother, who'd always had a man around to "protect" her. Lora had chosen to become a police officer because she refused to let fear rule her life.

Picking up the shirt and bra she'd dropped on her way to the shower, she shoved them into the hamper and muttered, "If he didn't like it, that isn't your fault."

"What isn't your fault?" Zhiruto's voice behind her made her jump.

Lora spun, gaze latching onto Zhiruto standing in the doorway. "God, don't sneak up on me like that."

Pepper hopped onto the bed, lying down with a huff.

"My apologies. I didn't mean to startle you." Zhiruto clamped and unclamped his fists at his sides. He'd refastened his jeans, but was once again shirtless like he'd been at the party. He still looked unhappy. "We must talk, Loragriffin."

She flicked a hand in the air dismissively. "Let's keep it in our pants from now on and focus on the investigation. I have an idea. Let's go downstairs to talk."

Shouldering past him, she exited the room. He tried to grasp her hand, but she evaded him and headed back down the stairs two at a time, trying to put some distance between them. At the bottom, she glanced back to see Zhiruto standing at the top looking down at her. Keeping her voice light, she said, "I imagine it's been a while since you've eaten. Are you hungry?"

"I must admit, yes."

Good. Food would help them both feel better. She headed to the kitchen to get her phone where she'd left it on the counter. Maise had called again, but hadn't left a message. *Boy will I have a story for her once this is all over.* Lora dialed a fried chicken joint that delivered all night, turning around to lean on the counter as Zhiruto followed her into the kitchen. The light from the living room backlit his broad shoulders and narrow hips, and a streetlight outside the kitchen window cut shadows across his face.

"Do you like breasts or thighs?" she asked.

His attention slid from her face to caress her chest and hips. "Both."

From any other man, she would've rolled her eyes at the cheesy pickup line. But when Zhiruto said it, electricity seemed to spark from her nipples to her clit. Good Lord, how did he continually make her feel like a horny teenager? She was still considering how to respond when the restaurant answered her call.

Swallowing, she looked at the menu flyer stuck to the fridge next to the photos and drawings from her nieces. She knew the menu by heart, but it gave her something to look at besides Zhiruto. She ordered a full bucket of fried chicken plus sides of mashed potatoes and gravy, biscuits, and coleslaw. Then she added a couple of fresh-baked chocolate chip cookies; she didn't usually let herself have dessert but felt like she needed it tonight.

Hanging up, she set the phone aside on the counter. "They usually take about twenty minutes. Want something to drink?"

"Do you have more of that bubbly drink from the auction?"

She raised one eyebrow. "Champagne's not on my budget." Yanking open the fridge, she pulled out two beers, twisted the tops off, and handed one to him. "Try this."

He sipped his hesitantly then tipped the bottle back and

drank it all. Damn, the guy must be thirsty. *Or he needs to take the edge off.*

She took several long swallows of her own. Maybe taking the edge off wasn't a bad idea. It felt as if the conflicting voices inside her head were engaged in a fistfight. *I need to do something to make things better.* Stop worrying about him. *But what if it's my fault?* It's not your job to make him feel good. *He tried to stop me and I kept pushing.* He backed you against the wall, not the other way around...

"I sense you're conflicted, Loragriffin."

The way he continually mashed her name together made her get all tingly inside, which only added to her conflict. She shrugged and looked toward Pepper sitting near the back door. Letting the dog out, she watched while Pepper trotted toward the lawn to do her business. "I'm worried about the assassin, that's all."

Zhiruto's warm presence heated her back, hovering just out of range of full contact. "Loragriffin, I've done something unforgivable."

Realizing an alien now stood in full view of her neighbors, she pivoted and put a hand on his chest to push him backward. "Jesus, don't stand where people can see you."

He didn't budge for a second as his hand slid up to cover hers. Then he stepped back into the shadows. The slow glide of his palm skimming the back of her knuckles was almost as erotic as his caress against her breast earlier.

She cleared her throat, trying to keep her head on straight. "What have you done?"

"You are my mate."

Stunned silence filled the kitchen as she blinked at him, trying to understand. *Holy shit, does he think we're married now just because we had sex?* Dread settled into her bones. "No I'm not."

Pepper padded back inside, and Lora closed the door with a hard thud.

Zhiruto continued to stare at her, his dark eyes glittering in the dim light. "We are bonded."

"Don't worry about it, really. It was just sex," she lied. Hell if she was going to admit it had been the best sex of her life, though she was also relieved to learn he hadn't hated the encounter like she'd first worried.

Downing the rest of her beer, she set the bottle on the counter and marched into the living room, careful not to brush against him as she passed. She flopped onto the couch next to Pepper, letting the dog remain on the cushions as a barrier to Zhiruto if he took the seat next to her. The coonhound put her head on Lora's lap, eyes rolling to look at Zhiruto as he followed them into the room.

The big blue alien remained standing. "I sense you're angry."

"I'm not angry. You're just confused. And you're on Earth now, so we have different rules." She knew she was being a bitch, but she couldn't help it. She didn't need a permanent man, didn't want one, and she wasn't about to buy into some alien code of honor about having sex. And as nice as it might be to have a hot, nearly seven-foot-tall, blue alien at her beck and call, she didn't want him to stick around because he was required to. He needed to back off.

A low hum that was almost too soft to hear reached her and Zhiruto's mouth tightened. He lifted his forearm. As before, a screen materialized above it, and the blue face of the alien she'd seen with Georgie appeared.

He and Zhiruto exchanged a few words in a language Lora didn't understand, then Zhiruto angled the screen to include Lora. "This human is a member of local law enforcement," he said in English. "She's helping me track the assassin."

Georgie's face appeared on the screen. "Lora?"

Lora shot to her feet, moving closer. Georgie's face glowed with multicolored lights that created a pattern over her skin, extending well below where Lora could see on the screen. "Georgie, where are you? What's going on with your skin?"

"Oh." Georgie lifted a glowing arm to admire it, an amazed smile twisting her mouth. "It's painted on, don't worry. I'm fine." She looked back up to meet Lora's eyes. "What's happening there? Is everyone okay?"

"Depends on your definition of okay. No humans seem to have been harmed, but there are a ton of dead aliens laying around." She explained everything that had happened except the sexual debacle. She wasn't ready to talk about it, especially with Zhiruto looking over her shoulder. Before Georgie could ask any leading questions, Lora asked, "Where are you?"

"I'm currently orbiting an alien planet, believe it or not." Georgie laughed, sounding surprisingly relaxed about it. "I'm heading back to Earth now. I should arrive in a few days."

"Girl, don't." Lora held up a palm, worry for her friend rising in her chest. "The NSA's looking for you. They consider you a person of interest, and they're assholes. You do not want to end up in their hands."

Georgie chewed her lip and glanced at the blue alien lingering beside her. "I guess I can stay here a while. But I'll be in touch. Take care of yourself, okay?"

"You, too." Lora blew her a kiss, and Zhiruto turned the screen back on himself, pacing away to speak a few more words.

The doorbell rang, making Lora jump. Pepper responded in kind, lurching off the sofa with a baying bark as she moved to the door. All this alien intrigue was making her twitchy, and she didn't like it. She wasn't timid or weak. She was a woman who took the bull by the balls. Still, she peered through the peephole to be certain it was the food delivery before she opened the door.

She carried the food to the kitchen and tore open the bags, inhaling the savory warm scent of fried chicken. The familiar scent was comforting, grounding. *Normal.* And it helped her understand what she had to do.

As soon as they finished eating, she was going to find the assassin and put both aliens on a spaceship back home.

CHAPTER TEN

Zhiruto was relieved the prince was safe, but the call had reminded him of his duty. First, he'd missed the transport window and was unable to escort his prince home. Now he'd been dallying with Loragriffin while the *burendo* was fortifying his disguise. Every second increased the assassin's ability to blend in with the natives.

At least his mate wanted to stay focused on the hunt. *Another reason she's my perfect match.* But talk about mate bonds could wait. He followed the smell of unfamiliar spices and oil into the kitchen where Loragriffin was assembling two platters.

She spoke without looking up. "So, my idea about finding the assassin sort of depends on you. If he's outside the park, do you think he'll still be shielding himself from your icky-whatever sense?"

"Iki'i," he pronounced. "Since there are not Kirenai

searching for him outside the park, there would be no reason to expend the energy, so I think not."

She thrust a full plate toward him. "Good." Picking up a large golden brown piece of food from her plate, she sank her teeth into it. He found himself mesmerized by the way she licked crumbs off her lips before chewing.

"Fried chicken." She gestured toward the plate in his hands. "Try it."

He looked down. There was a glob of white matter dripping with brown sauce, a small cup of something pale green flecked with orange, a circular item that resembled an unglazed *kazhitu* bun, and a golden brown item with a bone sticking from one end. His translator had identified 'chicken' as one of Earth's animals, so he selected the item with the bone and mimicked the way she'd taken a bite.

His teeth crunched down on salt and grease, then savory juices flooded his mouth. He chewed a few times and swallowed.

"Like it?" she asked.

"Very much."

"Good. There's more in the bucket if you want." She stuck a white plastic fork onto his plate and breezed by him into the living room. "Let's talk in here."

He followed, still munching on the chicken as she flopped onto the sofa and curled her legs up to one side. She'd changed into a new yellow shirt with sleeves that fell halfway to her elbows, the neckline hugging her collarbone. On the front was a swooped blue slash. He'd liked her better in the sleeveless tunic that exposed her skin, but the yellow of this one suited her rich auburn hair. She'd pulled it together at the back of her head, and he longed to let it down and run his fingers through its silky tresses. To strip her clothing from her and explore her body more thoroughly than he'd done during their previously rushed coupling.

Keep your distance, he told himself. Now that he'd shared the mate bond with her, all it would take was one playful glance from her and he'd want to pounce. He moved to a wooden rocking chair next to the window.

From where Loragriffin sat on the sofa, a flush of disappointment washed his way. He forced himself to ignore it. There would be time to lavish her with attention later, once they'd wrapped up this case.

Pepper skulked to the far edge of the sofa and lay down on the floor with her muzzle resting on her paws. He could sense both craving and resignation coming from the dog, but Loragriffin made no move to share her food with the animal.

"Tell me more of your plan, Loragriffin." He tore off another bite of chicken.

"First, we need to make you look a bit more human so I can get you into the precinct. It shouldn't be too hard—we have boatloads of people walking around town dressed as aliens, so all we have to do is make you look like someone wearing a bad costume."

He frowned. "Should we not try our utmost to disguise me well?"

"Most of the costumes are nothing more than plastic antennae and green face paint. Looking too perfect will draw attention." She stirred the fluffy white mound on her plate and then took a bite.

"Then I will defer to your judgment." If she thought a silly costume was all that was needed to mingle undetected among humans, then he had to believe her. But it meant the assassin would find it easier to hide, as well. He was beginning to lose hope of picking up a trail.

He focused on his plate. He'd always enjoyed sampling strange dishes during his travels with the prince—probably why the assassin had thought poisoning the food was a good plan. He hesitated a brief moment as he thought of the auction, then shrugged his concern aside. Loragriffin would never try to kill him.

Stirring the white mash as Loragriffin had done, he took a bite. The bland flavor was not to his liking, but he swallowed politely before picking up the thing that looked like a *kazhitu* bun. It had been split in two, and the center had been lavished with a rich yellow oil. He took a bite. "This is delicious. What do you call it?"

"That's a buttermilk biscuit. The white stuff is mashed potatoes, though I'm pretty sure they use instant, not the real thing. The little bowl is coleslaw."

He finished the other half of the biscuit in one bite, nodding at her in appreciation. She laughed. The sound sent a thrill of pleasure through him. He liked it when she laughed. He needed to discover more ways to make her happy.

"There's more of everything on the counter, and I have cookies for dessert when you're ready. Eat up." She stood, taking her plate toward the kitchen. "My brother left some boxes in my shed, and I think his clothes will fit you. Be right back."

The moment she was gone, Pepper rose and moved closer to sit in front of him, the animal's earlier resignation replaced by hope. He'd seen some of the females at the auction sharing food off their plate. Perhaps one was not supposed to offer until the quadruped asked? Scooping up a forkful of mashed potatoes, he held it out to her. "Would you like some?"

The dog leaned forward and swept out her tongue, licking the fork clean. An overwhelming sense of appreciation and delight filled Zhiruto's senses.

Zhiruto smiled. "I can see why the humans enjoy your species' company."

He sampled a bite of the green and orange flecked coleslaw. The slightly sour flavor reminded him of the *ayabe* his father used to make, and he finished it with gusto in between sharing bites of the potatoes with Pepper. By the time Loragriffin returned, her arms draped with clothing, he and Pepper had cleaned off his plate and helped themselves to seconds.

Loragriffin took one look at the dog's head in his lap and sighed. "Pepper, no begging."

The dog flinched and slunk back to the end of the sofa with her tail down.

Worried he'd offended, Zhiruto said, "My apologies. I saw other females at the party feeding their dogs, and Pepper seemed hungry."

A smile tugged the corners of Loragriffin's mouth. "She's a big fat liar, but it's okay. Just please don't give her any bones. And try not to make a habit of it."

"As you wish." He nodded and stood, setting his plate aside and eyeing the various colored fabric in her arms. "This clothing belonged to your brother?"

"Yeah. He stayed with me awhile when he and his wife were on the outs."

He liked the affection she radiated when speaking about her brother. "I've always wondered what it would be like to have siblings."

She tossed the clothes on the sofa and picked up a burgundy shirt. "You're an only child?"

"Most Kirenai are. Only rarely do bonded couples produce more than one offspring, and family units remain close throughout their lives. What about your parents? Do they live nearby?"

She shrugged. "My dad's not really in the picture. Never was. My mom lives with her current boyfriend in Tampa."

He'd been informed that humans made excellent mothers and had thereby assumed they and their offspring remained close for life, but Loragriffin's emotions when it came to her mother were more tolerant than affectionate. "I'm sorry you're not close."

"I'm as close as I'd like to be." She gave him a tight smile and held out the shirt. "I hope it doesn't smell too musty. Try this on."

He took the shirt she offered and pulled it over his head. Loragriffin liked his large muscles, and he'd purposefully exaggerated them for her benefit, but now they were making squeezing into the new clothing difficult. Concentrating on his matrix, he tried to condense himself to a smaller size and discovered he couldn't. The shirt was now twisted awkwardly around his shoulders, and he glanced with embarrassment toward her. She liked it when he was graceful, and at the moment, he was anything but.

But instead of disappointment, he was met with a rush of arousal.

Only then did he realize why he couldn't shift; when a Kirenai found a mate, his form was set, permanently held in the form his mate preferred. He was bonded to Loragriffin, which meant he was now and forever tied to this human shape.

Which also meant he could no longer serve as the prince's personal guard. His duties relied upon him being able to alter his appearance, to remain incognito along with the prince. His stomach roiled as if he was on a ship that had just lost gravity. If he could no longer adjust himself, he would have to resign. Who was he if he wasn't the prince's personal guard?

He tugged at the stretchy shirt, rolling his shoulders to make it fit. There wasn't time to wallow. Not now, when he was technically still on the job—the last job of his career. If he could now only look human, he planned to make the most of it.

He was going to locate the assassin at all costs.

CHAPTER ELEVEN

Lora watched Zhiruto pull her brother's old long-sleeved tee shirt over his head and tried not to drool over his flexing muscles. He stretched the shirt to maximum capacity, and she halfway wished she'd brought in a change of pants, too, just for a chance to get to see him step out of the old ones.

Stop it, she scolded herself. The guy was crazy enough with his talk of being her mate. She shouldn't encourage him.

Except she wanted to. They worked well together. The sex was amazing. Even Pepper adored him. Would it be so bad to make Zhiruto a permanent fixture in her life?

He finally got the fabric settled snugly over his torso and adjusted the tight arms across his biceps. She'd selected a plain shirt with no logo so as not to encourage anyone to read it when they ventured outside. But people were still going to look—his biceps were droolworthy, even beneath the cloth, and the deep burgundy color looked fantastic against his blue skin.

"That will do," she said, forcing her gaze away. "Let me grab some makeup. We'll need to cover some of that blue."

She hurried up the stairs and rummaged through her makeup drawer to find a tube of concealer. Gathering foundation, liquid blush, and several shades of lipstick, she stuffed them into a travel bag. Then she took a moment to check her own face, adjusting her ponytail and dusting her cheeks with some blush. *I'm not doing it for him. I'm doing it because we're going out soon.*

But she knew it was a lie.

She'd always told herself she was fine without a man, without the baggage of caring what someone thought or did. Yet deep inside, she wanted to please Zhiruto.

Returning to the living room, she discovered him lying on his back on the floor with his knees up. Pepper lay half-sprawled across his chest, nuzzling his jaw, tail wagging with pure affection. Lora's heart threatened to melt right out of her body. A man with a dog was sexy enough, but a man loving on *her* dog was downright irresistible, just like when she'd walked in and found him feeding Pepper off his fork.

Unable to restrain her smile, she bypassed them and went to the kitchen, bringing a chair back and setting it near the lamp. "I'm going to need you to sit here."

He pushed Pepper off his chest and rose, moving with a grace that made Lora's insides flutter. Pepper rolled playfully on her back, trying to entice him to return, then gave up and focused on her chew toy as Zhiruto relaxed into the chair.

She unscrewed the cap to her foundation. "Let's see if I can make you more human."

"I'm already human for you, Loragriffin."

She didn't know why, but the statement made her heart stutter. "Stop the flirting and hold still."

His hair was mussed from lying on the floor, and she ran her fingers through it to get it off his forehead, trying not to let her hand tremble at the familiarity of the gesture. Being around him felt strangely *right*. A weird mix of comfortable and uncomfortable at the same time. If she had to define the feeling, she might call herself giddy, not that she'd ever admit it.

She bit her lip as she dotted the applicator along his forehead at his hairline. The peachy shade was a complete opposite to his vibrant blue skin tone, and she had to put it on extra thick. If she made just a line around his face, it would look like his blue tone was makeup, and not the other way around. Using the tip of one finger, she blended it back toward his hair. His masculine smell pervaded her senses, and touching the warm, smooth skin of his forehead put her hormones in gear again. She smoothed the concealer toward his temple, breathing shallowly as she worked, though all she could think about was how close he was.

His eyes were closed, his face tilted slightly toward her, and his hands lay relaxed on his thighs. How could he look so damned comfortable when she was all fluttery inside? It wasn't fair.

She examined his slightly parted lips. Vivid blue, yet utterly kissable, surrounded by the perfect amount of scruff. Her own mouth tingled at the memory of that stubble against her face and neck, the way his kisses had felt. She wanted to feel his mouth on hers again, to experience his whiskers in unmentionable places, to smell herself on him as his arms embraced her...

His dark eyes popped open, full of a sudden hunger that took her breath away. *Stop being a silly schoolgirl. We decided to keep it above the belt.* But her imagination was all over the place when it came to this guy—especially the naughty places. Throat tight, she said, "We need to do something with your lips. They're too blue."

Stepping away from him, she pawed through her small bag of cosmetics, opening and closing several tubes of lipstick before settling on a rosy shade she thought might look natural. Trying to stay no-nonsense, she clipped, "Open up."

Still relaxed against the chair back and regarding her from beneath hooded lids, Zhiruto smiled and widened his knees.

Damn. That pushed every button she had. Her gaze fell to the bulge at the front of his pants—probably exactly what he wanted. *Or what I wanted.* She dragged her attention back up to meet his eyes. "I meant your mouth."

"I can do that, too." His voice had a low growl that seemed to connect straight to her pussy. He parted his lips.

She cleared her throat. Maybe she should leave his lips alone. Who'd really be looking at his mouth, anyway? But it would be foolish to go to all this effort and let her plan fail because she'd been a coward about one final detail.

Holding the lipstick out like a talisman, she stepped closer, feeling as if she was entering a trap as she stepped between his massive thighs. His eyes stayed locked on hers as she swiped the lipstick over his lower lip, then his upper. The way his flesh gave subtly under the pressure felt so erotic. She longed to smudge the lipstick with her fingers like she'd done the concealer. She could imagine his teeth gently catching her finger, his heated mouth sucking it gently...

She gulped, clutching the tube of lipstick tighter to keep herself in check. "Press them together."

His knees closed against her thighs. The heat of his breath penetrated the thin fabric of her tee shirt right over her breasts.

"I meant your lips," she choked out, realizing she'd put her free hand on his shoulder for balance.

He brought one hand up and wrapped long fingers around her forearm, turning his head slightly and running his nose down the inside of her wrist. "You smell amazing."

A shiver coursed through her. "Stop," she rasped. "We're on duty."

"You're right." He gently bit the base of her palm below her thumb, sending rockets of desire straight to her heart. "Let's get on with it." He released her arm and put his hands on her waist, pushing her back a step as he rose.

For a flash, she thought he'd said, "get it on." She could barely breathe, only let her head fall back to look up at his impressive height, her breasts barely brushing his chest. *What is wrong with me?* It felt like she was under a spell, dumbfounded and paralyzed. "Are you using some alien voodoo trick on me?"

"Voodoo trick? I don't understand." He frowned at her. "Do you feel unwell?"

"No, I'm just... not thinking straight. It's strange." She managed to take a step away from him and pick up a pair of aviator sunglasses and a pair of plastic devil horns she'd found in the shed. "Put these on and we're good to go."

He complied, looking like a cross between 007 and an extra in a low budget sci-fi movie. "You haven't told me the rest of your plan," he said, adjusting the elastic holding the horns to his head. "Why must we go to your precinct?"

"We need to use my desk computer to access the secure dispatch logs. The one in my car won't let me. Your assassin may be able to look human, but he's bound to do something strange or even illegal and get reported. I bet with a little elbow grease, we can pick up a trail."

Zhiruto chuckled. "Your elbows are not greasy, but even so, we don't need to go to your precinct to view the logs." He brought up his arm and opened the floating screen. "I can access it from here."

Of course he could. He'd hacked her car's navigation system earlier.

An interface just like the precinct computer screen floated in the air. He shifted closer and angled his arm to allow her to view it. "Are these the files you require?"

She pointed at a dropdown. "Go there."

After directing him through several steps, they located the logs. Within a few minutes, he'd run them through some sort of program that weeded out most of the irrelevant reports.

"How do you know they're not relevant?" she asked.

"We've been watching humans for a long time. There are certain tells." He opened the first file. "These are the incidents that potentially included our assassin. Good thinking, by the way."

She hated to admit it, but she beamed under his praise. "Let me see them."

The first file was a masked robbery. She doubted the assassin would bother to rob a convenience store, let alone wear a mask while doing it. Next up was a familiar address—Yappy Hour Dog Kennels and Grooming.

"Maise?" she gasped. "That's my friend's place."

"The female who took care of Pepper at the auction?"

"Yeah." She quickly read the log; the owner had called in to report a trespasser, but when officers arrived she brushed it off as a mistake. Guilt ran through Lora as she recalled the missed calls from her friend. "Something's not right. I need to call her." She rushed to the kitchen where she'd left her phone and dialed Maise. The call went to voicemail.

Zhiruto followed her. "We must go there immediately."

"I shouldn't have ignored her calls." She snatched her keys from the counter and stuffed her phone in her back pocket. "What if she's in trouble?" Yanking open the back door, she froze.

Agent Randall stood on her porch backed by two armed guards.

CHAPTER TWELVE

Zhiruto didn't understand why Loragriffin stood frozen in the doorway until she raised her hands and said, "Put away your weapons. No one here's a threat."

Striding closer, he saw Agent Randall outside, flanked by two men holding guns.

Pepper skulked up beside him and growled. She was feeling almost as protective as he was, and he put a hand on her head to communicate his shared purpose.

"Pepper, get back," Loragriffin commanded.

The animal obeyed but continued to growl.

"Get in the car." Agent Randall stepped backward off the porch and indicated a wheeled black vehicle parked behind Loragriffin's smaller car. "Both of you."

"We've done nothing wrong." She crossed her arms, belligerence thudding against his Iki'i.

"Incorrect." Agent Randall pointed toward Zhiruto. "You're harboring an illegal alien—literally. Now move."

Zhiruto put a hand on her shoulder. He didn't like the malice he felt from the three agents outside and wanted to put himself between her and the weapons. But Lora didn't budge from the doorway. His brave mate was trying to protect him.

But now wasn't the time for sentimental pride. He met Agent Randall's eye over her shoulder. "I'll comply if you leave Loragriffin behind."

"Afraid not," said Agent Randall. "She's in too deep to just walk away. Come with me before things escalate any further."

Loragriffin looked over her shoulder at Pepper. "Pepper, you stay." Then she stepped down the porch steps and strode past the agents. "This is going into my report."

Zhiruto loved how confident she was, but he was also frustrated she wasn't giving him a chance to defend her. He followed her cautiously down the porch steps. The oily sensation of Randall's satisfaction oozed over Zhiruto as he passed by.

"You're in front, *officer*." Agent Randall opened the passenger side door, emphasizing her title with zero respect.

She glared at him but got into the passenger seat without complaint.

Agent Randall slammed her door then yanked open the one behind it and indicated Zhiruto should get in.

Grinding his teeth, Zhiruto ducked inside. Randall nudged him to scoot over next to another agent before climbing in beside him, keeping his gun pointed at Loragriffin's back through the seat. "Everyone behave, now."

The other agent in the back seat held his weapon wedged against Zhiruto's side.

Zhiruto kept his voice calm and said, "Your concerns are with me, not the female. Let her go."

The third agent settled into the driver's seat and started the vehicle.

Agent Randal smirked as they backed down the driveway. "You're a long way from home and in no position to dictate terms. Do as we say and she won't get hurt."

"If you harm her, you will pay with your life," Zhiruto growled, hands balled into fists.

Loragriffin twisted around to look at them, but Agent Randall tapped the seat. "Eyes front."

She let out a frustrated breath and turned forward. "Listen, I think I know where the assassin is. We need to get there ASAP."

"You don't need to worry about the assassin anymore," said Randall. "He's back in orbit where he belongs."

Zhiruto clenched his teeth. He should've sensed there was something off when this man refused to cooperate with the investigation. "You let him go?"

Agent Randall sneered. "We received excellent compensation for not interfering."

Loragriffin twisted around again, eyes wide. "Were you part of the assassination plan all along? How could you just let all those people die?"

"Not people. Aliens," Agent Randall spat. "And I do what's necessary for my country and my species. The galactic confederation has continually denied us the means to defend ourselves, so I found a way to get what we need." His glittering eyes focused on Zhiruto. "And you're going to net us even more. The prince's personal bodyguard will be worth a lot to my contacts."

"Who are your contacts?" Zhiruto asked with artificial calm. He couldn't fight back at the moment, but he would find a way out of this. Any information he could gather would be useful.

Agent Randall made a clicking noise with his tongue. "Another instance of you aliens assuming humans are stupid. I'm not going to monologue about all my deepest secrets then let you escape. And you're not as clever as you think. Pretending to die was such a cliché. Your assassin escaped notice by doing the same thing."

Zhiruto groaned inwardly as the pieces came together. The poisoned Kirenai's lack of pain, the worry the poison could be transferred through touch, the false lead about a *burendo* that probably didn't even exist. "The survivor was faking illness."

Agent Randall grinned. "So much for advanced alien technology."

Zhiruto was getting really tired of the man's condescending smirk.

They whizzed past the gate to the park, and a feeling of alarm shot toward him from the front seat. "That was the park," Loragriffin said. "Where are you taking us?"

A flash of uncertainty rose in Agent Randall before slipping beneath the smug surface once more. "Let's just say it's a good thing you like aliens, because I understand you'll be getting familiar with a lot more of them."

"What the hell is that supposed to mean?" she asked.

Zhiruto balled his fists against his thighs. He knew what it meant. Why had it not occurred to him that humans might be feeding their own people to the slavers? "You do realize that the contacts you're working with are some of the most wanted criminals in the galaxy, don't you?"

Agent Randall remained stiff in his seat. "You call them criminals, but they consider themselves freedom fighters. And they're willing to help Earth compete in the galactic hierarchy. A handful of our women is a small price to pay."

"Oh, my God," whispered Loragriffin, once more turning to look at Randall.

The man was vile, more so than Zhiruto could've imagined. He let out a slow breath, never breaking eye contact. "Do your leaders know you've been selling your own females on the black market?"

The other two men had remained surprisingly unemotional this entire time, but Zhiruto didn't have time to probe for deeper feelings. Agent Randall slid his gun between the window and the headrest, pressing the muzzle to the back of her neck. "I said eyes front."

Loragriffin grudgingly turned around to face the oncoming streetlights. "You're a fucking monster."

"Call me what you will, but I'm doing it for the good of humanity. Just like you soon will be. We usually select women who won't be missed, but I'm sure we can find a way to link your disappearance to the assassination. Hell, maybe I'll have you take the fall for it."

"Nobody will believe you." A frantic worry filled the vehicle as Loragriffin processed Agent Randall's words.

It was all Zhiruto could do to keep from strangling the man. Loragriffin could not be handed over to slavers. She was his mate. Like a blow from a sunda lizard's tail, an idea came to him. There was a way to convince Randall to let her go. "Loragriffin will be worthless to slavers."

Agent Randall narrowed his eyes. "What are you talking about?"

"Slavers want human females as breeders. I've claimed Loragriffin as my mate. They will offer you nothing for her when they learn of it."

Randall barked out laughter as the vehicle merged onto a wide street packed with other vehicles moving at a fast pace. "Nice try, alien."

Confusion now mixed with Loragriffin's worry.

Zhiruto continued, wishing he'd been able to have this conversation with his mate in private. "She's already been given the genetic markers that make her unable to bear children for anyone but me. Your buyers will detect this the moment they scan her."

Agent Randall sneered. "Not every alien wants to breed; she's attractive enough to make someone a nice plaything. Hell, they can send her to work in the mines for all I care, as long as they pay me."

"You're pure evil." Loragriffin shook her head, her voice trembling with a mixture of terror and fury.

"Don't judge me. The slave trade was happening long before I got involved. I just found a way to take advantage of the situation. If the emperor would give us the weapons we need instead of closing our planet to trade, we wouldn't have to do it this way. We'd be able to defend ourselves. But he denied our entrance into the confederation, and the only contact we have is with the black market, whether we want it or not. At least this way we get something out of the deal." Agent Randall sat up straighter in his seat. "The women we hand over serve humanity, and the technology they're earning us means soon we'll no longer be at the mercy of the slave traders. We'll stand up for ourselves and join the confederation of planets as we're meant to do."

"You don't really think slavers are going to provide you with technology that can defeat them?" Zhiruto asked. "They want to maintain their trade here, and the last thing they're going to do is arm the natives."

"They think they give us nothing but baubles. Harmless toys and trinkets to numb our minds and soothe our pain. But humans are great at thinking outside the box, and our nation's best scientists have already innovated what they've learned and created weapons that outpace our rivals here on Earth. Eventually, we'll develop weapons that will rival that of any species in the galaxy."

Zhiruto laughed harshly. "You're deluding yourself, Agent Randall. The members of the Senburu who are supplying you are delighted to see you humans squabbling among yourselves. Your inability to get along with one another on your own planet is what keeps humans out of the confederation."

"We'll see about that," said Randall. The vehicle turned down a ramp, leaving traffic behind.

Loragriffin said, "It's not too late to do the right thing, you know. Let's talk about this."

"Shut up, or I'll have you gagged and put in the trunk."

They passed through a small town where all the windows were dark, and soon they turned onto a narrow road lined with overarching trees. The sharp beams of the headlights cut through the darkness, giving them glimpses of small fluttering insects mere moments before pulverizing them.

The driver turned sharply and bumped down a rutted path between the trees. He pulled to a stop in a small clearing.

"Get out." Agent Randall opened his door and climbed out, yanking open Loragriffin's door.

The other agent kept his weapon aimed at Zhiruto. The driver also got out, keeping watch over all of them from the other side of the car while shining a big Maglite toward them.

"That way." Agent Randall jabbed the nose of his gun into Loragriffin's back and herded her down a narrow path between the trees.

Zhiruto's guard said, "Follow them."

The threats were too spread out for Zhiruto to act without risking Loragriffin's life. He stepped onto the uneven trail. This was his first visit to Earth, and the night air smelled cool with a hint of something sour, like rotting vegetation. He wished he was more familiar with what that might mean as they followed the terrain between large, rough-barked trunks.

The two agents at his back maintained a respectable distance, but he could feel their unwavering presence against his Iki'i. He had to do something... and soon. Once they rendezvoused with the slave ship, the traders would have weapons far more deadly than the projectile throwers the humans held.

Although every fiber of his being wanted to resist the idea, a plan began to take shape. He was the one the Senburu wanted, not her. If he resisted or started a fight, it might give her just the break she needed to get away. But he needed to target Agent Randall for this to work.

Picking up his pace, he hurried to catch up.

CHAPTER THIRTEEN

The trail ahead was barely visible in the flashlight beam from several yards behind them, and Lora tried not to trip over the many roots. Every time she thought things had gotten as weird as they possibly could, the universe threw her into a new tailspin. The maniac with a gun at her back was planning to sell her off as some sort of alien sex slave. And what was this mate thing Zhiruto was talking about? No children except with him had to be a lie to try to protect her.

She put a hand against the trunk of a nearby tree to steady herself as she stepped over a root. At least the agents were cocky enough that they hadn't bothered to tie her hands. She was biding her time for an opportunity to disarm Agent Randall, but it would have to be just right or one of the other men would surely shoot her or Zhiruto.

A shout behind her made her spin in time to see Zhiruto tackle Agent Randall from behind. The agent remained obstinately sure-footed as Zhiruto drove him sideways into the tree, grappling for the gun.

Zhiruto's eyes met hers. "Run."

Agent Randall yanked the muzzle down and fired, the shot deafening at close range. Something warm splattered Lora's arm, and pain pinched her side. *Am I shot?* She dropped to a crouch as the men continued to struggle.

Pressing a hand to her waist, it came away sticky, yet she was in surprisingly little pain. *It must just be a flesh wound.* Watching the other agents to make sure they weren't paying any attention to her, she crept around the wide tree trunk into the underbrush.

Another shot rang out, but she couldn't tell from where. One of the agents said, "Get in there. I'll cover you."

Her heart thundered in her ears, and her hands and feet tingled with the need to move. To fight. Her side was beginning to throb, but she pushed the pain aside. She had to act fast if she was going to save Zhiruto. Glancing around the trunk again, she saw one agent edging forward, his attention trained on the men now tussling in front of him. The flashlight lay on the ground behind the third agent, turning the men into silhouettes with their weapons focused on the grapplers.

Her best bet would be to take out the man providing cover, so she tiptoed through the underbrush beside the trail, keeping one hand pressed to the growing stitch in her side. She hoped to spot a branch or rock she could use as a weapon, but what little she could make out on the dark ground showed only a thick layer of leaves.

She came out on the trail behind the man in the rear and

paused. If she tried to sneak up on him, he'd likely turn the gun on her, which would only end badly. But if she swept in fast enough, she might be able to take him down with the first blow. She'd done plenty of mat tumbling in her kickboxing lessons, but she wasn't sure she could take him down with her fists alone, and her wound was making her feel woozy.

Her gaze dropped to the flashlight. It would make a decent club if she could reach it.

Taking a few quick breaths, she darted forward, doing a tuck and roll to grab the mag-lite. Her fingers wrapped around the long handle, and she rocked back to her feet, gritting her teeth as she swung a wide arc toward the man's head.

A resounding thud filled the air as the metal shaft made contact. He dropped like a stone, his pistol cartwheeling into the leafy underbrush.

The other agent rounded on her, the muzzle of his pistol seeking a target. Dropping the flashlight, she dove into the darkness beside the trail. A deafening shot split the forest, close enough behind for her to feel the rush of displaced air. Barely daring to breathe, she belly-crawled through the brush toward the men.

The agent shouted, "Damn bitch came in behind us. Richmond's down."

Zhiruto yelled, "Loragriffin, run!"

No way was she going to leave Zhiruto here to face them alone. After all they'd been through, he was her partner, and she refused to leave him behind. Through the trees she could see the agent half-lit by the reflected glow from the flashlight and panning his gun along the treeline where she lay hiding. She halted her crawl, hand pressed to the growing wetness on her side. She should check it and staunch the bleeding, but there wasn't time.

Agent Randall gasped, "Ignore her and get this fucking alien off me."

Reluctantly, the agent turned toward where Zhiruto had Randall pinned, one knee on his chest, the other on a wrist while he grappled with the gun in Randall's free hand.

The agent who was still on his feet fired. A blast shattered the air and the gun bucked. Zhiruto's chest blossomed into a hole.

"No!" Lora screamed, scrambling to her feet. This couldn't be happening.

But Zhiruto didn't let go of Randall's weapon hand. Instead, the hole shimmered, then closed up, just like in a scene from a Terminator movie. A stream of curse words left the agent's mouth, and he fired twice more—once to the head and again to the chest. Each blast opened a gaping hole. Each wound shimmered closed.

"Fuck me!" the guy yelled, and started backing toward her, firing at Zhiruto again and again.

Lora didn't have time to be shocked. Now was her chance. She sprinted out of the bushes and barreled into him. The gun went flying as he stumbled forward.

But instead of falling, he spun and struck the base of his palm into her collarbone. She heard a snap, and pain lanced down her arm. Gasping, she side stepped, barely dodging his next blow.

The agent bent his knees and brought his hands up, looking for a chance to strike.

She went into a half crouch, shuffling sideways to keep him in front of her. He'd obviously had martial arts training, and her kickboxing would be no match, but she had to try. She aimed an uppercut toward his jaw with her good arm.

He danced out of the way, aiming another jab toward her solar plexus.

Pain lancing through her from shoulder to hip, she lurched out of range in the nick of time. When the man darted forward again, she brought her knee up, aiming for his crotch.

He caught her behind the thigh with one hand, the other landing a blow to her cheek.

Her head rocked to the side and stars blasted across her vision, but she kept her balance as she yanked her leg free. Her broken collarbone was sending blinding white lightning into her chest and down her arm, and she could barely take a full breath.

From the corner of her eye, she caught sight of Zhiruto with Randall's head between his hands, bashing it back against the ground. But then she had to focus on her own opponent again as he bared his teeth and advanced. She widened her stance, staying on her toes. His hands were up, ready to strike. He was good.

By the look in his eyes, she realized he thought so, too. And it was just the weakness she needed. Guys like him were like cats; they loved to play with their prey.

Be the wounded bird. Not hard to do with the pain in her side and collarbone. Gritting her teeth, she forced her left arm up as if to throw a punch and whimpered, keeping her weight on the balls of her feet. When his attention shifted, she snapped her foot out in a switch-kick to his jaw.

The stars must've aligned just right, because her foot made solid contact. He rocked back, eyes glazing, then sank to his knees and toppled to his side on the forest floor. *Knockout.*

Except the pain in her side was now an agonizing knife in her gut. She doubled over, good arm clutching her middle. Looking down at her shirt, she realized it was soaked with blood, as was the arm she now pressed against the wound.

Her eyes refused to focus. She sank to her knees, panting as she tried to lift her shirt. But her fingers wouldn't cooperate. She looked up, trying to spot Zhiruto. The darkness felt like it was squeezing her, reducing her line of sight to pinpricks.

She slumped sideways onto a hip, barely able to support herself on her good hand. The ground felt so solid and good. She knew better than to sleep, but she needed to rest.

She'd only closed her eyes for a minute...

CHAPTER FOURTEEN

Lora opened her eyes to a pale purple ceiling. For a moment it felt as if she floated in thin air. Then she lifted her head slightly, taking in a narrow bed with soft raised bumpers on either side of her. The mattress was deliciously comfortable. She let her head fall back down. Where the hell was she? Her memories were a blur, but the last thing she recalled was kicking someone in the face...

Zhiruto moved into view above her, his dark eyes full of relief. He was shirtless, as usual, his broad shoulders and molded pecs as perfect as ever. "You're awake, Loragriffin."

The way he smushed up her name still made her heart flutter. She exhaled slowly. "Where am I?" Pepper's nose poked over the edge of the mattress, her urgent whine insisting on immediate attention. Lora scratched behind the dog's ears. "And how did you get here?"

"I retrieved her for you. We're on the IDA ship in the medical bay," Zhiruto said. "How do you feel?"

She had to admit, she felt pretty darn good considering she thought she might die last time she was awake. "I'm okay. Did you say we're on a spaceship?"

As if to prove just how weird her surroundings were, he pulled a floating stool over and sat down. "Yes. The healers extracted a bullet that had perforated your digestive system."

Remembering darkness and blood, her hand left Pepper's warm fur and reached for her own stomach. Her fingers met strange material, not quite silk and not quite velvet. She looked down and saw she'd been dressed in a soft cream-colored nightshirt. Sliding the hem up, she checked both sides of her abdomen; her skin was unblemished.

Then she realized her collarbone no longer ached, either. A broken collarbone would take weeks to heal. A gut shot even longer. *Thank God he remembered about Pepper.* "How long have we been here?"

"Two days."

Surprised it hadn't been longer, she sat up and looked around, fully taking in her surroundings. The walls were the same purple leaf-like texture she'd seen in the background on the video with Georgie. To her right, recessed shelves held an assortment of unidentifiable items. Another wall held a panel of blinking lights. She really was on an alien spaceship, and she really had been miraculously healed.

Then she remembered the way the bullets had gone through Zhiruto, creating holes that closed almost instantly. She turned her attention to him. "You took bullets, too. Are you okay?"

"I'm uninjured. Simple projectile weapons are ineffective against Kirenai. Our matrix can also absorb all but the most extreme blunt force trauma." He said it with pride, and she had to admit, it was sexy to have a boyfriend who was impervious to bullets.

Is that what he is? My boyfriend? Her thoughts felt both strange and right at the same time. "Thank you for remembering Pepper."

He smiled. "Of course. She's important."

She smiled back. He was thoughtful, protective, and sexy all at the same time. Squeezing her eyes closed, she fought back what had to be post-surgery brain fog. There were a whole lot of unanswered questions she needed answers to before she let these mushy feelings overcome her. "What happened to Agent Randall and his men?"

"His men are in stasis and awaiting justice. The emperor does not condone non-consensual servitude, and anyone caught participating in the black market trade will be punished." He looked away, his face grim. "Agent Randall is dead."

"You killed him?" she asked softly. She'd never killed someone in the line of duty or otherwise, but she'd met plenty of officers who had and knew there could be aftereffects.

"He was a vile representation of your species. I don't regret it."

She looked at him a heartbeat longer to be sure, then asked, "What about the assassin? Did you find him?"

Zhiruto shook his head, his lips forming a thin line. "Unfortunately not. Agent Randall put the creche holding the assassin on a separate shuttle, and no one seems to know where it went."

"Have you interrogated his men? We might at least be able to get a name."

Brushing his knuckles softly down her cheek, Zhiruto's eyes softened. "I was waiting for you to wake up."

She swallowed, feeling a bit stunned. Usually the men she worked with jumped at the chance to claim victory on an investigation.

She swung her legs over the edge of the bed. "We should talk to them right now. The trail's getting colder even as we speak."

"As you say."

She planted her bare feet on the strangely textured floor. "Where are my clothes?"

"I had some made for you." He guided her toward the blank wall and ran his fingers over some strange bumps. A panel opened up, revealing a narrow closet full of clothes. He pulled out a forest green tunic and matching slacks and handed them to her.

The fabric was as soft as the nightshirt she wore and stretchy like spandex, embroidered with a subtle wave pattern in silver along the seams. She eyed it dubiously, knowing it would cling to every curve, but it would at least be better than the long nightshirt she now wore. "Thanks. Where can I change?"

He pressed more bumps on the wall and a door slid open to reveal what looked like a motorhome lavatory. "My apologies for the poor accommodations. The IDA could offer no better options. Feel free to shower—I have not used our water allotment today."

She stepped inside and looked at the fixtures which were somewhat similar to Earth, but not entirely. "How do I turn on the water?"

He stepped into the small space behind her and reached around to point to some largish bumps on the purple wall. His nearness against her back made her skin heat with awareness; his blue, muscled arm was close enough that her own breath bounced back against her cheek.

Without even thinking, she leaned closer and kissed the inside of his elbow. "Thank you for saving me."

Two muscular arms wrapped around her from behind, pulling her back against him, and he nuzzled his face in her hair. "Thank you for not dying."

He felt so warm and solid, so alive, she couldn't help herself. She turned and put her arms around his neck, lifting her face to his.

Without hesitation, he claimed her mouth in a deep, satisfying kiss. His lips moved against hers, and his tongue stroked forward with soft yet sure movements that soon had her panting with desire. He backed her slowly against the wall, one hand rising to cup her jaw while the other cradled her waist.

She let her head fall back against the hard surface as he pressed small kisses to the corner of her mouth and up her jaw.

Her hands splayed over his back, loving the play of his corded muscles as he moved.

He nibbled her earlobe, sending a delightful shiver through her, then ran his hot tongue down her throat as the hand at her waist rose to find her breast. He cupped its heaviness before kneading gently until the nipple tightened in a hard peak. Rolling the bud between his fingers, he sucked at the base of her throat, his hard tongue massaging. She was probably going to have a hickey, but she didn't care. It felt amazing, like he was worshiping her.

She widened her stance, and he responded by leaning closer between her legs so she could feel the hard length of his arousal against her center. Her fingers clawed into his back as she flexed her hips, grinding herself against him.

He growled low in his throat, sending vibrations along her skin from his mouth. Dropping his hand from cradling her face, he hoisted her nightshirt up, pulling back only long enough to yank it easily over her head and off her arms. Then he claimed her mouth again, his kiss ferocious and intense as he plunged his tongue between her lips.

She realized she wore nothing underneath and now stood naked against him. His bare chest had a slight dusting of course hair that teased her nipples to excruciating awareness, and the heat between her legs was now an ache that needed to be filled.

Sliding her hands down to his waistband, she discovered he was somehow already naked. She didn't take time to worry about it and slid her thumbs along the slight indentation of muscle beside his hipbones to the top of his heavily muscled thighs. His hard shaft prodded against her belly, and she pressed it down until it tunneled between her legs.

He rocked his hips slightly, rubbing himself against her, and wetness flooded her pussy. His hands roamed her body, skimming delightful shivers over her skin as he slowly pushed his thickness deeper between her legs, sliding along her slit again and again until he was slick with her juices.

She was going to die if she didn't have him soon. Hitching a leg up around his hip, she reached for him, angling the head of his shaft into her opening. She gasped as he entered her, the fullness bringing her close to orgasm almost immediately.

Zhiruto hooked both hands under her ass and lifted her, settling her onto his cock as he stared into her eyes. Still inside her, he marched from the small bathroom back to the bed. He lowered her onto it, and the moment of broken contact made her whimper. "I want to taste you, Loragriffin."

Before she could reply, he placed his hands against her thighs and spread them, burying his face against her pussy. His tongue stroked up her slit and circled her clit before delving back down to plunder her with deep, penetrating strokes. Up and around he licked her, driving her crazy with desire until she was squirming on the mattress.

His lips wrapped around her clit and sucked while he dipped a finger inside her, the quick rhythm of his penetration pulling an unexpected orgasm out of her. She shuddered, legs going stiff as waves of pleasure raced through her.

Then he kissed her belly, pulling his finger out and climbing up her body until they were face to face. His stubble smelled like her, but she didn't mind as he kissed her, his hard muscles covering her with his strength and his cock settling between her legs. In a well-aimed stroke, he entered her, filled her completely, and she sucked in a breath of pure ecstasy.

He ground his hips, pulled back, and pounded in again, picking up a rhythm that had her crying out with every breath. The pressure inside her was rising to nearly unbearable heights as she lifted her hips to meet him, fingers digging into the tight muscles of his ass. She loved feeling it flex as he thrust, loved pulling him deeply inside her until there didn't seem to be enough air in the room.

Then her climax broke—the wave of her orgasm crashed down around her in a cascade of pure bliss. Her surroundings disappeared, and she knew nothing but him.

He drove hard into her, taking a few more strokes to find his own release, the hot jets of his seed filling her. When at last he collapsed on top of her, his heavy breathing a match to her own, she feathered her fingers down his flanks and kissed his shoulder.

He nuzzled her back. "My perfect mate."

The warm fuzzy feeling that gave her was almost enough to put her to sleep. Almost. "You told Agent Randall something about me having genetic markers. What did you mean?"

"I have implanted you with genetic markers that secure our mate bond."

A cold realization swept through her and she pushed against his chest to make him get off her. "Hold on. You implanted me something in me?"

"Yes, I told you after our initial intercourse." He lifted his head to look into her eyes. "You're the only one for me. I've claimed you as my mate."

There was that word again. Her heart fluttered and the familiar giddy feeling swept through her. But she wasn't going to let it take away her sense. Did he think he owned her now? She squirmed away from him and got to her feet, backing away toward the bathroom.

From where she lay near the door, Pepper raised her head, alert to the new tension in the room.

"I thought we already had this discussion. The auction wasn't selling slaves."

Zhiruto sat up, raising his palms as if to placate her. "Not my bondservant. My mate. Humans don't require permanent bonds in order to procreate, but it is the only way for most Kirenai."

She snatched up the discarded nightshirt and shrugged it over her head. "I'm not procreating with anyone."

"I'm explaining myself badly." He rose, his gorgeous blue body catching the light in all the right places. "We don't have to produce children. The genetic material we share will grant you longevity to match my own. We're bonded for life."

Her chest felt tight and her mouth dry. "Is that why I feel this way around you? Because you put some sort of DNA drug in me?"

His blue face had gone still. "Loragriffin—"

"It's Lora. Just plain Lora. And I'm serious. Get me off this damn spaceship, and take me home this instant. I want this disgusting genetic marker thing gone. Out of me. Now."

He stared at her a long moment before dropping his gaze.

"You're right. I overstepped. I'll take you back to Earth immediately."

Right before her eyes, his nakedness disappeared, dark blue slacks and a shirt materializing over his body like magic. Without another word, he strode to the door, bent to briefly run a hand over Pepper's head, then was gone from the room.

And Lora wondered if she'd just made the biggest mistake of her life.

CHAPTER FIFTEEN

The maelstrom of Loragriffin's emotions against Zhiruto's Iki'i was indecipherable, but her body language was very clear. She felt angry. Betrayed. And rightfully so.

He'd formed a mate bond without her permission.

He deserved to be forever separated from the one person who could share his heart. She obviously didn't want to share hers with him. He wondered if it had something to do with the human capability to bear children without a mate bond. Such a bond meant nothing to them.

Unfortunately, his genetic markers were part of Loragriffin's DNA now and could never be removed. But she didn't need to know that. She didn't want to have children, so she'd likely never notice it was there. Because she obviously didn't love him.

She would be happiest back on Earth. He would report back to the prince. After that, who knew? He would hopefully be able to find a new job, a new purpose.

He ordered the ship's transport technicians to teleport Loragriffin—*no, just Lora*—and Pepper back to Earth. He didn't go to the transport chamber with her. He couldn't bear to face her, to see the distaste in her eyes when she looked at him. It was better to let her go without any more contact. *But I will always ache for her.*

A cup of Hypawan brew in hand, he paced the galley and waited for the techs to tell him she'd returned safely home. Once she was gone, he'd take a military shuttle back to Kirenai Prime. He still didn't know how he was going to break the news to the prince. He'd failed his mission, would have to resign his post, and had absolutely nothing to show for it. Kirenai almost never had a mate reject them, especially after the bond had been set. The shame of his situation was almost too much to bear.

Staring at the nondescript purple walls of the galley, he took another long swallow from his cup. The strong alcohol did little to dull his feelings, and for the first time, he understood why people sought out the smoky mindlessness of the many *ahen* dens on Sireta Prime. It would be so good to feel nothing right now...

"She's safely at the coordinates you provided, sir." An IDA tech spoke from the doorway, keeping a good distance between them. Zhiruto had barked at the techs earlier when they'd asked if he wished to transport with Lora.

"Thank you," Zhiruto attempted to infuse his Iki'i with gratitude. Much as he wanted someone to blame for everything that had gone wrong, the techs had been compliant with his requests, and the IDA medics had saved Lora's life. They deserved better than his ire.

He teleported over to a royal military shuttle for the long ride back to Kirenai Prime. The shuttle wasn't as fast as the prince's personal vessel, and he wasn't sure if he should be glad for the chance to think things over or worried he'd go crazy with the wait. As the ship was preparing to enter FTL, his personal comm alerted him that he had a call. He assumed it was from Prince Arazhi, but it was from the empress herself. Knowing this didn't bode well, he told the pilot to wait and answered.

The empress's alabaster face was lined by worry. "Zhiruto, there's been another assassination attempt on Arazhi."

Guilt flooded through him. He should've been there to protect his prince. "Is he all right?"

"He's in a regeneration pod, and the healers say he should recover. We've been told the attempt was actually aimed at the human he brought back, most likely to keep her from breeding. Not that that's an issue, since she's barren. Did you secure an alternate female as I ordered?"

Zhiruto grimaced. He hadn't liked the empress's order the first time, and he liked it even less now that he'd met the humans in person. "The auction was not for bondservants as we believed, empress. I was unable to convince a female to return with me."

She leaned closer to the camera. "You know what my son likes in a female. You must return to the planet and bring back a fertile human my son will accept."

His throat tightened as he remembered the condom during

his interlude with Loragriffin. "Are you certain the one he chose is barren? Humans practice something called birth control."

The empress's lips curled with frustration. "Yes, we're certain. The healers tested her and said she's incompatible."

Zhiruto dropped his gaze. This was unexpected and terrible news. But he couldn't return to Earth. It would be too painful. "I will pursue the assassin, empress, but I can't return to Earth. I'm not welcome there." It wasn't the exact truth, but it was all he could offer. "And I'm afraid I must resign from my post. I am no longer fit to be the prince's security officer."

"Why would you choose to resign now?" She scowled. "You've been a loyal officer for most of my son's life. He needs you now more than ever. Whatever happened on Earth can't be that bad."

He found he couldn't meet her gaze. "I have taken a mate."

There was a long pause. "And?"

His heartbeat thundered against his ribs. "She rejected me."

"*Kuzara.*" The swear word coming from the empress's mouth was enough to make him look up. Her face was a mask of fury. "These humans are nothing but trouble. Fine. I'll send another emissary to secure a female. But you're still not allowed to resign. Arazhi needs you. Come back immediately." She ended the call.

Zhiruto lowered his arm. The empress might want him to stay at his post, but only the prince had the power to choose his guard. Once Arazhi learned of Zhiruto's many failures—especially his inability to change shape—the only logical choice was to let him go.

Heading to the shuttle's small galley to look for a drink, Zhiruto wondered if he might find any *ahen* on board.

CHAPTER SIXTEEN

Lora felt like Dorothy in the *Wizard of Oz* as a gut-wrenching whirlwind seemed to yank her off her feet. One minute she was standing on the purple floor of an alien spaceship, and the next she was on her knees in the long grass of her front yard. She retched dryly, and Pepper shook as if trying to clear water from her floppy ears.

"Officer Griffin, are you all right?" Lora's neighbor called from her driveway.

The last thing Lora wanted right now was to deal with a nosy neighbor asking questions. Forcing a smile and waving cheerfully, Lora called, "Yeah, thanks."

Rising shakily, she hurried to her back door. The moment Pepper was inside, she closed the door and leaned against it, breathing hard as she stared blankly at her kitchen. Someone— most likely Zhiruto when he'd retrieved Pepper—had cleaned up the containers of fried chicken, but other than that, everything looked untouched. Her cell phone lay dead on the counter near the back door, so she plugged it in, staring at the screen as the battery charged.

Her mind kept rolling over and over the past few days. She should be more worried about what was going on here on Earth, but all she could think about was Zhiruto.

We're bonded. His words were branded in her mind. *You're perfect for me.*

He'd saved her life. Stopped a slave ring. And taken care of Pepper while she was unconscious. Fuck, he'd even been willing to let her lead the investigation, right down to putting on that silly disguise. And he'd respected her enough to let her go when she'd asked.

Bonded didn't mean bound.

Nausea welled up inside her. She looked at Pepper, who watched her from where she lay in the doorway between the kitchen and living room. "Think I made a mistake?"

Pepper whined softly, tail thumping the floor.

She glanced back at her phone, nausea intensifying as she realized she had no way to contact him. Did aliens even have phone numbers?

Powering on the phone, she waited for everything to load, hoping for a message. There were several, but none from Zhiruto. The precinct had left a voicemail checking on her—apparently Zhiruto had let them know she'd been injured and wouldn't be in for a while. Another thoughtful gesture that made her belly knot with regret. The last message was from Maise. "Lora, I really need to talk to you. There's weird stuff going on. Please let me know you're okay."

Lora grimaced, feeling terrible for putting her friend off so long. She hit auto-dial, but after several rings, the call went to voicemail. Figuring Maise might be up to her elbows in sudsy dog fur, she dialed the kennel.

Maise's assistant answered, "Yappy Hour Grooming and Dog Kennels."

"Hi, Ted. Is Maise around?"

"No. Haven't heard from her in a few days," said the young man as dogs barked in the background.

Lora scowled. "She lives right upstairs, Ted. Did you think to check on her?"

"Hey, what she does is her business. I babysit dogs, not people."

Frustrated, Lora hung up and grabbed her keys. Then she realized she was still wearing only a nightshirt, so she hurried upstairs and put on a uniform. If there was trouble ahead, she wanted to be prepared.

After loading Pepper into the back of her car, she drove to the small apartment above the kennel where Maise lived. When no one answered her knock, she glanced around before stretching to retrieve the spare key from the little birdhouse wind chime near the door.

Inside, nothing looked out of place. A used coffee cup sat in the sink. The dog bowl held some kibble that Pepper immediately gobbled up. And the unmade bed could've been slept in last night. "Dammit, Maise, where are you?"

Lora pulled out her cell phone and dialed again. The tune for *Bad Boys* started playing in the bedroom—Maise's personalized ringtone for Lora. Cold dread filled her.

"Shit." She spotted the phone plugged in on the bedside table.

Was it just coincidence Maise had gone missing right after the auction?

No. Lora knew in her heart that there had to be a connection. It could be anything from an alien kidnapping to Agent Randall selling her off before he died. For a fleeting moment, she wished Zhiruto were here to back her up. *Stop it. You don't need him.*

Pepper was pawing at some dirty laundry in the corner.

"Good idea, Pepper." Picking up some socks, Lora put them into a plastic bag, then hooked Pepper back to her leash. "We're going to find Maise."

They went outside, and Lora offered the open bag to Pepper to smell. "Go find her."

Pepper immediately put her nose to the ground and started down the stairs. Lora expected Pepper would head to the parking lot and the trail would go cold because Maise had been forced into a car, but the dog led her around the back of the kennels and down the sidewalk into a nearby neighborhood. Now that the aliens were officially gone, the city seemed to be returning to normal, although a few yards still held signs offering paid parking.

They walked at a quick pace, Pepper trotting along as if she knew exactly where to go. They crossed the bridge that led to the pulp mill. The air was breathable, but the sour stench grew more pronounced as the houses thinned to nothing and the weedy fields surrounding the plant took over.

"Are you sure this is Maise's trail, Pepper?" Lora shoved the socks under the dog's nose again.

Pepper bayed and pulled harder against the leash, tracking off the road toward a stand of young trees near the plant's fence. Someone else had been this way recently; there was a barely noticeable line of crushed stalks just off the trail.

Lora's heart thundered as she contemplated what she might find at the end of this path. The scene was feeling a lot like the true crime podcasts she listened to, and she felt for the gun at her waist, reassured by its weight.

They wended through the trees until they came upon a dry creek bed. Pepper easily trotted down the steep incline while Lora picked her way down more carefully. Then it was all she could do to keep up with the dog as Pepper bayed again and began running. Lora's feet pounded the earth, and she prayed over and over that Maise was all right.

They climbed out of the creek bed and went through more trees, finally emerging into a clearing in the middle of the woods. Pausing, Lora gaped at the perfect circle of crushed grass in the middle. In the center sat something that looked a little like a pale purple rosebud the size of a city bus.

Pepper bayed again and pulled against the leash.

Lora gulped. "Maise?"

Whatever she was looking at had to be alien. She imagined the rosebud opening and swallowing her friend whole, like something from *Little Shop of Horrors*. Was this thing a monster, an invasive plant, or something else entirely?

"Maise? Are you here?" She let Pepper pull her one step forward onto the crushed grass.

Without warning, the rosebud lifted off the ground. An invisible force rolled outward, shoving Lora off balance. She landed hard on her backside at the edge of the circle. Pepper yipped and cowered beside her. The rosebud hovered a moment, completely silent, then shot straight into the air and disappeared.

Lora realized her mouth was hanging open as she looked at the now empty clearing and sky. That thing had been a spaceship.

And she was certain Maise had been on it.

CHAPTER SEVENTEEN

By the time Zhiruto reached Kirenai Prime, a lot had changed; the royal healer, Elthos, had been implicated in the assassinations, and Arazhi's mate, Georgie, was not barren after all. Now a royal wedding was in the making, and Zhiruto was torn between jealousy and happiness for his friend.

He strode toward the prince's chambers for his first meeting, taking in the familiar gray stone walls and purple doors of the palace. Kirenai in all shapes and sizes passed him in the hall, and he was once more surrounded by the flow of his people's Iki'i. It was good to be home, yet it also no longer felt complete. He was missing a vital piece of his future. He was missing Loragriffin. *No, Lora. Just Lora.*

His throat tightened. Now he was about to relinquish the last thing that meant anything to him; his position as the prince's personal guard.

He entered the prince's chambers to find Arazhi at his desk, several interfaces open above it. Dappled blue daylight played over the floor from the tall windows facing a veranda, and the sharp scent of *kuro* tea rose from a steaming pot nearby. The prince stood as Zhiruto entered the room, his blue-skinned human form dressed in what appeared to be gray slacks and a button-down shirt that matched the styles Zhiruto had seen on Earth. Arazhi and he had been close even before Zhiruto had accepted the position as his guard, and the familiar warm touch of the prince's Iki'i surrounded him like an embrace.

He returned the greeting along with a small bow. "My prince."

"I'm relieved you're back." Arazhi waved a hand at his desk. "This whole assassination conspiracy has been a nightmare, and I have no idea how to run the palace guard."

"I regret I wasn't there to properly protect you and your bride." Zhiruto cleared his throat preparing to voice his resignation, but Arazhi continued speaking.

"No need to be sorry. You were following another thread. Tell me what happened while you were on Earth." The prince moved to the table with the tea and poured a cup for Zhiruto before sitting in a padded chair that had a view of the patio. "You said the assassin was a *burendo* last time we talked."

Zhiruto sighed and sat down opposite the prince. *May as well provide my report first, then resign.* He stared out toward the shady blue trees, trying to find his center. He'd never had to shield his Iki'i from his friend, but his roiling emotions were too raw to share. So he fortified his walls. "The report of a *burendo* was a clever misdirection designed to take me away from the center of activity." The memory of the supposedly poisoned

Kirenai rising from the transportation creche just long enough to deliver the lie still stung. "I'm ashamed to admit it came from the assassin himself—I spoke directly to him without realizing it."

Leaving out the more intimate details about Lora, Zhiruto explained everything that had happened. When he got to the part about Agent Randall trading unwilling women, Arazhi sucked in an angry breath. "Reprehensible."

Zhiruto nodded. "Yes, he was an evil man. I'm not sure why I didn't sense his intent from the start."

Arazhi took a sip of his tea. "Might it have something to do with that pretty human you were with during our communications?"

Heat infused Zhiruto's face. "Did the empress speak to you?"

"My mother and I are not on the best of terms at the moment." Arazhi knit his brows. "Why?"

Now Zhiruto understood why Arazhi hadn't asked about Lora from the start. Picking up his teacup, Zhiruto stared down at the inky liquid. "You aren't the only one who found a mate on Earth."

"Aha!" Arazhi set his cup down with a thunk. "I wondered why you seemed to be so fixed in your human form."

Zhiruto's normal form at the palace was that of a Hypawa, his mother's species, with slender limbs and a mane of hair that grew all the way down his spine. The vertebrae between his shoulder blades itched with the memory. Strange and demoralizing to think he would never assume that familiar form again. He wondered what he was going to tell his mother.

The prince jarred him from his thoughts with a clap on the shoulder. "This is excellent news! Where is she? Georgie will be delighted to have a human friend."

The shield around Zhiruto's Iki'i slipped, spewing forth some of the guilt and shame threatening to consume him. "She did not wish to come with me."

Arazhi leaned back, but compassion flowed from him. "Well, humans are difficult. Georgie took a lot of convincing to accept me. Keep trying."

"I can't." His next words nearly wouldn't leave his constricted throat. "I claimed her without permission."

A spike of alarm flashed from the prince. "*Kuzara.*"

Zhiruto rose, keeping his eyes downcast. "She was very clear that she does not wish to see me again. I betrayed her by what I did, and I don't blame her for being angry. I also don't blame you for dismissing me from your service."

"Dismiss you?" Arazhi sliced a hand through the air like a blade. "Never. You are my most important, most trusted advisor. This has nothing to do with your ability to serve me."

"But I'm now trapped in this form." Zhiruto looked up, sure he'd see disgust in his prince's eyes.

Instead, he saw resolve. "I'm also human now, so it's a fitting form for you," said Arazhi. "You're to remain in my service. We will not speak of this again." The prince rose, moved back to his desk and pointed to a list of names on one of the interfaces. "These are the guards who were part of my security detail during the latest assassination attempt. Were you able to learn any names from the humans who were working with the assassin?"

Focusing back on work helped dull the ache in Zhiruto's chest. "No. But I've gone over the IDA's records and there's one person unaccounted for from the guest list—a Kirenai named Iroth. He's listed as a 'shipping expert' and I suspect he may run one of the smuggling rings transporting illicit slaves."

"How did a smuggler manage to get an invitation to the event? I thought the IDA required referrals."

"My guess is that someone tampered with the invitations. I need a warrant with your seal to dig deeper into the IDA's secure files."

"Done."

Just then a female voice spoke from the chamber doorway. "Arazhi, can I interrupt you for a minute?"

The human held a data pad in one hand and wore a pair of glasses that made her eyes look larger than usual. Her pale blonde hair hung loose around her face.

Arazhi broke into a smile, and a wash of love filled the room. "Georgie, come meet Zhiruto, my personal security officer."

"Good to meet you." She granted Zhiruto a tight smile before returning her attention to Arazhi and hurrying forward. "I've been inviting my friends to the wedding, and I can't reach Maise. Lora thinks Maise was abducted. Here, I want you to talk to her."

Loragriffin. Zhiruto felt as if the world were in slow motion.

Arazhi reached for the data pad. "This is Prince Arazhi."

Loragriffin's face appeared on the interface. From the angle of the data pad, she couldn't see anyone except Arazhi. "Hello, your highness. Thank you for speaking with me. I worked with your security officer here on Earth."

The prince shot Zhiruto a concerned glance. "Thank you for your assistance. What can I do to help you now?"

"My friend Maise was carried away in a spaceship. We need to find her before she's turned into a sex slave."

Zhiruto's stomach clenched. He'd been so concerned with escaping Earth, he hadn't considered that the slavers Agent Randall had been meeting were likely still on the planet.

Arazhi asked, "Why do you think she was abducted?"

"Pepper and I tracked her to a field by the pulp mill." Pepper's muzzle appeared briefly on the interface. "We found a spaceship. A weird purple thing that looked like a rosebud. It flew away before I could stop it. Can you track it down?"

The prince grimaced and shook his head. "Tracking a ship after it enters FTL is nearly impossible. We'll scour the shipping lanes, but I'm afraid you should prepare for the worst."

Georgie shook her head and stepped forward, a spike of anxiety slamming into Zhiruto. "No! We have to find her."

"There must be something you can do," Loragriffin added.

Zhiruto snatched the data pad from his prince's grip, turning it so he could look into Loragriffin's chocolate brown eyes. "This is my fault, Loragr—Lora." He caught himself before he said her full name. "I will find her, I swear to you. If it takes the rest of my life, I will find her."

CHAPTER EIGHTEEN

Lora stepped off the spaceship onto the ramp, gaping at the spectacular blue forest all around the landing pad. The wedding was in a few days, and she'd come to Kirenai Prime to help Georgie with last minute details.

Three weeks had passed since she'd spoken to Zhiruto, and since then, his updates on the search for Maise came through Georgie. If Lora asked to speak to him directly, she was told he was otherwise occupied. *Classic blowoff.* But she couldn't blame him. She'd acted without thinking, without giving him time to properly explain. She was pretty sure she might've called him disgusting. If their roles were reversed, she'd probably give him the cold shoulder, as well.

But she couldn't get him out of her head. *Does he even still think of me?*

"Please proceed. I will bring your bags." A blue alien with long eyestalks and fingers like a gecko gestured down the ramp. The small crowd of Georgie's extended family was shuffling across the tarmac toward the huge stone palace like a flock of confused geese.

"Thank you," Lora replied in strange syllables that definitely weren't English; during the two-day trip here, she'd received a chip that allowed her to not only understand but also speak other languages.

She gripped Pepper's leash and moved forward. The dog stayed close to her side, ears pricked and nose sniffing a mile a minute. She'd been a bit dubious about bringing Pepper, but with Maise still missing, she didn't want to leave her fur baby at the kennel.

Variously shaped and colored aliens had gathered on the tarmac to either side of a path kept open by two orderly rows of guards. Many onlookers held parasols or wore large hats, and as the sun beat down on the top of her head, she understood why. She'd been warned the planet was hot, but now she wondered if her suitcase full of strappy tank tops and shorts had been the right choice—even SPF 100 wouldn't protect any exposed skin from this sun.

Ahead, the looming stone walls of the palace were covered in blue vines and magenta flowers. The massive purple doors looked like they were made of the same material as the spaceship she'd ridden to get here and opened to a courtyard shaded by tall blue trees. Gravel that looked like pearls created pathways through the moss growing around the bases of the trunks, and small yellow flowers sprouted with abandon across the grounds.

She'd barely taken two steps inside when Georgie broke from the swarm of her relatives and swept in for a hug. "Lora!"

"Georgie!" Lora squeezed her friend back, delighted to see her in person at last. "I can't believe I'm walking on an alien planet."

"I know right?" Pepper was having a conniption, whining and wiggling in her excitement. Georgie bent and rubbed her ears. "Hi, Pepper. How are you, girl?"

Georgie's dad came over, a gleam of sweat sheening his bald head. "Georgie, Aunt Bev has some questions about sleeping arrangements."

"Of course," Georgie said. "Let me show you the way."

Lora'd been cooped up on a ship with Georgie's family for two days, and though she didn't mind them in limited doses, she was ready for a breather. The shade here in the courtyard was nice, so she let the family go on without her. Pepper tugged her toward a small brook and lapped up a drink, then squatted and did her business on the moss.

Cringing, Lora glanced around to see if anyone had noticed. She didn't have any cleanup bags. But a stocky blue alien with massive sideburns seemed to appear out of nowhere and cleaned it up as if this sort of thing happened every day.

"Thank you," she said.

He bowed and moved on without a word.

She entered a small doorway into the palace where the others had disappeared. The minute she stepped inside, Pepper let out an excited whine and started pulling toward an open doorway to the left. The hall was a straight shot forward, and the noise the family was making would be easy enough to follow, so she let Pepper pull her over to see what was inside.

A familiar set of broad shoulders and long blue hair stood like a statue in the middle of what looked suspiciously like a small, unlit storage room. *Zhiruto.*

He wore a form-fitting white tunic and slim black pants with orange piping down the front crease.

Lora couldn't seem to inhale. Pepper's leash slipped from her numb fingers and the dog lunged forward, her entire body wriggling with joy.

Reaching down to rub the dog's head, Zhiruto didn't break his gaze from Lora's. "Lora."

His use of only her first name felt like a punch in the gut. She found herself saying, "You can call me Loragriffin if you prefer."

Something in his eyes shifted, a flash of emotion that was gone as soon as it had appeared. "I haven't yet located your friend. Please forgive me."

She shook her head and stepped forward, unsure how to respond. He was so stiff. So formal. The room was tiny, and his spicy, masculine scent permeated the air. "I believe you're trying. But I also know Prince Arazhi said it might be impossible."

"I won't stop until I find her." Taking a backward step, he edged around her and left the room.

Trembling, Lora remained still, trying to process what had just happened. Why had he been hiding in a storage room? The most logical explanation was that he was trying to avoid bumping into her. She rubbed the back of her neck. This was going to be a long and agonizing visit if he couldn't even manage to look at her.

Feeling shaky and uncertain, she hurried down the hall toward the chattering voices of Georgie's family.

The next week was a flurry of activity helping Georgie finalize things for the wedding. The few times Zhiruto was in the same room with them, he barely looked at her and always found an excuse to escape as soon as possible. Even Georgie noticed the tension, despite being wrapped up in her planning.

"What's going on between you and Zhiruto?" Georgie asked as she stood still for the dressmaker's final adjustments. Her bridal gown was gossamer thin, and millions of pearls had been affixed to the surface using some sort of alien technology to keep them from weighing the fabric down.

Lora shook her head. She hadn't told her friend anything because she didn't want her drama to ruin Georgie's big event. There would be time after the wedding. "I can't talk about it yet."

Georgie's pale eyebrows rose. "I can ask Arazhi to dismiss him until after the wedding."

"No!" Lora grabbed her friend's hand, receiving an annoyed glare from the dressmaker weaving a line of pearls along the hem. "Please don't say anything."

"Then tell me what's going on."

Lora looked away. "It's complicated. I promise I'll tell you later, okay? Let's just concentrate on you and the wedding."

Georgie let out a sigh. "All right. But if you change your mind, let me know."

Forcing a weak smile, Lora nodded. "Thank you."

That night was the rehearsal dinner, and after several run-throughs in the enormous amphitheater where the wedding was to be held, everyone headed to a small banquet hall in the palace. Georgie's Aunt Bev clucked over everything like a mother hen and had insisted on a formal seating arrangement. Which of course placed Lora smack dab next to Zhiruto at the dining table. Her heartbeat fluttered so erratically she thought she might pass out as she settled into the seat next to him.

He wore somewhat human-looking clothing, and the white button-down shirt hugged his biceps and shoulders as if they were tailor-made just for him. He'd pulled his long blue hair into a man bun, and the blue stubble along his jaw had been well-trimmed to frame his sensuous lips. Not that he turned her way to allow her a full assessment. He kept his gaze straight ahead, and the rigid set of his shoulders and corded lines of his neck very clearly conveyed his displeasure at her nearness.

She picked at the strange food on her plate, her appetite non-existent. Everyone laughed and chattered around them and their bubble of silence. The carbonated drink they were serving reminded her of champagne, but all she wanted was a beer. Which, of course, made her remember Zhiruto tilting back the bottle at her house. Made her long to go back in time and have a do-over.

Then an epiphany washed through her. She was stewing over what a man thought of her—just like her mother. The exact opposite of who she'd sworn to be. She shouldn't blame herself for his responses. She was the one who'd been wronged when he mate-bonded her without permission, and Zhiruto had no right to treat her like a pariah—to refuse to look at her or even speak to her.

For the first time all night she turned to look directly at him. "You could at least pretend to make small talk."

His throat moved in a swallow. Slowly, he pivoted to face her, all restrained muscle and broody eyes. "If you wish. What would you like to discuss?"

Her mouth went dry. *God dammit, why does he have to be so spectacularly handsome?* She clutched at the gossamer threads of her indignation. "Well, you might start by apologizing."

"For what?"

"For avoiding me. Everyone notices, and it's embarrassing."

His gaze roamed her face as if he was trying to memorize every curve and hollow. "I apologize. I find it difficult to be near you, but I will try harder if that is what you want."

She swallowed. He couldn't stand to be near her? Her heart felt like it was made of glass and was about to shatter. "Well, being around you is no walk in the park for me, either."

He leaned forward a fraction, still looking at her face. "I can't stop thinking about you."

A jolt of awareness raced through her. Her breath caught, and she had to force out a response. "In a good way or a bad way?"

"Both. I'm truly sorry I rushed our courtship." Beneath the table, his leg touched hers. Stayed there.

Oh, God, there was that giddy, fluttery feeling all over again. "I don't think you can call our time together a courtship."

His hand slipped from the tabletop and rested gently on her thigh. Heat from his palm seemed to radiate straight into her belly, and her nipples hardened. He licked his lips, and she couldn't help staring at the glide of his blue tongue over his sensuous mouth. "I would very much like your permission to try again."

The suddenness of this change frightened her and thrilled her at the same time. She glanced toward the others, who seemed oblivious to the sexual tension circulating between her and Zhiruto. They had a connection even she couldn't deny. A connection she craved. She met his gaze again from beneath her lashes and nodded. "Let's talk about it after the wedding."

His hand withdrew, leaving her bereft, but her heart swelled at the change in his demeanor. He smiled at her, actually smiled. "As you wish, Loragriffin."

CHAPTER NINETEEN

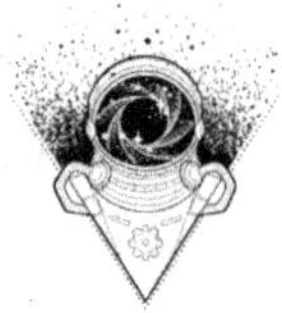

Zhiruto didn't sleep a single minute between the rehearsal dinner and the wedding. Loragriffin was giving him a second chance. Whatever it took, however long she needed, he would find a way to be by her side. She made him want to be the best mate possible, and he would never stop seeking to please her.

He performed his duties for the prince, making sure everything was secure for the wedding. With over fifty-thousand citizens in attendance, he'd arranged many layers of protection to keep the royal couple safe. Now, standing beside his prince at the altar, he was impatient for the ceremony to be over so he could once more focus on his mate.

Loragriffin emerged ahead of the bride and glided down the aisle toward them. His cock hardened at the sight of her shapely legs appearing and disappearing through the long slit in the skirt of her magenta gown. Not even the bride in all her splendor could eclipse the stunning beauty of his mate, and he kept his gaze on Loragriffin during the entire ceremony.

She shot him shy glances throughout, and he could feel her yearning for him within his Iki'i. He'd kept himself closed off from her ever since their meeting in the supply room the day she'd arrived. Now he reveled in her attention. He would not waste another moment of their time together.

The wedding official pronounced the royal couple husband and wife, and Arazhi swept Georgie into a kiss that made the amphitheater thunder with applause from the audience. Then they turned and hurried toward the carriage Zhiruto had arranged to take the four of them away. Georgie had insisted on something called a "honeymoon," although apparently no honey or moon were required. He and Loragriffin would escort the royal couple to a secure location and remain nearby for the duration.

And he planned to use every scrap of free time wooing his mate back into his arms.

As thousands of glowing balloons fell from the amphitheater ceiling and the crowd continued its deafening roar of approval, he stepped toward Loragriffin and held out an arm.

She beamed at him with tears in her eyes. "That was so beautiful."

"Yes." He threaded her arm around his and led her down the path behind the prince and his mate.

He'd arranged for multiple carriages to act as decoys and ushered his mate into the one with the royal couple. As the carriage started forward and the royal couple were engrossed looking into each other's eyes, he turned to Loragriffin. "Are you ready to talk, Loragriffin?"

She smiled, affection warming his Iki'i. "Shut up and kiss me, Zhiruto."

Enraptured by the permission to touch her again, he slid his palm along her jaw to cup the back of her neck. Her skin was so soft, her hair like fine silken threads between his fingers. She was delicate yet strong. Resilient in ways he'd never imagined. That she was willing to even think about forgiving him for what he'd done was a miracle, and he would cherish her every glance, her every word.

But right now, she didn't want to speak. She leaned into him, chin upturned, and he brushed his lips over hers before claiming her mouth in a penetrating kiss.

EPILOGUE

Lora tossed the last bite of her *kazhitu* bun to Pepper and sipped the cool, fruity drink the funny alien named Deshel had given her. He reminded her of a house elf from *Harry Potter*, and she was tempted to give him a sock every time she saw him. But apparently slavery was an accepted thing on this side of the galaxy, and people willingly—even gladly—entered into contractual servitude.

Not Maise, though. Lora looked up at the brightening sky, feeling guilty for sitting here being waited on by servants while Maise was...

Lora didn't want to think about what Maise might be enduring.

"What are you thinking, Loragriffin?" Zhiruto set aside his data pad. They'd been working on open communication since getting back together; there had been too much misunderstanding between them already, even with his ability to sense her emotions.

"Worrying about Maise." She'd given up her job at the precinct to join a galactic task force focused on finding abducted women. Her team had managed to track down and rescue several human women, but none had been her friend.

He moved his chair closer and put an arm around her shoulders. He didn't say anything, just held her. They'd already been through his guilt and her worry a million times, and he knew all he could offer was a hug.

The cell phone in her pocket started playing *Jaws*, and she groaned. Her mom still insisted on using her cell number to reach her, and Zhiruto had arranged for calls to be routed through the interstellar communication relays to reach her. Although Lora would've have been just as happy to ignore it, Zhiruto insisted family was important, so she answered without looking. "Hey, Mom."

"Lora?" Static made the breathless voice unrecognizable, but she could tell it wasn't her mother.

"Yes? Who is this?"

"It's Maise."

"Maise!" Lora pulled the phone from her ear to look at her friend's face on the display. "Where are you? Are you all right?"

Maise's raven hair hung loose around her face, and her eyes were red as if from crying. "Lora, we need your help."

IROTH

Iroth is stranded on a backwater planet called Earth. Forced to assume the shape of one of the human's primitive four-legged pets, he seeks temporary refuge with a breathtaking human female - and his plan to escape goes to the dogs...

CHAPTER ONE

Keeping his Iki'i shielded so any nearby Kirenai couldn't identify him, Iroth adjusted the formal human clothing covering his matrix and took a moment to gather his senses. Using the teleport always left him woozy, and the transportation web around Earth had obviously been set up in a hurry, without the usual buffers to mitigate discomfort.

He inhaled slowly. The warm night air was full of the sound of chirping insects. Beneath his feet, fine blades of vegetation had been shorn to an even length, though he couldn't discern the color in the feeble light coming from the poles several paces away. A few other Kirenai in the shape of blue humans were already moving along a concrete path toward the sounds of a gathering crowd.

He straightened his shoulders and stepped onto the trail. Tonight, he was on an exclusive guest list full of high-ranking dignitaries and wealthy merchants. The teal-blue human shape he now wore was similar to the one he grew up using—his mother was Fogarian—though his current form was taller, less hairy, and lacked claws and fangs. But it wasn't the shape that made him uncomfortable, it was the role he needed to play.

Normally, he preferred to do his jobs as a servant or underling, blending in with the natives. He was a *burendo*, able to change both color and shape, though for this job he was to be obviously Kirenai. He charged his clients exorbitant prices, making a very comfortable living infiltrating events to gather diplomatic intel or smuggling contraband. Tonight he was after different cargo. *Live* cargo. And the only reason he'd agreed was because the purchase would be legal, for a client who didn't want the transaction made in his own name.

Striding along the path, Iroth examined a pair of females who stood shoulder-to-shoulder as they watched the guests pass by. He'd worked with the black market long enough to have heard rumors about human captives capable of inciting passion in the most reticent partners. Tonight marked the first legal event for human bondservant contracts, and competition would be high.

The females he looked at now each wore a long dark gown, one with sparkles and the other with a skirt that turned sheer at mid-thigh to reveal shapely legs. *Not bad looking*, he acknowledged, smiling at them as he passed. The one in the sparkly dress locked eyes with him, and he opened his Iki'i briefly to feel her emotions.

She was curious and a bit nervous. He understood how she felt—the first job he'd hired himself out for had been thrilling and nerve-wracking, and he'd been glad when it was over. He could hardly imagine wanting to sell himself long-term to a single person.

He continued past them, heading toward a raised platform illuminated by lights. His gut churned and his matrix wanted to contract into the smallest form possible at the sight. No matter how many times he saw a stage, he always battled those feelings. *You're not revealing yourself to anyone,* he reminded himself. He wouldn't be changing color or escorted away by his parents in shame.

No one here knows what you are.

Still, he sat at a table at the outer edge of the audience, taking some comfort in knowing he could bolt at a moment's notice. Although the emperor had forbidden ship landings on the planet and restricted access through the teleportation web, Iroth had managed to land an unmanned, cloaked ship outside the city several days ago. He'd only used the transportation web tonight in order to be documented as a bidding guest. But ever since he'd had a job go sideways and leave him stuck in the slums on a G'naxian moon for six revolutions, he made sure he always had alternate ways to get off-planet.

A human male approached his table carrying a tray with tall thin glasses of a golden beverage, and another human offered a selection of local food. Iroth politely took one of each but set them aside untouched. He'd never enjoyed foreign foods very much, plus he was too busy examining the human females gathering to one side of the stage. Each one possessed a quadruped, either on a leash or cradled like a baby. He hadn't been warned this species required accommodations for an additional life form, and made a mental note to demand additional payment when he delivered the female.

A small white quadruped put his front paws against the legs of the female holding its leash, stubby tail wagging. It reminded him of a baby *nezumi* he'd found as a child, a downy creature with a stubby tail and long floppy ears. It had been cowering in one of the space station's condenser pipes. Most residents considered the creatures pests, and the poorer families on the station hunted and ate them. But he'd put the baby into his pocket and taken it home, sneaking it crumbs of their precious food. When his father found out, he was furious. They'd eaten *nezumi* soup that very night.

Iroth shook off the memory and refocused on the human females. Now was not the time to fall into dark thoughts.

A black-haired beauty in a sleeveless burgundy dress caught his eye. The fabric was shimmery without being gaudy, and detailed with layered pleats across the bodice and a smooth skirt that draped effortlessly from her hips. Her rich golden brown skin reminded him of well-polished *amai* wood and made him wonder if she smelled as sweet.

The quadruped on her leash had thick red-and-black fur over its back and a heavy white ruff that continued down to its front feet. The animal's mouth hung open in what looked like a smile, and though his Iki'i was closed, he imagined the complete adoration the creature must have for the female.

Bid on her, a voice inside him urged. He pictured how she'd look splayed across the silken sheets of his bed, dewy-eyed and yearning for his next touch. Except he wasn't buying a bondservant for himself. His client wanted breeding stock, and the woman in the burgundy dress deserved better. He forced his gaze away, examining the other females.

The lights went down, and the auction began with the booming voice of an auctioneer rattling off information too fast for his universal translator to process. Spotlights appeared across the stage, and the women paraded out with their pets as a group, performing some sort of rehearsed strut in time to a pulsing tune. Then they retreated to the sidelines.

Iroth folded his hands in his lap and waited as the women reappeared one-by-one, letting the first two come and go without bidding. The guests were competitive, and the bids were high. Iroth's client had provided a generous allowance for the auction and said Iroth could keep whatever he didn't spend, but at this rate, winning a female would require him to spend the full amount. *Another reason to charge extra for the pet.*

Sighing, he bid on the next woman and lost. He eventually won a small female in a pink dress named Susan, who had luscious curves and perfectly straight white teeth. She bounced down the stage steps, followed by a black quadruped with droopy ears and a long tail. The animal trotted up and stuck its head on his lap while the female set a tall green bottle and two empty glasses on the table. "Ish fremmich zeze genzuln!"

He blinked, trying to decipher her words while pushing the quadruped's muzzle out of his crotch. The damn universal translator must be on the fritz. Glancing around to be certain any nearby Kirenai were otherwise occupied, he unshuttered his Iki'i a fraction, hoping it would allow him to glean some of her meaning. She was friendly and seemed to want to begin her bondservant duties by providing him a drink.

He smiled and nodded.

She set the bottle down and pulled out the chair next to him, scooting it so close that they brushed elbows. Her animal lay on the ground under the table, hot breath fanning his shins. Now that he had secured a female, he was ready to depart, but it would draw undue attention to leave before the auction was over. So he continued to smile and nod as the female chattered incoherently.

On stage, the woman in the burgundy dress appeared, knuckles white as she gripped the leash to her quadruped in both hands. The animal seemed to sense her mood, and nudged the back of her knee, herding her forward. His estimate of the creature's value increased.

She slowly walked to the front of the stage as two Kirenai and a Khargal began a bidding war for her contract. He could barely contain himself from joining in. But what would he do with a second female? After a few volleys of bidding, the auctioneer declared a Kirenai at a table in the center the winner, and the woman descended the steps to greet the new owner of her contract. Jealousy heated Iroth's center.

The female he'd purchased nudged his arm. Turning his head to look at her, his mouth collided with something that left a paste on his lips. He drew back instinctively, realizing she held a brown disk of food topped with a pale creamy substance.

"Servi." She cringed and popped the item into her mouth, chewing. "Is good," she said around the food.

She was pulsing with anxiety, struggling hard to make him like her. He licked the residue from his lips. The flavor wasn't unpleasant, slightly sweet with a hint of oil. Her wash of relief reached him, and she smiled, raising her flute expectantly. He lifted his, and she clinked the glasses together before drinking. He sampled the bubbly alcohol, finding it acceptable, though he preferred tea.

The auction ended on an overpriced female in a blue dress, garnering a deafening roar of applause from the audience. Then a band struck up a lively tune.

"I leeb dis zong! Tancen?" Without waiting for his reply, his female grabbed his hand and pulled him toward a grassy area where two other couples were moving in time to the music.

Reminding himself this was likely the last evening the female might ever have on her home planet, he let her guide him through some rhythmic steps.

A scream shattered the music.

Iroth twisted toward the sound and saw a woman backing away from her chair in horror.

At the table next to her, a Kirenai half rose to his feet, quivered for a fraction of a second, and collapsed into his resting state. Another woman fell over backward in her chair.

Iroth stared, horrified. Kirenai didn't shift to their resting states in public. Ever.

Humans began screaming and fleeing as Kirenai at other tables also collapsed. The two Khargals grabbed their females and flew up to the stage. A Fogarian tunneled into the ground. The two Kirenai who'd been dancing next to Iroth shuddered, turning into puddles right before his eyes.

He opened his Iki'i to the fullest, looking for an explanation. *Are they dead?* His species weren't easy to kill. But he could detect no emotion, no signature coming from the Kirenai nearby. This was a massacre unlike any he'd known.

He looked for his female, intending to flee with her, and realized she was gone. He glanced back toward the tables. Only two other Kirenai remained standing besides himself. The nearest one stepped closer, and Iroth felt the sharp prod of inquiry along with a sense of ammonia against his Iki'i as the Kirenai sought his identity.

Kuzara, his Iki'i was open. He shut it down, but not before sensing a brief whiff of satisfaction from the other.

Iroth's insides quivered. *You're going to be blamed for this.* No one trusted a *burendo*.

Then, to his relief, the Kirenai shuddered and collapsed along with the others.

Feeling queasy, Iroth glanced toward the single remaining Kirenai who was now striding his direction with fury in his gaze. *You can't stick around for questioning.* He had to blend in. It was what he was good at.

Taking a deep breath, he sealed his Iki'i deep inside and let his matrix relax, joining the rest of the fallen. Only a medical scanner could now tell he was alive.

He hoped he'd get a chance to slip away unnoticed before the real investigation began.

CHAPTER TWO

Maise pressed her back against the stage and gaped at the puddle of goo that moments ago had been her alien date. Her sheltie, Bixby, stood steadfastly at her side, warm thick fur pressed against her skirt as people screamed and ran, toppling chairs and shattering champagne flutes. Mounds of quivering alien remains dotted the grass.

She'd been the first volunteer for her friend Georgie's charity auction, glad to help the animal shelter outside of donating services from her pet grooming business. The event had brought in an exorbitant amount of money.

Except dead aliens can't pay. She felt guilty about the thought even as it flitted through her mind.

An escaped poodle sped toward her, and Maise instinctively stepped on its leash, stopping it in its tracks. The owner raced up, breathless, thanked her, and grabbed the leash before continuing her flight.

Maise returned her attention to the puddle near her feet. Was there anything she could do to help? She wasn't a doctor, but had spent the past eight years taking night classes to become a vet. Gathering her courage, she stepped closer to for a better view and grimaced. All the veterinary training in the world couldn't prepare her for how to perform triage on something that looked like a giant blue amoeba. She shuddered and backed away again. No way was she going to touch it without gloves.

"Sorry, dude. Wish I could help." She bit her lip and looked around, hoping to spot one of her friends. Everyone had already fled.

The two horned, gray aliens had jumped onto the stage behind her and now roared in what she could only assume was aggression.

She decided it was time for her to get out of here, too.

Bixby stayed in a close heel as they avoided the various splotches of blue goo scattered around the tables. There was no way any of these poor aliens were alive. She pressed a hand over her middle, wondering how many had been disintegrated.

As they passed by one of the tables, Bixby paused and emitted a low whine. The sheltie had failed service training as a medical alert dog because she was too friendly with people, but she still had a keen sense for when something was wrong with someone.

Maise stopped, wondering if she'd found a survivor. Lifting the edge of the tablecloth, she peered beneath it.

An enormous Great Dane Maise emerged, its gray fur covered in slick, dark blue goo.

She recoiled. "What have you been rolling in?"

The Great Dane froze, trembling.

"Aw, you poor scared baby." She unhooked Bixby's leash and created a noose, knowing the sheltie would stay by her side without restraint. Patting her thigh, she said, "Come here, Big Boy."

The massive dog didn't move, regarding her with turquoise eyes. He didn't look aggressive, but she knew better than to assume he wasn't. A dog his size could probably take her out with one swipe of his massive paw.

"The big ones are always the shyest, aren't they?" She spoke in a soft voice, maintaining eye contact. "Come on, Big Boy."

The dog inched forward as if pulled by a thread, stopping just out of range. His tail wagged slightly.

Bixby darted out behind him and nipped at the Dane's heels, driving him forward. Heart racing, Maise looped her spare leash around his neck and cinched it, preparing to keep the bigger dog from turning on Bixby.

The Great Dane gave the sheltie a withering glance and turned back to Maise. She gripped the flimsy leash, knowing it wouldn't stop him if he really wanted to get away. He must've slipped his collar somehow. "Stick with me, Big Boy. We're gonna find your momma."

"Ma'am, are you all right?" A voice behind her made her jump, and she turned to see a man in a dark suit approaching. A helicopter thumped past overhead.

"I'm fine." A small cluster of women moved past her, shepherded toward the stage by another man in a suit. "What's going on?"

"We're gathering survivors. Please come with me."

Survivors. Her stomach churned thinking about how many people she'd seen dissolve. "How many are dead?"

"Don't worry, ma'am, it looks like just the blue aliens were affected."

She didn't like his cavalier attitude, but didn't have a chance to respond as a labradoodle ran up to them dragging its leash. She grabbed it, adding the dog to her menagerie before joining the other women at a table that'd been pulled away from the others. The gray aliens were no longer on stage, and armed men in uniforms were extending ribbons of caution tape between stakes in the grass.

"Please hand over your cell phones," said a man with a clipboard and a bin.

"Why?" asked one of the other dates from the auction, planting her hands on her hips.

"A matter of national security, ma'am." The man held out his hand expectantly. "Please don't make us search you."

The woman harrumphed and handed over her phone. Maise reluctantly did so, too, a sense of foreboding settling over her. She'd seen enough TV shows to suspect she could end up locked in some secret government facility where no one saw the light of day. *I wish I'd called Mom and Dad one last time.*

A familiar "baroo!" split the air, and Maise turned to see a Redbone Coonhound leading a guard toward them.

"Pepper!" she called, scanning the dimness behind him for her friend Lora.

The coonhound pulled the man straight over and began nuzzling Bixby.

"This dog belong to you?" the guard asked.

Heart thundering, she said, "She's my friend's."

He shoved the end of the leash into Maise's hand. "Here. You can take her then."

"Wait, what about—" But the man was already striding away. She scowled. "Asshole."

The dogs had to sniff each other, and within moments, all four leads were tangled. Maise moved to a grassy spot nearby to give the animals more room to play. At the edge of the police tape, someone else was arguing about having her cell phone taken, and a woman in a black strapless dress sat at a table with her face in her hands.

A tall, blue, bare-chested alien approached, escorted by two suited goons. A familiar auburn-haired woman in a crimson gown limped beside him.

Pepper bayed in recognition, and relief flooded Maise at the sight of her friend. "Lora! Over here!"

Lora was a police officer, and if she had anything to say about things, nobody would be locked in a secret government facility. Her friend met her at the police tape. "Thank God you found Pepper." Lora bent to let the wriggly whining coonhound nuzzle her ear. "Can you watch her for a bit longer? I'm on duty."

"Sure." Maise had faith that her friend would soon set things right. "Whatever I can do to help."

Maise went back to the grassy area with the four dogs. Pepper and the labradoodle resumed rolling around, chewing on each other's ears. Usually, Bixby liked to be in the middle of the fray, but she snuggled up next to the Great Dane who had laid down with his massive head morosely on his front paws.

Bixby kept checking in with Maise, as if expecting her to do something.

Lowering herself to sit cross-legged on the ground next to the giant dog, Maise gingerly rubbed behind his ears. His fur felt sticky and the slight odor of men's cologne hung around him —either the mess he'd rolled around in had been wearing it, or his owner was male. *What if his master was someone who'd melted?* Her chest tightened and tears pricked her eyes. "You worried about your master, Big Boy?"

He sighed, a shiver rolling across his sleek gray coat.

The other dogs wore themselves out, eventually lying down around her on the lawn. Maise grew sleepy, too, and lay back on the grass, wishing she could get out of this constricting dress. She startled awake at the sound of Lora's voice calling for attention nearby.

"We're going to speak to everyone individually about the events this evening," said Lora, addressing the gathered women. "Then we'll let you go home."

Maise headed over, and Lora reached for Pepper's leash. "Thanks for taking care of her, Maise. I'll talk to you first."

Several women grumbled about playing favorites, but Lora led her to a small table at the bottom of the stage stairs.

Maise looped the leashes of the other three dogs on the railing before joining her friend. "Do you know what happened to Georgie? I haven't seen her."

Their friend had planned the entire auction, but Maise hadn't seen her since the disaster. She hoped Georgie had been able to get away before things took a turn for the worse.

Lora rubbed the back of her neck. "She's, ah, on a space ship with an alien prince. I glimpsed her when Zhiruto Facetimed them or whatever aliens call it."

"A space ship?" Maise gasped, glancing toward the dark sky. The faintest glow of dawn lit the horizon. "Is she okay?"

"Yeah, I think so. At least, Zhiruto says she's not in danger."

Maise turned her gaze back to her friend. This was the second time Lora had mentioned that name. She thought of the shirtless alien Lora'd been walking beside earlier. "Who's Zhiruto? Your alien bodyguard?"

Lora flushed. "He's working for the prince. I'm just his NSA liaison."

Maise wiggled her eyebrows. Leading an investigation with a hot, shirtless guy was probably like a dream date for Lora. "Ooh la la."

Lora crossed her arms and scowled. "There are more than a dozen dead aliens only footsteps away. Definitely not the time to be thinking of hot guys."

"You're right." Maise dropped her gaze guiltily. "This entire thing is awful."

"Let's get on with a few questions so I can let you go home, okay?"

Maise nodded.

"Does everyone here seem normal to you? I'm looking for anyone who seems less shocked than they should be. Or more shocked. Anything strange at all."

Maise thought for a second. "I think people are acting pretty normal. Heather's been crying non-stop. Meg's her usual bossy self. I suppose Tammy's been a little quieter than usual, but I think she's in shock. I overheard someone say she and her date were kissing when it happened." She glanced to where poor Tammy sat with her knees up and a wool blanket over her shoulders. "You should probably talk to her next so she can get out of here."

"Thanks, Maise." Lora rose. "I'll let the guards know you're clear to leave."

"Thank you. Call me when you get a chance." Maise gathered the dogs and moved to the guard with the confiscated cell phones. She'd put the labradoodle and the Great Dane in the Yappy Hour kennels until she could swing by the shelter and borrow the chip scanner. Hopefully, she could get them back to their owners.

A man in a suit flashed her his NSA credentials, warned her not to speak to the press, and gave her a number to call immediately if she began to feel ill or unusual.

"You mean if I feel like I'm about to dissolve into a lump of Jell-O? Because I'm pretty certain no one had time to make a call before they dissolved."

The guard looked at her blandly. "If we thought you were in danger, we wouldn't allow you to leave."

Yet another guard escorted her to her Jeep in the parking lot and left her to load up the dogs. The back of her Jeep wouldn't hold all three animals, and she had to put the massive Great Dane into the passenger seat. It was now four in the morning, and all she wanted to do was sleep. She headed to the Yappy Hour and pulled up to the service entrance. With the enticement of a handful of kibble, the labradoodle pranced happily into a kennel. The Great Dane wasn't so easily swayed.

"Come on, Big Boy." She rattled a stainless steel dish. "Aren't you hungry?"

She could swear he shook his head no as he sat on the floor between the cages. He lay down with his head on his front paws.

Bixby nosed him, then began licking his face. Maise frowned. Bixby wasn't a licker, but it was what she'd been trained to do during her service days to alert her owner of an oncoming seizure.

What if whatever he rolled in is what's making him sick? "Oh, God. Bixby, no. Get back."

She pushed the sheltie aside. She had to get that stuff washed off before he became more seriously infected or infected anyone else.

Tugging on his leash, she got him to his feet and led him through the kennel area to the washing stations. She had the Dane hop onto the table and tied off the leash, then stepped out of her restrictive gown. There was no one else here, and Ted wouldn't be in until nine.

Dressed in nothing but a strapless bra and panties, she turned on the water.

CHAPTER THREE

Iroth's breath caught at the sight of the female's bare skin. Long, golden brown legs. A smooth flat abdomen with a perfectly dimpled navel. Pert breasts covered with brown fabric that he yearned to push aside so he could gaze at what lay beneath. *Kuzara,* how he wished he didn't have to hide behind his current shape.

The Great Dane had been an excellent choice for a disguise, despite how difficult it was to maintain a quadruped. He'd even felt a bit smug when the prince's bodyguard had looked straight at him and moved on. But as the night progressed, he'd begun feeling unwell. Keeping his matrix compressed into a smaller size was causing his exterior to leak interstitial fluid like a film of sweat, and he could no longer shield his Iki'i. His head throbbed, and he shivered with the need to resume a more familiar shape.

"It's okay, Big Boy. You'll feel better after we get you cleaned up," the woman called Maise said as she filled a bucket with soapy water.

He was glad the universal translator seemed to be working now, but despite the female's words, he felt her worry like a knife. Maise was as kind as she was beautiful. Her gentle touches behind his ears and the soothing tone of her voice made him want to curl up around the fullness of her body and enjoy her in other ways.

She poured warm water over his neck and shoulders. The soap smelled like sun-warmed citrus flowers, mingling with her feminine musk as she leaned close to scrub his coat with a red, nubby thing. Her touch along his back and over his sides felt so good. Under other circumstances, he would've enjoyed such attention. Returned it by stroking his palms over her curves, licking the tender spot between her breasts, wrapping his arms around her waist and pulling her close...

Kuzara. The core of his matrix roiled, seeking to resume an easier shape. His mouth was dry, and his eyes felt like they might explode from the growing pain in his head. He had to expand, to release himself from the confines of this quadruped body. The pressure was something he could no longer deny, witness or no witness.

With a shake that rolled through his shoulders and down his spine into his legs, he let himself shift.

"What the..." Maise dropped the nubby thing and stepped backward until her legs bumped the low table behind her.

He knelt with both palms planted against the stainless steel surface. Sudsy water dripped down his arms and legs, and he glared at his clawed blue hands, trying to make them more human. He'd transformed into his Fogarian body, an adult version of the one he'd grown up using, and was powerless at the moment to shift to a less familiar form.

"Help me," he said, staring downward at the table. If he spoke directly to her, she'd see his fangs, and he wasn't certain how she'd respond to that.

Maise hesitated only a heartbeat. "What can I do?"

"Water." His mouth felt dry, and it was the first thing he thought to ask for.

He snuck a glance as she hurried over to a desk where a monitor and keyboard were nearly buried in papers. She bent to open a small cube beneath it and returned with a plastic bottle. Uncapping it, she held it out. "Here."

He lifted a hand to take it and nearly fell on his face as his other palm skidded across the soapy table.

She reached out and caught his shoulder, helping him stay upright. She withdrew just as quickly, her uncertainty clashing against his Iki'i.

"Thank you," he said, still not looking at her as he settled back on his heels and tipped the bottle against his lips. The cool liquid burned all the way down his parched throat.

From the corner of his eye, he saw her attention fall to his lap and realized his genitalia were completely exposed. Luckily, the Fogarians were similar to humans in overall anatomy. But her interest made his cock stir.

She made a choked noise and her golden skin flushed russet.

Grabbing a nearby cloth, she clutched it over her half-clothed torso, then pointed to a hose nozzle at the head of the table. "You can rinse off if you want." She grabbed another handful of cloths. "And here are towels."

Disliking the way his hand shook in front of her, he reached for the nozzle. He felt woozy, unbalanced. He wanted her to see him as strong and in command. Squeezing the handle released a warm spray, but his exhaustion was too much. He dropped the nozzle, letting it swing back against the pipe with a clang, and fell forward onto one hand.

"Shit," she breathed and stepped forward.

Warm water sluiced over his shoulders and back. He closed his eyes as her fingers threaded the back of his curly hair and brushed along his thick sideburns with the spray, helping remove the soapy residue.

She set the nozzle back in its holder and draped a towel over his shoulders, rubbing gently to dry him off. Her touch was comforting. Even more so was her concern for him as she helped him step off the table and wrap a towel around his waist.

"Please tell me what's going on," she said. Though her voice and actions seemed calm, he sensed her inner turmoil, the trembling uncertainty of facing the unknown. He had to admire her strength.

He'd intended to slip away when her back was turned, and hadn't bothered to fabricate a cover story, but since it was obvious that he'd need to spend a little more time with her while he recovered, he knew he had to come up with something fast—if she learned he was a smuggler, she'd turn him in.

Stalling for time, he answered, "My name's Iroth."

"Okay, Iroth. We need to get you to a doctor."

"No. Human doctors can't help me. Please, I'm in danger. No one can know I'm here."

She frowned. "Why?"

He expected her to be wary, suspicious. But his Iki'i only sensed confusion and concern. A desire to tell her the truth infused him.

But he buttoned down the urge. No matter how understanding she seemed, once she understood what he was, she'd turn on him, just like everyone else. Most *burendos* were detected early and eradicated—he'd survived by being quick on his feet. And he had to do that now if he wanted to keep surviving.

He concentrated hard on retracting his pointed teeth, making his Fogarian face as human as possible before meeting her gaze. He'd heard the woman who interviewed Maise say that there'd been an assassination attempt on the prince. Perhaps he could use that information to keep her silent. "I was a decoy for the prince. He suspected an assassination attempt might happen."

Her marvelously green eyes widened. "Why didn't you come forward during the investigation?"

"I was instructed not to reveal my true identity to anyone," he lied. "The royal family doesn't know who to trust."

She covered her mouth, her distress palpable even without his Iki'i. "My friend Lora is helping one of his bodyguards. Do you think she's in danger?"

He shook his head. "I'm sure she's fine as long as she doesn't know anything that might compromise the prince."

Nodding, she offered him another towel.

He wrapped it around his waist, marveling at the ease of this conversation. He couldn't recall ever meeting anyone as inherently trusting, as innately *good,* as this human female. Guilt ebbed up his spine, a feeling he hadn't felt in a very long time.

But if he wanted to survive, he had no other choice but to deceive her. "I need a place to recover until I can get back to my ship."

She bit her bottom lip and nodded. "My apartment's upstairs. You can rest there for a while."

He let out a sigh of relief. "Thank you."

Leaning heavily on her shoulder, he exited the building and ascended an exterior staircase, clutching the towel around his waist. Her small quadruped followed close behind, satisfied the female had interpreted its signals.

They entered the domicile, and he collapsed onto a sofa, barely taking in the cluttered space. Maise offered him another drink and put a hand against his forehead.

He seldom got close enough to anyone to be touched, and his eyes drifted closed in satisfaction. It was hard to think of anything but her. He'd always taken for granted his natural Kirenai resiliency. "You really need a doctor. Are you sure there isn't anyone we can call?"

He shook his head and repeated, "No one can know I'm alive."

Sighing, she pulled a blanket from the back of the cushions

behind him and tucked the edges around his body. "I can't believe I'm doing this." She smiled wryly. "Don't you dare die on my couch."

He smiled back, gratified that she could find irony in the situation. Then he closed his eyes and hoped he wouldn't wake in a royal military brig.

CHAPTER FOUR

Ever since Mom started calling her a dog whisperer, Maise had been inclined to help any living thing; dogs, birds, even people. And one thing was sure—this alien needed her help.

She watched him sleep on her couch for a long time. It was difficult to believe he'd looked like a Great Dane less than an hour ago. If she hadn't seen him transform before her very eyes, she wouldn't have believed it herself.

At the moment, he didn't look at all dog-like. His features were broader than a human's and slightly flattened, and his dark blue facial hair reminded her of photos of her father back in the seventies when bushy sideburns were in style. Although his hands each had five fingers, his fingernails were curved and sharp like claws, and he had thick, fur-like hair on the backs of his knuckles.

Her attention drifted lower over the lap blanket that

barely covered his naked legs and towel-wrapped hips, remembering other parts of his anatomy she'd glimpsed. The very thick, dark blue mat of hair on his chest tapered toward his crotch, and she could still envision the massive shaft of his cock stirring to life under her gaze. Her body flushed as she realized he'd seen her nearly naked as well. A brief fantasy of what it might've been like to press their bodies together flitted across her mind.

She shook off the image, wondering what was wrong with her. She rarely liked hairy men, and this guy—no, this *alien*—had what looked like a pelt on portions of his body. Not to mention he'd been a dog not so very long ago. She shouldn't find him remotely attractive. Maybe it was because he smelled so damn good? The scent of men's cologne still hovered around him, a pleasing smell like musky pine that reminded her of walks in the woods. She'd always found good quality men's cologne a turn on.

Sighing, she tiptoed back to her bedroom, closed the door, and threw on a pair of leggings and a long tee shirt. Then she sat on the edge of the bed, staring at the nearest travel poster on her wall. What if he didn't get better? What if he died? She recalled with horrifying clarity the way her date had turned into gooey blue gel. She had to help Iroth before he got worse, while he still had a body to heal.

But she had no clue why he might be sick or if it was even related to what had happened to the others. She needed more information. *Lora's working with an alien.* Perhaps her friend could offer information that would help. Maise would simply need to be careful not to let anything slip about the alien on her couch in case the NSA had tapped their phones. She dialed Lora's cell.

"You've reached Officer Lora Griffin with the Springfield Police Department. Leave me a message and I'll get back to you."

Maise sighed and hung up. Lora was most likely still at the crime scene. She'd ring back as soon as she had a chance.

Looking around for Bixby, Maise realized the dog had stayed with Iroth. The sheltie was a lot like her, interested in people and driven to help. They'd met when Bixby's service animal trainer had brought the dog in for grooming. A service animal needed to stay focused on her owner, but every new person who walked in the door had garnered Bixby's attention. "I just can't train it out of her," the trainer complained. "She loves people too much. I think I'm going to have to list her for adoption."

"I'll take her," Maise offered, then cringed over the adoption cost. But she'd pulled together the money. All she knew was that she and Bixby understood each other on a fundamental level. They'd been constant companions ever since.

It made sense that Bixby wanted to help the alien as badly as Maise did. Either that, or the sheltie had a crush on the Great Dane.

Girl, same. That thought made Maise smirk, but she sobered quickly. A body double for a prince seemed like the perfect job for an alien who could change shape—until someone tried to assassinate him. Did Iroth look like the prince now, or was he in his own shape? "So weird," she muttered.

She rose from the bed and cracked open the door just as her

phone began to cluck like a mother hen. Quickly closing the door again, she answered, "Hi, Mom."

"Darling, did I leave my jacket at your house?"

Mom hadn't been to her apartment above Yappy Hour in over a year. Her progressing dementia made seeing the veterinary clinic she'd run for twenty years now relegated to pet grooming and boarding, no matter how often Maise assured her it was temporary.

Maise quickly texted her Dad—*On phone with Mom. She's confused.*—while still talking to her mom. "Are you and Dad going somewhere?"

"It's Sunday, Maise." The reproach in her mother's voice was clear. "Church starts in an hour and I'm supposed to do the reading. That's why I need my jacket."

She's dressing for church, she texted. "Ok, I'll look around for it. Have you eaten breakfast?"

There was a pause as Mom considered. "I don't remember."

Maise heard Dad's indistinct rumble in the background, and Mom replied to him, "I'll be there in a minute." Her voice once more returned to the phone. "What did you need, darling?"

"You answered my question." Deflecting her had been easy for once. "Thanks, Mom. Love you."

"I love you too."

As she hung up, Maise bit her lip and stared at her phone. "She's getting worse." Dad could not take care of her on his own forever.

But that was a problem for another day. Right now, there was an alien on her couch who needed help. She dialed Lora again and still got her voicemail. Hanging up, she texted, *call me,* and grabbed a blanket from her bed before returning to the living room.

Bixby watched from where she was curled up on the floor near Iroth's head. The tip of her tail wagged slightly in greeting.

"Good dog." Maise lay the bigger blanket on top of the small lap blanket, wishing she could take his temperature or other vitals to understand what might be wrong. But she didn't know what a normal temp would be for an alien, let alone pulse rate or respiration. He seemed peaceful enough lying there.

She put the back of her hand against his forehead. As before, he felt slightly feverish compared to a human, but that could be normal.

For now, she set the water bottle within his reach, rubbed behind Bixby's ears, and retrieved her notes from her toxicology class. One of the top reasons pets needed urgent care was because they'd eaten something poisonous. Perhaps she'd find something useful for Iroth in her notes.

She kicked up the footstool on her recliner and began reading. Her eyes were bleary, though, and her attention kept drifting to the couch. She watched his chest move slowly up and down, reassured by its steadiness. Slowly, her eyes drifted closed.

CHAPTER FIVE

Iroth battled fevered dreams of himself wearing traditional Kirenai *happa* bark armor and being pursued by a giant, growling *nezumi*. Of shifting and shifting and shifting. All while being watched by a pair of green eyes. In between, he woke to water against his lips. A female's gentle hands and soothing words.

He didn't know how long he lay there, fighting to keep his matrix cohesive, but he finally cracked open his lids and kept them open.

Sunlight slanted through the slats covering a nearby window, low on the horizon, and it took several minutes to remember where he was. On the wall facing him hung a media screen with multiple wires snaking down to small electronics on a low table below. A piece of plush furniture suited for a single person sat beside him. Another wall held a set of shelves overflowing with books, and on the opposite side of the room four chairs made of what looked like sticks surrounded a small table scattered with more books and papers.

He pushed the blanket aside and sat up. He felt like *kuzara*, but the pounding in his head seemed to have receded. A female's scent hovered around him, making his cock stir despite his weakened state. *Maise.* The human had placed an extra blanket over him at some point, and a bottle of water waited on the floor beside the couch. He drained it before attempting to stand.

Maise's quadruped, Bixby, rose to greet him, bumping her muzzle beneath his palm. The dog was as nurturing as the human, and he could sense she wanted approval, so he patted the fur between her pointed ears. Was it morning or evening? It didn't matter. It was time for him to leave.

Then he realized he couldn't. The moment he left, Maise would call the authorities. Which left him in an unfortunate position. He needed everyone to believe he'd died with the others. To keep his secret, he had to silence her. He wasn't a killer, which left him only one option—kidnap her. *She'll be worth a lot of money on the black market.*

A fierce protectiveness rose inside him at the thought. Humans were traded on the galactic black market as breeders, and Maise deserved better. She'd rescued him, sheltered him without hesitation, probably saved his life. But what the *kuzara* was he going to do with her if not sell her?

He'd come up with something later. Right now, he had to figure out how to take her with him.

The domicile appeared to extend beyond this room, so he padded toward the hallway, the nappy fabric beneath his feet reminding him of the moss on Kirenai Prime. Not that he'd spent much time there, but when he'd visited, he'd always enjoyed the lushness of his species' home world. His mother's planet, the one of his early youth, had been one of rocks and lichen.

He reached the kitchen, and the room seemed to spin around him, forcing him to pause with one arm against a cupboard. Bixby nosed his hand as if trying to tell him something, and he realized he was starving. Whatever had been wrong with him had sapped his strength. He would require sustenance to reach his ship.

But many species shared communal space, and he didn't want any surprises; he couldn't eat until he'd examined the rest of the domicile.

Passing the kitchen, he headed toward two open doors at the end of the hall. The first was a bedroom lit by filtered light from a curtained window. A large mattress took up most of the space, and a dresser against the far with a drawer hanging open. Maise lay on top of the covers, face relaxed in sleep and one hand clasped over the top of a notebook.

He stood in the doorway, admiring her finely defined nose adorned with a sparkling gem at the crease of one nostril, strong eyebrows, and perfectly fanned crescents of eyelashes. He yearned to run a finger along the seam between her full lips, to see if they were as soft as he imagined. His gaze drifted down to where her nipples jutted like beacons against the thin fabric of her pale yellow shirt. Shapely legs ended with bare feet, toenails painted a deep burgundy.

Every aspect of her was breathtaking, and his cock stirred

against the rough fabric of the towel around his waist. He looked down, suddenly self-conscious about his Fogarian body. His most naturally assumed form was also the one he most avoided. It had too many memories attached. And while Maise had been curious about him, he couldn't recall feeling attraction.

His throat tightened as he realized he wanted her to desire him. *It would make it easier to get her to my ship.*

Peeking into the other open door, he recognized the windowless room as a lavatory. He searched the nearby wall for atmospheric controls and found a pair of simple toggles that activated a light and a fan. A wide mirror spanned the wall behind the sink.

He quickly stepped inside and closed the door before Bixby could follow. The animal was intelligent, and Iroth preferred to make adjustments to his form in private. He was immediately struck by the image of his father looking back at him: flat features, thick sideburns, heavy brow. He grimaced and leaned closer to the mirror, noticing that his teeth were blunt, more like a human's than a Fogarian's. At least he'd managed to hide his fangs.

Concentrating, he retracted his bushy sideburns and the pelt covering his chest, leaving only a cap of thick hair over his scalp. He also changed his claws to flattened fingernails. He leaned heavily on the countertop, panting. The effort of changing had almost been too much to handle. But now when he looked at himself, he might pass for human—except for his color. His skin was still a deep teal, with dark blue hair and eyes.

He looked down at the towel that parted below his hips, showing off one of his muscled thighs. He often created clothing with his disguises, finding it easier to alter them than remove them if he had to make a quick change. But he'd barely been able to make himself look somewhat human. Clothing was out of the question at the moment.

A vibrant pink robe hung from a hook on the back of the door. It smelled of Maise as strongly as the blanket she'd thrown over him. Leaving the towel on underneath, he forced his arms into the robes' sleeves and tied the sash. The garment was too small to close across his chest, but it covered his lower half better than the towel.

When he opened the door, Bixby stood waiting, her tail sweeping back and forth. Why was this quadruped so interested in him? Shouldn't she be paying attention to Maise? He edged around her and headed toward the kitchen. Once he'd eaten something, he'd feel better.

He opened a large humming cupboard that looked different from the rest and discovered cold food storage. Perfect. The most familiar items would be whole foods that required chilling rather than the packaged, shelf-stable items likely to be in the cupboards. He picked up a clear plastic rectangle and pried open the lid, revealing what he believed might be vegetable matter mixed with spices. A bottle of red paste smelled tangy, and another bottle held the bright red juice of a sour fruit. A tall rectangular carton appeared to hold the mammary excretion of some animal. He opened a cellulose carton and discovered two rows of white eggs and sighed with relief. Eggs were a classic food throughout the galaxy, with variations in flavor and texture.

He set the carton on the counter, wondering what stage of

development they were in. He preferred his eggs cooked and investigated the appliances until he discovered one with coils that produced heat. There were several metal pans in a nearby cupboard, so he set one to heating.

Then he noticed Bixby standing expectantly in front of a pair of empty metal bowls. She met his gaze and did a small dance on her four paws, then froze again next to the bowls, waiting.

He smiled despite himself. Her dance was entertaining. Sensing she was thirsty, he picked up one bowl and filled it at the sink. She lapped at the water, gratitude thrumming against his Iki'i. He felt like a child again, hand-feeding his baby *nezumi*. He clamped down the memory and turned back to the heating pan. *Do not get attached.* Attachment led to trust, and trust led to betrayal, even if that betrayal only meant one of them ended up on the dinner table.

Cracking an egg into the pan, he was delighted to discover it was in a pre-fertilization stage of development, with a golden yolk and delicate albumen that turned white when heated. He cracked several more, stirring slightly and adding some sodium chloride crystals he'd located in a shaker nearby. He was just sliding the eggs onto a ceramic plate when a voice made him jump.

"Good morning." Maise stood next to the cold storage unit, smiling at him. Relief saturated the space around her, along with mild humor as she took in the pink robe. Then her eyes lifted to his face and a flood of attraction rushed toward him. "You shaved."

His own satisfaction made him smile back. She liked the

changes to his form. He held out the plate. "Would you care for some eggs?"

"Mm, that would be lovely. Thank you. Take them to the table and I'll bring plates."

Bixby did her little dance again, hunger pricking his Iki'i. He looked at the eggs, not wanting to share. "Your pet is hungry, too."

Maise laughed and opened a lower cupboard next to Bixby's dishes. "I'm sure she is. Sorry girl, no eggs for you. Bixby gets kibble."

He couldn't help but stare at Maise's nicely rounded backside as she poured something from a bag into the empty dish, filling the small kitchen with a tinging sound. He loved watching her move, feeling the comfort she exuded, the self-confidence in her own space. The way she welcomed him into it made him happy.

A sudden wave of vertigo swept through him, and he nearly dropped the plate.

She grabbed it and set it on the counter behind him. "Are you okay? Go sit down. I'll bring things over."

He nodded, ashamed of his weakness. Her concern for him was like a heavy blanket wrapping around his shoulders; a welcome weight that made him want to curl up and sleep again. Yet at the same time, he was guiltily forming a plan to use Maise's compassion to get her onto his ship. Regret burning his throat, he went to the chairs and sat.

She followed close behind and shoved aside papers and books to make room for the dishes. "Sorry for the mess. I've been studying for my exams."

"What sort of exams?"

"I'm almost finished with veterinary school. I want to open my own practice downstairs." She divided the eggs onto their plates and sprinkled tiny black specks over hers before taking a bite. "Mm, good eggs."

He took a bite of his own, satisfied by the creamy texture and rich flavor. They chatted about what she was learning. He'd never finished school, and found her many years of dedication to study intriguing. "All of this so you can take care of species that are not your own?"

She shrugged. "I grew up helping Mom run the clinic. I think I spent more time with the dogs than with my family. Mom really wanted—wants—me to become a vet."

He nodded, sensing in her a bitterness that matched his feelings about his own family. "I think I understand."

They finished their eggs, and she rose. "Do you want more?"

He put his hand over hers, startled by a jolt of awareness at the feel of her soft skin under his palm. "No, thank you. But I need to ask for your help again. I must inform the prince about what I know." He hated himself for what he was about to do, but he had no other choice. "Will you take me to my ship?"

She frowned and sat back down. "Of course. Where is it?"

"Near the outskirts of your city. Hidden in the trees near an enormous building that bellows foul-smelling steam."

"The pulp mill." She nodded. "I can drive you there, no problem. Are you certain you're well enough to leave?"

"It doesn't matter. I must leave Earth immediately. I know who was behind the assassination attempt." He rubbed his thumb over the back of her knuckles. His Iki'i felt her attraction for him like a caress. He had a momentary fantasy of leaning forward and tasting her lips. Cupping the swell of her breast—

The inner coil of his matrix spasmed and pulsed, as if on the verge of losing cohesion. He pulled his hand from hers, worried he might collapse into his resting state right before her eyes. "I need to leave as soon as possible."

Her lips thinned and regret knotted the space between them. She picked up the dishes. "I'll dig up some clothes for you and we can go."

As she returned to the kitchen, he made a point of leaning down to pet Bixby so he wouldn't be tempted to watch the sway of Maise's hips.

CHAPTER SIX

Maise drove Iroth to the pulp mill and parked just inside the fence around the parking lot. Thankfully, the plant's workers were in the middle of a shift and there was no one standing around the scattered parked cars. She looked over at the passenger seat. Iroth had exchanged her hot pink robe for an old, paint-splattered flannel shirt and sweats that strained around his thickly muscled arms and thighs. A black baseball cap with the Yappy Hour logo on the front and sunglasses shaded his face. It seemed the tall blue alien could look sexy no matter what he was wearing.

"Where do we go from here?" she asked.

"Through those trees." He indicated the woods on the other side of the fence, a line of vegetation that followed the river to the right before rising into craggy foothills.

Over the past two days, she'd fretted over him, worrying that he might die at any moment. According to the news, not a single blue alien at the auction had survived. She hadn't been able to reach Lora or Georgie for advice and hated not knowing what to do to help him. She'd even toyed with the idea of calling the number the NSA agent had given her; social media was rife with fear about aliens coming to take revenge on humanity for the massacre, and Iroth was the only one who knew the truth about what had happened.

But she'd resisted, remembering how adamant he'd been that no one could know he was alive.

When she'd discovered him making breakfast in her kitchen, she'd been overjoyed. And despite her determination to help him report back to the prince, she wondered where things might've gone if he didn't have to leave right now. He was such a good listener, and every time he touched her, she felt a little thrill of attraction. After he was gone, she'd be fantasizing for weeks—maybe months—about being holed up in her apartment with a hot blue alien.

You need to get back to class so you can graduate, she reminded herself. Though, to be fair, she wasn't looking forward to tying herself to a vet clinic for the rest of her life. It'd been fine for Mom, but Maise had always dreamed of travel. And after this bit of excitement, the course of her life seemed even more boring.

Iroth got out of the car and leaned on the mirror as if about to fall over.

Worry flared in her gut, and she hurried to his side, stuffing her keys into the front pocket of her hoodie.

He met her gaze, his turquoise eyes full of strain. "I wasn't going to ask, but would you mind helping me walk the rest of the way? It isn't far."

She sighed, furrowing her brow. "I sure hope you know what you're doing. Stay here a sec so I can let Bixby out."

Opening the back of the Jeep, she let the sheltie hop down, opting not to use a leash since there was no one around to complain. The dog waited patiently as Maise put one shoulder under Iroth's arm, then trotted along beside them as they walked through the gate toward the trees.

Iroth was barefoot, since none of her shoes would fit him, and he stepped carefully across the uneven ground. His cologne had been intriguing from the moment she'd met him, but for some reason now it was downright sexy. *Maybe because he'd shaved?* The longer she knew him, the more attractive he seemed. She could even swear he was taller than she first remembered.

They followed a dry creek bed, and she adjusted her arm around his waist to help him down the incline, her insides fluttering as her fingers contacted the muscle peeking from beneath the too-small shirt.

He paused when they reached a clearing, tightening his arm around her shoulders. "Here we are."

She liked his arm around her, adding it to her fantasy repertoire as she gripped his waist and looked around at the grass and weeds. Several yards away, Bixby was pacing and sniffing the ground. "Where's your ship?"

Iroth let go of her shoulders and tapped a spot on his wrist, speaking in a language she didn't understand. The air in the middle of the clearing shimmered, and something that looked like a purple butterfly chrysalis appeared.

She gasped.

The thing was about the size of a city bus and rested with the pointed end slightly elevated above its bulbous base. One edge unfolded like a petal, forming a ramp to the ground, and she realized it didn't look like a chrysalis so much as a rosebud.

He smiled, once again leaning on her shoulder. "Help me up the ramp."

Her heart thudded hard against her breastbone. She was looking at a real live space ship. Helping a real live alien.

Bixby sniffed the ramp, then trotted ahead. Maise stared in awe at the delicately veined floor and walls as they ascended the incline.

Inside the cramped space, a pedestal rose from the floor in the center in the same lavender-colored material as everything else. The entire interior seemed to glow with ambient light rather than from overhead fixtures. A row of four seats was molded into one wall. She touched the arm of one, rubbing the leathery texture. "Everything looks organic—made of leaves or something."

"You're correct." He moved to a waist high console and ran his fingers over its bumpy surface. Multicolored lights appeared among the bumps, and a screen on one wall lit up to show the trees outside. "Most advanced technology has a biological component."

No one was ever going to believe her when she told them about this. She had to take pictures. But when she searched her pockets for her phone, she remembered she'd left it charging by her bed. *Crap.*

The floor vibrated beneath her feet, as if he'd started the engine, and she knew it was time for her to go. Biting her lip, she put a hand on his arm. "Guess this is where we say goodbye." She didn't know why, but she felt sad thinking she'd never see him again. "If you ever visit Earth again, look me up, okay?"

He turned to her and pointed to the seats, his face an unreadable mask. "Please sit over there."

A wave of doubt swept over her. She turned toward the door and discovered Bixby pacing the spot where the opening had been. Maise spun to face Iroth. "What's going on? You need to let us off!"

His features remained calm, one hand resting on the bumpy console. "I'm sorry that I must do this. But if you don't sit down, I'll be forced to restrain you."

She stuck her hand into her hoodie pocket and gripped her keys, as Lora had taught them in self-defense class. "Go ahead and try. You can barely stand up!" But even as she said it, she realized how stupid she'd been. He'd been faking his illness. This was the oldest serial killer trick in the book, and she'd fallen for it. The only thing that might've worked better was if he'd claimed to have a sick puppy on board. And escaping from an alien space ship was going to be a lot more difficult than escaping some creeper's abduction van. "You tricked me."

"Yes, and I deeply regret it. Now sit."

She glanced at Bixby, who now lay against the wall, a soft whine coming from her throat as if begging to be let out. *So much for canine protection.* Maise hated the tears filming her vision. "But we rescued you. Why are you hurting us?"

"I will not hurt you. But if I leave you here, you'll tell the authorities. Everyone must think I died along with the others."

"I won't tell, I swear." She thought of the various messages she'd left for Lora, the vague hints that something weird was going on.

His eyes were like stone. "I'd like to believe that, but I know better."

Her throat tightened with another suspicion. "Are you the assassin?"

He turned his attention to the console. "No, but it doesn't matter. I was there."

Gritting her teeth, she reached for bumps and lights, hitting as many as she could and praying the door would open.

"Stop." He grabbed her wrist and grimaced, flashing pointed teeth.

She stumbled backward, heart stuttering in terror. Where had those come from?

Still holding her wrist, he advanced a step. "Sit."

Her gaze went to her wrist, where his fingers once more ended in claws instead of fingernails. It had all been a disguise. A human-like façade to make her feel comfortable. Even his face had once more sprouted hair, though it was more like human stubble than the bushy sideburns he'd had the first time.

Trembling, she fell back into a seat. The cushioning enveloped her like a bean bag gone wrong, suctioning around her. She thrashed, but it refused to let her go. On the screen, she saw Lora appear in the clearing with Pepper tugging on a leash.

"Lora!" she screamed.

But it was too late. All she could do was watch as the ground fell away beneath them.

CHAPTER SEVEN

Iroth cloaked the shuttle and hurtled into orbit toward his ship, sending an encrypted message to Zhinko, his ship's AI, that he was on the way. He'd been on the surface too long, and the crystals used for the cloaking device were nearly spent. Keeping the cloak operational while moving would use even more, and he hoped there was enough to hide the shuttle until they reached his ship.

As they exited the atmosphere into the inky void of space, his gut churned with regret about tricking Maise, but it wasn't like he had a choice. No one could know he'd survived. It didn't matter that he'd never hired himself out for assassinations—his name was on the IDA guest list. He'd be front and center of the galaxy's most wanted boards if anyone discovered he'd survived the massacre, because everyone would assume a *burendo* was to blame. Just like when he was nine and got blamed for stealing lunches at school or his adolescence when he'd been invited to a party and got accused of forcing himself on a girl.

He synchronized the shuttle controls with his ship's AI and let the computer take over guidance into the cargo bay, the horrific memory still clawing inside of him. He'd kissed that girl once that night in a game. His very first kiss. But someone else had done more than kiss her. And no amount of words from him would convince the authorities it hadn't been him.

Worse, even his parents had doubts. Their disappointment weighed heavier than anything he'd ever imagined possible. "It doesn't matter if you did it or not, Iroth," his father had said as they left the juvenile detainment unit. "You were there, which makes you guilty."

Right after that, his family had moved. Again. It had felt like hopelessness took up most of the room in their suitcases. That was the moment he'd decided that if he was going to be blamed for breaking the rules, he no longer needed to follow them.

Iroth Sanoko needed to wink out of existence, and so did Maise. She knew his name, what he looked like in his most familiar form, even what he smelled like; all things that might be used to track him down before he could secure a new identity.

Ahead, the starlit void shimmered, and a shaft of light appeared as the ship's cargo bay doors opened. As the shuttle settled to the docking bay floor, his insides convulsed. He gripped one arm across his middle. Despite his long rest in Maise's domicile, he was not yet fully recovered. He needed time in his resting pod and possibly medication. He opened the shuttle's hatch and lowered the ramp.

Still cushioned in the jump seat, Maise looked ashen, lips

pressed into a thin line. His Iki'i sensed her nausea, which wasn't helping with his own roiling insides. He closed off his senses before he embarrassed himself by vomiting breakfast. "I'm sorry the ride was rough. The cloaking device interferes with the shuttle's stabilizers. But we've reached my ship now, and I think you'll find it quite comfortable."

Although the circumstances weren't ideal, he was excited to show her his domain. He'd worked for a long time to afford a small luxury liner of his own, and longer still to outfit it with the latest FTL drives, black market cloaking technology, and an AI bondservant. The AI had been the best investment of all, able to care for the ship and keep it from being marked for salvage if Iroth had to be away for extended jobs. The vessel was Iroth's sanctuary.

Releasing Maise from her jump seat, he held out a hand to help her stand.

She batted it away and struggled to rise on her own. "Don't touch me, asshole."

He sighed, unable to deny her anger.

Zhinko's even tenor voice floated up the ramp. "Welcome back, Captain."

Stepping to the open hatch, he spotted the small, black, egg-shaped module that acted as Zhinko's hands on board the ship hovering at the base of the ramp.

"You were gone longer than expected," Zhinko said. "Would you like me to prepare a meal for you and the female?"

"Not right now," Iroth said. "I need my resting pod. Will you please ready it for diagnostic protocols?"

"Of course, Captain." The module backed away but

remained hovering nearby, ready to assist with other tasks while its main ship processors prepared the resting pod in the medical bay.

Maise still stood at the top of the ramp, one white-knuckled hand gripping the edge of the hatch opening. Bixby sat at her feet, leaning into Maise's leg and looking upward as if awaiting instructions. Both of them pulsed with uncertainty, though Maise was also generating fear and anger. "Please, Iroth. Take us home. You don't want to do this.He understood her desperation, but there was no going back now. At least he could make her as comfortable as possible. "I've reserved the best room for you." He patted his thigh in invitation, as she'd done when they'd first met. "Come this way."

Bixby took a few steps down the ramp, then turned back to Maise as if to ask if she was coming.

Maise remained planted at the shuttle doorway. "I'm not your dog, and I don't respond to hand signals." She patted her leg, calling Bixby back to her side. "Will you please at least let me call my family? If you tell us how much you want, we'll try to come up with the money."

His throat grew tight. "Your family can provide nothing I need." He marched up the ramp and gripped her arm, using all his will to transform his claws into blunt nails. "It will be okay. Come with me now."

"Ow!" Maise tried to pull away. "You're hurting me."

Bixby growled, and Iroth glanced at the beast with surprise. She had her feet planted wide and was exposing her teeth. It was the first sign of aggression he'd sensed from her, and although the emotion was directed at him, he approved. He'd use his fangs and claws to defend Maise if she was threatened as well.

He let go of her arm and raised both palms. He'd wanted to show her the room himself rather than leaving it to Zhinko, but the instability in his matrix was growing more insistent. Interstitial fluid leaked from his pores like sweat. "I didn't mean to hurt you. Perhaps it would be better if I allowed my bondservant to escort you." Stepping back, he said. "Zhinko, please settle our guests in my private quarters."

The black egg floated forward. "There is no need to use your personal quarters, Captain. I have prepared one of the other rooms in anticipation of our cargo."

The other rooms on the ship were adequate lodging, but were intended for bondservants, with a shared lavatory and no exterior view screens. "My quarters, Zhinko. And give them any luxury they desire, but no access to core systems, communications, or the shuttle."

"Understood, Captain."

"What's going on?" Maise asked. "What are you saying?"

He remembered then that she didn't have a universal translator. He'd have to pick one up for her as soon as he got a chance. "Zhinko, please access universal translation file 86LF7 and introduce yourself."

The AI rotated in a circle, as if to face the newcomers. "Greetings, Maise and Bixby. Welcome on board," Zhinko said in Maise's native tongue. "My name is Zhinko, and I am honored to serve your needs. If you will allow me, I will show you to your accommodations now. If you are hungry, we have a fully outfitted galley and I would be delighted to prepare an excellent meal for you."

As Zhinko was speaking, Bixby trotted the rest of the way down the ramp to circle beneath the AI, looking up with her tongue lolling from one side of her mouth.

Reassured that at least Bixby would be happy, Iroth backed down the ramp while speaking to Maise. "You're free to explore anywhere except the lower level. Engineering's down there, and you could get hurt."

With that, he turned and strode toward the medical bay. It felt as if his bones would soon refuse to hold him upright, and a blue haze was sliding over his vision. He only hoped he made it to his resting pod before Maise saw him collapse.

CHAPTER EIGHT

Maise followed the thing that looked like a black floating egg away from the shuttle and through a door into a narrow purple hallway. Bixby trotted just behind her, content as usual. The dog's protective response when Iroth had grabbed Maise's arm had been short-lived, but that was to be expected—Bixby didn't have a suspicious bone in her body.

Just like me, thought Maise with disgust. And look where that got them.

"Can I make a phone call?" she asked the egg's back—assuming the thing even had a back. Or a front, for that matter. "I should let my parents know where I am, and I have a test tomorrow that I need to reschedule—"

"I'm sorry, but the captain has instructed me to restrict your access to the communication system. Is there something else I can provide for you?"

"How about a shuttle back home?" muttered Maise, knowing it was a futile request.

"Unfortunately, the shuttle and the ship's core systems are also prohibited," the egg answered as a panel in the hallway slid open to reveal a large room with a low bed covered by a deep red coverlet. An enormous window over the head of the bed looked out at velvet blackness and twinkling stars.

A moment of vertigo rocked Maise, and she put out a hand to support herself against the doorframe. *Holy crap, I'm actually in outer space.*

Bixby stopped moving as well, pressing her warm, furry flank comfortingly against Maise's leg. A wet nose nudged Maise's free hand.

Maise rubbed between the dog's ears, grounding herself in the familiar sensation. At least the room was nice, not some serial killer hole in the ground. She stepped slowly inside. "What does Iroth intend to do with me?" she asked the egg.

"He is under contract to deliver a human female to a client in the Pudari asteroid belt."

Icy dread flooded Maise. He intended to sell her? To who? And why? "He has no right! I'm not a slave, and he doesn't own me."

"You will have to address that with the captain. I am merely here to serve. He obviously considers you a prime specimen, however. I have never seen him offer his personal quarters for a passenger."

She glanced around at the artwork decorating the shelves and walls. A trio of red and violet statues that looked like they were covered in feathers sat in an alcove next to what might be a desk, and a painting of a burning red sunset between looming dark rocks resembling clawed fingers hung on the wall. Smaller figurines and artifacts lay scattered among the other shelves.

"These are his personal quarters?" she asked, wondering if he planned on sleeping here, too; just because he planned to sell her didn't mean he didn't also intend to sample the goods.

"Indeed. Would you like to see our selection of virtual entertainment options?"

No way was she going to kick back and watch a movie right now. She needed to find a way off this ship while there might still be a chance of reaching Earth. "Are there other crew members on board?"

"Captain Iroth and I are the only crew."

Maise sighed. So much for appealing to the mercy of a crew member. She doubted there was much she could say to a robot egg to convince it to set her free. *Perhaps I can change Iroth's mind.* All Maise needed was time and interaction to make him change his mind.

"Where's Iroth?" she asked. "I want to speak with him."

"He's in his resting pod recovering. It seems he encountered something poisonous on your planet and requires a detoxification protocol."

"Poison." That made sense, considering how many aliens had been affected. They wouldn't have realized they were eating or drinking poison until they all got sick. *Or died.* Her heart hammered against her ribs as another thought occurred to her. "What happens to me if Iroth dies?"

The egg rotated slowly. "I do not believe he has made

provisions for your contract in the event of his death. I would be honor bound to deliver you to our client in his stead."

She gulped. Was there no way out of this damn situation? "Will you please keep me informed about Iroth's recovery?"

"Absolutely." The egg bobbed as if performing a bow. "Might I suggest you join your companion and rest now? I will alert you when it is time for dinner."

She looked over to find Bixby had hopped onto the bed and now lay there with her eyes closed. "Traitor," she muttered and turned back to the egg. "All right. Thank you."

"Should you have questions, simply ask and I will assist you."

The egg floated through the door, which slid closed behind it.

Maise waited a few minutes, then approached the door, curious if she'd been locked inside. It slid open automatically at her approach.

The egg's voice floated through the room. "Did you think of something you need?"

"Oh," Maise flinched and looked around. The hallway outside was empty. *Of course there are cameras.* Good to know. But at least she wasn't locked in. Iroth had said she was free to explore. "I was just looking around."

"Very good."

Stepping back inside, Maise went to the desk. If these were Iroth's personal chambers, perhaps she'd discover something to help her convince him to take her home. She regretted not asking more questions about him during breakfast this morning.

He'd been such a good listener, and she'd done nothing but talk about herself. *Stupid me.*

She touched the desktop, and a virtual screen winked to life above it. Symbols blinked on the screen, none of them decipherable. She moved on to examine the other items scattered about the room.

The feathered statues were knee high looked more like red and purple six-legged crabs than birds. The shelves held figurines of alien creatures and other indecipherable shapes that seemed to be made of gemstones. A small box contained what looked like puzzle pieces, and a plant with tiny leaves shivered when she touched it, producing a strange harmonic note that brought Bixby to her side, tail wagging.

"I don't know what it is, either, Bixby." She touched it again, this time creating a discordant note. One entire branch trembled so violently, she thought it might fall off, so she decided she'd better not touch again.

She opened a door and discovered an opulent bathroom with surprisingly human looking fixtures. Besides a wide sink and commode, there was a shower with four spigots, and when she ran her hand across some bumps on the wall that looked like they might be controls, the shower heads turned on and a fruity smell filled the air.

Not in the mood to shower in fruit juice, she wandered back into the bedroom and frowned at the shelves. No clothing. No books. "Why aren't there any photos?"

The egg's familiar voice answered, "We have a selection of photos in the ship's database." The virtual screen on the desk began a slideshow of landscapes. "Is there a particular place you would like to see?"

"Computer, are you always listening?"

"I am Zhinko, the ship's onboard intelligence. It is my duty to anticipate the needs of everyone on board."

No chance of sneaking around and finding an escape, then. Which only left convincing Iroth to let her go. Maise moved to the desk and watched the images float by.

"Are there any pictures of people, Zhinko?"

"We keep a database of client photos. Would you like to see those?" What looked like alien mug shots began appearing on the screen. Bug eyes, green skin, slitted noses...

"Do you have an image of the client who bought me?"

The passing images settled on an alien that resembled a blue-scaled lizard. "Uragi Rhimono, a prominent member of the Senburu."

She shuddered, contemplating what a creature like that might want with a human female. "Do you know how much he paid for me?"

"I am not at liberty to discuss the captain's finances."

Of course not. "Do you have any personal photos? Like Iroth's family or friends."

The screen went dark. "There is only one historic image I am aware of in our database. It has no label."

"Show me, please."

The image of what Maise assumed was a family appeared on the screen; a blue man with bushy sideburns similar to Iroth's when he'd first appeared to her, a woman with fiery crimson hair and thick eyebrows, and a small, teal-skinned child between them, baring his pointed teeth in a smile. Behind them loomed craggy black rocks that rose like claws from the ground, as if ready to clamp down on the family's heads.

"Do you know where this picture was taken?"

"There is a ninety-eight-point-eight percent chance this was taken at the Tasigrad Spires on Fogaria."

She sat in the padded chair facing the desk. "Those must be his parents. Do you know anything about them?"

"No. Iroth does not speak of his family."

She looked closer at the child, wishing she knew more about him so she could build empathy. That was the only way she was going to convince him to let her go. But he had a family, and that would be a starting point. Next time they talked, she was going to be the one asking the questions.

CHAPTER NINE

Iroth couldn't find rest, despite the soothing feel of the regeneration fluid bathing his matrix. He'd been listening to the news while he recovered, and it turned out the *Khensei* toxin his diagnostics equipment had found in his system was the same one reported to have killed the guests at the auction.

"We are fortunate you avoided a lethal dose," Zhinko said. "I do not want to look for a new owner."

Unable to respond while in his resting state, Iroth silently agreed. Yet even surrounded by the news of the massacre, speculation about the prince's well-being, and the ongoing search for the assassin, all Iroth could think about was Maise.

She thinks I'm a monster. And not just for kidnapping her. When he'd reached the medical bay and seen his own face in the reflective glass above the counter, he'd been horrified to see that portions of his features had reverted to his Fogarian form, fangs and all. No wonder she'd been so terrified when he'd grabbed her arm. He needed to reassure her he wouldn't harm her. The problem was, he had no idea what he was going to do with her after that.

Zhinko floated into his field of vision next to the sparsely stocked medical shelves. "Your diagnostics indicate that your matrix is fully purged, Captain."

Iroth pulled himself into a basic humanoid structure and sat up. "How long was I in here?"

"You entered your resting pod approximately three jiros ago."

Three jiros was almost seven hours in Earth time. "What's Maise been doing?"

"She has been looking at photographs and having me translate information about Fogarian culture."

His stomach clenched. She was definitely trying to figure out what sort of monster he might be. He assembled his features into the human form he'd worn during their breakfast together.

"Would you like me to prepare a meal?" Zhinko asked in a hopeful tone. For some reason, the AI enjoyed cooking, even though it couldn't eat, and Iroth kept the ship well supplied with fresh foods.

Maise enjoyed our breakfast together earlier. Perhaps sharing another meal would bring back good feelings. "Yes, please. Make sure everything is safe for humans." Iroth recalled Maise's insistence that Bixby was to eat something special. "Do you have a recipe for kibble?"

"I would be delighted to find one, Captain."

Standing, Iroth glanced down at his naked body. The clothing Maise had loaned him lay in a crumpled heap on the floor between his resting pod and the med bay shelves. She'd found amusement in the items, but he didn't want to be seen as amusing. "Have the replicator prepare human clothing for me. Male specific, common, no ornamentation."

"Understood," said Zhinko. "Please be advised we are almost to the designated rendezvous point in the Pudari asteroid belt."

"What?" Iroth froze halfway out of his pod. He hadn't specified a trajectory when they'd fled Earth's orbit, so of course Zhinko had followed through with the original plan to deliver a female to their client. "Turn us around. Plot a course to the station near Sireta Prime." He had contacts there that could forge a new identity for him.

"Would you like me to reserve a slot for the female with the bondservant broker on the station?"

"She's not for sale," Iroth clarified.

"I see." Zhinko bobbed as if thinking. "What about her companion?"

"No. They're both guests."

"Guests!" Lights flashed over Zhinko's dark surface. "How delightful. I will finally be able to use my hospitality programming as intended." The AI glided toward the door. "Oh, dear. Captain, I'm afraid our guests have ventured onto the engineering level. They will be here in—"

Maise and Bixby appeared in the doorway. Her eyes widened and her gaze slid down his chest to his groin before slinging back upwards. "We were wondering, um, how you were."

Kuzara. It seemed she was destined to see him naked. But at least she hadn't seen him in his resting state. Her dark curls were loose about her face, and dust smudged one cheek.

Putting both hands on her shoulders, he turned her around to guide her back the way she'd come and growled, "I told you to stay off this level."

As he followed close behind her, he realized he'd instinctively made himself taller than his usual size, tall enough to loom over her. Yet her nearness threatened to bowl him over. Her heady scent reminded him of musky *amai* wood incense, a popular aphrodisiac. His cock swelled, no longer in his control.

"How much are you selling me for?" She glanced over her shoulder at him. "I want a chance to counter offer."

He stopped walking. "Zhinko told you?"

She turned her head to look over her shoulder, keeping her gaze locked on his face. "Yes, and no matter what happens to me, I want to make sure Bixby's taken care of." Her voice remained firm, but her anxiety trembled against his Iki'i. "Don't let her end up on someone's dinner table or used for medical tests or something."

He stiffened. "I would never allow anyone to hurt Bixby. Or you."

"But you're selling me to a lizard man. How do you know he won't do something awful?"

"I'm not selling you."

She narrowed her eyes. "You're not?"

"I didn't buy you for our client. I don't own your contract."

She brightened. "So I can go home, then?"

"No."

Her attention slid once more to his groin where his shaft

was now at full attention, impossible to ignore. Both unease and arousal spiked against his Iki'i. "If you're not selling me or taking me home, what are you going to do with me?"

He wasn't sure of the answer. All he knew was he wanted to cover her body with his, to feel the softness of her curves against his angles. He couldn't help himself. Stepping closer, he pressed her back against the narrow corridor. "You're mine."

Green eyes lifted to meet his, and she whispered, "You just told me I'm not your slave."

But she didn't squirm or try to run. Didn't push him away. Her breathing was fast and shallow, and her arousal was now strong enough to smell. She was conflicted, flustered, and he sensed that a nudge from him would tip her over into passion.

Inhaling deeply, he dropped his chin until their foreheads met and stared into her eyes. His erection bumped her stomach, the slight friction making him throb. Her breasts were two perfect pillows against his chest. Even her lips looked soft and utterly kissable. Slowly, he lowered his mouth toward hers—

"Did you not find the clothing to your liking, Captain?" Zhinko's voice jarred him back to the moment. "I can program something different if you prefer."

Iroth spun to face the hovering AI. It held a pair of blue denim pants and a plain white shirt dangling from one of its extendible arms.

"These will be fine, thank you." Iroth stepped quickly into the pants and pulled the stretchy shirt over his head.

"I'm going back to my room." Maise edged past him, her hands shoved into the front pocket of her shirt.

"I'm preparing kibble for dinner," Zhinko volunteered. "But

I have been unable to decide on a beverage pairing. Do you have any suggestions, Maise?"

Maise stopped and frowned. "Kibble... For all of us?"

"Yes, at the captain's request."

Iroth shook his head. "I meant for Bixby, not us."

Zhinko laughed, a sound Iroth wasn't certain he'd ever heard before. "That explains why it was so difficult to find a recipe for human-grade kibble. I understand now. I will revise the menu accordingly."

The unit lifted toward the ceiling and zipped toward the galley.

Bixby pranced a few steps after it, then seemed to remember herself and returned to Maise's side, gazing down the hall with longing.

Maise edged farther down the hall toward the lift, shoulders hunched and hands still in her pockets. "Well." Her throat bobbed. "Thank you for thinking of Bixby."

"Anything I can do to make you more comfortable."

Nodding slightly, she turned and fled, the dog at her heels.

Iroth remained standing in the hallway until she disappeared around a corner. His body still trembled with lust. She'd felt it too, stoked his desire with her own. There could be no denying the magnetism between them, which would only increase the longer they were on the ship together. And *burendo* or not, he was still Kirenai, driven to pleasure a partner both in bed and out.

There was no reason either of them had to deny themselves. He just had to win her trust.

CHAPTER TEN

What the hell is wrong with me? Maise wondered as she hurried back to her room. She'd almost kissed Iroth just now, even after all he'd done. She hadn't been here long enough to develop Stockholm Syndrome, had she? Her gaze roamed the desk and shelves full of curios before falling on the immense bed with its satiny red coverlet. Did he intend to join her here later?

You're mine. His words lingered at the back of her mind, making her pussy ache and her heart beat faster. She imagined herself falling back onto the mattress, the weight of Iroth's body between her legs. His breath against her skin. The subtle hint of his cologne filling her senses. The enormous erection that had been sandwiched against her belly instead pressing between her thighs...

She clutched her arms around herself. Her own response to Iroth scared her more than his obvious attraction to her. He was delicious in his human form, but he'd also appeared like a hairy beast with fangs. Who knew what other shapes he might take or which one was even real? *Banging a beast could be fun.* Holy shit, what was she even thinking?

As if sensing her distress, Bixby nudged her hand.

She looked down into the dog's warm brown eyes. *Kibble for dinner.* Beast or human, he was considerate enough to have thought of Bixby, which made him even more attractive. "I think I'm going crazy."

Closing her eyes, she tried to find a rational thought, one not wrapped up in feelings and intuition. Following her instincts had gotten her into this mess. If she wasn't careful, she'd end up doing something she regretted. *Think, Maise.*

Zhinko's voice entered the room. "Dinner will be ready soon. Would you like to freshen up? We have a wide selection of clothing designs in our replicator database." The screen above the desk began scrolling with images of clothing.

"You can just make clothes on demand?" She watched a designer pencil skirt and jacket set whisk by.

"Whatever you desire, however, our human clothing record is not yet complete. Earth's current fashion trends include many clothing items imprinted with words, which will take some time to compile."

"Can you make a pair of jeans and a simple turtle-neck sweater?" She figured that was classy without being sexy.

An alcove near the bathroom lit up. "Is this to your liking?"

Maise retrieved a pair of jeans and a deep purple sweater that felt soft as cashmere.

"If you prefer something else, simply ask and I will make it for you."

"This should be fine, thank you." She pulled her hair tie from her pocket and pulled her curls into a messy bun before stepping out of her old clothes and into the new. As she did, she watched the door, praying Iroth didn't show up while she was half naked.

An entire wall transformed into a mirror without warning. "Would you like to examine your appearance?"

Maise stiffened, momentarily startled, then regrouped and looked at her reflection. The jeans hugged her ass with precision, and the turtleneck enhanced her curves more than it ought to. *So much for not being sexy.* She considered requesting a baggier set, but then the door slid open.

Heart thundering, Maise spun, expecting to see Iroth. Instead, Zhinko's egg hovered there. "You look exquisite! It would be my honor to escort you to the dining room."

Maise couldn't help the smile that twitched her mouth. Was the AI offering to be her chaperone and protect her honor? She doubted the little egg could—or even would—stand up to Iroth if the need arose, but having him on her side felt nice. "I'd appreciate that."

She followed the AI around a bend into an open area with a massive view of the stars along one wall. A long table suitable for eight or ten people had been set for two—one at either end. Two stainless steel bowls rested on the floor near one chair, and Bixby immediately trotted over and began crunching on what Maise could only hope was the promised kibble.

Iroth stepped from behind a bar at one side of the room,

carrying two martini glasses filled with something pink. He was even more handsome than before, looking like a casual, teal-blue James Bond in a white tee shirt that molded across his well-muscled chest and jeans slung low across his hips. He held out a glass. "Would you like a drink?"

She accepted it, sniffing what smelled like vodka and cranberry juice. "Is this a Cosmo?"

"If you prefer something else, I will try to make it."

She gripped the glass tightly, wondering if it was coincidence he'd made her favorite drink, or if he'd been stalking her. "This is fine, thank you."

He gestured with one hand toward the table. "This way."

She let him pull her chair out for her and sat. He moved to the chair at the other end of the table. "Do you enjoy looking at the stars, or would you prefer another view?"

"I didn't realize the view could be changed." She'd been avoiding looking at the enormous screen in her bedroom because the vast open space made her dizzy.

He said, "Something more grounded, perhaps." Suddenly, the view changed to large trees dappled in soothing blue and magenta leaves. "The forest of Kirenai Prime."

She'd learned the name of Iroth's species from Zhinko, but hadn't seen images of their home planet. Anything she could learn about Kirenai might help her convince Iroth to let her go. She smiled. "That's beautiful."

Zhinko arrived carrying what looked like a platter balanced across two thin metal arms protruding from its egg-like body. "I thought you might enjoy freshly baked tartlets and a selection of roasted and glazed vegetables. All suitable for humans."

A third arm rose from a panel at the top of the egg and placed three tiny tarts on her plate along with some green, yellow, and orange bits covered in shiny golden sauce. Then the AI glided over and did the same for Iroth.

Realizing she was famished, Maise picked up a tartlet and nibbled one edge. The filling tasted savory and delicious, so she quickly devoured the entire thing. She'd never been a fan of vegetables, but they smelled good, so she ate them, too.

"Did Zhinko not offer you food while I was recovering?" Iroth said from the other end of the table, eyebrows raised.

She froze, suddenly realizing she'd been scarfing like a hungry dog. Swallowing, she sat up straight and set her fork aside. "Yes, but I wasn't hungry then."

Zhinko whizzed over with another tray in hand, nearly dropping it on the floor as the unit came to a halt near her chair. "Oh, dear. I allowed you to go hungry. I have been a terrible host."

"No, Zhinko, you've been wonderful. I just didn't realize I was hungry until now."

"You are our first guest on this ship, and I fear I may be out of practice with my hospitality programming." One of Zhinko's arms whisked her dish away while another arm placed a new plate loaded with what looked like a steak and purple mashed potatoes in front of her. "Please enjoy the main course tonight— *ijin'en* tenderloin and whipped *fahwe* root with herbed butter sauce."

Her mouth watered at the savory smell. "Did you actually cook all this, Zhinko?"

"I was originally programmed to perform hospitality on a

G'naxian cruise liner. Unfortunately, the liner is no longer in business." The AI's tone dropped as if sad, and Maise wondered if alien computers had feelings. She'd have to be careful how she spoke to it from now on, just in case.

"Be sure to save room for dessert," Zhinko continued, more brightly this time. "I made *goviberry* pie and ice cream."

"Masterful as always," said Iroth, lifting his fork. "Thank you Zhinko."

Maise watched the AI leave. She hadn't been provided with a knife, but the steak was tender enough to cut with the edge of her fork. Taking a small bite, she nearly moaned out loud at the buttery succulence. Whatever *ijin'en* was, it was delicious.

Iroth sipped his Cosmo, his turquoise eyes following her every move. "How do you like your room?"

Her stomach turned, and she set her fork aside. It would be easy to get comfortable here if she allowed it. "It isn't my room."

He lowered his gaze to his plate. Was he ashamed? He seemed determined to keep her prisoner, yet he also seemed to want to please her.

She rose and approached his side of the table, taking a seat next to him. "Why won't you let me go home, Iroth? I won't tell anyone about you, I promise. I helped you back on Earth. Didn't ask too many questions. Took you at your word. Can't you take me at mine?"

He eyed his glass. "I don't think you understand what's at stake. The prince is looking for an assassin, and I'm the obvious culprit."

It was as if a lightbulb went off in her head. "My friend Georgie knows the prince! She was on his ship last I heard. And my friend Lora is working with his security person. Once I talk to them, I bet we can get the prince to listen to your side of the story."

"Stop." He spoke sharply enough to make her shrink back in her chair.

She gulped, just now realizing that any connection she might have to prince might make Iroth more wary of her, not less. "I—"

"I'm the bad guy and always will be. No one will ever give me the benefit of the doubt, no matter who you speak with."

She could feel her jaw trembling and the prickle of tears behind her eyes. The thought of never going home, never seeing her parents again, never finishing school or laughing with Lora and Georgie made her want to cry. But giving up wasn't something she was good at, otherwise she'd have quit vet school years ago.

Reaching over, she touched the back of Iroth's hand with her fingertips. "I haven't known you very long, but you don't seem like you want to be bad. I understand you think I'm a liability if you let me go. But will you please at least let me call my mom? She's sick, and I'm worried about how she'll do without me. You can listen in and stop me if I say anything you don't want. I'm begging you."

It was a long shot, and she was certain he was about to say no. But then he stood. He set his napkin aside and stood next to her chair. "Kiss me, and I'll let you make a brief call."

She sucked in a breath. "K-kiss you?"

He raised an eyebrow, a mischievous glint in his eye, as if he was daring her.

"You don't think I will, do you?" She pushed her chair back and stood on unsteady legs. Although he was holding her against her will, she didn't think he was a monster. He was just scared and trying to survive. If a kiss would allow her to call her mom, what was the harm?

Swallowing, she nodded. "One kiss."

CHAPTER ELEVEN

Using Maise's request to call her mom as leverage for a kiss was low; even a rogue like Iroth knew that. He'd expected her to reject him. To barter. And definitely he expected her to emanate disgust.

But as she rose to face him, he felt no disgust coming from her. In fact, he felt anticipation that matched his own. He could barely breathe. Allowing her to have contact with her family was probably a mistake, but there was something about Maise that made him want to please her, to help ease her sadness, no matter how irrational and careless that made him. He yearned to crush her against him, clamp his lips over hers, taste her sweetness and feel her warmth.

But he didn't. He remained perfectly still. Taking a kiss was not the same as being given one. She had to come to him, not the other way around.

She locked gazes with him for what felt like an eternity, as if waiting for him to move. His Iki'i felt her growing nervousness. It was as delicious as her arousal had been earlier.

Slowly, she put both hands on his shoulders and lifted onto her toes so she could reach his mouth. Her lips brushed his. A feathery touch, barely more than a breath.

His control fled.

He wrapped his arms around her waist and pulled her against him, leaning into her kiss and sweeping his tongue across her lips.

She gasped, going momentarily stiff. But her nipples hardened against his chest. Her fingers curled behind his neck and the tension fled her body as she molded herself against him.

He slid one palm up her spine to the base of her skull, tilting her closer. She tasted slightly of berries, and he probed his tongue into her mouth with broad strokes. She responded by opening wider and rolling her tongue around his as he thrust.

Oritzu, she was delicious, intoxicating. Irresistible. He let his other hand glide downward to cup her nicely rounded ass, grinding his insistent erection between their bodies. He'd been with women before, but never experienced any feeling except release. Maise made him want more than just release. So much more. He yearned for connection. For sanctuary. A safe place to rest. He'd give anything to feel her heat clamped around his cock, to drive into her until she cried out in ecstasy.

But then she broke the kiss. In a breathless voice, she said, "Okay, I kissed you."

His entire body was rigid with desire. He wasn't certain he had the strength to stop. *You've been reprobate enough for one evening,* he chastised himself. She'd fulfilled his request. If he took more now, that would be the end of any growing attraction she might have for him. They were going to be shipmates for a long time, and he didn't want her to hate him.

Dropping his hold, he stepped backward. "One kiss. One call."

She licked her lips and looked down to straighten her sweater. He could see the sharp points of her nipples even through the plush knit, and it made his cock throb harder. They were going to be together on this ship for a long, long time. If he didn't control his urges, he would eventually end up doing something stupid. *Like agree to let her make a call?*

He picked up his drink and took a long swig, the reality of what he'd promised now slipping over him like a shroud. But a deal was a deal.

Hoping he wasn't about to make the biggest mistake of his life, he said, "Zhinko, make a connection to Earth's cellular satellite system and place a call to Maise's mother. Audio only."

A few moments later, Zhinko said, "Ready, Captain."

A trilling sound repeated itself three times before a woman answered. "Hello?"

"Hi, Mom, it's Maise." Maise's voice was higher than usual, and he narrowed his eyes, ready to sever the connection if she so much as hinted at betraying him.

"Oh, hello, darling," the other woman said, her voice an older version of Maise's. "Did you want to come over for dinner? Your sister's here."

Maise's eyes looked glassy as she sank into her chair again. "Thanks, Mom, but I can't. I, um, I'm going to be out of town for a while. I wanted to let you and Dad know."

"Out of town? What about school?"

Other voices in the background sounded curious, and there was some shuffling before a male voice said, "Where're you going, Maise?"

"I... got a last-minute offer for a work-study program abroad. I'm going to be in and out of communication." She glanced toward Iroth.

He knew she was hoping for future opportunities to call, and licked his lips, unable to stop thinking about what she'd traded him for this one.

She flushed and dragged her gaze from his. But his Iki'i felt her desire.

"That sounds interesting," said another female he assumed must be Maise's sister. "Where will you be studying?"

Maise cleared her throat. "Lots of places. Mostly off grid. I hope to get to work with some exotic animals."

"How long will you be gone?" asked her mother. "What about the clinic?"

Frustration circled Maise like a dust devil and she rubbed a hand over her face. "My business manager has it handled, don't worry."

Her father said, "Come over for a goodbye dinner before you go. I'll grill burgers."

"I can't." The strain was coming through in Maise's voice. "I'm already en route. I had to jump, or I'd miss out."

"Oh, that is last minute!" Her father chuckled. "I hope this helps satisfy your travel bug."

The family talked a little more about Maise's imaginary trip, and Iroth had to give her credit; she was a good storyteller. Her parents seemed happy about her success. By the time the conversation ended, Maise was fighting tears, and he was swallowing guilt.

"Okay, I love you guys," she said.

"We love you too," said her father.

"Call again as soon as you can. We can't wait to hear all about it," her mother added.

The moment she hung up, a sob broke from her. "They're going to be heartbroken when I never come back."

Iroth gritted his teeth. He'd left his own family without a word, and the few times he'd checked on them, they were doing just fine without him. It'd been a mistake to open this wound for her. She'd be better off never contacting them again. Never being reminded of what she'd left behind. "They have another child to nurture. You'll be surprised at how quickly they'll get over your loss."

She lifted her splotchy, tear-stained face and scowled. "You're a bastard, you know that?"

Shoving her chair back, she rose and rushed toward the door with Bixby at her heels.

Zhinko entered as she was leaving. "Don't go yet. I've brought dessert!"

But she disappeared without a word, leaving the dining room hollow.

"She doesn't need dessert," said Iroth, tipping back the rest of Maise's Cosmo and stalking to the bar to pour himself something stiffer. He knew from experience she'd find little joy in anything for a good long while.

CHAPTER TWELVE

Maise paced the bedroom floor, tears she refused to let fall burning behind her eyes. *They'll get over your loss.* "What an asshole." She looked at Bixby where the dog stood near the door, watching her pace. "I can't believe he said that."

Maybe he was a monster, no matter how much she wanted to deny it. No matter how good he kissed, or how much he catered to her and Bixby's needs. He was keeping her against her will. And now her parents weren't even looking for her. Why had she bothered to make up such a plausible story? They were thrilled she was finally getting to travel. If they only knew the half of it.

She looked at the window over her bed, taking in the thick spray of stars across the blackness. Was she to be stuck on this ship for the rest of her life?

"Gah!" Picking up a glittering green figurine, she threw it

across the room as hard as she could. It left a gash in the purple wall. "See how fast you get over that, Iroth." She got the sense he valued his ship more than anything.

Except right before her eyes, the damaged wall knitted itself back together as if it'd never happened. She stalked over and picked up the figurine. It was fine, too, made of emerald or some equally unbreakable stone.

"Argh!" She dropped it and flopped backwards across the bed.

Bixby hopped up beside her and laid her head on Maise's stomach.

She rubbed the dog's soft ears and imagined her parents and sister sitting around the dinner table, talking about the adventures she must be having. How long before they started to worry and called the police to start looking? Not that any Earth authorities could do much since she'd been abducted to outer space. And she imagined even alien space police might have a hard time finding a single ship among the millions of stars.

Over the next two days, she spent her time dozing or reading, expecting Iroth to show up at her door any minute. But he stayed away. Zhinko, however, was at her beck and call. The AI brought food and drinks, taught her how to play alien board games, and even turned out to be a decent conversationalist. She learned a lot about Kirenai, Fogarians, and the many other sentient species populating so many fascinating planets. *Well, you wanted to travel.* Would she ever actually get to walk on one of these exotic worlds?

But by the third day, she grew tired of being cooped up. Bixby was even more antsy. Maise stared at the closed door, contemplating leaving, even if only for a walk around the hallways. Except she dreaded running into Iroth. "You can't avoid him forever," she muttered to herself.

Before she could step forward, a knock sounded at her door.

Her heart leapt to her throat. Zhinko didn't bother knocking, which meant it could only be...

Iroth's muffled voice said, "If you're done being angry, I would like to show you the holo suite."

Maise crossed her arms, then sighed and stepped forward. The door opened. Iroth stood there wearing a checkered maroon button-down shirt under a black leather vest. She glared at him. "I'll never stop being angry at you. What's a holo suite?"

He closed his eyes and nodded once, as if absorbing her heated emotions. "A place Bixby will be able to run."

Her crossed arms relaxed slightly. "That would be nice."

"Come, then." He walked down the hallway.

She hesitated only long enough to take a deep breath, then followed. He led her to the lift she'd discovered on her earlier forays of the ship. She stepped inside after him, keeping as far to the other side of the car as possible. Bixby kept to her knee, a fuzzy wall between them. His cologne permeated the small space, and she forced herself to keep looking straight ahead instead of at his broad shoulders and square jaw. Why did her hormones threaten to take over every time she was around him?

The doors slid open, and he stepped from the car ahead of her. He threaded them through a room full of odd-looking furniture and a big platform that could be an alien version of a billiard table. A door in the far wall opened for him automatically to reveal a massive room with curved walls and grid lines that gave her a moment of vertigo. "Come stand here," he said, pointing to a spot next to him. "What's Bixby's favorite terrain?"

Maise approached slowly, unsure why he asked. "An open field, I guess."

Suddenly, they were no longer in a room. They were outside on a flat plain. Minuscule mahogany-colored leaves blanketed the ground. Barely visible in the murky distance, what looked like sharp mountain peaks rose into the azure sky, and a huge red sun burned overhead.

"Oh, my." Maise gaped at the vast expanse. A hot wind gusted past, and far in the distance, a herd of running creatures disappeared behind a swale.

Bixby barked happily and took several steps in that direction, pausing to see if Maise wanted to follow.

Maise said, "This is incredible." She raised one hand and walked forward, trying to recall how many steps would take her back to the door. "How do you keep from bumping into the walls?"

"You will never encounter a wall. The program has a looping function and the floor is designed to slide so you can feel like you're walking forever. When you finish, simply say 'end program'."

The landscape disappeared.

She grinned, her previous anger evaporating under a glow of excitement. "What else can it do? A beach? I'd love to walk on a beach."

Glittering gold sand appeared under their feet, lapped by gentle turquoise waves. The smell of salt filled the air, and a tiny, bluish sun that was barely more than a star created a sort of twilight across the entire sky. Even so, it was delightfully warm, making Maise want to roll up her pant legs and wade in the surf.

She bent and picked up a curled white shell the size of her thumbnail. "Holy crap, this feels real." She looked at Iroth. "What happens if I try to take it out of here?"

He smiled. "You can't. This is simply a sensory immersion program. Nothing's real. You can swim in the water, and when you leave, you'll be fully dry."

She laughed and stepped into the waves, soaking her tennis shoes in very real-feeling warm water. "Come on, Bixby." Bending, she peeled off her shoes and socks, wanting to feel the sand underfoot. "Let's run!"

The dog barked once and splashed into the water joyfully. Together, they took off down the beach. It felt so good to run, to breathe the warm salt air. She kept expecting to hit the wall, but Iroth was right. She ran and ran, Bixby zig-zagging up and down the beach ahead of her.

Iroth jogged up behind her, grinning and obviously pleased she was enjoying this. "You may come here any time you like. There are many worlds programmed in our database."

She stopped and pushed her hair away from her eyes, breathing hard. Sweat rolled down her sides beneath her sweatshirt. Recalling the photo of him with his parents, she asked, "Will you show me Fogaria?"

His smile faded. "Why do you want to go there?"

"I saw a picture of you and your parents there."

His mouth formed a thin line. "Where did you find this picture?"

"In the ship's database—"

"Zhinko, erase the photograph."

"Wait, what? No!" she grabbed his wrist.

"My past is dead." He said through clenched teeth, the cords of his neck like thick ropes. The anguish in his eyes made her heart ache. What had happened to make him so desperate to leave his past behind?

She gripped his wrist harder. "Why are you so determined to be rid of anything connecting you to your past? Tell me the truth, Iroth. Are you the assassin?"

"No." His nostrils flared as he looked down into her face.

"Then why are you so desperate to disappear?"

He pulled his arm from her grip and turned to look out over the waves. "When I parted ways with my parents, I took a job hauling freight in the slums of Sireta station." He picked up a small stone and tossed it into the ocean. "It was backbreaking work, and the pay was terrible, but I was young and desperate. Most of us working there were. Our overseer was like a father to us. He protected and sheltered us. Even when he discovered I was a *burendo*, he treated me with respect and swore that as long as I worked for him, he'd never reveal my secret. But one day his son got caught stealing from the deliveries." His upper lip curled into a sneer. "Next thing I knew, I was in a detainment cell serving time while his kid went free."

"That's terrible! He framed you?" Maise shook her head. "And what's a *burendo*?"

Iroth thrust out one hand. The teal blue skin faded to gold, then deep ochre up to where his bicep disappeared under his sleeve. "Most Kirenai can assume the shape of any species in the galaxy, but not color. I can do both. I'm a mutation. A freak."

"Why would changing color make you a freak?" She examined his arm in awe. "I'd say that's pretty damn cool."

"That's not how the galaxy sees us. *Burendos* are dangerous. Unpredictable. Inclined toward crime." His arm resumed its teal color and dropped it to his side.

She shook her head. "But that doesn't mean they're right. People say pit bulls and rottweilers are inherently aggressive, but they're strong and loyal and protective and a lot of wonderful things if they're taught how to use those qualities for good. Sure, they can be trained to be bad, but so can any dog."

His nostrils flared, and he released a loud breath. "Are you comparing me to a dog?"

She flushed, realizing that's exactly what she'd done, even after throwing a stink at the shuttle about not being his dog. "I'm just using an example of how DNA doesn't define who we are on the inside. I mean, look at Bixby. Shelties aren't known for being interested in anyone but their owners, but she makes friends with everyone she meets."

He raised an eyebrow. "You just did it again."

She threw up her hands, the heat in her face intensifying. "I'm sorry, but dogs are what I know, all right?"

He grinned. "I forgive you. But if I make the mistake of using one of your dog signals again, you're not allowed to get mad."

She pursed her lips, trying not to grin back. "I can if you're being a jerk."

"Agreed." His smile turned lazy, and he tucked a loose curl behind her ear.

Suddenly, the way their gazes were connected felt alive with sparks, and Maise's breath caught in her throat. He stood close enough to kiss her if he wanted to. *Or for me to kiss him.* Except kissing him was the worst idea in the world, even if she wasn't all gross and sweaty under her shirt from her run on the beach.

She stepped back and looked for her dog. "Hiding like you are makes it look like you're guilty. You should stand up for yourself. I'll vouch for you if you let me go home."

He let out a heavy sigh. "It would do no good. The galaxy only views me with fear. I can't risk being tied to the massacre. Which means I can't let you go home. I'm sorry."

Bitterness resumed its place in her heart, but at least she understood where his fears were coming from. She patted her thigh and Bixby trotted over. "Come on, girl, time to go. End program."

The holo suite paradise winked out of existence. As she left the room, she felt Iroth's gaze at her back like a drowning man crying for help. But she couldn't help someone who wasn't willing to help themselves.

CHAPTER THIRTEEN

After Maise had gone, Iroth stood alone in the barren, gridded room, heart aching. Innocent or not, he was a monster. A deviant. A creature shunned by all who met him.

Maise doesn't think so.

She wanted him to stand up for himself. Had even offered to vouch for him.

He shook his head fiercely, clearing it of vacillation. He'd been lied to before. Coming forward would only result in his death. No matter who spoke on his behalf, the prince would never believe him, let alone the rest of the galaxy. Nobody believed a *burendo*, let alone one who'd been at the scene of the crime.

Yet a softness for this human female had crept into his resolve. He set the ship's systems to Earth's rotational cycle, and over the next days, he watched the news with her, hoping beyond hope someone caught the assassin. If the culprit was caught, he'd breathe a little easier. Perhaps even return Maise to her family, though his entire being balked at that idea for all the wrong reasons. He couldn't seem to get enough of her.

As time passed, she sat closer. Touched him more often. Even laughed at his stories when they weren't dark. He was surprised by the number of fond memories he could recall, encouraged by her sweet smile and addictive laughter. He adored her laugh. Lived for the brightness in her eyes. And his Iki'i sensed a growing affection he yearned to make permanent.

They spent many days in the holo suite, exploring different worlds. He discovered she enjoyed learning about cultures and art, and showed her the artifacts decorating his room, explaining how he'd discovered them. She shared her love of animals by showing him documentaries from Earth. In turn, he opened up the galaxy to her by showing her the galactic web, full of more information than she could ever consume.

When news of a royal wedding reached them, they sat next to each other on a plush sofa to watch her friend make her first public appearance on the arm of Prince Arazhi himself. Maise had her legs crossed on the cushions, her knee touching Iroth's thigh. Every time she touched him, all he could think about was pulling her even closer. He watched her while she watched the screen, her eyes glittering with excitement.

She covered her mouth with both hands. "Oh, my God. I can't believe Georgie's marrying a prince." Maise leaned forward and pointed to another woman with auburn hair in the background. "Look, there's Lora, too!" She sighed. "I wish I could be there."

Although she didn't say it as a request, he felt the tug on his resolve just the same. He wanted to give her everything.

"Would you like to call your family again?" he asked.

She turned to him, eyes wide. "Really?"

He nodded. "Just be careful what you say."

After the wedding ended, he turned off the screen and had Zhinko place the call. "Audio only, please."

On the first ring, her father answered. "Maise? Thank heaven you called. I'm in the hospital with your mom. She fell and hit her head." His voice hitched. "The doctors say it doesn't look good."

A wave of terror and grief slammed into Iroth's heart, and Maise's face turned ashen.

Bixby whined and licked the back of her white knuckles gripping the edge of her seat.

"Is Alison there?" she asked.

"Yes. Can you make it back? It might be..." her father's voice cracked again, "the last chance you get to see your mom."

Maise glanced at Iroth before burying her face in Bixby's ruff. Sobbing, she said, "I don't think so, Dad. Will you hold the phone to her ear?"

Iroth felt like he was encased in ice as she sputtered words of love and regret. His Iki'i resonated with her pleas for forgiveness, her gratitude, her grief.

And at that moment, Iroth knew. He knew everything he'd done was wrong. He'd been cruel and evil and self-serving. Maise had saved him. Even now, she continued to be faithful to her promises. She was good and kind and didn't deserve to suffer just to keep him safe, any more than he deserved to be blamed for crimes he hadn't committed. A fresh realization spiked through him with a solidity he'd never expected. *I love her.* He'd kissed her but once, had never enjoyed the pleasures of her body, yet he loved her. Maise was his mate, he was sure of it. And he was going to do what he could to make her happy, no matter the cost.

The moment she told her father goodbye, he said, "I'm taking you back to Earth."

She sucked in a breath and looked up, eyes red with tears. "What?"

"I'm taking you home. You should be with your family."

Her face crumpled, and fresh tears spilled from her eyes. "Thank you, Iroth." She threw herself into his arms. "Oh, thank you. You won't regret it. I'll never tell a soul about you. I swear to God."

He held her tight, breathing against her hair as she cried, his Iki'i warmed by relief and gratitude. Was this what it felt like to be a hero? It was likely the closest he'd ever get. His own heart was breaking, both at her pain and at the realization he'd no longer have her around to talk to. But it was the right thing to do.

Maise could hardly believe that after all this time, he was letting her go. She only wished it hadn't taken her mom's accident to convince him. But he apologized again and again as she clutched his chest, letting her sob, stroking her hair as they sat on the couch where they'd spent so much time together over the past few weeks.

He commanded Zhinko to turn the ship toward Earth, and she let a last shuddering breath ease from her chest. She felt so wrung out. And his arms were a comfort. His scent, familiar and warm.

She tilted her face to meet his gaze. The concern softening his eyes made her heart melt. Needing more comfort and unable to resist, she traced her lips across his mouth.

He smiled softly and closed his eyes. He'd never asked for another kiss after that first exchange. She might've thought he hadn't enjoyed it, except every look he gave her was full of desire. Desire he never acted on. Desire she never responded to. Even now, she could feel the bulge at his crotch nudging her hip while they hugged. *This could be your last chance.*

What she was thinking was probably a bad idea, but the comfort of a man's arms sounded like exactly what she needed right now. Swallowing nervously, she kissed him again, more firmly.

It was like a spark on gasoline. His posture shifted, the mood in the room suddenly heating.

She cracked her eyelids to find his eyes blazing with passion. She put her fingertips to his cheek. "Kiss me, Iroth."

Without hesitation, he dipped his head and claimed her lips like a thirsty man at a well. Her lips parted with a moan, and he slipped his tongue inside. They sparred, tongues tangling, lips twisting together. His hands spread across her back, pulling her tighter against him as if he never intended to let her go.

Gasping for breath, she broke the kiss, but only long enough to readjust herself so she straddled his lap. She needed to lose herself in this comfort and to find relief from her worry about her mother's accident. His muscles were hard, his thighs like granite boulders under her legs, and the lump at his fly pressed and throbbed against her jeans-covered center.

He planted a frenzied line of kisses along her jaw and down the curve of her throat.

She curled her fingers around his neck, tilting her head to one side and offering herself to him. Clawing at the back of his shirt, she raked it up over his head.

He shrugged free of it, then reached for hers, tearing it free before moving quickly to her sports bra to do the same. Her nipples puckered in the air, and he reached for her breast, hand cupping the mounded flesh as he bent his head to suck.

Rockets of sensation exploded through her and she arched her back, fingers in his hair as he nipped and sucked first one nipple, then the other. "Yes," she gasped.

He flicked open the button to her fly, then his large hot fingers slipped down the front, sliding to the top of her slit where her clit was already throbbing with need. With slow, gentle pressure, he circled, inching deeper and deeper into her folds. She widened her legs, but it wasn't enough. She wanted more. Needed all of him.

Standing, she shucked out of her jeans and panties at the same time, pushing them down around her ankles and stepping free. Standing naked before him, she looked up to find him sitting back, sucking on his finger, turquoise eyes blazing with desire. His bare chest flexed as he slowly rose from the couch and put a hand to the button of his jeans.

"Is this what you want, *itoshi?*" he asked, his voice a deep, throaty growl that made her pussy tremble.

Wetness flooded between her thighs. "Yes."

With a quick twist of his hand, his fly was open. His cock sprang free, massive and gorgeous, deep blue with a shiny bulbous head and a deep slit at the top already leaking white pearly liquid. His jeans slithered to the floor as if made of silk, and he stepped forward, pulling her against him, roughly claiming her mouth once more in deep, compelling strokes.

He tasted as good as he smelled, fresh and woodsy, and their naked skin pressed together ignited her body in places she hadn't known existed until this moment.

Clamping one arm around her waist, he lifted her feet off the floor and pivoted to lay her on the couch. He looked into her eyes for only a moment before he began worshipping her body with his mouth. He licked and kissed down her throat, along her collarbone, over her breasts and belly. When he reached her sex, he inhaled deeply and buried his face there, tongue snaking between her folds while his hands roved her legs, drawing her knees up around him. He kissed her inner thighs, running the rough edge of his jaw against the tender skin, then returned to her center, his fingers parting her lower lips as he delved deeper with his tongue.

She gasped and arched into him, her hips moving in a steady rhythm that matched his probing. He sucked her clit, and a thick finger entered her. Her vision flooded with a sea of stars as a sudden climax overwhelmed her and she exploded with pleasure. After stroking a few more times as her micro-shocks subsided, he climbed up her body and kissed her throat.

She panted, hands kneading his thickly muscled shoulders. He was driving her crazy with need, turning every square inch of her into an erogenous zone. Even her toes tingled as she ran the soles of her feet along the backs of his muscled calves.

His cock pulsed at the crease of her thigh, and she reached down, needing to feel him. Her fingers circled his girth, the velvet skin hot under her touch. He groaned and shifted his hips, thrusting against her.

"I want you," she gasped, angling the head of his shaft toward her entrance.

He pulled back, claiming her mouth as she centered him against her opening. In short, stuttering thrusts, he entered her, his tongue mimicking the thrusting as he stretched her, filled her, his heated length finally seating itself fully inside her with satisfying pressure.

"Maise," he murmured against her lips, continuing to worship her mouth while his hips pinned her against the cushions.

She bucked and squirmed, wanting—needing—him to move inside her. Needing to feel his long stroking thrusts entering her again and again.

He pulled back, plunged forward again, his rhythm increasing until he was pounding into her, his pubic bone meeting her clit every time he filled her.

The pressure building inside her was massive, an unbreakable thing. Her entire body trembled with the need for release. But every time she thought she might reach the cliff, he shifted his position, his rhythm, somehow taking her even higher.

She clawed at his back, cried out his name, thrashed her head from side to side, sure she couldn't take anymore. Then he rolled his hips, drove deeper than she thought possible, and she crashed over the edge.

A growl rose from him, and she felt something prod her ass as she shuddered. Then it was gone, and he was grunting as jets of heat filled her. She opened her eyes only long enough to see him staring down at her face, teeth clenched and lips pulled back as he came inside her, pulsing, pulsing. It was enough to send her into another wave of pleasure.

When they both could finally breathe again, he wrapped her in his arms and curled onto the couch behind her. She'd never felt this cared for, this cherished. But her contentment was bittersweet. This would soon be nothing but a memory.

She was going home.

CHAPTER FOURTEEN

Iroth stood on the bridge with Maise beside him, her small fingers interlaced with his. Earth's transportation web was still disabled, and traffic to the surface was forbidden by royal edict. Two royal military cruisers patrolled in high orbit for unauthorized shuttles attempting to land. But the rest of the solar system was no longer off limits to travel, and commercial sightseeing cruisers and personal recreation vessels hovered in Earth's orbit like carrion birds.

He and Maise had spent the two days of travel to reach Earth enjoying each other's bodies. With each coupling, his desire to bond with her had grown, but he was proud he'd resisted. He was sending her home. Alone. He wouldn't secure the bond. He was a *burendo*, and mating him would only bring her shame. She should be free to pursue happiness without him.

A spiny gray G'naxian cruiser slid across the view screen,

and Maise shook her head. "Why are there so many spaceships here?"

"They're curious. Earth is on the verge of being opened to travel, and they all want to see what has been hidden for so long. The emperor is wise to restrict travel, or they would flood your planet with visitors." *And probably black market traders.* His gut clenched at the thought of Maise being abducted and sold as a breeder. The emperor would try to stop the illegal trading, but undoubtedly some would slip through. "Be very cautious if you ever speak to an alien again."

She smirked and gave him a sideways glance. "Worried about me being abducted?"

"Yes." He met her gaze with as much seriousness as he could muster.

Her playful aura subsided, and she nodded. "Believe me, I won't fall for the wounded alien thing ever again."

"Good." He turned to where Zhinko hovered near the door. "Do we have enough cloaking crystals to get her home undetected?"

He'd transmitted a forged vessel signature to mask his ship's identity so he could mingle with the other spacecraft; they had to be in shuttle range if he hoped to get Maise home. But moving a shuttle to the surface without being detected would be a challenge, even with the cloaking technology. The military cruisers had advanced sensors, and he'd need to time her departure just right to avoid detection.

"I have scavenged the remaining crystals from the main ship's cloaking device," said Zhinko. "We have the capacity to fly the shuttle down and back."

"Getting her home is the priority," Iroth said. "If we end up leaving it behind, that's a sacrifice I'm willing to make."

A shard of Maise's fear pierced his Iki'i. "Are you sure I won't be shot out of the sky?"

He turned and took her shoulders so he could look into her eyes. "I wouldn't risk it if I thought there was a chance that would happen."

She took a deep breath. "Thank you." Wrapping her arms around his waist, she laid her cheek on his chest. "This means everything to me."

He hugged her tightly, resting his chin against the top of her head, breathing in her scent. He would never again smell *amai* wood incense without thinking of her. "I would do anything for you, *itoshi*."

He led her to the cargo bay where the shuttle waited.

At the base of the ramp, she paused. "Will I see you again?"

Sighing, he shook his head. There would be no more dishonesty between them. "No."

Indecision and regret tasted bitter against his Iki'i. She put her fingers over her lips a moment, pinching them as if doubting what she should say. Then she dropped her hand and took both his. "I enjoyed our time together, Iroth. Even if things started off on the wrong foot, you opened a galaxy of possibilities for me, and I'll cherish the time I spent with you."

The unfamiliar sensation of tears prickled behind his eyes. He held himself stiffly as he answered, "Your kindness was my undoing. I will never be the same, *itoshi*."

Her eyebrows pinched, and she tilted her head. "You've called me that several times now. *Itoshi*. What does it mean?"

He pressed her hands to his mouth. "Beloved one."

A small sound escaped her throat, and her green eyes filled with tears. "You love me?"

There was no sense in denying it. He nodded curtly. "Wherever you go, whatever you do, please take care of my heart."

She dropped her gaze, and doubt flooded his Iki'i. But it no longer bothered him. What she felt didn't matter. He loved her and would do anything for her. He nudged her toward the ramp. "Go on now. Your mother is waiting."

Without warning, she wrapped both arms around his neck and pulled him down to meet her mouth. This kiss was softer than the passion they'd shared over the last few days, yet just as urgent. He shared her breath, memorizing every play of her lips against his, the way her hands felt on his shoulders and neck, how she leaned into him, curves against planes.

When they finally parted, she said, "If you ever get a chance to come to Earth again, find me, okay?"

He knew he wouldn't be back. He hadn't committed the crime, but he could never return to the scene of it. Still, he nodded. "I promise."

Smiling, she stepped onto the shuttle and sat in the jump seat. Bixby nudged Iroth's hand, as though asking if he intended to come along. Iroth scratched behind the canine's ears and then urged her toward the ramp. "Not this time, Bixby. Take good care of her for me."

Bixby looked toward Maise, then back at him before slowly turning to join Maise on the shuttle. As the door closed and the ramp retracted, he felt like his heart was shriveling inside his chest, a heavy, useless weight he would never use again.

Turning, he left the cargo bay and everything that mattered behind.

Engulfed in the awkward beanbag jump seat again, Maise watched the ground loom closer until the shuttle settled into the clearing near the pulp mill. *Right back where I started.* Only she was no longer the same person who'd left Earth. Her chest felt tight, but how much of that was from the flight and how much was from her regret about leaving Iroth, she couldn't tell.

The jump seat released her with a whoosh, and Zhinko's voice filled the cabin. "Welcome back to Earth, Maise."

She struggled out of the seat. "Thank you, Zhinko, and good luck. I hope I get to talk to you again some day."

"Likewise, Maise. You and Bixby were a delight to have on board."

Bixby was already halfway down the ramp, apparently eager to get home.

Maise hurried after her. As expected, her Jeep was no longer in the pulp mill's parking lot, and she had to walk back to her apartment. About a half an hour later, she stood outside Yappy Hour. The brick-walled building seemed smaller than she remembered, more like a prison than a kennel. The stairway up to her apartment thudded hollowly under her feet as she went to retrieve her phone. Luckily, it was still there, plugged in next to her bed as if she'd only been gone a day.

But the apartment smelled disgusting, with a rank odor coming from her fridge. She didn't dare open it That was something for future Maise to take on, after she'd seen her mom.

She dropped Bixby off at the kennel downstairs, called an Uber, and within a few minutes was headed to the hospital. Her dad and sister were sitting outside the ICU.

"Maise!" they both cried together, sweeping her into a group hug.

She gripped them back fiercely, emotions too raw to speak.

Her father cupped her cheek and pressed a kiss to her forehead. "I'm so glad you could make it back."

"Me too, Dad," she choked out. He looked rumpled and tired, his gray polo shirt stained by what looked like mustard, and a haze of gray stubble sprinkled across his chin. "Can I see her?"

"The nurse should be finished by now." He led the way to a small room where Mom lay as if sleeping, a tube beneath her nose and IV lines running to her arms. Her head was bandaged, but a big purple bruise peeked from the edge near one temple.

Throat tight, Maise took her mom's hand, noting how papery and light it felt. Tears blurred her vision. "Hi, Mom. It's me, Maise. I'm here."

The slow, steady beeps from the monitors were all that answered.

"Sorry I was gone so long." The words would barely leave Maise's throat. "But I'm here now. I've seen so much, done so much. I can't even begin to describe..." she tapered off, knowing her father and sister were listening. Instead, she pressed her lips to the back of her mother's frail hand.

The small room was crowded with all of them there, but the nurses overlooked the two-person minimum and brought in an extra chair. The family sat with Mom well into the night, reminiscing about things with both laughter and tears.

Some time in the wee hours of the morning, when the conversation had subsided, and they were all in a half-doze, the monitors went static. A low beeeeeeep filled the room.

"No!" both Maise and Alison gasped. "Mom! Don't leave us. Please, mom."

The monitor continued to sing its mournful note.

Dad, stoic as ever, bent and kissed his wife's cheek.

Maise frantically went to the door, looking for a nurse, but her dad put a hand on her shoulder. "She didn't want to be resuscitated, remember?"

Tears choked Maise's eyes and throat. Mom had signed a living will years ago, before her dementia had taken over. But all Maise wanted was to once more see the strong and vibrant mother of her youth.

She and her sister held each other, sniffling, and watched the nurses come in, turn off the machines, and pull Mom's IV and oxygen tubing. Mom looked as if she was sleeping.

As soon as the nurses were gone, Maise lay her head against the mattress beside her mother's body and sobbed.

Eventually, a warm hand touched her shoulder, and her dad's voice said, "They need to take her now, Maise. Come on."

She left the hospital in a daze and went back to her parents' house. Everything looked the same, as if Mom might come back at any moment. A basket of half-finished crochet work near the recliner, ready for her to pick up where she left off. Family photos on every wall.

Dad went to bed, and Maise and Alison curled up on either side of him, holding hands across his chest.

When morning came, they went with him to the funeral parlor. He and Mom had made arrangements long ago, and after signing the papers, Maise took her dad to lunch at a sports bar close to Yappy Hour. Mom used to order takeout from here when she ran the clinic, and everything on the menu made Maise want to cry.

"I'm sorry I wasn't here, Dad."

He smiled at her. "Mom understood. You know she was thrilled for you, right? I know she gave you a lot of pressure about the business, but she was happy that you were following your dream."

That brought a fresh bout of tears and a shitload of guilt. If Mom only knew. But Maise couldn't say a word about what she'd really been doing, and Dad wouldn't understand if she did.

"Can you stay for the funeral?" he asked.

She swallowed and looked away. How was she supposed to tell him she wouldn't be going back to a dream veterinary sabbatical that had never existed?

He took her hand, concern creasing his face. "I hope you didn't burn any bridges to come back here. She'd want you to be happy, Maise. We both do."

Taking a shuddering breath, Maise shook her head. "It's too late to go back."

"Naw, that can't be." He squeezed her fingers. "Whoever's

running things will understand, I'm sure. You just need to talk to them."

Numbly, she nodded. If only she could. She had no way to contact Iroth, and even if she did, he wouldn't be able to send the shuttle for her.

The shuttle. She sat up straighter. Iroth had said getting the shuttle back to the ship would be tricky. That he was willing to abandon it, but he planned on trying to find a window when the military ships weren't watching. If it hadn't left yet, she could try to call him. Or perhaps even return to his ship and surprise him. Would he want to travel the stars with her?

She stood so quickly her chair almost toppled. "I love you, Dad. Thank you."

"Of course, honey." He chuckled as she kissed his cheek. "Go on. I'll get the check."

She rushed back to Yappy Hour and grabbed Bixby.

Her assistant held his hands out in question. "Am I the only one who works around here?"

"You're in charge, Ted. Tell Monica I'm giving you a raise."

And with that, she was rushing back to the clearing and praying she made it in time.

CHAPTER FIFTEEN

Iroth had lingered in orbit longer than he should, delaying the order to bring the shuttle back to the bay. He told himself he was waiting to be sure the military ships wouldn't spot it. But in reality, he just wasn't ready to leave. The taste of Maise's kiss on his lips was like a lifeline to another definition of himself, one he'd never believed could exist. Preparing to leave felt like preparing to cut off a limb.

He scrubbed his hands over his human face, wondering if he'd ever have the will to shift out of this body again. He liked how this form felt, the ease it gave him around Maise. Each muscle and plane had a memory for him now, her fingertips tracing here, her lips kissing there.

Then it occurred to him. Shape wasn't really the issue. What if he didn't try to look less human, but *more*? He stared at the glowing blue and white planet below, suddenly realizing how much of an idiot he'd been. He wanted a new identity.

Creating one on Earth would be easy if he looked fully human. Galactic databases had not yet catalogued earth's individuals.

He could make a life with Maise.

He extended his teal-blue hand and focused on changing color. The skin faded, becoming pale, then blossoming golden brown similar to Maise's skin tone. *Easy.*

Excitement making his heart race, he asked, "Zhinko, how soon until the shuttle can return?"

"The shuttle just returned to the cargo bay, Captain. Maise is on board and wished to surprise you. But I fear we have another urgent matter. We have been boarded, Captain."

Feeling like he had whiplash, Iroth scowled. *Maise is back?* His ship was being invaded? "*Kuzara!* By whom? And how?"

"The invading shuttle is registered to Senbur Uragi Rhimono. They were cloaked and slipped inside when I opened the door for the shuttle. I have suggested Maise hide in the shuttle's smuggler's hold."

Iroth snatched a kinetic pistol from the locker on the bridge and ran toward the cargo hold. Uragi was the client who'd wanted a human female from the auction. *He probably wants the down payment back.* His blood turned cold. *Or he wants Maise.* He had to keep them from finding her. He reached the hatch to the cargo bay and skidded to a halt.

Three Kirenai and a pink scaled Qalqan stood on the docking bay floor beside a second, smaller shuttle, weapons drawn. And they were headed straight for Maise's shuttle.

"Hey!" Iroth shouted, stepping into the cargo bay. "The authorities are on the way, so I suggest you get the *kuzara* off my ship while you still can."

The Kirenai leader was in the shape of a Qalqan, as well, with a long, blue lizard snout, scales and a stubby tail. He leveled the muzzle of his gun at Iroth, lipless mouth gaping in a facsimile of a smile. "I seriously doubt you called the authorities, *burendo.*"

Iroth gripped his pistol tighter and took a step closer. "I don't have your money, if that's what you're after. Go talk to the IDA."

"The money isn't my concern." Uragi waved a dismissive claw before placing it reverently over his chest. "I'm here to protect the empire." His voice dripped with sarcasm, and an identifying sensation that reminded him of ammonia reached Iroth's Iki'i.

Like a flash, the final moments at the auction swept through him; his gaze locking with a fellow Kirenai, the fleeting sense of ammonia, then the other Kirenai collapsing. Uragi had faked his own death?

Just like I did.

"You were at the auction," Iroth accused.

Uragi lifted his chin and chortled. "You're the only guest unaccounted for, *burendo.* The transportation web logs will verify it."

Iroth felt like he'd been frozen in ice. The contract had been a setup. Uragi hadn't wanted a human female—he'd wanted a scapegoat for the assassination. And Iroth had played right into his hands.

"You set me up," Iroth gritted between his teeth.

Uragi made a ticking noise and shook his head. "That's not how the emperor will see things. I'm about to be a hero." He pointed to a pair of Kirenai detention manacles in the Qalqan's hands. "Come now. You know you can't win in a gunfight."

Iroth's attention fell to Uragi's weapon. A laser pistol, not kinetic. The Kirenai guards behind him held matching weapons. Lasers were one of the few weapons deadly to Kirenai, and even a ship's self-healing *popotan* bulkheads could be irreparably destroyed by laser fire. Most captains banned such guns from even coming on board.

If it'd been only his own life at stake, Iroth would've fought claw and fang before surrendering. But he couldn't afford a laser fight on deck, not while Maise was in the shuttle. The best thing to do would be to get Uragi and his men off his ship as soon as possible.

Stepping forward, he let the manacles clamp over his wrists. Pain flared up his arms, followed by a wave of nausea. He frowned. He'd been manacled before and expected the familiar wash of chemicals that would temporarily prevent him from changing form. This was not that. Yet it was also familiar.

Uragi gestured toward the shuttle. "In there."

Maise. Iroth surged forward. "Just take me and go—"

A guard slammed a fist into his gut, doubling him over. Then a knee to his head made the deck spin out from under him. The nausea he'd felt from the manacles now turned to vertigo. His matrix shuddered. His vision narrowed to a pinpoint, then blackness.

I'm losing my form, he realized.

The last thing he remembered as he fell to the deck was the sound of a dog barking.

The shuttle thunked to the deck, and the jump seat released Maise before the floor stopped vibrating. She struggled to her feet. On the shuttle's screen, another shuttle smaller than the one she was in sat on the opposite side of the deck, this one shaped more like a bullet than a rosebud. A group of aliens were climbing out of it, three blue and one that was bright pink.

"Zhinko, what's happening?" she asked.

"I apologize for the discomfort, but I must ask you to hide in the smuggler's hold. The ship has been boarded." A panel popped open beside her jump seat.

Fear settled in her chest. "By who?"

"I believe it is Uragi Rhimono," said Zhinko. "The client we were supposed to deliver you to."

Shit. Was Iroth going to get in trouble for not fulfilling his contract? Maise pushed Bixby into the small space that had opened. "Can't we just give him his money back?"

"He does not appear to want money."

Maise gulped. If he didn't want money, that probably meant he wanted a female. *Me.* She tried to squeeze into the small space beside Bixby, but there wasn't room for both of them. Feeling panicked, she said, "There isn't room in here, Zhinko."

The row of jump seats separated, revealing a long crack at the base of the wall. "Then I suggest one of you hide in the engineering compartment."

"Bixby, lay down," she commanded.

The dog obeyed with her ears tucked back, sensing her owner's terror.

Maise hurried to the other compartment. She had to lie on her stomach to squeeze sideways into a coffin-sized area amidst the wiring and something squishy she didn't want to think about. Then the seats slid back into place, leaving her in darkness.

Heart beating loud in her ears, she tried not to gag at the sharp, oily smell surrounding her. What was happening to Iroth? Was he going to be all right?

The sound of booted feet thudded outside her hiding spot.

She held her breath, staring blindly into the darkness. *Please don't find us.*

A deep voice rumbled in a language she didn't understand, and someone started pounding on walls. She felt like she was about to suffocate.

Then Bixby began barking.

"No no no!" Maise whispered, hands clenching into fists near her head.

Bixby yipped and went silent.

Bixby? Maise gasped for air. What had they done? She needed to get out, but couldn't move in the small space.

The deep voice rumbled again and boots thudded away.

After a few minutes, the jump seats parted. Maise struggled out. Bixby's panel was still closed, and she rushed over, dreading what she might find inside. "Open it!"

The panel slid open, but the only thing inside was a scrap of gray fabric and some broken glass shoved into the back corner.

She spun, looking around the rest of the shuttle as her entire body trembled with adrenaline. "Where's Bixby?"

"I am sorry," Zhinko's voice sounded like a whisper. "They have taken her."

"Did they kill her?" Maise rushed from the shuttle.

"She appeared to be alive," said Zhinko.

The docking bay door was closed and the bullet-shaped shuttle was gone. "We need to go after them! Where's Iroth?"

Maise spun to look for him and spotted a gelatinous blue puddle. Her throat tightened. She'd seen this before. At the auction. She fell to her knees beside the puddle. "Iroth?"

The gel rose, as if trying to reach for her, then collapsed again. "Zhinko!" she screamed. "Zhinko, he's still alive! Do something."

She could barely breathe.

Zhinko whooshed in from the hallway, trailing what looked like a plastic tub. "Medical emergency protocols engaged. Please stand back."

Gulping back hopeless tears, Maise scrambled out of the way. It was Iroth. She knew it. This was happening because he'd brought her home. Uragi had come looking for her and probably taken Bixby as a consolation prize. And now Iroth...

Within moments, the AI had levitated the gel into the tub and rushed back through the halls and into the lift. Maise squeezed in beside them. The doors opened on the lower level, and Zhinko said, "The captain has forbidden guests on this level."

She pushed past and stepped off the lift. "Yeah, well, he's not here to stop me this time."

The AI didn't say more. It rushed them to a small room dominated by a large open coffin that looked as if it was made of stone. Zhinko emptied Iroth into it and, in a flurry of arms, began connecting tubes and pushing buttons.

She gripped the doorframe. "What's wrong with him?"

"It appears he is poisoned again. Beginning detoxification."

Why would Uragi poison Iroth instead of shoot him? It didn't make sense. "Will he be all right?"

The AI flashed with multicolored light. "I am uncertain. We used a significant portion of our medical supplies during the last purge process."

Maise swallowed, trying not to hyperventilate as she stared at the coffin. He couldn't die. She wouldn't let him. "If we need medicine, how do we get it?"

"The captain usually trades for supplies on Sireta station."

"How long will it take to get there?"

"Several of your Earth days, but I fear he will not survive that long."

Fighting panic, she thought of all the ships in orbit around them. "What about the ships nearby? One of them probably has what we need. We could call for help. And we need to get Bixby back."

Zhinko said, "The captain has ordered that you are not to have access to communications or other core ship systems."

She scowled. "Screw the captain's orders. This is an emergency."

"I'm afraid my programming will not allow me to disobey. We are to maintain our cover identity until I receive orders."

She stepped into the room and gripped the edge of the stone tub. "Iroth, if you can hear me, you have to give me control of the ship. You have to trust me."

The gel shuddered. Pulled together then parted with a sigh. "Yesss."

"You heard him, Zhinko." She glared at the egg-shaped robot. "He said yes."

"Acknowledged. Who would you like to call?"

She ached with relief, yet remained clenched with terror. Iroth was dying while she was arguing with a machine. "Just send a general request for the medicine."

"Please be advised that a general transmission will alert the royal military ships. They will be the first to arrive, and will undoubtedly place Iroth under arrest."

Her jaw trembled. *I'd rather see Iroth in jail than dead.* And if anyone was likely to have the right medicine, it was a military ship. "Do it. Tell them that Uragi stole my dog while you're at it. I want Bixby back."

"Right away, Maise."

"Iroth, you're going to be okay." She'd come back to the ship full of hope, full of dreams to follow, full of love for a big, blue-skinned alien with a chip on his shoulder. She had to save him. "I want to see the stars together. Hold on for me. Help is coming."

CHAPTER SIXTEEN

Iroth fought for consciousness. Fought for life. He'd given control of his ship to the only person in the galaxy he trusted and now he was under arrest.

But he was alive.

He faded in and out of consciousness as unfamiliar healers looked into his resting pod. Medication burned through his matrix. The dizzying nausea of dialysis swept through him again and again.

All the while, all he could think was that his worst fears had come to pass. But he also knew Maise hadn't betrayed him on purpose. She'd come back to him. She'd done what she could to save him. If he died now, he'd die knowing his one true love didn't hate him. She was alive and well. And that was worth dying for.

His matrix tightened and separated, solidified and melted. Finally, after long agony and uncertainty, he cracked open his eyes. He'd resumed his human form, lying on a bed and staring up at a pale gray ceiling. The air felt like torture against his raw skin, and the soft white light in the room may as well have been a million suns blazing against his eyes.

He groaned and sucked in a breath. The fruity smell of regen fluid. A faint whiff of *amai* wood incense. A soft voice.

"Iroth?"

He turned his head to find a goddess's green eyes focused on him from a seat beside his bed.

She leaned forward. The love that bathed his Iki'i was as healing as any medicine.

"Maise?"

She smiled, and a cool hand touched his burning cheek. "Welcome back."

"Where am I?"

"The royal infirmary."

He blinked, trying to make sense of her words. "Prison?"

"No. The emperor's palace." Maise bent and kissed him, her relief against his Iki'i strong enough to make him swoon. She gently stroked the back of his hand. "You've been in and out of consciousness for days."

"What happened?" He didn't understand. He'd expected to be dead, or at the very least, in prison.

"Uragi tried to frame you." Holding his hand, she explained everything, her love never wavering.

The manacles hadn't been detainment manacles, they'd injected him with the poison used in the massacre. Then Uragi's men had planted a broken poison bottle on the shuttle as evidence. The only reason Uragi hadn't discovered her there was because they'd come across Bixby first. "The asshole took her captive as a cover-up for why he'd visited your ship. He tried to tell the authorities he'd bought her from you."

Apparently, Uragi had intended to wait long enough to let Iroth die from the poison, then alert the authorities that a *burendo's* ship was in orbit. With the planted evidence, everyone would assume Iroth was the assassin responsible for the massacre on Earth and that he'd been accidentally killed by his own toxin.

Except that Maise's quick call for help had saved his life. "Zhinko had video footage of Uragi's minion planting the evidence and abducting Bixby. After you were arrested, I had Zhinko call Lora and Georgie. We made sure you got a fair trial."

He took a moment to glance around the sterile room, his mind reeling. "Where's Bixby? Is she okay?"

Maise grinned. "She's fine. She's with Lora's dog, Pepper, in the gardens right now. I think she'll be a little more cautious about strangers from now on, though. She lost a tooth trying to bite the asshole who captured her."

He had to smile. *Good dog.* "And Uragi? Did they catch him?"

"He and his henchmen are locked up on a prison moon. I guess the emperor is planning a formal execution. There are still more collaborators on the loose, though. I guess the conspiracy runs pretty deep."

A male voice interrupted, "We still have some questions about that, if you don't mind."

Iroth turned his head and saw a blue human with long hair

standing at the doorway: Zhiruto, the prince's bodyguard from the auction.

Maise smiled at him, affection obvious against Iroth's Iki'i. His heart threatened to crack. How long had he been unconscious? Had she transferred her affections so easily? *She's mine.* He sat up, breathing through the dizziness threatening to bowl him over.

"*Oritzu*, take it easy." Zhiruto stepped inside.

Behind him, another Kirenai waited in the hall, one who could only be Prince Arazhi, dressed in a black and yellow tunic and wearing a narrow crown on his head. Maise's human friend, Georgie, stood at his side, her blonde hair held back by a circlet of gold.

"Come in." Maise stood, making room for the newcomers. "Where's Lora?"

"She received information about another black market slave ship and went to manage the rescue team," said Zhiruto.

The prince stepped forward, gaze entirely on Iroth. "I understand you're a *burendo*."

Ah, here it is. The moment of truth. When Iroth's real fate was decided. He gripped the edge of his mattress and swung his feet off the edge. "I am."

"I'd like to offer you a job," the prince said.

Iroth frowned, confused enough that he momentarily considered lying back down. "Why?"

The prince cut a glance toward Maise. "I've been told you're trustworthy."

Maise was holding Georgie's hand and biting her lower lip. Had she arranged this?

He returned his full attention to the prince. "What kind of job?"

"My spy network could use a man like you. Someone who can truly blend in. The royal healer who tried to kill the emperor is still on the loose."

Iroth shook his head slowly. "I'm not really a palace guard sort of guy. More of a smuggling, thieving, espionage sort of guy."

The prince chuckled. "That's why you're perfect. No one will suspect you're on our side. But you're free to say no, of course."

Iroth took a deep breath. 'Free to say no' didn't always mean free to go. "And if I decline?"

"Then as soon as you're ready, you can leave. Your AI is waiting in orbit with your ship."

He looked again at Maise. All he cared about was her. And if she thought that a job with the prince would somehow make the galaxy accept him, she was wrong. He needed her to understand that. "Can I think it over?"

"Absolutely." The prince nodded. "I'm glad to see you've recovered."

Georgie kissed Maise on the cheek and whispered, "I'm glad he's okay."

Once everyone had gone, Maise sat beside him on the bed.

He adjusted his legs to face her. "What's going on? Do you want me to work for the prince?"

She shrugged. "I don't care who you work for, as long as you don't have to hide anymore."

He took her hands in his and looked at them, admiring her

golden brown skin and finely shaped nails. His greatest desire was to bond with Maise. To give her the future she dreamed of. But she didn't understand what it would mean to bond with a *burendo*. "Even if I work for the prince, I'm still a monster. The prince will never trust me. The guards will never trust me." He swallowed thickly, hating what he was about to say. "If we're together, everyone will as shun you as they do me."

She squeezed his hands. "That's not true. The prince does trust you, or you wouldn't be here. We have my friends. And I'm a firm believer that the way to gain someone's trust is by trusting them first." She winked at him. "Just take you and me as an example."

He shook his head, still full of doubt. She had come back to him, even after what he'd done and despite what he was. If Maise wanted him to do this, he would try. He would do anything for her. Kill for her. Suffer for her. Die for her. She held his heart whether he willed it or not and was the one person in the universe who saw through what he was and into his soul. And she had faith in him.

Nodding, he said, "All right. I'll give it a try."

EPILOGUE

Georgie had tried to talk Maise into a big wedding on Earth, but small and intimate was more Maise's style. So they were holding the ceremony on board Iroth's ship with a handful of her family and friends. Iroth had managed to get the holo suite to look exactly like her parents' church, right down to the snag in the carpet at the door to the sanctuary.

Now she stood ready to walk down the aisle, her father next to her in his best Sunday suit. Bixby had just carried the ring pillow saddled to her back down the aisle, and it was time for Maise to go.

Dad held out his arm. "Ready?"

She glanced down at her simple, cream-colored gown and nodded. She'd tried on what felt like hundreds of wedding dresses before settling on the silky, off-shoulder wrap gown with a small, ruffled fold at the waistline that made it feel elegant without being gaudy. Gripping her bouquet of violet and cream roses in one hand, she took her father's arm with the other and started down the aisle.

As they passed the empty pew where she'd spent many childhood Sundays with her head in her mother's lap, her eyes pricked with tears. It wasn't really their church, but she knew her mom was here. That she'd approve, even if it didn't include becoming a vet.

Taking a deep breath, Maise turned from her past and focused toward her future.

Iroth stood waiting at the altar in a classic tuxedo, a small spray of red and purple *jargoth* feathers on his lapel. The feathers were Fogarian, the same ones that covered the statues in his room. She'd tried to get him to contact his family for the wedding, but he wasn't yet ready to reunite with them. Someday, she hoped, but he would do it in his own time. Meanwhile, he had her family, who already loved him to pieces.

She reached the altar, and he gave a deep bow to her father before accepting her hand. After several family meals together, Iroth and her dad had hit it off, arguing about classic spy movies. They'd ended up in the living room binge watching Alfred Hitchcock movies three nights in a row.

Zhinko hovered beside the groom with a boutonniere affixed to its black casing, proud to have the title "Best AI." At first, Lora had laughed at Iroth's choice of Best Man, but Maise pointed out that Zhinko was it. Iroth had lived in solitude and had no friends. But he was developing camaraderie with Zhiruto and Arazhi, who were serving as groomsmen to match Maise's bridesmaids: Alison as Maid of Honor, plus Georgie and Lora, all resplendent in their deep purple gowns.

"You look gorgeous," Iroth said in a low voice as she took her place beside him.

She beamed, glad they'd instructed the church pastor to make the ceremony short. When it was time for the vows, Iroth turned to her with the most serious expression she'd ever seen on his face. He took her hands and locked his gaze with hers. "Maise, I don't deserve you. Your kindness and optimism have changed my life forever. You've seen me at my worst, and love me even so. Thank you for taking a chance on me. Thank you for inviting me into your family. And most of all, thank you for teaching me to trust again. I'm honored to be your mate from now until the end of time."

Her throat felt tight as he placed a ring with a diamond the size of her thumbnail on her finger. Her dress might be simple, but Iroth had insisted on the ring after seeing a "diamonds are forever" commercial while watching Hitchcock.

She licked her lips and poised a gold and diamond ring that was almost as gaudy as hers over his finger. She wasn't as eloquent as he was, but every word she spoke came straight from her heart. "Iroth, I promise to love you forever and to trust you with my heart. I look forward to a lifetime of adventures together."

The pastor smiled and nodded. "Congratulations. I now pronounce you mates for life."

The music began once more, and they raced down the aisle together under a shower of holo suite rice. The church doors gave way immediately to a ballroom—unlike the real church back home. Zhinko had prepared food, and hours of drinking and dancing later, Maise was glad to collapse into bed next to her husband, still buzzed from champagne.

He stroked her curls away from her cheeks and kissed her nose. "My beautiful bride."

Happier than she'd ever imagined possible, she smiled as his hand curled around her ear and trailed down her throat with a feathery touch that made her giggle. "I think I drank too much."

His stroking stopped. "Would you like to wait?"

He'd insisted they shouldn't form the Kirenai mate-bond until the human ceremony was complete. She was pretty certain it was because he was giving her the option to change her mind right up until the last minute.

"Absolutely not," she said, putting his hand on her breast and making him pinch the nipple through her satin chemise.

He made a low, sexy noise and leaned in to kiss the curve of her throat.

A shiver rocked her. She slid her hand down his arm to his chest and lower, slipping inside his silk boxers to find his thick primary shaft already throbbing and ready.

They'd been intimate many times before the wedding, and she'd discovered he had a second cock just below his primary one. His mating shaft, he called it. Apparently, when he used it, it would share his DNA with her and form an unbreakable bond that would give her health and long life.

But right now she gripped his primary shaft firmly, feeling it pulse and swell beneath her palm. "God, I love this thing."

He flexed his hips, pumping against her, and nibbled his way up her throat to find her mouth. His tongue was firm and insistent, prodding her lips apart and delving into her mouth with seductive sweeps.

She loosened her hold on his cock and slid her hand around to find the smaller shaft below. It was stiff and shorter than his primary shaft, about the thickness of her thumb. He shuddered at her touch and pulled back. "Not so fast, *itoshi*. Let me prepare you."

He rolled her onto her back and cupped her breast with one hand, rolling and pinching the nipple while he kissed her again. She wriggled underneath him, dragging her chemise up over her head and tossing it aside. "I don't want any barriers."

He dipped down and sucked a nipple hard into her mouth, sending electric jolts straight to her pussy. His hands were like fire, blazing against her skin. He dragged a palm down her ribs and circled one hip, kneading her ass cheek as he moved down her body with small, biting kisses. She wore no panties, and he licked her right between the thighs before sucking gently on her clit.

She gasped, flexing her hips toward him. Spreading her knees farther apart, he brushed his tongue over the nub again and again, circling and teasing until she was panting, bucking up in time to his rhythm as her legs trembled and her nails dug into his shoulders.

Right as she was on the verge of orgasm, he thrust his tongue deep into her channel. She came, throbbing hard as his tongue stroked in and out.

He climbed back up her body, running his stubbled chin gently over her stomach. He sucked hard on a nipple, then moved to her throat, his erection prodding her slick folds. As he claimed her mouth, she rocked her hips, trying to take him inside. His tongue had been amazing, as always, but she needed all of him.

The head of his cock teased her opening as she writhed, satisfaction kept just out of reach. She growled against his mouth, "Stop it, you tease."

Chuckling, he penetrated her, quick and deep.

She gasped and flexed, taking every hot inch until his pubic bone crushed against her clit. He felt so good, she almost came again. Her ridges fluttered around him, and she pulled his mouth to hers to kiss him once more.

With a slow building rhythm, his hips began to move. He pumped in and out, pressing her into the mattress, body hot and heavy between her legs. He pushed into her harder and faster until she was panting his name, her juices slippery between their bodies.

She was near climax again when he reached around her backside, his fingers finding her slickness. He eased one digit against her ass as he continued to pump, more slowly now, deeper and deeper. Her impending orgasm doubled in size, tripled until she thought she might burst.

"Are you ready, *itoshi*?" his voice was a choked off growl.

"Yes, yes." She lifted her knees and spread her legs wide, opening herself to him.

He pulled back, and his finger left her ass. Then he sank forward again, both shafts penetrating her, filling her. They pulsed and swelled, a perfect unison of sensation as he drew back and entered her again.

Her eyelids fluttered. Moaning a long, loud cry, she

shattered, her entire body clenching and releasing in a wave of pleasure so intense, the universe seemed to tilt. Her legs shook, her breath stopped, her heart pounded so hard and fast she thought it might burst.

She was vaguely aware of Iroth growling her name, a long deep note that resonated with her shuddering body. He continued pumping into her hard and fast, skin slapping skin until heat jetted from both his shafts. An aftershock rocked her, taking her almost as high as the first release.

He collapsed on top of her, breath heavy against her ear as they floated together for long minutes.

After their breathing eased and their skin cooled, he propped himself onto his elbows and looked into her face. His turquoise eyes were shining with love. "Are you ready to see the galaxy with me, *itoshi?*"

She snuggled against his chest. "Absolutely, my love. But can we get some sleep first?"

Dear Reader,

I had a ton of fun creating this unique, shapeshifting species, and hope you enjoyed them, too. The fun continues in the next installment, Starship Romantasy!

Join the Bloom sisters on the cruise of a lifetime - in space!
You'll meet hot alien men, visit dangerous uncharted planets,
and die laughing over hilarious cultural misunderstandings.

Get your copy from your favorite bookstore now!

XOXO, Tamsin

INTERGALACTIC DATING AGENCY

Looking for more out of this world romance? Your local Intergalactic Dating Agency can help! These strong, smart, sexy aliens are on the prowl for mates, and humans like you are exactly what they're after. Jump in with Book 1 of any standalone trilogy from our crew of rock star SFR authors and make steamy first contact! Warning: abductions may or may not be included!

Grab more hunky alien action here:
http://romancingthealien.com

ALSO BY TAMSIN LEY

SCI-FI ROMANCE

Galactic Pirate Brides series

Kirenai Fated Mates (Intergalactic Dating Agency) series

Khargals of Duras

FANTASY ROMANCE

Mates for Monsters series

PARANORMAL ROMANCE

Alaska Alphas series

AUDIOBOOKS

BOX SETS

BOOKS IN GERMAN

Gefährten für Monster

Alphas in Alaska

Bräute für die Alien-Piraten

Versteigert an die Aliens

POST APOCALYPTIC SCI-FI written as Tam Linsey

Botanicaust series

ABOUT THE AUTHOR

Once upon a time I thought I wanted to be a biomedical engineer, but experimenting on lab rats doesn't always lead to happy endings. Now I blend my nerdy infatuation of science with character-driven romance and guaranteed happily-ever-afters. My monsters always find their mates, with feisty heroines, tortured heroes, and all the steamy trouble they can handle. I promise my stories will never leave you hanging (although you may still crave more!)

When I'm not writing, I'll be in the garden or the kitchen, exploring Alaska with my husband, or preparing for the zombie apocalypse. I also enjoy crocheting while binge watching Netflix, playing video games, and enjoying family time during our weekly D&D session.

Interested in more about me? Join my VIP Club and get free books, notices, and other cool stuff!

www.tamsinley.com

bookbub.com/authors/tamsin-ley

goodreads.com/TamsinLey

facebook.com/TamsinLey

amazon.com/author/tamsin

www.ingramcontent.com/pod-product-compliance
Lightning Source LLC
Chambersburg PA
CBHW060756210726
48292CB00013B/203